Julia James liv~~es~~ ~~in a~~ peaceful verdant ~~corner~~ of Cornwall. She ~~loves the Mediterranean~~— so rich in myth an~~d history, with its~~ sunbaked landscapes and oli~~ve groves~~, ancient ruins and azure seas. 'The perfect setting for romance!' she says. 'Rivalled only by the lush tropical heat of the Caribbean—palms swaying by a silver sand beach lapped by turquoise water… What more could lovers want?'

Jackie Ashenden writes dark, emotional stories, with alpha heroes who've just got the world to their liking only to have it blown wide apart by their kick-ass heroines. She lives in Auckland, New Zealand, with her husband, the inimitable Dr Jax, two kids and two rats. When she's not torturing alpha males and their gutsy heroines she can be found drinking chocolate martinis, reading anything she can lay her hands on, wasting time on social media or being forced to go mountain biking with her husband. To keep up to date with Jackie's new releases and other news sign up to her newsletter at jackieashenden.com.

EXPECTING
HIS HEIR

JULIA JAMES

JACKIE ASHENDEN

MILLS & BOON

First published in Great Britain 2025
by Mills & Boon, an imprint of HarperCollins*Publishers* Ltd,
1 London Bridge Street, London, SE1 9GF

www.harpercollins.co.uk

HarperCollins*Publishers*, Macken House, 39/40 Mayor Street Upper,
Dublin 1, D01 C9W8, Ireland

Expecting His Heir © 2025 Harlequin Enterprises ULC

Accidental One-Night Baby © 2025 Julia James

Boss's Heir Demand © 2025 Jackie Ashenden

ISBN: 978-0-263-34451-6

02/25

ACCIDENTAL ONE-NIGHT BABY

JULIA JAMES

MILLS & BOON

For all the donkey sanctuaries and welfare charities
for the wonderful and vital work they do.

CHAPTER ONE

VINCENZO GIANSANTE STOOD looking down at the woman in his bed. She was asleep still, and he did not wish to wake her.

But it needed to be done.

For a moment, though, he went on looking down at her, only half covered by the quilt, exposing her sculpted, naked back. She lay on her front, one hand near her slender throat, the other flung wide, across the empty side of the bed. Her long dark hair streamed over the pillow, and her face was turned towards where he had until recently lain.

His face was expressionless, but thoughts moved behind his eyes. Had he really done what he had the night before? The evidence was here in front of him, in the dim light seeping past the hotel room curtains, shafting from the lit en suite bathroom. She'd slept through his shower and getting himself dressed for the day ahead. But then, after all, there had been little enough sleep during the night…

He pulled his mind away. Best not to think back that far. Best not to think of how he'd slowly, sensually peeled from her the short, clinging dress that had so perfectly moulded her perfectly proportioned body…how he'd slipped the catch of her bra so that her ripe breasts spilled free for him to cup them with his palms, feel how they engorged and crested at his touch…how she'd leant back into him, her mouth reaching for his, her hand winding around his neck, lips opening to his…

Fatally, he felt memory impacting his body, making him want to reach down and stroke the silken mass of her tumbled hair, move down beside her, scoop her lissom, yielding body to his again, taste and take all that she had offered him last night…all that they had both so lushly indulged in…

But that was not possible—and would not be wise.

Why had he succumbed as he had the night before? Whatever had it been about her that had made him focus on her at that party in one of the hotel's private function rooms, when his plan had only been to network with those who might prove useful to him in business here in London?

Whatever it had been, the allure of those wide-set, long-lashed, sea-blue eyes with their intriguing hint of green had made him want to look and look again at the face that somehow combined a fine-boned delicacy with dramatically contoured cheekbones and a lushly curving mouth. At the slender but oh-so-shapely body, and the clinging dress with its deep cleavage, its thigh-skimming hemline that exposed the length of her stockinged legs, their length emphasised by the five-inch heels that had brought her closer to his own six foot height.

Whatever it had been, and whyever he had made the decision to let himself indulge in her—and an indulgence it had been—he knew now that it was necessary to call time on it.

He reached out a hand, lightly touched her bare, exposed shoulder. She barely stirred, so he said her name.

'Siena…'

Her name had been the means of extending their initial conversation, after he'd made his split-second decision not to rebuff her. To allow himself the indulgence of talking to her, looking her over. Just as she had been doing to him. He'd been aware of it immediately, in the widening of her eyes, in the tell-tale colour flaring briefly across those sculpted cheekbones, the slight but revealing parting of her lips, the even more revealing breathiness. All had told him that she was reacting to him as strongly as he was reacting to her.

Their subsequent conversation had merely been a means to an end. Her Italian name, given after the Tuscan city of the same name, had provided a link to his own nationality, leading her to ask where he came from in Italy, which had led on to why he was in London, which had led on to yet more anodyne exchanges that had allowed them both to continue with the actual purpose of their conversation— which was, after a suitably appropriate and not too unsubtle interval, to allow him to suggest that if she had no pressing reason to linger at the party they might remove themselves to dine at the hotel, in order to continue their acquaintance away from the noise of the party.

And that would lead to one place only—as both of them had known. The Falcone restaurant had been only across the lobby. She had come with him—why would she not?— and from then on the decision had been made.

And now…?

Now he must make another decision. Had already made it—must simply abide by it. Execute it. Without further hesitation. Without reconsidering. Without any second thoughts at all.

Without regret.

Regret was not something he could indulge in. He'd indulged in quite enough already. Time to be tough—including on himself.

No more prevarication.

'Siena?' He said her name again, his voice a little louder. This time she stirred. She was waking, he could tell. She lifted her head, looking up at him. Her wanton hair tumbled around her bare shoulders as she raised herself on her elbow, eyes blinking as she focussed on him.

'I have to leave now,' he said. His voice was cool, matter-of-fact. 'But for yourself there is no hurry. Please order breakfast when you will—it is all chargeable to the room.'

He did not wait for her to say anything—he did not want to hear it. What he wanted was to move on with his day. His schedule was full, and his first appointment—a breakfast meeting at a London club—imminent.

He walked from the room, his stride unhurried, picking up his briefcase as he went. He was booked to stay here tonight, but would not return till late. Then he would be flying back to Milan, where he was based.

And the night he had just spent would slip into the past.

He closed the room door behind him and headed for the elevator, his mind already going to the business meeting ahead of him. It was occupying all his thoughts. Putting the night that had passed behind him.

Siena lowered herself back down to the pillow, soft behind her head. She felt cold, suddenly, but did not pull the duvet higher.

She stared up at the ceiling.

Aware that her heart was thudding.

Aware that she was completely naked.

Aware that she had just spent the night with a man she had met only the previous evening. Aware of so much...

A sudden heat knifed through her.

Dear God, had she really done what she thought she had?

Her gaze went around the room. Luxuriously appointed. But then this was the Mayfair Falcone, so of course it was luxurious. As elegant and upmarket as the restaurant where she'd dined, with its famous chef and famous reputation and sky-high prices. As elegant as that swish party in one of the hotel's opulent function rooms which her old school-friend Megan, whom she was staying with in London, had dragged her to, insisting she needed something fun and carefree and hedonistic after all she'd been through, and insisting, too, that she look the part for so glamorous and fashionable a venue.

So Megan had loaned her one of her own designer cocktail frocks, in mauve shot silk. It was a size too small, but Megan had said she'd looked a knockout in it, and then sat her down and done her hair and nails and make-up—far more extravagantly and glamorously than Siena was used to. Then she'd handed her a pair of strappy evening shoes with sky-high heels, thrust a satin evening bag at her and, looking a knockout herself, had piled them both into a taxi to whisk them from Megan's flat in Notting Hill to Mayfair, to disgorge them at the Falcone.

'It's part work, part social,' Megan, who was a high-flyer at a fancy PR company, had told her of the party she was taking her to. 'And it's just what you need after all these tough years. You put your life on hold—and, yes, I know why you did it, and applaud you for it—but now you're starting your life again. Off to art school in the autumn—finally! Just like you always dreamt. And a flash bash like tonight's will get you back into the swing of things. You haven't had a social life for years!'

She'd squeezed Siena's hand in the taxi, her voice sympathetic.

'So let your hair down tonight! Be someone different—go crazy…indulge yourself. Who knows? Meet someone!'

As Siena sat back against the pillows, alone in the bed,

alone in the room, a hollow opened up inside her and found a chill was replacing that flush of heat.

Meet someone...

Megan's words echoed in her head, and the hollow inside her gaped wider.

Instantly he was in her vision. Just as he had been last night when, gingerly taking a glass of champagne from a passing server, she had been inadvertently jostled by someone, making her reverse sharply and step against another guest. She'd turned to apologise—and the apology had died on her lips.

She'd felt her eyes widen, her mouth open, colour flare.

The most lethal-looking male she had ever seen in her life...

He was tall, wearing black tie like every other male there, and as her eyes had gazed helplessly she'd registered dark hair, a narrow face, bladed nose, sculpted mouth and eyes... oh, eyes that were dark, and deep and—

'I'm... I'm so sorry!' Her voice had been breathless, because all the air had been sucked from her lungs.

For a second he had not responded. Then: 'Not at all,' he'd said politely.

It had been perfect English, but with a trace of an accent in it...something that had only added to her breathlessness.

She'd wanted to move away—there had been no reason not to. But she'd seemed quite paralysed.

He'd given a slight nod. 'It's quite a crush, isn't it?' he'd said.

Again, she'd heard an accent in his voice—an accent, she'd realised, that went with his Mediterranean skin tone. And there had been something about him—maybe the cut of his tuxedo, or the groomed style of his hair, or just that cosmopolitan air... She'd given a silent gulp. Or maybe it had been the fact that he had openly let those dark, deep eyes rest on her in a way that drove yet more air from her lungs.

'Yes, it is,' she'd heard herself reply.

'There's more space over by the French windows,' he'd said.

He'd gestured with his hand—an elegant, effortless movement which had let Siena see that he was also holding a glass of champagne.

She'd moved in that direction, and realised he was moving as well.

'Definitely better,' he'd said. And smiled at her.

And the air which had just begun to creep back into her lungs had vanished again...

After that it was almost a blur—and yet every moment was crystal-clear.

He'd asked her name, and told her his own, and then asked if she'd ever been to the city she'd been named after. She'd said she'd never been to Italy, and asked where he came from...

And then, at some point—and she didn't really know why, or when, or how—she had been walking into the Falcone restaurant with him, trying to move gracefully on her towering high heels. And then, when he'd wined her and dined her, she'd found—though she didn't really know how—that he was ushering her into one of the elevators and she was going up to his room...

How, she might not have known...but *why*, she burningly did...

She felt her face flare now, even as the rest of her body, naked and bare, grew cold.

Because she had never, in all her six and twenty years, met anyone like him before...anyone who had had the slightest measure of his impact on her—raw, visceral...sensual...

Making her pulse throb, her pupils dilate, her breath catch with an overpowering awareness of his physical appeal—an irresistible appeal…

So she had not.

She had not resisted him.

Because I could not resist him. Because he only had to look at me the way he did, with those heavy-lidded eyes that seemed to be turning me inside out and outside in, melting me down to the core…

Desire—that was what it had been. A sensual white-out…

She felt her cheeks flare again with the memory of it. Never in her life had she done what she had done last night—but then never in her life had she ever encountered a man like that. A man she had been completely, totally enthralled by. Helpless to resist…

Resistance had been the very last thing she'd wanted to impose on herself. Instead, she had given herself, all-consumingly, urgently, to all that he skilfully, seductively, meltingly aroused in her, from his first sensuous kiss to the moment of hungry, almost unbearable pleasure that had flooded her body as it had fused with his, pulsing through her, wave after incredible wave, as her body had arched beneath his, her head thrown back, crying out aloud…

Again, and again, and again…

All night long.

And now…

Now there was no more heat—only a chill spreading through her that was not just physical…

He was gone.

After their night together—after *that* night together—he was just…gone.

The chill turned to cold. Filled her veins.

CHAPTER TWO

Six weeks later...

SIENA TOOK A BREATH, short and sharp, and summoning up her courage stepped into the lift that would take her to the one man in the world she did not want to see again.

Vincenzo Giansante.

Megan couldn't get why she didn't want to see him. She'd stared uncomprehendingly at Siena...

'Of course you have to tell him! I've looked him up—he's loaded! A hotshot financier worth a tonne!'

Siena's mouth had tightened.

'That isn't the point, Megs—'

She couldn't care less whether he was rich or not—the only reason she knew she had to tell him was because, like it or not—and she did not like it...not one little bit—he had a right to know.

That and that alone had brought her here, to this swish City office suite that Vincenzo Giansante used when he was in London.

Megan had found out for her, using her PR contacts, and also found out that he'd be in London this week. She had brazenly phoned to check he would be in this afternoon. She hadn't gone so far as to make an appointment, after warning Siena that if he knew she was turning up, he might balk at seeing her.

'He'll think you're chasing him—and he's made it clear he's done with you.'

Siena's mouth tightened. Vincenzo Giansante had, indeed, made it crystal-clear that he was done with her—had walked out in the briefest way possible in the bleak light of the morning after the night before.

Well, now she was walking back into his life—to tell him what she could still scarcely believe herself, ever since seeing that thin blue line form on the test stick.

He has a right to know—any man does—whether I want him to or not.

The lift jerked to a stop, the metal doors sliding open. For a moment she wanted to be a coward, and jab the 'down' button again. Then, steeling herself, she walked forward.

Vincenzo terminated the call he'd just finished, mentally processing the conversation he'd had about a prospective investment. Yes, it would do. He'd give it his assent.

OK, so what was next?

He glanced at the crowded diary page that was maxing out his brief visit to London, flexing his shoulders as he sat back in his capacious leather executive chair. He'd put in a workout at the end of the day—the hotel he was booked into had good gym facilities, and a pool as well.

His expression changed fractionally. This time around he was not staying at the Falcone, but at a hotel on Piccadilly. And this time around he would not be socialising— even for networking. And what he would most definitely *not* be doing this visit was what he'd done on the previous one. Something he'd never done before. Spending the night with a woman he had only just met, taking her to bed within hours of meeting her. Indulging himself in her.

For a second, memory flared—hot and humid—of their white-out night together. Then he shut it down.

He had walked out on her and put it behind him.

It was over and done with.

His attention went back to his diary for that afternoon. His next phone appointment was in twenty minutes—time enough to scan the relevant file and note the key points.

As he clicked to open it, his desk phone sounded.

'Yes?' His voice was brisk as he answered.

But when his PA told him who was asking to see him, his expression hardened like stone.

Siena wanted to turn and bolt, but again she steeled herself not to. The female sitting at the desk in an outer office, dressed in a tailored suit and with perfect hair, had displayed the greatest reluctance at her request. Signor Giansante, she'd informed Siena disdainfully, saw no one without an appointment. Let alone a female turning up in a chainstore skirt and sweater, her face bare of make-up and her hair pulled back into a tight, plain knot. That had been her implication. But Siena had stood her ground, repeating her request.

'Please let him know I am here.'

All but rolling her eyeballs, the woman had done so, and then, with a highly displeased air, had replaced the handset and told her she could go in.

Siena was now doing just that.

Her chest as tight as a drum.

Vincenzo let his eyes rest on her. They were completely inexpressive, but behind them he was reacting. Reacting in multiple ways. First and foremost was the thought that if the name had not been so unusual he would not have known who she was. Second, and far stronger, was the reaction that had hit him when his PA had given her name. That was uppermost now.

He got to his feet as she walked towards him.

'This is unexpected,' he said.

It was a statement, nothing more.

She stopped in front of his desk and he resumed his seat. He did not invite her to sit down. He did not intend this… visitation to be of any duration.

Did she not get the message when I left her that morning? That I am not interested in continuing any liaison with her?

Because that was why she was here—that much was obvious. It always was. Ever since he'd started making money— serious money—he'd been a target for women keen to have him spend it on them.

The way they'd targeted his father. Battening on him.

The old, familiar, bitter stab of anger came at how his hapless father, wanting only to find a woman to love after the tragedy of losing his wife when Vincenzo was a young child, had been easy prey. Right to the very end. The end that had been fifteen years ago now, when Vincenzo had just started at university, having spent his boyhood watching one woman after another exploiting his father, leeching off him, until one of them had managed to get a ring on her finger—and a lot more than that.

Get all that was left of my father's money by then.

As for himself—he'd got nothing. He'd had to start from scratch, building up his own business, making his own money. Money that no avaricious female would get her greedy claws into.

By any means.

His eyes rested now on the woman in front of him. She could not have looked more different from that evening at the Falcone. Then she had been dressed to kill—advertising her allure on all frequencies. Now, instead of that low-cut, clinging cocktail dress, she wore a knee-length denim skirt, flat shoes, a cotton sweater. Gone was the loose, lush hair and full make-up. Her hair was knotted plainly at the back of her head and her face bare.

Yet even without any adornments, he was conscious of her beauty…

He dismissed it ruthlessly. It was irrelevant now.

'Yes, I know,' she answered. Her voice was staccato. 'I apologise for turning up like this,' she said, her voice still staccato.

'Do you?' Vincenzo murmured. His face was still inexpressive.

Something flashed in her eyes, then was gone. Her hand tightened over her canvas shoulder bag, which looked as cheap as the rest of her appearance. In one part of his brain he speculated on why she had turned up looking as she did. If she thought to entice him again, she should have come better packaged.

Then, with her next words, he realised that she had quite a different strategy in mind.

'Yes,' she said tightly.

For a moment she was completely silent. And then Siena Westbrook, who had once provided him with a memorable but unrepeatable one-night-only of exquisite sensual pleasure, took a visible breath and continued in the same tight voice.

'I'm here to tell you that I'm pregnant.'

Oh, God, she had said it!

Siena's hand tightened on her bag even more tightly.

'I'm sorry just to announce it like that, but there isn't any other way of doing it,' she made herself say.

She looked directly across at him—made herself do so. It was hard to do it—memory was burning through her now she was seeing him again. His impact on her was as overwhelming now, all these weeks later, as it had been that night at the Falcone. But she had to ignore it. It was as irrelevant to the moment now as was his wealth, that Megan was so focussed on.

'No, I imagine not,' he replied.

His voice was that murmur again—the one that she instinctively took exception to.

'Permit me to offer you my congratulations.'

His voice wasn't a murmur any longer. It was smooth. But smooth in the way that the water flowing over the edge of Niagara Falls was smooth. Deadly smooth…

He was still sitting back in that massive leather chair of his, one hand resting on the chrome and leather arm, one on the mahogany desk's surface. He was quite immobile, his face completely expressionless. His eyes unreadable.

Those eyes had once, that fateful evening, flickered sensuously over her, telling her that they was liking what they saw, quickening her pulse, making heat beat up inside her…

Now, she only frowned. 'Congratulations…?'

'Yes.' His voice was still smooth. 'This must be a happy time for you—and for the father.'

She stared at him. Not understanding.

He lifted his hand off the desk, holding it up as if to silence her when she was already silenced.

'Whoever he may be,' he said. His expressionless eyes rested on her for a moment. 'You cannot expect me to believe I am the only candidate for that honour?' he said softly.

'After all, you were in my bed within hours of meeting me.' His voice was a murmur again. 'How many other men have enjoyed a similar…felicity since myself?'

The breath went from Siena's lungs—instantly sucked out by what he had just said to her.

What she could not *believe* he had just said to her.

He went on speaking. His hand still raised to silence her. He looked completely relaxed, but there was something in his inexpressive face, his expressionless eyes, that chilled her even more than his words.

'Do not, I beg you, seek to verbally contest the logic of my statement. Instead, what I would recommend is the following course of action. Get your doctor to request a paternity test for all possible candidates, and when the result is known, proceed on that basis.'

He got to his feet, walked around the desk. But not towards her—to the double doors leading out of his office.

As he walked, he went on speaking. 'You have had a wasted journey. This matter could have been dealt with remotely, in the way I have just recommended.' He reached the door, opened it. 'And now you must leave. I have an appointment in a few minutes.'

He held the door open for her.

Siena, frozen where she stood, jerked forward. There was emotion inside her, but what it was she did not know. Her feet carried her across the thick carpet, past him standing there, then past the PA at her desk in the outer office, and then on out on to the corridor beyond. She jabbed numbly at the elevator button, saw the doors sliding open to allow her to step even more numbly inside.

The lift dropped down.

And as it did, hollowing her out, she felt two overpowering emotions flooding into the hollow like a suffocating tide.

Mortification.

And an anger so great it made her shake with it.

Vincenzo walked back to his desk, resumed his seat in his capacious chair. His face was still without expression, and yet emotion was scything through him. Silently and lethally.

This was not the first such try-on he'd experienced. There'd been an ex in his early twenties—a decade ago— who had claimed she was pregnant. It had been when he'd first started making money, and the connection between the two had not been lost on him. He'd called her bluff and waited it out. She'd turned out not to be pregnant at all.

So, is this one pregnant?

He stared out across the room, his eyes hard. Well, time would tell. If she really was pregnant then it would not be long before he'd get a request for a paternity test. And then...

He sliced the thought away. He would deal with it as and when—and, above all, *if.*

Until then she would cease to exist for him—again.

Megan eyed Siena warily.

'What did he say?' she asked, even more warily.

Siena was walking around the room—striding around it. Megan's sitting room was small, but handsomely appointed, leaving very little space for walking about, let alone striding.

'Oh, he was very economical with his words! Didn't waste a single one! He recommended sending out paternity tests to all the candidates—'

'*What?*' Megan's voice sounded stunned.

'You heard me! He pointed out that since I'd fallen into bed with him the same evening as meeting him for the first time, it showed there must surely be other candidates.'

'He *said* that to you?' Megan was aghast. 'But…but what did you say?'

Siena stopped her striding and whirled round to face her friend.

'Nothing. I got thrown out!'

'Thrown out?'

'Which was totally unnecessary as I'd have gone any-way—like a bat out of hell!' Her face worked. 'I wish to God I'd never gone there! I had to force myself to go, and that…*that*…was what I got!'

She felt her fists clench. Fury lashing through her.

Megan was still eyeing her warily. 'So…so what are you going to do?' she asked.

Siena stared. 'What do you mean, "do"? You mean apart from storming back there and slugging him from here to Christmas!'

'Well, yes, apart from that,' Megan said. Her expression changed. 'OK, so I'm not excusing him—' a choking sound came from Siena's throat, and Megan hurried on '—but to be honest it's only to be expected he'd want some kind of proof, as in a paternity test. Any man would in those cir-cumstances.'

Siena's eyes flashed dangerously. 'You mean the circum-stances of a one-night stand?'

'Well, yes. I mean—'

'What you mean,' Siena supplied, and her voice was as dangerous as the flash in her eyes, 'is that I am, in fact, the kind of female who would drop into a different man's bed every day of the week!'

Megan looked uneasy. 'Obviously I know you're not, but he doesn't—'

Another noise escaped Siena's throat.

Megan hurried on. 'It's just biology, Si—it can't be

helped. Have sex with more than one man in one month and how can you tell which one—?' She held up her hands placatingly. 'Don't get mad at me, Si! You had one night together, and he walked out in the morning.'

Siena's eyes burned with a brightness that was coruscating. 'Thank you for reminding me—yes, he walked out in the morning—because he'd got all he'd wanted. So it was *Wham, bam, Thank you, ma'am*—except that he was conspicuously short on either the thank-you or any other politeness! He just told me he was off, and I could stay in the room and charge my breakfast to it—'

She broke off, her voice choking. Memory burned like acid, etching into her skin. Talk about the morning after the night bef—except she didn't want to talk about it, or think about it, or remember it.

She threw herself down beside Megan on the sofa.

'Oh, God, Megs, how could I have done what I did?' Her voice was a toxic mix of rage and memory.

Megan patted her arm in an attempt to be comforting. She'd already had the post mortem weeks ago, when Siena had got back that morning, and had done her best to show Siena that having a scorching fling with a gorgeously irresistible Italian—even if one-night-only—was a well-deserved celebration of her new freedom.

OK, so the gorgeously irresistible Italian in question had been graceless in his leave-taking, and certainly had not followed through—which was a shame, because a slightly longer fling, even maybe a romantic escapade in Italy, was really just what Siena needed now, after the last grim years. But now it had all gone pear-shaped. All that was possible was damage limitation.

'I don't really know anything about how to get a paternity test organised,' she began now, in a voice she hoped was encouraging, 'but I guess you go to your doctor first and explain—'

Siena reared back. 'You're not serious!' she shot out.

'It's the only way to—'

Siena cut straight across her. Voice vehement. 'You don't seriously think I am going to go *anywhere* near that vile, disgusting man ever, *ever* again, do you?'

'Si, I know it's galling, but it's the only way—'

'No. No, no, no, no and *no*! I forced myself to go there because I genuinely thought it was the right thing to do—that a man has the right to know if he is to be a father, even in circumstances like these! But I did have to *force* myself to do it. It was humiliating and mortifying and deeply, deeply embarrassing, damn it! Even before he looked at me like I was something the dog dragged in! And now, after the way he reacted, the way he treated me, I would stick *pins* in my eyes before I'd go *anywhere* near him again. He can rot in hell—go down a hole in the ground—take a running jump—go and boil his head...'

She moved on to some explicit but anatomically impossible manoeuvres for him to contrive, and then, with gritted teeth, got to her feet. Her hands, she realised, were still clenched.

'Vincenzo Bloody Giansante can take himself back to Italy, the sooner the better. And the bigger the distance between him and me the better! I should never have fallen into bed with him, never gone to see him today, and I will never, as God is my witness, have *anything* to do with him for as long as I live.'

She took a shuddering breath, making her fists unclench. She pressed both hands across her still-flat abdomen.

'As for my baby...' Her voice changed, but only she could feel the tremor in it. 'It is *my* baby—'

She turned and walked out of the sitting room, closing the door behind her. There was a storm in her breast and steel in her heart. Cold, hard steel.

CHAPTER THREE

SIENA SIGHED DESPONDENTLY. She'd just been told by the art school's accommodation officer that the hall of residence where she had a room reserved, subsidised by a bursary for mature students, did not cater for parents, and nor did any college accommodation. She must rely on the private rental sector.

Siena sighed again. That would be far more costly—and when the baby arrived there would be childcare costs too. Would the legacy from her parents that was to pay for art school stretch that far? Doubt filled her. And resentment too.

How could her life have changed so dramatically?

So disastrously.

Just because of that one damn night.

One night—and it's changed my life for ever. Destroyed my dreams.

It had been wonderful beyond all things to get into this ul-tra-prestigious, world-famous London art school as a mature student, with a subsidised room in a hall of residence. But if she could not afford to live in London and pay for childcare too, how was it going to be possible to take up her place?

She couldn't stay indefinitely in Meg's flat—she was only here doing some temporary office work at the PR company where Meg worked because Meg's flatmate, Fran, had taken off for the summer. It was meant to have tided her over until term started and she moved into the hall of residence. But now that wasn't going to be possible.

As for getting council accommodation… For single mothers, the waiting list was a mile long, and it would probably be little more than a grim bedsit or hostel.

She gave another sigh, deeper this time, and more despondent. In the face of such difficulties a decision was forcing itself upon her—one she didn't want but had to accept, with heavy reluctance and resignation. There was no other option.

She made herself tell Megan when her friend came back from work that evening.

'I'm calling it quits, Megs. Giving up my place at art school. I just can't afford it. I'll move out of London…find somewhere loads cheaper to live. I'll work until the baby arrives, then live on my parents' legacy until I can sort childcare for when the baby's older. As for art school… Well…' she gave a shrug '… I gave up on it once before and survived. I'll do so again.'

Megan looked at her, dismayed. 'You mustn't do that, Si,' she said emphatically. 'I know what you went through…giving up your place all those years ago. You lost your dream then—you must not give it up again.'

Siena looked at her sadly. 'I've no alternative. It just isn't financially viable. And it's my own fault, isn't it? I got myself pregnant—'

'No, you didn't *"get yourself"* pregnant,' Megan began forcefully. 'The man you refuse to contact again got you pregnant.'

Siena held up her hands, wearied beyond measure by her friend's pointless insistence. 'Megs, please, please, *please*—just don't. Look, I've made my mind up. I'm chucking art college, starting my life afresh—again—and moving out of London. I'll start checking out where rental prices are cheapest, but somewhere decent enough to raise a baby. I'll be fine.'

Megan's expression changed. 'There is another option, you know,' she said slowly. 'You could choose not to have this baby...'

'No!' Now it was Siena's voice that was forceful. 'I won't do it—I won't even think of it!'

Megan bit her lip, looked uneasy. 'I know... I know it's because of...well...because of...what you went through with your family.' She halted, then went on, her voice lifting. 'But what about adoption? There are plenty of couples who would love—'

Again, Siena cut across her. 'I couldn't do that either. Megan, I'm honest enough to admit I don't want to be pregnant—but I am, and it is my responsibility from now on.'

My responsibility. No one else's.

To her relief, Megan didn't argue any more. But as she headed into the kitchen her expression was set and determined...

Vincenzo was watching the yachts criss-crossing the bay, skimming the azure waters. He was in Sardinia, meeting up with a CEO in whose company Vincenzo was considering investing. Meeting done, he was having lunch at his hotel, prior to flying back to Milan that afternoon.

As he ate on the shady open-air terrace overlooking the azure bay the yachts made a peaceful scene.

They also brought back memories—mixed memories.

As a teenager, he'd wanted to learn to sail—wanted to step aboard one of those light, almost winged craft and skim across the waves. Carefree...

But his teenage years had not been carefree. Even from

a younger age he'd been aware of how much of a soft touch his widowed father was…had watched women making up to him, getting him to squander his money on them. Finally, one of them had become his wife—and then the spending spree had really started. Ending with his increasingly stressed father dying, leaving everything to her. She'd seen to that…

Vincenzo's expression hardened. He'd learnt a lesson from his father's sorry experience…his lack of judgement when it came to women and their ambitions.

His thoughts flickered. He'd heard nothing more from that woman he'd spent a single night with who had then claimed he'd got her pregnant. Clearly it had been nothing but a try-on. But the fact that she'd tried it on at all showed him that he'd made the right call, that morning at the Falcone, to walk out as he had. Not to take things any further with her.

However alluring her charms…

He reached for his wine glass, memory spearing. She really had been something…right from the first moment he'd set eyes on her, looking at him wide-eyed, lips parted, as obviously drawn to him as he to her. And when he'd taken her into his arms, slowly and sensuously peeled that tightly clinging dress from her soft, sensual body…

Sheer indulgence on his part.

But one he had enjoyed—even though he'd been right to keep it to a single night. A night that had been as out of character as it had been memorable.

He pulled his thoughts away, draining the last of his wine. That night and the unpleasant follow-up scene in his office, tainting what otherwise would have been a pleasing memory of their night together, were done with. Over. He could draw a formal line underneath them.

Time to head for the airport—get back to Milan.

As he moved to stand up, his phone rang. Sliding it out of his jacket pocket, he frowned. Why should the account director of the PR company who handled his media comms be contacting him? He kept a low press profile overall, and there was nothing in the offing.

He answered the call, intent on disposing of it as swiftly as he could, whatever it was about.

His voice was short—the voice at the other end, however, was the opposite, apologising for disturbing him and then hesitantly venturing, 'Does the name Siena Westbrook mean anything to you?'

Vincenzo froze.

'You did *what*?' Siena stared, aghast—more than aghast— at Megan across the breakfast table.

It was Saturday, and Megan had been out late the previous night, on duty at a corporate client's dinner for journalists. Now she'd surfaced and was fessing up to Siena, who'd gone pale.

'I did what needed to be done,' Megan said defiantly. 'And it's no good getting on your high horse about it! I'm not letting you screw your life up!'

Siena fulminated visibly. 'It's *my* life to screw up if I want—and anyway, I am *not* screwing it up! I am making a perfectly rational decision—'

'No, you're not!' Megan cut across her. 'Look, it's not as if you hadn't decided to tell him in the first place!'

'And how I wish to God I hadn't!' Siena's eyes glowed with remembered fury, exacerbating the anger spearing her at what her friend had just told her she'd done.

'Well, you did tell him,' came Megan's rejoinder. 'And just because he proved to be a total jerk about it, it does *not* let him off the hook. Which is exactly what I told his press office!' She went on, her voice more emollient now. 'Look, I know how this stuff works, OK? I'm in PR, and I know what levers to pull. So that's what I did. Pulled a lever that your precious Italian jerk really wouldn't like being pulled!'

Her voice changed, and Siena, furious though she was, could hear satisfaction in it.

'And even I think it was a lulu! I simply told the guy that his precious Signor Giansante could look forward to reading the headline *The billionaire and his bedsit baby.* He didn't like that—didn't like it one little bit! Oh, he prevaricated, and went all smooth and evasive, but I'd got him ruffled all right!'

Siena went on staring at her, but now her anger was subsiding, to be replaced by unease.

'Megs, I know you meant well...' it cost her to say it, but it was true '...but this guy, Vincenzo Giansante—well, he's not some patsy. You've poked a tiger, and—'

Megan stood her ground defiantly, not letting her finish. 'Si, he got you pregnant and has treated you like dirt!'

'Yes, and because of that I don't want *anything* to do with him!'

'You don't have to have anything to do with him!' Megan remonstrated heatedly. 'All you have to do is accept a maintenance payout from him! That's all. And, given he's so loaded, any payout will pay for you to live in London, go to art school and afford decent childcare while you study—not to mention when you graduate. The whole thing can be done through lawyers, and you'll never have to set eyes on him!'

Siena's face worked. Oh, dear God, why had Megan gone and interfered like that? Didn't she understand?

I don't want anything to do with the man! I don't want him

*coming near me—or my baby! And he can take his money
and choke on it for all I care!*

'Megan, I don't want to be beholden to him in any way
at all! I don't want his money—and I don't need it!'

*If I take any money from him at all he'll just feel it proves
that's what I was after all along, and I won't give him the
satisfaction of despising me for it!*

She made herself take a steadying breath. Getting upset
wasn't good for the baby. She reached for her mug of tea—
but before she could lift it, the flat's doorbell rang.

'I'll get it,' she said, standing up. She was dressed, and
Megan was still in her dressing gown.

It was probably a delivery, and some other resident had
obviously let them in at the main door on their way out.

She unbolted the security lock and opened the door.

Vincenzo Giansante stood outside.

For a moment, Vincenzo thought she was going to pass out.
Instinctively he reached for her arm to steady her as she visibly swayed, slumping against the doorframe. He felt her
jerk violently away, stumble backwards. Heard her give a
strangled cry.

A voice called from the room beyond the hallway.

'Si, who is it? Si...?'

Someone was emerging into the hallway—another female, wearing a loosely tied dressing gown and with messy
hair.

She gave a gasp as she saw him. Frozen in the doorway.

'Get out!'

The words were hurled at him—but not from the woman
in the dressing gown. From the one now slumped against
the wall. The woman he had last seen stalking out of his
office as he dismissed her from his presence.

She looked white as a sheet, except for two spots of high colour in her cheeks. Absently, with a part of his brain that was completely irrelevant to his purpose, he registered that she was making him want to look at her just as powerfully as she had the very first time he'd laid eyes on her that fateful evening.

An evening that had brought him here, now, right in front of her.

He ignored her hissed and equally irrelevant outburst.

'Where can we talk?' he demanded. 'Privately.'

'I said, get out!'

He ignored her again, turning his attention to the woman in the dressing gown, who was looking as if she could not believe her eyes. He smiled inwardly, grimly, and entirely without humour. He could see a sitting room of sorts behind her—that would do.

He turned back to the woman he had flown from Sardinia to see.

'I want this settled,' he said. His voice was quelling. Intentionally so. Necessarily so. 'And I want it settled now. You, or your representative, have made an allegation and threatened me with damaging publicity. You will either withdraw or substantiate your allegation. Which is it to be?'

She didn't answer him. Instead, her face contorted again. 'I have absolutely nothing to say to you! Nothing except get out!'

Vincenzo drew in his breath sharply, ignoring her imprecation, walking into the room beyond.

He heard the woman in the dressing gown speak, her voice urgent. 'Si! This is it—he's here now. God knows how… He moves fast—including finding out where I live, because how else is he here? Look, let's just do this! Commit to nothing, just hear what he's offering, then hand the whole thing over to lawyers to hammer out so it's watertight.'

Dark rage fleeted in Vincenzo's eyes. Rage had filled him from the moment he'd heard his media comms account director say her name. It had brought him here and he would not be leaving. He watched, his face stony, as Siena Westbrook walked into the room, the other woman's hand propelling her.

He threw a quelling glance at the other woman, who lifted her chin and crossed her arms assertively.

'Whatever you intend saying, you're saying it in front of me as well,' she said fiercely. 'It was me who talked to your media comms guy yesterday—and I meant what I said. I promise you that!'

He made no reply, his eyes going to the woman who'd confronted him in his London office last month with the claim she had made. The claim, his expression tightened, that she must now either prove or withdraw.

His eyes rested on her for a moment. Did she look pregnant? No more than she had in his office. She was wearing jeans now, with a baggy tee shirt—both cheap. Her hair was in a plait, and she wore no make-up. Two spots of colour still burned in her cheeks. Her eyes glowed—but only with anger. Absently he noticed that they were still that same dark blue-green that had so intrigued him that fatal evening at the Falcone…

He dismissed the memory summarily. Frowned. Why did she want him to get out? Her PR friend had clearly been the one to bring him here by the means she'd used so effectively twenty-four hours ago. So why object to his arrival? Did she think his lawyers would be easier to deal with? If so—tough.

He cut to the chase.

'If you want to claim maintenance you must prove paternity. I told you that in my office. Since you have not done so, I have drawn my own conclusions.' He spoke briskly, and coldly. 'Now, however, you are pursuing that claim. So, which is it?' He levelled his gaze at her.

She didn't answer—the other woman did. The one who'd made the call yesterday. Megan Stanley was her name, he recalled.

'Mr Giansante,' she said, eyeballing him. 'You are, without doubt, the father of Siena's baby. As such, she is entitled to maintenance from you. She is perfectly prepared to substantiate that claim, and an *in utero* paternity test will do so. All that is required is for you to provide the appropriate DNA blood sample for her claim to be verified. Then it is simply a question of the level of maintenance required by Siena from you.'

Vincenzo turned his laser gaze on her, saying nothing. He saw her start to quail, for all her bravado. Then another voice cut across.

'There will be *no* paternity test—now or ever! And *no* claim for maintenance!'

Vincenzo's eyes snapped back to Siena. 'Because,' he directed at her quellingly, 'you know perfectly well the baby is not mine.' It was not a question—it was a statement.

Something flashed in her eyes. He'd seen it in his office, and now he was seeing it again.

'Because,' she echoed, 'you are the very *last* man on *earth* I would want to be the father of *any* baby—let alone *mine*!'

He saw her take a heaving breath and point towards the hallway.

'So, having established that, you can now give me the *only* thing I want from you—and it is *not* your precious money!—which is for you to *get out*!'

She stalked ahead of him and he saw her yank open the front door. Hold it pointedly open.

He did not hesitate. He walked out of the room, across the hallway. He paused by the door and looked into her face. Anger was in it…and something more. For one long, timeless moment he held her eyes. Then he walked out.

Decision made.

He heard the door slam shut behind him as he headed downstairs.

Siena slumped back against the wall. Her heart was racing, her breathing shallow, her colour high.

Megan came hurrying out, and Siena turned on her. 'Well, now you know why I will not—*will not!*—have *anything* to do with him!'

'No,' Megan bit back, 'I do *not* know why.' Then her voice changed, sounding quite different. 'But I'll tell you something for free. I know exactly why you fell into bed with him! Dear God, but he's just *lethal*!'

Siena's teeth gritted. '*Lethal* is exactly the right word. And, no, I don't mean it the way you damn well mean!'

Megan made a face. 'Well, the one adds to the other,' she said. Then her expression and her voice changed again. 'Oh, Si…why on earth did you send him packing? OK, so I never dreamt he'd actually turn up like that—I assumed he'd be too high and mighty to want to do anything except through lawyers. Speaking of which—what I said back there is absolutely what you must do next. I know a good law firm who will sort it for you. Yes, it will cost, but since he'll have no option but to concede to pay maintenance, once the paternity test is done, you'll cover the legal costs with that, so—'

Siena held up a hand. When she spoke her voice, still shaky, was nevertheless adamant. 'Megan, I know you mean well, but just stop. Stop interfering in my life. I am abjectly grateful he *doesn't* think he's the father! Because I meant every word I threw at him. He's the last man on earth I want to have anything to do with either me or my baby. I am *done* with him.'

She went back to the breakfast table, her hand still trembling, she could see, as she picked up her now cold mug of tea. Her heart rate was subsiding, but slowly, and shock waves were still going through her.

She must calm herself down...it would upset the baby.

My baby—as in mine and mine alone.

It was sentiment she clung to for the rest of the weekend. Until, on Monday morning, by registered hand delivery, she received a summons to co-operate with a claim for paternity or face legal action for refusal.

It seemed, she thought, with a hollowing out of her insides, that she might be done with Vincenzo Giansante, but he was not done with her.

Or with the baby she carried...

Vincenzo sat behind his desk in his London offices, staring at the screen of his computer. His face held no expression, yet behind its frozen surface emotions were scything.

He was the father of the baby Siena Westbrook was carrying. The baby conceived on that single, fateful night with her.

Despite the evidence on the screen, disbelief still sliced through him. More than disbelief.

What the hell had she been playing at, Siena Westbrook? Why come here—stand right here, in front of this very desk—tell him she was pregnant and then never follow through on paternity tests?

Why had she not simply included him in the round of

DNA testing she had presumably been instigating since their confrontation here? Why get that termagant in PR to do what she had? Threaten a press scandal? Why had that been the slightest bit necessary? It made no sense.

His mouth thinned, his frown deepening. Just as it made no sense that she should throw that hysterical outburst at him when he'd confronted her at the termagant's flat—telling him she wanted nothing to do with him. That wasn't the message he'd got when she'd told him she was pregnant, or she wouldn't have turned up here in the first place.

He thrust it aside. It was irrelevant. As irrelevant as her objecting to his demand for a paternity test—refusing to co-operate until, losing patience, he'd instructed his lawyers to exert the necessary pressure to get her to comply. Eventually, she had. He'd left her no option but to do so, or be hauled—expensively—into court. So finally she'd had the required blood test, and he had had the required cheek-swab. At this stage of pregnancy, nearing the end of her first trimester, there were sufficient foetal cells circulating in her system for the test to be completely non-invasive—and for the results to be ninety nine point nine percent accurate. No room for effective doubt.

He stared at the screen, emotion still scything through him.

He'd been so sure the results would be negative. So completely sure...

And yet—

Into his head one last question shaped itself. The one that he could not avoid.

So what the hell do I do now?

CHAPTER FOUR

'HE WANTS TO take you out to dinner to discuss the future.'

Megan's voice was neutral, but her observation of Siena as she made this declaration was wary.

'It's none of his business,' came the terse reply. 'And I told you not to have any more contact with him!'

'If you won't, I must!' Meg shot back. 'Look, Si, he's got responsibilities—to the baby and to you. He knows he has to sort maintenance out—'

'No, he does not. Megan, stay out of this. I won't have him anywhere near me or my baby. He's a vile, despicable jerk and he can go to hell and stay there!'

Siena's voice was vehement. She shut her eyes. Megan kept going on and on about maintenance…

But I'm not taking a penny from him! Not a single damn penny! Not now, or ever—not after the way he's treated me!

All she wanted to do was plan the future she was facing, find a decent enough place to live—far away from London and a million miles from Vincenzo Giansante!—see out her pregnancy, have her baby in peace, all by herself.

'Si, *please*… Just meet him and *talk*—' Megan started again.

Siena's eyes snapped open. OK, maybe that was what she should do—tell him to his face that he could go to hell. Get him off her back—and Megan too.

'So, where and when does he want to meet?' she heard herself asking.

'Tomorrow night. La Rondine—and that's a hell of a fancy restaurant, by the way. In my job I know just about every fancy restaurant in town!' Megan's voice relaxed. 'I'm wondering if it's significant that he doesn't want you to meet at his hotel...' Now she gave a wicked laugh. 'Maybe he's worried he'll fall for your charms all over again and haul you up to his room! I have to say, Si, that you are looking totally gorgeous. You know, pregnancy really is making you bloom—just like they say it does!'

Siena threw her a fulminating glance. 'That isn't funny,' she said brusquely. 'What time does His Lordship want to summon me?'

'Half-eight. What are you going to wear? Like I say, La Rondine is a pretty fancy place. Borrow something of mine—you can still fit into just about anything, so make the most of it before you turn into a barrage balloon!'

Siena didn't find that amusing either. 'I am not dressing up for him. I'll wear whatever comes to hand first.'

She did just that—deliberately dressing down. Deliberately choosing the very top and skirt she'd worn when she'd gone to his office. Would he recognise it? Probably not—but it gave her a sense of satisfaction to do so. The only sense of satisfaction she could find right now. That and the prospect of telling him to go to hell and take his precious money with him.

She left for the restaurant, put into a taxi by Megan, with Megan's final admonition ringing in her ears.

'See what he's offering but agree to nothing—that's for the lawyers.'

Siena hadn't bothered to answer.

All she wanted was this evening over and done with.

Then never to set eyes on Vincenzo Giansante again.

* * *

Vincenzo sat on the leather banquette at the table he'd reserved. Megan Stanley had just texted to tell him Siena was on her way. He reached for his martini. Emotions were stabbing at him, but he was ignoring them. This was about what had to be done—not what he was feeling about it. His feelings, whatever they were, were not relevant.

Yet despite the control he was exerting over them, he could feel them stabbing. Wanting release.

He took a shot of the strong, dry martini and set down the glass, his glance going again to the reception area where the desk clerk was checking in new arrivals.

And there she was.

Vincenzo observed her approach, keeping any expression out of his face, the way he preferred.

She looked tense.

She also looked out of place.

She was wearing chain store clothes… His eyes narrowed. Yes, exactly what she'd worn when she'd turned up at his office to disclose her valuable information to him. That was surely no coincidence.

His expression darkened.

He got to his feet as she reached the table. Face tight, she took her place at the far side of the curved banquette from him, so they were a semi-circle apart.

'Thank you for agreeing to come tonight,' he said, keeping his voice rigidly civil and neutral as he resumed his seat.

He got a brief nod in response, but that was all. She set her handbag down beside her.

'I have no idea why you've bothered—' she started. Her tone was openly belligerent.

He cut across her. 'You've never struck me as stupid,' he said. 'So of course you know why you are here.'

Her eyes flashed. She wasn't wearing a scrap of eye make-up, but that did not lessen their impact. The same impact they'd had when he'd first set eyes on her.

And that's ended up with me here, like this...

He pushed the pointless observation away. He was here for the reason he was here—and so was she.

'I'm here,' she said, 'to get you to accept that I make absolutely no claim for maintenance, and that you are, therefore, completely free of this entire situation.'

The words were ground out from her. He heard them, and let his eyes rest on her for a moment. Why was she being like this? What did she hope to achieve? A higher sum?

She'll get only what I'm prepared to offer—there will be no bidding war.

Whatever she hoped.

A waiter approached, wanting to know her choice of drinks and carefully placing menus in front of them both. She asked for mineral water and an elderflower spritzer, and the waiter disappeared again.

Vincenzo flicked open his menu. 'I suggest we keep our discussion for the meal,' he said. He kept his voice civil, still neutral. He lowered his eyes to focus on the menu options. After a moment, she did likewise. Then, making his decision, he shut the menu with a snap, beckoned the waiter over again.

'Have you decided?' he addressed Siena.

She looked up. 'I'm not hungry,' she announced.

Vincenzo's mouth tightened. 'Starving yourself will not be good for the baby,' he said.

Something flashed in her eyes. Absently—and quite irrelevantly—he registered that the flash only made them more striking. Again, he blanked their impact. It was not relevant.

'I'll be the judge of what is good for my baby,' she snapped back.

'*Our* baby,' he corrected tightly.

She stared balefully at him. *'Mine,'* she riposted.

The waiter's arrival silenced him, and he simply gave the man his order, not bothering with a starter. Whether Siena Westbrook ate or not, he didn't care. But she had clearly changed her mind, ordering grilled fish with vegetables.

The waiter glided off again, and the wine waiter took his place. Siena shook her head, so Vincenzo simply ordered a glass for himself.

They were left to themselves finally, and he sat back, letting his eyes rest on her. He kept his face expressionless, though he was more than conscious of the tension inside him. But how should there not be? He was in an unprecedented situation.

'So…' he opened. 'Maintenance.'

'I don't want any,' came the automatic response.

He ignored it.

'My lawyers have put forward a reasonable proposition,' he went on, naming the sum in question.

He saw her eyes widen, and grim satisfaction went through him. Yes, that was more like it—she was realising just how rich the pickings could be. She would not be turning them down.

She did.

And in words as clipped as they were concise. Adamant.

'It could be triple that—I don't care, and I'm not taking a penny. Please stop wasting my time and get that through your head.'

Vincenzo felt his teeth gritting. 'I have responsibilities and I will not walk away from them.'

'Well, you can—with my blessing. I don't want you or

your responsibilities.' She lifted her eyes to him, eyeballed him. 'Just leave me alone, Mr Giansante.'

'*Mr Giansante?*' He echoed her formal address disbelievingly.

Something flashed in her eyes again. 'Well, what else are you to me? The man I called Vincenzo I only knew one night.'

Vincenzo's eyes glinted darkly. So that was the cause of her hostility—the fact that he had wanted nothing more than a single night with her. Her female vanity was offended. Insulted.

'I am based in Italy,' he said stiffly. 'Whatever the… charms of that night, anything more would have been unworkable.'

Even as he spoke, he knew he was simply feeding her something to allay her vanity.

'You should not take the…brevity of our time together as an insult,' he added for good measure. His tone was deliberately sardonic.

He saw her jaw set, and her eyes were not flashing now, but like steel.

'Oh, really? So I'm just imagining that you put it to me, on that memorable day in your office, that I had fallen into bed with any number of men after a bare few hours of acquaintance with them?'

There was anger in her voice—tight, hard and vicious.

He set down his martini glass with a click.

'The sole purpose of that observation was to point out to you the fact that you might have any number of candidates responsible for the pregnancy you claimed.' His tone now was not sardonic, merely dismissive. 'It was not,' he went on, 'to indicate any criticism of your sexual behaviour.'

Her face worked. 'Well, that is very good of you! I'm *so*

grateful! You all but called me a slut to my face!' She leant forward. 'Well, let me point out to you, Mr Giansante, that it takes two to tango. You fell into bed with *me* within hours of meeting me—what does that make *you*? Some kind of ultra-masculine stud to be admired and applauded?'

Vincenzo took a sharp breath. Anger, answering hers, flared inside him, but he would not give it space. Instead, he said, his voice tight, control rigid, 'I cast no such aspersions—on either of us! It was simply a question of whether there might be other candidates for the claim you were making.'

'Well, there weren't! If there had been, why the hell would I have come to your office as I did?' she demanded hotly.

'Because,' Vincenzo replied silkily, 'I just happened to be the richest candidate...'

He saw her throw herself back against the squabs of the banquette. Eyes flashing like gunfire. Directed straight at him, full-on.

'Ah, now we have it, don't we?' Her tone was withering and scornful. 'This isn't about babies, or sex, or anything else at all, is it? It's about your money! And you think I want to get stuck into it! Well, I've told you—and I will tell you again and again if I have to—that I am *not taking a penny from you*! So go and take a running jump and *leave me alone*!'

She moved to push herself to her feet, but the waiter was just arriving with their meal, lowering plates, making a fuss over them, and then the wine waiter was there with his glass of wine, making a fuss over that too.

He could see her fulminating, but she stayed seated. Vincenzo used the time to take several deep breaths and regain his composure. She had an ability to rile him that got right under his skin...

For the next few minutes, as they started to eat, neither of them said anything. Then, knowing he had to resume battle, he spoke again.

'Whether or not you wish or don't wish to accept maintenance from me, I shall create a trust fund for the child.'

'We don't need anything from you!' she retorted, barely glancing up from her food.

'It will pay out when he or she reaches majority,' he went on.

She didn't answer—just went on eating. Not looking at him still. For a moment he let his eyes rest on her. His expression darkened, his jaw tightening.

'Siena, please co-operate on this,' he said tautly. 'I have acknowledged paternity. I acknowledge the responsibility that comes with that.'

'I absolve you totally of that responsibility.'

She spoke indifferently, and something snapped inside Vincenzo. He set down his knife and fork abruptly.

'That,' he gritted, 'is not within your remit. As you said only a few moments ago, it takes two to tango. Now that I know the child you carry is mine, you are *not* the sole arbiter of what is to happen. So be sure—be very, very sure—that I will not hesitate to resort to the law, if necessary, to claim my right for involvement.'

Her eyes snapped up then, and she looked straight at him. 'Are you *threatening* me?' she bit out.

'I am warning you,' he corrected.

He could feel anger rising within him—or something that he thought must be anger…anger at her obstinacy, her obstructiveness, her dogged, relentless opposition to him.

'I would far prefer not to have had to give you that warning, and would prefer even more not to be given reason for making my claim in that manner. But make no mistake: I am making that claim. And nothing you can do, or say, or attempt, will prevent that. Understand that, or things will become highly unpleasant.'

She glared across at him. 'They already are,' she said bitterly.

Her expression changed. Became questioning. She looked at him, frowning, and when she spoke her voice had changed, incomprehension in it now.

'I don't understand why you are making such an issue of this! Look—we met, we fell into bed, we had a single night of torrid sex and then you left, never to see me again. The last thing you want is to leave me—or any female you have sex with—in such circumstances! Pregnant. You went into total denial when I came to your office, and you couldn't have made it clearer that you didn't want to know. And now that you've insisted on a paternity test—completely against my will and consent, as I have made very clear to you—and the results are what they are, you are equally insistent on bringing money into the situation. When I have told you to your face I don't want a single penny of it—neither for me, nor my baby. And yet you are...just going on and on about it! Give me a piece of paper, right now, and I'll absolve you of all responsibility—past, present or future—in writing! I'll sign it in blood if it makes you any happier!' she bit out. 'I will do anything and everything to get you *out* of my life and out of my baby's life!'

'Why?'

She stared across at him. The single word seemed to have silenced her.

'Why?' he said again.

He wanted an answer.

He got one.

He saw her expression change. 'Because,' she said, enunciating the word, holding his gaze rigidly, 'you are a total and complete jerk. And falling into bed with you was the worst mistake I have ever made in my life.'

She dropped her eyes, picked up her knife and fork, and went on eating. She looked calm, but obviously she was not. The white-knuckled grip on her cutlery showed him that.

But then neither was he calm either. Anger was trying to break free—anger at her obduracy, her insults, the very fact that he was in this damnable situation.

He felt his teeth grit again as he spoke, his voice tight.

'I suggest we leave such puerile comments aside,' he said dismissively, resuming his meal. 'Understand and accept that, whether you want it or not, I *will* have an involvement in your pregnancy—and thereafter. All that is required, therefore, is for us to reach agreement on it. Starting with your accommodation. I will find an apartment for you, where you can live at least until the baby is born. We can use the time to discuss what is to happen once he or she makes an appearance.'

She didn't answer...only took a slug of her elderflower spritzer.

He went on talking. At least she wasn't arguing back, or giving him her pungent, if entirely irrelevant, opinion of him.

'I will cover all the expenses of the apartment—rent, taxes, utilities and so forth. I am also willing to make you an adequate monthly allowance to cover your costs during your pregnancy. I will also cover private medical costs for you, so you are not reliant on the NHS.'

She made no reply—only set down her glass, and picked up her knife and fork again.

An impulse just to get up and walk away knifed through

him, but with rigid self-discipline he repressed it. This was not a situation he could walk away from.

Nor for the rest of my life.

He thrust the thought from him. He could not deal with it—not right now. It was enough just to handle the situation at hand.

He made himself continue. 'I was thinking that the Holland Park area might be suitable. It is not far from Notting Hill, and your friend Megan, and it also has close access to the park there, which will be pleasant for you. How does that sound?'

He strove to make his voice civil.

Her response was an indifferent glance.

Something snapped inside him.

He dropped his cutlery abruptly.

'Do you think you might *possibly* bring yourself to pay attention? Bring yourself to deal with this situation—unprecedented for both of us—in a way that is co-operative and not intransigent?' he demanded scathingly, his patience at an end. 'I have acknowledged paternity, I am acknowledging my responsibilities for the child, and I am doing my damnedest to make your life easier so that you can have a healthy and safe pregnancy! So damn well stop stonewalling me!'

That got a response. She looked across at him. Anger was flaring in her eyes again.

'Am I supposed to be grateful? I *forced* myself to come to your office that day. Forced myself! I didn't want to—I didn't want anything more to do with a man who hadn't even had the courtesy to behave with some basic level of civility after our night together! But I thought that I should tell you—thought that I had no right to deny you knowledge of your own child. And all I got for my pains was insults and contempt! If you had said then that a paternity test might be prudent, but in a polite and civil manner, then I would have understood. But you just went straight for the jugular! You couldn't wait to throw me out! Like I was dirt on your shoe! And now—now that you can't evade paternity— you have the temerity to talk about my being *co-operative*? Don't make me laugh!'

Vincenzo's face was set. 'That was then…this is now— we have to deal with the situation.'

'I *am* dealing with it! I'm telling you I want nothing from you and nothing more to do with you. I am telling you I absolve you of all and any paternal anything! So just leave me—walk out the way you walked out on me the morning after the night before! Leave me to get on with my pregnancy and raise my child.'

'The child is mine as well. You cannot ignore that.' Vincenzo's voice was terse.

'Believe me, I'll do my level best—I promise you!'

She fell silent and drained the rest of her elderflower spritzer. Then she crushed her napkin onto her side plate and got to her feet.

'This has all been pretty pointless, but at least it's sorted things out between us. You go back to Italy and I'll look after myself. Like I say, I'll sign any documents you like, absolving you of any responsibility—especially financial— and then we'll be done with it all.'

She picked up her handbag, slung it over her shoulder, and prepared to walk away.

Vincenzo's next words stayed her. Where they came from, he did not know—but he heard himself say them all the same.

'There is an alternative outcome,' he heard himself say. 'That we marry.'

* * *

Siena stilled—and stared at him disbelievingly.

'We spend one night together—*one night*—and now you say we should *marry*?' Incredulity filled her voice.

'As I say, it would be one way of addressing the situation. Of course I would require you to sign a prenup, but since you have been at pains to tell me you are not interested in my money, that should not be a problem for you.'

She could hear the open sarcasm in his voice, and it grated like nails on a chalkboard.

Her eyes flashed. 'You must be insane to think I'd marry you!'

'Then accept my offer of accommodation and an allowance.'

His voice was implacable, his gaze on her relentless.

She sat down heavily again, placing her hands on the table either side of her empty plate, and leaned forward. There was a tangled knot of emotions inside her…like a bunch of snakes.

'I will say this one more time.' She spoke slowly, in a staccato voice, enunciating each word as if it was bitten out of her. 'I do not want anything more to do with you. I should never have had anything to do with you in the first place! I bitterly, *bitterly* regret that night!'

He was looking back at her, his face grim, eyes dark.

'Do you think I don't?' he retorted starkly. 'But it happened. And now we have to deal with the consequences. You will have to accept that you carry my child,' he said, and his darkened eyes had a dangerous anger in them. 'And you are not walking away with it.'

He drew a breath—a harsh, heavy one. That dark expression was still on his face, and she didn't like it. Not one little bit.

Suddenly, it was all too much. She couldn't cope—not one minute longer. Not with one more vicious, biting exchange.

She heaved herself to her feet. She was done here. Done, done, done, and *done* with Vincenzo Giansante.

She stood, her face working, and he looked back at her.

'Go to hell,' she said. 'Just go to *hell*!'

Then she walked out.

Before she collapsed.

CHAPTER FIVE

'SO,' ASKED MEGAN, 'what are you going to do? Did he really offer to marry you?' Incredulity was mingled with another emotion—several of them, Siena thought cynically, of which envy was only one.

She gave an inner sigh. Megan was pitifully impressed by Vincenzo Giansante—that was obvious.

'It was a play, Megan, a totally transparent one. Marriage would give him control over me. And he must be insane to think I'd even give him the time of day!'

Megan laughed shortly. 'Any other woman would snap his hand off at the offer. All that money and all those lethal looks!'

'And all that charm…' Siena rejoined with acid sweetness.

'So, are you at least going to move into this apartment he's rented for you? He sent me the details—it looks pretty good.'

'No, of course I'm not,' Siena returned.

'But why not?' Megan pursued. 'Look, you can move in at the weekend—I'll help you.'

'Megan, no.' Siena's voice was adamant. 'That's final. I've got a roof over my head till Fran gets back—time enough to decide where I'm going to move to and get a place to rent there.'

Till then she'd stay here and keep on with her temporary clerical job at the PR firm Megan worked for, earning some useful money.

But when she got back from work on Friday evening, it was to find the bed in her room pulled away from the wall, all the furniture swathed in a dust sheet, another dust sheet on the floor, and paint pots on the chest of drawers.

Megan's attitude was unapologetic. 'I've decided this room needs a little sprucing up, Si.' Her tone was sympathetic, but determined. 'Just move into the apartment Vincenzo's taken for you—he's had the keys delivered to me, and I'll come with you this evening to settle you in. It's all furnished and kitted out. We just need to take basics, like milk and tea. We'll get a takeaway, and you can go food shopping tomorrow. I've even packed your things for you.'

Siena stared at Megan in dismay.

Megan patted her arm encouragingly. 'You know it makes sense, Si. It gives you somewhere to think things through. And I hope—I really, *really* hope—you'll decide to stay there and take up your place at art school. I'd hate to see you give it up!'

Siena's face worked. She knew her friend was trying to be helpful, but—

But right now, however galling it is, I have no choice but to do what she wants. I don't even have a bed to sleep in tonight!

Grimly, she let Megan have her way.

And Vincenzo Giansante was getting his own way too.

Her face darkened. She would stay in his damn flat *only* until she got her life sorted out. Then she'd be gone.

And he'll be out of my life.

The way, after all, he obviously wanted *her* out of *his* life…

Her expression became even grimmer, memory stabbing of how he'd walked out on her that morning after their searing night together.

He hadn't wanted anything more to do with her then, and if it weren't for the baby he still wouldn't. That was the blunt, hard truth of it…

Vincenzo gave a tight smile of grim satisfaction as he read Megan's text.

She's here—we're ordering a takeaway. She's not in the best mood, so I'd give her a day to accept what's happened.

He took her advice, waiting until Sunday before turning up at the apartment. As the taxi dropped him off he glanced around. The street on the park side of Holland Park Avenue was quiet and expensively residential. The apartment block was small and twentieth century, compared with the surrounding nineteenth-century stucco-fronted houses, but it was well maintained, and close to the park entrance. It was costing a pretty penny, but that was only a fraction of the future expense this whole damn situation would put him to.

A lifetime of expense. A lifetime of responsibility that he could not shirk, nor avoid. That he must assume, whatever it took. And right now that was getting Siena Westbrook to see sense.

That, at least, seemed to have started happening. She was here, in the apartment he'd taken for her. Now he had to move things on from there. Make some kind of acceptable arrangement for the future, however pointlessly and inexplicably obdurate she was being.

He frowned. Why had she not jumped at the financial

offer he was prepared to make? Let alone his offer to marry her. His thoughts darkened. Why was she protesting? Refusing?

Well, whatever she was playing at, he would deal with it. He had no choice but to do so. This was not about her, or him. It was about the baby that in six months would be making its appearance. That was all he must focus on.

His expression as he paid off the taxi was set.

He had his own keys for the apartment, bestowed upon him by the letting agent, and he let himself into the lobby, ignoring the lift and vaulting lightly up the two flights of stairs. Then, without pause for thought, because thoughts were only unwelcome, he let himself into the apartment.

From the hallway he could see into the reception room, from which came the sound of the television. He walked in.

Siena was lounging on the sofa, a cup of tea on the side table, a paperback beside her, and sunshine streaming in from the window overlooking the garden at the rear.

As he walked in she sat bolt upright.

'What the hell—?' The words broke from her, shock and consternation in her face.

Two emotions knifed through Vincenzo. One was the same grim satisfaction he'd felt when he'd learnt she'd moved in here, fight it though she had. The other was completely different.

It knifed through him again.

The sunshine was turning her hair to a glossy mahogany, glinting off it gloriously, and even though she was lounging in nothing more than pale blue cotton trousers and a yellow top, and hadn't done a thing to her face, he still felt his senses kick in response. The same kick that had come that first, fateful evening when he'd seen her for the first time. Seen her—and wanted her.

He crushed the reaction down. It had been that damn re-action that had brought him to this predicament now.

'Buongiorno,' he said civilly, though he could hear the jibe in his own voice.

She grabbed the remote for the TV, flicking it to mute. It was some old black and white Hollywood movie, he could see.

'What are you doing here? And why have you just let yourself in?' she demanded.

'I came to see how you've settled in,' he said. He glanced around the room. 'Does it suit you, this place?' he asked.

She glowered at him. 'No, because I didn't choose to be here—you fixed it with Megan.'

He didn't bother to reply.

'Do you have any coffee?' he asked.

'I'm pregnant—no caffeine or stimulants,' she answered, her voice clipped.

He went into the kitchen, resolving to have a coffee machine delivered before his next visit. As it was, he opted for tea—only to discover that that, too, was decaffeinated. He made himself a cup, then went back into the living room, cup in hand. She was still curled up on the sofa, looking tense and baleful.

He lowered himself into an armchair, crossed one leg over the other, and made a start on his cup of tea.

'Your friend Megan told me you have not lived in London long,' he opened. He was going to stay civil, whatever the provocation. Anything else was not helpful. 'You never did mention, when we first met, what you do for a living.'

He saw two reactions in her. One was a distinct flare of colour in her cheeks as he referred to the evening when they had first so fatefully encountered each other. The other was a tightening of her expression—as if she didn't want to expound on the subject.

'I've been doing some casual office work for the PR company Megan works for,' she replied, but he could tell she said it with reluctance.

'Do you plan to continue?' he asked. He kept his voice studiedly neutral.

'I don't know,' she replied. 'I don't know what I'll be doing. Other than having a baby.'

Vincenzo let his eyes rest on her a moment. So, here it was, then—what he had been expecting. For all her vehement protestations that she didn't want anything to do with him, she did, in fact, expect him to keep her.

He didn't reply, only went on calmly sipping his tasteless tea. Letting his gaze rest on her. Letting himself be deflected from his purpose by something that was completely irrelevant.

She truly is beautiful—radiantly so.

His glance went to her waistline. Nothing showed. Yet within her body his child was growing...

He felt something go through him, but he did not know what it was. He set it aside. He had enough to deal with.

He finished his tea. On the still silent screen he could see the old film end, and Siena reached absently for the remote and turned the TV off.

He got to his feet. 'It's a fine afternoon—pleasantly warm for England. How about taking a walk in the park?' he asked.

He crossed over to the sofa, picked up her own empty tea mug, and took them both through into the kitchen. Then he returned to the living room. She hadn't moved.

She looked up at him. 'You've seen I'm OK, so why don't you leave now?'

'Because,' he said pointedly, his gaze levelled on her just as pointedly, 'we have things to discuss.'

Her face tightened. 'No,' she said, 'we do not.'

Vincenzo took an impatient breath. 'Stonewalling is pointless. There are practicalities to be decided upon.'

She shook her head vigorously. 'No, there are not. I am only in this damn flat until I find somewhere else. After that you can wash your hands of me.'

'But not,' he said even more pointedly, his gaze boring down at her, 'of the baby.'

Anger flashed in her eyes—and frustration too, he could see. She opened her mouth again, and he was pretty sure she was going to offload the same diatribe—tell him that she wanted nothing to do with him, that he should clear out and get back to Italy.

Well, that was not going to happen, and she had better take that on board.

He held up a hand.

'Let us walk and talk at the same time,' he said, making an effort to keep his voice even. He gestured towards the door. 'Shall we?' he said.

She got to her feet with visible ill grace, slipping her feet into the canvas shoes on the rug in front of the sofa. Silently he handed her her bag, lying on a sideboard within his reach. She all but snatched it. He went through into the entrance hall, holding open the door for her. She marched through, head high, making straight for the stairs. Vincenzo locked the door and followed her.

Of all the women in the world he knew, of every one of them with whom he had ever had sexual relations, it was this bristling, critical, obstreperous and supremely unco-operative and unappreciative one that he'd got pregnant.

He couldn't have made a worse choice.

But we did not choose, did we? We got landed with it, that's all. And now, somehow, I have to try and find a way forward.

That was all he must focus on.

As they made their way into Holland Park Siena was churning inside. Vincenzo walking in like that had been a shock, unexpected and totally unwelcome. Why the hell couldn't the man stay away? Stay in Italy. Wash his hands of the whole damn business, like she kept telling him to. He should be *glad* she didn't want anything to do with him!

Her eyes darkened. He thought her a slut for falling into bed with him the way she had, and now a gold-digger, trying to get a free meal ticket off him because she was pregnant.

Well, I am neither, thank you! And you—her glance went malevolently to him as he fell into step beside her, heading towards the nearby park—*are a total jerk!*

She waited for anger to fill her again—the anger that had been spearing in her ever since that hideous afternoon when she'd been thrown out of his office. It had more than enough, to feed on. And yet right now all she could feel was a deflation of her spirits. A dullness and tiredness and sense of depression.

About everything—just *everything*.

This was all wrong. Wrong, wrong, *wrong*. She should not be pregnant, and she shouldn't be staying in an apartment which the man responsible had forced her into—the man who obviously thought she was after his money.

This wasn't what I wanted—none of it!

Even as she thought it she felt guilty, and that only added to her darkness of mood. The creation of new life was precious—she should not feel so bitter, should not so resent what had happened. How could her poor, innocent, hapless baby be to blame for anything? How could she blight the start of its existence by wishing she were not pregnant at all?

Yet still something cried within her.

This is not how it should be!

Babies should be born into joy and happiness, welcomed and rejoiced over, bringing blessings and being infinitely blessed themselves. To grow in love, become happy, healthy children…

Yet the cry inside her came again.

This is not how it should be!

But this time it was an echo. A terrifying echo. She felt it clutch within her, like a vice around her heart, her lungs, her throat. Memory stabbed at her, infinitely painful.

'What is it?'

Vincenzo's voice pierced her dark thoughts. He was walking beside her, along one of the paths in the park.

She didn't answer, and he spoke again. 'What is it,' he repeated.

She gave a shake of her head. 'It's nothing,' she said.

She didn't want to talk to him, to walk with him, to be with him at all. She wanted absolutely nothing in her life right now—the life that had finally been heading in the direction she had waited so long for it to go in, and which had now been derailed. *Again.*

She felt her arm taken, and halted in her pacing. Vincenzo stepped in front of her, looking down at her. His face had a taut expression.

'It is not "nothing",' he said. 'It is not "nothing" that both you and I find ourselves in a situation neither of us wished for.'

'No? But you think I'm definitely thinking it's a bit of luck for me, don't you? It's got my greedy little fingers into your nice rich pie, hasn't it? A meal ticket for life! That's what you think!'

His brow darkened and he dropped her arm.

Siena's mouth set tight. 'Despite my repeatedly telling you to walk away—that I don't need your financial support or want it!'

'So how will you support yourself?' he countered immediately. 'Live on state benefits in a council-paid bedsit? That was the graphic image painted by your friend Megan to get my attention,' he said witheringly.

'She acted totally without my consent!' Siena threw back instantly. 'I never wanted her to interfere. Just as I never wanted you to come anywhere near me again! And just as I do *not* want any of your damn money!' she bit out. 'Just believe me when I say I've got enough to live on.' She took a slicing breath. 'If you really want to know, I've inherited some money and it's safely banked. It's quite enough to let me live somewhere a lot cheaper than London and look after my baby, so I neither need, let alone want, a single penny from you!'

Dear God, how many times had she got to say that before he got the damn message?

But it seemed he was set on moving on to a new subject.

'Even setting that aside—for the moment at least,' he said repressively, 'there is more to the situation than financial considerations.' Vincenzo's voice was still tight. 'I told you I would not walk away—and I do not mean only from my financial responsibilities.'

Siena started to walk again. The vistas of the park all around were scenic, but she had no appreciation for them.

Vincenzo fell into pace beside her again. 'We cannot avoid looking ahead,' he was saying now, as if he were forcing himself to do so. 'To beyond the child's birth and babyhood.'

She felt her mind sheer away. She couldn't even cope with being pregnant, let alone thinking beyond it to an unimaginable future. One she had never, in all her days, thought she would be landed with.

Depression weighed down on her. All around were people enjoying the park—families, couples, singletons young and old. Yes, maybe they had their own problems, but all she could focus on were her own. Her pace slowed, energy draining from her.

At her side, Vincenzo spoke again, glancing at her. 'We should find a café, and you should sit down,' he said.

They made their way to one with outdoor seating which overlooked a small fountain, and Siena was glad to sit down. Her energy levels fluctuated these days—her mental energy levels too. She knew it was not good for her to be so agitated—but what else could she be in the circumstances?

Vincenzo got coffee for them both, and she sipped her decaf without enthusiasm. As he sat opposite her at the small table she was acutely conscious of his physical closeness, the strength of his body, and she caught the scent of masculine aftershave. Memory assailed her, of that night she'd succumbed to his seduction.

I went along with it willingly—oh, so willingly! And now...

'Do you have to drink decaf all the time?' There was a frown on Vincenzo's face as he put the question to her.

'Standard recommendation when pregnant,' she said flatly, resenting the note of criticism. 'Like no alcohol and no smoking.'

'Is it so very bad for you?' Vincenzo pursued, stirring his own coffee. 'Pregnant women have drunk caffeinated tea and coffee for generations and no harm seems to have been done. The rules seem very strict these days. Banning all alcohol too...'

She gave a shrug, not wanting to debate it. She hadn't issued the damn guidelines, so why should he be challenging her? It set her teeth on edge.

'We are supposed to do nothing that risks the baby,' she said. 'Even though—'

She broke off.

Some risks have nothing to do with the mother's lifestyle...

No, she must not think of that—it was too upsetting. And it served no purpose but to weigh her down yet more. She knew she should—she must—be thankful, but the thought oppressed her all the same, however stringently she sought to repress the memories that assailed her. It made her feel guilty that she was resenting a pregnancy that was seemingly healthy when—

Vincenzo was speaking again, bringing her thoughts back to her predicament. Once again Siena got the impression he was choosing his words carefully,

'Stress is also bad. Stressful emotions.'

She eyeballed him, feeling on edge again. 'What are you getting at?'

He looked directly at her. 'Anger, hostility, resentment—these are all negative emotions. They cannot be doing you any good. Nor the baby.'

'Are you *criticising* me?' Siena's anger shot to the fore. 'Don't you damn well preach at me!'

He held up a hand. 'Do you deny that you are seething with anger at me?' he returned implacably. 'That that is your dominant reaction to me ever since your friend Megan took matters into her own hands to bring me here?'

Her eyes flashed with the very anger he was accusing her

of. 'How should it be otherwise?' she threw at him witheringly. 'After that delightful scene in your office!'

A dismissive expression filled his face. 'What were you expecting?' he retorted scathingly, his expression hardening. 'You turn up, out of the blue, demand to see me, then drop your bombshell on my desk. Were you expecting me to shout with joy and sweep you into my arms and promise undying love?'

'I was expecting *civility*,' she ground out tightly—as tightly as she was gripping her coffee cup.

He made a rough sound in his throat, as dismissive as his expression. 'I dealt with the situation as required. Rationally. Until paternity was established, there was no point in any further conversation at that time.' He sat back, took a mouthful of his coffee. 'But now that it is established we can move forward—as we must.'

His gaze levelled on her.

'Tell me, have you thought through what I put to you the other evening? That one option appropriate to the situation would be that we marry.'

Siena stared at him. 'Even as a joke, that is not humorous. As a serious suggestion—and I cannot believe it to be as such—it is, as I've told you already, *totally* insane!'

She saw his face darken. He hadn't liked her answer, and it was obvious why. Presumably she should be melting all over him and planning a hideously expensive wedding as an excuse to start spending all his money on herself.

'There are practical advantages—' he began.

'No,' she said. She wanted this conversation stopped— right now.

His dark eyes flashed angrily and he held up a hand. 'Hear me out before you give me an infantile rejection!

Marriage would regularise the situation…provide far more security both for yourself and the baby, and enable us to—'

'I said *no*,' Siena ground out. Her own eyes flashed with anger. 'The *only* reason you want to marry me is to control me—and my baby. So don't feed me any garbage to the contrary!'

For a moment she saw an expression on his face that almost silenced her. But she would not be silenced—she would *not*! Emotions were boiling up in her, tangled and knotted, vehement and vicious.

'It's bad enough you feel you have any say about my baby—let alone expect me to walk into the noose you're dangling in front of me. So get this, and get this once and for all—finally! I will *never* marry you! I will *never* have anything to do with you of my own free will. Because of this baby I am handcuffed to you—shackled to you! And I resent it and I hate it. *Hate* it—'

She broke off, churning inside. Heart thudding. She pushed her pallid, undrunk coffee aside. She got to her feet, looked down at him. Her face contorted with the emotion heaving inside her.

'I can't *bear*,' she said, 'that it's you who got me pregnant.'

She walked away. Eyes blind. Crushed and hopeless.

Words went through her head—as crushed and hopeless as her spirit.

It's all a mess—such a mess.

Such a hopeless, hopeless mess.

CHAPTER SIX

VINCENZO SAT AT his desk in his office in Milan. He should be working, but he wasn't. He was brooding. That was the only word for it. His expression was a study—a darkened one—and his hands were resting tightly on the arms of his custom-made leather chair. His eyes were seemingly fixed on a focal point that did not actually exist in the spacious, beautifully appointed and ferociously expensively decorated executive office, with its modernistic grey leather sofas facing each other across a low chrome and glass coffee table, backed by the floor-length plate glass window looking out over the city skyline.

In his head was circling the memory of visiting Siena two days ago. Baleful and benighted. What had it achieved? Nothing. It had only sunk them further into the impossibility of their situation. A situation neither of them wanted.

His mouth thinned.

Shackled to each other—that was what she'd said. And that was the blunt truth of it, all right. This baby, that neither of them wanted, was handcuffing them to each other. He could resent the fact that it was so all he liked—but it changed nothing.

Nothing could change the situation.

His hands tightened over the leather arms of his chair. He was trying, damn it. Trying to take the necessary responsibility, to make the necessary plans for the future. What else could he do? And for his pains she was stonewalling him totally. How did he get past that? How did he get her to drop her relentless hostility towards him? Because somehow he had to...

Resolve steeled in him. Anger, as he had said to her face, was her predominant emotion towards him—well, he had to defuse it. Bring down that wall of implacable hostility. Do whatever it took to do so.

He reached forward, lifted his desk phone, and spoke to his PA in the outer office. He told her to cancel the week's appointments and book him a flight to London tomorrow morning.

He was going back. Whether Siena Westbrook liked it or not, wanted him or not, he was going back.

Not for him, and not for her, but for the one person who was overweeningly more important than anything he or she might want—who deserved better than a pair of angry, hostile, irresponsible adults throwing their resentment at each other.

The baby she carried.

The only thing that mattered in all this sorry mess.

Siena was kneeling on the floor, leafing through her portfolio, her spirits sinking as she did so. So short a time ago her future had been bright, finally taking off. And now it had crashed and burned. She had given up on her future once before—and now she was doing it again. Instead of looking forward to starting a new term she was scouring the Internet for affordable rental properties in places—anywhere at all—where she might want to live as a single mother of the baby that was on the way.

With a sigh she leant the portfolio back against the wall of her bedroom, then leaned back herself as well, stretching out her legs. Her hands went to her midriff. Already there was a change in her body—a rounding discernible to her, even if her clothes still hardly showed it. Within her body a hapless little baby was forming, day by day, its tiny body taking shape, limbs and organs and tissues and heartbeat… so desperately tiny, so desperately vulnerable…

So entirely and totally dependent on me.

A wave of fierce protectiveness went through her, and her fingers splayed out like a net to keep safe the tiny soul inside her.

Poor little mite… None of this is your fault, yet you are going to be the one who suffers—born to two irresponsible, selfish people who thought their own fleeting sexual plea- sure so important…

She looked out across the room, but she did not see it at all. Her face was a mask of self-condemnation. Yes, she wished with all her being that she had never conceived that wretched night, but it had happened, and now she must do whatever it took not to blight the totally innocent life within her.

I've got to protect you…make it better for you, little one. I've got to! Make the best I can out of the mess that this is. I've got to at least try. I owe you that…

And if that meant coping—somehow—without getting so angry, so upset, so destructively emotional with Vin- cenzo…well, she would have to.

Because only one person mattered now. And it wasn't her, and it certainly wasn't Vincenzo Giansante.

Her hands pressed protectively again.

It's you, little one—only you…

* * *

Vincenzo's fingers hovered over the text message he was composing. Siena had walked out on him twice now—in the restaurant and in the park. He had to get past that. Get past the wall of her hostility.

Would what he intended achieve that? Well, he would find out soon enough.

He reread the message, then hit 'send'.

I am back in London. I would like to come and see you again. I have something to say that needs to be said.

The reply came briefly.

What is it?

He tapped back.

In person. This evening? I will come to the apartment for eight.

Her reply took longer. But it came, and at least that was something.

You're paying the rent. I can't stop you.

His mouth tightened. Would she even be there?

Siena was pacing up and down. It was seven fifty-seven, and she was on edge. She didn't want to see Vincenzo again. And at the same time she knew she must.

I can't just pretend he doesn't exist. I might want to, but

I can't. And whatever it is that he says he wants to say to me, I need to know it.

He was, as she knew, a man perfectly prepared to be ruthless. Ruthless enough to not even stick around for breakfast with her that morning after the night before. Ruthless enough to say to her what he had when she'd told him she was pregnant. Ruthless enough to throw her out of his office. Ruthless enough to threaten her with the law when she refused to co-operate on a paternity test. Ruthless enough to rent this flat and then commandeering Megan into manipulating her into moving in to it.

Ruthless all round.

A sudden longing to pour herself a glass of wine and knock it back assailed her. Going without alcohol was hard when it came to moments like this. She wondered whether to make herself a cup of tea, and see if that helped at all, but she didn't have time to drink it. He would be punctual, she knew.

He was. She heard the front door open and turned around, facing the door into the hall.

Vincenzo walked in.

She felt tension bite inside her—or something bite, at any rate. Every time she saw him she felt his impact.

No wonder I fell for him—fell into bed with him...

No, there was no point thinking that, or remembering it. It was, after all, what caused her to be standing here now, nerves on edge, in an apartment whose rent she couldn't have afforded for a week, let alone a month, and pregnant by the man now walking into the room.

He was wearing a business suit, pale grey, perfectly tailored with Italian flair to his lean, tall frame. His shirt was white, his tie pale grey, his hair clipped short. His features possessed whatever chemistry it was that made her—and doubtless every other female—gulp openly.

Not that she did—but she could feel the impulse to do so all the same.

She crushed it down. Vincenzo had turned up to talk to her—he had something to say, he'd said. She had to brace herself for it.

And I won't let myself be upset by it—whatever it is. I won't—I can't! I have to think not about myself, only about my baby.

That was the resolve she'd made, sitting by the now useless portfolio that had won her a place at art school she could no longer take up. Letting Vincenzo upset her wasn't good for her—let alone the baby. Vincenzo himself had told her that—and, gall her though it did, he was right.

I have to stay calm—not let my emotions boil over. Whatever he throws at me.

His eyes—dark, long-lashed and quite unreadable, so no change there, she thought resignedly—were resting on her.

'How are you?' he asked, his voice cool and accented.

'The baby,' replied Siena pointedly, because the question was not about her, and she knew that perfectly well, 'is fine.'

A frown flashed briefly, as though her answer, and the pointedness with which she'd made it, displeased him.

'And yourself?' he pursued.

She gave half a shrug. 'Fine,' she said. 'I'm having, it seems, a very healthy pregnancy.'

She took a breath, wanting to cut to the chase, not wanting to let her fragile, flammable emotions flare up when she was trying so hard to stay cool and calm—the way he was being. For now, at least.

'Your text said you had something to say to me.'

Tension had entered her voice. She could hear it. So, it

seemed, could he. Because he made a slight gesture with his head, as if to negate her reaction.

'Yes, but not right now.' His voice was clipped. His stance changed, and so did his tone. 'Tell me, have you eaten?'

Siena shook her head. Was she supposed to provide dinner for him?

'In which case,' he went on, 'there's a restaurant nearby on Holland Park Avenue that appears tolerable.'

'OK…' she said guardedly.

Eating out was preferable to eating in—and, whatever it was that Vincenzo wanted to say, doing so in public might be preferable too.

She glanced at him. 'I had better change first,' she said.

She was wearing cotton pedal pushers and a long-sleeved tee shirt—not good enough for a swanky restaurant. Memory darted, of how she'd deliberately not dressed up the previous time. But that had been to make a point. A point she didn't need to make a second time.

'I'll be two minutes,' she said.

She kept to it, too, having simply swapped what she'd been wearing to a pair of smarter, dark blue trousers and a blue striped shirt, worn loose. She didn't think her pregnancy showed much, but it definitely wouldn't in the shirt. She didn't bother with make-up, simply brushed her hair, drawing it back with a barrette. Then, staring at her reflection, she grabbed some lip gloss after all and touched it to her lips. Then she stared again.

Memory intruded suddenly—of how Megan had dolled her up that fateful evening, for that swanky party at the Falcone. Squeezing her into that tight dress, doing her make-up—*over*doing it, by Siena's standards—leaving her hair loose and tumbling down her back, seeing her legs lengthened by the high heels she'd persuaded her to wear.

She'd looked totally vamped. Sex on legs…

It wasn't me.

It hadn't been her. The reflection that had gazed back at her that evening, with its deep eyes, lavishly lashed, scarlet mouth, wanton hair and skin-tight dress. Dressed to kill.

No wonder he thought I was up for it…

She swallowed. She *had* been up for it, hadn't she? She could hardly deny it.

She shut her eyes to block out the memory of what she'd looked like that evening. Then opened them again.

Now she looked nothing like that.

Thankfully…

She grabbed a cardigan, threw it around her shoulders, slipped her feet into flat pumps, and went back out. She didn't know what Vincenzo wanted to say to her, but she knew she had to be ready for it. She nerved herself accordingly.

He was by the sitting room window, looking out, his face in profile to her. He looked severe, but as she came in he turned. Whatever he was thinking, she didn't have a clue.

He nodded, in lieu of saying anything, and crossed to the door, holding it open for her. She walked through into the entrance hall, opening the front door, picking up the handbag lying on a pier table next to it. They didn't speak as they went down to the lobby, nor as they went out onto the pavement. The sun had gone and it was very slightly chilly. She was glad of the cardigan.

He still didn't speak, and neither did she, as they paced beside each other heading for Holland Park Avenue.

The restaurant, looking swish enough for Vincenzo, was on their side of the busy road, and this early in the week was not full at this hour. She took her place at the table they were shown to, and then the business of presenting menus and ordering drinks took place, so it was some minutes before they were left alone.

Vincenzo glanced at the closed menu, but did not open it. Instead, he looked across at her. His face still had that reserved expression on it, now even more pronounced, and Siena felt a sudden shaft of apprehension. Whatever it was he'd come back to London to tell her, it was not going to be good. Nothing he ever said to her was good...

As she braced herself, Vincenzo's inexpressive gaze rested on her, quite unreadable. Then he spoke.

'I owe you an apology,' he said.

Vincenzo saw Siena's eyes widen. Whatever she'd been expecting, it hadn't been that. But then, he thought sardonically, that was hardly surprising. Had he not resolved to say it, he wouldn't have expected it himself.

'I owe you an apology,' he said again. He kept his gaze levelled on her. 'It has been owing to you,' he said, 'for some time.'

He paused, as if he might be waiting for her to say *What for?* But that look of surprise was still paramount in her widened eyes.

'I have behaved badly to you, for which I apologise.'

He took the slightest of breaths and kept going. This had to be done.

'My reception of the news you came to tell me in my office was not acceptable. I apologise for it completely. Unreservedly.'

There was silence. Complete silence.

Then Siena said slowly, 'You came to England to tell me this?'

'Yes,' he said.

The slightest frown creased her brow. 'Why?'

'Because,' he said, 'my apology has, as I say, been owing for some time.'

The frown did not lighten. 'Why now?' she said.

His right index finger smoothed along the length of the knife at his place-setting. He was trying to find the words— first in Italian, then in English—that would answer her question. They did not come easily. But they came all the same. Feeling his way with every one of them.

'Because...' He spoke carefully, feeling his way with every word, conscious of the tension in his voice, his jaw, his throat—his expression. His eyes were levelled, by an act of explicit will, on her closed and shuttered face. 'Because it was holding things back—holding us apart. Because...'

He made himself go on in the same tight and guarded tone, saying what had to be said, what needed to be said, what was necessary for the future that only the words he was saying now could create. A future that had to exist. Because it was the only one that would do any justice to the reason she and he were yoked together as they were.

'Because without it, it will be impossible for us to have any kind of...acceptable relationship within the situation in which we both find ourselves.'

A glint was suddenly in her eye. A steely one.

'Do you mean it?' she asked. 'That apology?'

He would have had to have been deaf and stupid not to hear the edge in her voice—and he was neither. And he would have had to have been stupid indeed not to know that only one answer was permissible.

Whether or not I believe it myself does not matter. All that matters is the fact that it is the only means to the end I have to achieve.

'Yes,' he said. He paused, his eyes still levelled on her. 'Do you accept my apology?'

For a moment her face was unreadable, her eyes masked now. Then she spoke.

'Yes,' she said.

Siena heard herself say it, but she wasn't sure it was real—had she really said it?

But she had, and she knew why.

For the same reason he had brought himself to apologise to her. To make an apology she had never, for a moment, thought to hear.

But he'd made it all the same.

And I have to bring myself to accept that apology.

Because if she didn't...

Everything that had passed between them since the moment she'd walked into his London office to tell him she was pregnant flashed before her eyes. Every ugly, vicious, biting, hostile expression of enmity and anger. Of bitterness and resentment and loathing.

It was draining from her every residue of the energy she still possessed. Draining her and destroying her...

I can't go on like that—I just can't.

However justified her reaction to him...

I have to let it go—I have to.

It was the same sense of deeply unwilling resolve that had gone through her as she had sat by her portfolio, hunkered down on the carpet, her hands cradling the tiny, innocent life within her. It, alone of all involved in the situation, deserved to be their priority.

We've got to do this—Vincenzo and I. We don't want to—we wish each other to perdition. But we can't go there, either of us. Because it isn't just ourselves we'd be there...

She heard him speaking now, this man who was the other

half of the tiny life growing inside her, depending on her so absolutely.

'Thank you,' he said.

The waiter was returning with their drinks. Vincenzo hadn't bothered with a cocktail—he would drink wine with the meal—and for now matched Siena with her obligatory soft drink. Iced water was placed on the table as well, along with rolls and butter.

'Shall we order?' Vincenzo said, opening his menu.

Siena did likewise.

It was a strange moment…a strange atmosphere. So little had been said verbally—but he knew it was more than that. He felt as if he'd gone through a barrier that had not been visible, only tangible. Tension was still making his shoulders stiff, his expression severe, but now it came not from knowing that he had to say what he'd just said, but from not knowing how she would be with him now.

He busied himself scanning the menu options, giving her time to do likewise. Then, seeing her place hers flat on the table, closed his.

'Chosen?' he asked.

Memory suddenly hit him. That was exactly what he'd asked her when they'd removed themselves from that party to have dinner at the Falcone restaurant. When both of them had been radiating a force field neither could resist—nor had any wish to resist—and that searing sexual desire had flared between them.

For a second it almost overwhelmed him, the vividness of that memory, and of what it had led to when they'd been alone in his room, desire flaring…blazing to white-hot flame…

He slammed it down. Slammed down the memory as if to crush it out of existence.

Except its echo mocked him. The very fact that memory existed was the very reason he was here now...

With a start, he realised she was speaking.

'Yes, I'll have the sole Veronique,' she was saying.

He nodded, deciding almost at random on the lamb. Then he turned his attention to the wine list. A glass or two would suffice...no need to order a bottle.

'What will you drink?' he heard himself asking.

'Just another of these.' She indicated the glass she'd been sipping from.

'When will you be allowed alcohol again?' he asked.

This total ban seemed alien and unnecessary to him. Did pregnant women in Italy deprive themselves so? He had no idea—he did not socialise with pregnant women either in Italy or here, or anywhere. They were an unknown species to him.

'When I stop breastfeeding,' came the answer.

He looked across at her. 'You intend to breastfeed?' he asked.

He strove to keep the question neutral, not wanting her to pick up any criticism, implied or not, in any answer she might give. This entire purpose of the evening was his attempt—finally, wearily, resignedly—to get them beyond the warfare that raged between them.

Warfare that was as wearying as it was pointless.

In his head, memory stabbed again—not of the fateful night that had led to this moment, but of her words, hurled at him repeatedly, telling him that he should leave her and go back to Italy, get on with his life, have nothing more to do with her...

Or the child she carried.

His child.

Does she really want me to do that?

She was speaking again, and he made himself pay attention to her and not to his turbid thoughts.

'Yes, unless there's some kind of problem. It's nature's way, after all…breastfeeding. It helps the baby's immune system develop. And anyway—' she made a face '—from what I've read so far it seems to be a lot easier than faffing about with sterilising bottles all the time.'

'Does it not tie you to the baby?' Vincenzo heard himself ask.

She levelled a look at him. 'Since I don't have anything else planned *except* looking after my baby, that isn't exactly a problem,' she said.

He frowned. 'You mentioned previously that you'd inherited some money, so could afford to support a child.'

Whatever the sum was, judging from her clothes, it clearly did not run to anything lavish.

'Yes,' she acknowledged.

She added nothing more. He tried to draw her out.

'You never did tell me what your line of work is—other than temping at your friend's office.'

'No, I didn't,' she answered shortly.

He looked across at her, trying to recall their conversation that first night over dinner at the Falcone. But there had been nothing about her life in England. They'd talked about Italy in general, and the city she was named after but had never visited. She'd been interested, and made conversation, and had not been unintelligent in her questions to him.

The waiter was there, hovering, ready to take their orders, and it was a timely distraction. As the man departed, Vincenzo drew breath. He needed to keep going with this new, tenuous neutrality between them.

'So, what did you do before—?' he started, and then re-alised the only way to finish the sentence was by saying *before you found yourself pregnant by me*.

But he didn't have to say it. She said it for him.

'Before I found myself in this unholy mess?' she said.

She hadn't said it angrily, or accusingly. But there was a bleakness in her voice that he could not help but hear. He could feel it reaching him, settling around them like a thickening mesh, winding around them, binding them.

Another spike of memory came, from that episode in the park—her saying, so vehemently and so bitterly, that they were handcuffed together...shackled...

Rejection flared in him. He wasn't going back to that. He'd come here tonight specifically to get beyond that. Whatever it took.

'Does it have to be a mess?'

He heard the words fall from him.

CHAPTER SEVEN

SIENA'S EYES FLASHED to him.

'You have another name for it?'

She didn't say it angrily—she wasn't going to get upset. But she wasn't going to whitewash it either. 'Mess' was—bluntly and bleakly—the only word for the situation.

His eyes were levelled on her. She could not read them.

'I think,' he said, and his voice matched his eyes, his expression, 'that we must find one.' He paused, his eyes still on her. 'Because it is not…helpful to call it that. To think of it as that.'

She saw him take a breath, a thin one, and it pressed his mouth for a moment before he went on.

'We must get beyond it.'

His eyes dropped from her and he reached for his wine. For the second time that evening Siena wished she had a glass of wine to turn to as well. Instead, she took a mouthful of her soft drink, slightly effervescent. Memory shot through her of how the mousse of the champagne she'd knocked back at that fateful party had filled her mouth… her senses…her blood… Loosening her inhibitions, making her impulsive, adventurous, daring…

Reckless.

Landing her where she was now.

She set down her glass with a click, eyeballed Vincenzo.

'How?' she said bluntly.

There was a careful, watchful air about him as he answered her.

'We have made a start,' he said. 'I have given you an apology that you have accepted, and we are dining together in a civil fashion.' His mouth twisted suddenly. 'That is a definite start. Something to build on.'

She kept on eyeballing him. 'And just how,' she rejoined tautly, 'do you intend we do that?'

She could feel the tension building inside her again. She didn't want it to.

And now he was answering her, and she knew he was picking his words carefully.

'We should get to know each other better,' he said.

Siena's eyes widened. 'Really? Don't we know enough? The essentials? You are rich and I am pregnant. Isn't that what it boils down to? For you, at any rate.'

It was her turn to twist her mouth.

His expression changed again. As if what she'd said so bluntly had been more blunt than he would have preferred.

'I have already apologised to you on that score,' he said stiffly. 'So perhaps we could move on from there?' His tone was pointed.

'Move on to where?'

'As I say, to knowing each other better,' he replied.

She sat back. 'So, what do you want to know?'

If it helped to stop her tension rising, then she would go along with him. Maybe...

He lifted a hand slightly. 'Well, I made a start, asking you about your work. You chose not to answer me.'

She gave a shrug, helping herself to a bread roll. She was hungry suddenly. 'Because there isn't much to say. I don't have a glittering career—unlike Megan.'

'So what have you been doing with your life so far?' he continued.

She busied herself buttering her roll. She didn't want to talk about having hoped to go to art school. Let alone second time around. Let alone why it was second time around.

She felt memories from those anguished years seek to intrude, painful and difficult. But she must not let them. There was no reason now, in her condition—healthily pregnant—for such haunting, such apprehension.

It's nothing like it was for them—it's all quite different. Quite different for my baby...

Vincenzo was speaking again, and she found herself glad of the distraction from thoughts—fears?—she did not want to have.

'Did you grow up in London?' Vincenzo put to her.

Siena shook her head. This was safe enough, surely? 'No, I'm a country girl, born and bred.'

'What part of the country?' he pursued.

'East Anglia…a small country town.' Without her being conscious of it her voice softened as she remembered her happy childhood. 'My father was a vet, my mother his veterinary nurse. My brother trained as a vet too, ready to take over the practice in due course—' She broke off.

It wasn't that safe after all…

She was aware that Vincenzo was resting his gaze on her, and that it still had that careful, watchful quality to it.

'Have you told your family you are pregnant?' he asked.

'No,' she said. She tried not to let her voice sound short. 'My parents—'

She stopped, took another drink from her glass, her mouth suddenly dry. She looked away, out over the restaurant, which was now starting to fill up.

'My parents did *pro bono* work every year. My father was

an equine vet, and he and my mother went out to North Africa regularly, to help at a donkey charity they supported. Donkeys are crucial to the livelihoods of most of the rural population in that part of the world—but sadly their owners often don't have the means to look after them properly. My parents gave their own services to the charity, and helped to train local practitioners as well. They did it for years… Except that one year—' She stopped again. Took a painful breath. 'One year, while they were out there, there was an earthquake.'

She felt her throat tighten, reached for her glass again.

'I'm sorry.'

She heard the words, spoken quietly, but she could not look at him. Nor could she say anything.

Into the silence he spoke again, careful still. 'You mentioned a brother—?'

'He lives in Australia,' she said quickly. 'We're not estranged or anything…' She could hear the awkwardness in her voice and tried to speak over it. 'But, well…it's the other side of the world.'

That was all she wanted to say. But inside her head thoughts were running that she did not wish to think. Thoughts about her brother. At some point she must tell him that she was pregnant. It would not be easy…

She looked up at Vincenzo, setting down her knife. 'What about you?' she asked, turning the tables on him. Deflecting questions away from herself.

Did she even want to know anything about him?

If they were going to get beyond their destructive, exhausting hostility she must make an effort to.

He's apologised—I've accepted it. Now we move on.

He did not get a chance to answer her. At that moment their food was arriving, and Siena quickly made a start on her fish. It was delicate, and delicious, the tiny new potatoes and fresh peas served separately equally delicious. Across from her Vincenzo was eating his lamb—which looked, to her mind, too rare for her palette.

'How is your sole?' Vincenzo asked politely.

'Very good,' she answered, equally politely.

For a few minutes they did nothing but make inroads into their dinner, then Vincenzo resumed their conversation.

'You asked about me,' he said, picking up on the question she'd turned on him. He took another forkful of lamb before he went on.

Was it an effort for him as well? Siena wondered. His voice sounded stilted, but he was answering her all the same.

'I cannot claim to be a country boy—I grew up in the suburbs of Milan. My background was not as...' She heard him hesitate suddenly, then continue. 'Not as affluent as my life is now. I have improved it since then.'

Siena looked across at him. There had been an edge to his voice as he'd finished that sentence—she'd have had to be deaf not to hear it.

'How?' she asked.

His wealth was clearly of prime importance to him, and he guarded it from wannabe pregnant gold-diggers, so presumably it was a subject dear to his heart—and his ego.

And his fears...

Just in case I get my sticky, greedy little fingers into it...

'Hard work,' he came back succinctly. 'I studied, took an interest in economics and finance—because that, after all, is where the money is. I worked to earn money during the day and studied by night. I got my qualifications, and went to work for one of Milan's finance houses—it is the financial centre of Italy, as well as its fashion capital—and then, when I felt I had learnt enough to try and make my own fortune, I set up for myself.'

She looked at him, frowning slightly. 'What is it exactly that you do?'

'I make investments,' he said. 'I started by using my own money to accumulate sufficient funds by making investments on the Milan stock exchange. Then I used profits from that to invest in other companies, other ventures. I persuaded others to contribute as well, and made money for them as well as myself. Money,' he said, and now Siena could hear not just an edge, but a dryness to his voice, 'makes money. Once you have it, it is easy to make more of it.'

His voice changed, and now the dryness had gone, but not the edge. The dryness was replaced by something that might even have been bitterness.

'The challenge is the initial capital formation,' he said. 'That is where the hardest work is.'

'You started from nothing?' she asked.

She saw him reach for his wine, take a mouthful, set the glass back with a decided click.

'More or less,' he said.

There was no mistaking the bitterness in his voice now. She let her eyes rest on him. His face had closed—that was the only word for it. Instinctively, she moved the subject away.

'You asked about my family,' she said. 'What about yours?'

But his expression remained closed and he turned his attention to his lamb.

'None worth mentioning,' he answered tersely.

Then he set his knife and fork down abruptly, looked

straight across at her. There was a strange expression in his eyes now, one she could not make out.

'Apparently,' he said, 'we have something in common. Neither of us comes with a large family around us.'

Words rose in Siena's head. Words she did not want to hear and would not say. But they said themselves inside her head for all that.

Yet between us we are making a family.

Immediately, instantly, she refuted them—rejected them. No, that was *not* what they were doing. There was nothing of 'family' about their situation. Nothing at all.

We are strangers who fell into bed in a moment of reckless, unthinking lust—and that does not, cannot, must not, should not have anything at all to do with 'family'!

She broke eye contact, dipped her head again. She got stuck back into her sole Veronique…stabbed a potato with the tines of her fork.

As if she could stab the words that had just forced their impossible, unnecessary and totally *wrong* way into her head.

Vincenzo heard his own words echo in his head.

'Apparently we have something in common.'

His mouth tightened.

Something else besides the child she carries.

Doggedly, he went on eating, though for an instant the tender lamb tasted like cardboard in his mouth. He swallowed it down, reached for his wine. This whole evening had been his idea, and he must stick with it. It was…necessary.

Necessary to have made that apology to her, whether or not he'd meant it.

Necessary to attempt civil conversation with her.

Necessary for them to talk to each other. Get to know each other.

Because one day soon we will be parents.

It seemed impossible to believe that a single night had turned them into what they would be for the rest of their lives.

He pulled his mind away, finished off his lamb, pushed his plate away from him. He took another mouthful of wine. Time to make conversation again. To get to know each other a bit more. The way they had to.

He frowned inwardly. Her parents had been professionals, and so was her brother, it seemed. Had she really not done anything similar? Just worked as a clerk, or whatever, in her friend's office?

He gave a shrug mentally. What did it matter? She wasn't going to be working at all now. Courtesy of her pregnancy and his wealth.

No, don't go there again. It is as it is. You will be funding her existence because you are funding the existence of the child that is yours. And you can afford it, so if she benefits from it, why care?

She had finished her fish and the waiter was gliding up again, carefully placing the dessert menus on the table, whisking away the empty dishes.

Vincenzo picked up his menu. 'Do you care for dessert?' he asked.

Memory shot through him again. That night at the Falcone she had ordered an iced *parfait*, he recalled now. And he had watched her spooning little mouthfuls, openly relishing them. He recalled that frisson now, untimely and unwelcome though it was, of watching her sensuous enjoyment. It had only fuelled his impatient desire for her, his wanting the meal to be over and the real purpose of being with her that night to begin.

He put the memory from him. It was inappropriate.

She'd picked up her menu, was scanning it assiduously.

'I'm torn,' she said. 'There's a lot to choose from…' she mused.

'I see there is a raspberry parfait on offer. You had something similar at the Falcone,' Vincenzo heard himself saying, and instantly wished he had not.

Yet even as he cursed himself for referencing that fateful evening he became aware of something else he wished he had not done. And it wasn't about the unwelcome outcome of that night.

It was about what had led to it in the first place.

Now that wall of hostility that had been there since she'd walked into his office to drop her bombshell all those weeks ago had gone, other things were taking its place. Things he did not want. Oh, he wanted a degree of basic civility between them—just as he'd told her when he'd made himself apologise, and when he'd said they must get beyond it—but now more was happening. Some line of self-defence had been breached. Something he'd been holding at bay. Something their mutual hostility had kept at bay…

But now it was running again…

He felt his gaze fasten on her. Though she looked very different from the way she'd looked at that party, her image now—nothing like a siren flaunting her sexuality—did not mean he could not see just how appealing her looks were. She might be wearing no make-up to enhance those blue-green eyes of hers, she might have her hair drawn back into a simple ponytail, and she might be wearing an open-necked shirt not designed for allure, but he was increasingly aware that it did nothing to detract from what nature had endowed her with.

If anything, it enhances it—shows off her natural beauty...

He felt it reach to him—not with the full-on, seductively sensual allure he'd been unable and unwilling to resist indulging in that night at the Falcone, but with a pull that made him want to go on letting his eyes fasten on her, appreciate what she had on show.

It was having an effect on him—an effect he did not want. Because it was irrelevant. His attraction to her, overpowering as it had been that night, was what had landed him in this situation—the very last thing he wanted now was for that to rear its head again.

He shifted in his seat, forcing his gaze away, wishing to God he'd not made that damn remark about their dinner together that evening.

'In which case I'll definitely avoid it!' he heard her say, and by the way she said it she knew she had found the reference unwelcome as well.

His mouth tightened again. Something else they apparently had in common...

Not wanting to remember that night—think about it at all...

The waiter had glided up again, ready to take their orders. Vincenzo specified cheese, in a voice curter than he would usually have used. Then he heard Siena say, her voice as tight as before, 'And for me the *tarte citron.*'

She handed her menu back.

'And coffee,' she added. 'Decaf. Thank you.' Her voice was staccato now.

Vincenzo, not looking at her, ordered coffee for himself. 'Not decaf,' he stipulated.

The waiter moved off again.

For a moment there was silence.

Vincenzo cast about for something neutral, anodyne to say. The trouble was he couldn't think of anything.

As if she had come to the same conclusion, Siena spoke abruptly. 'So, we don't really have anything to say to each other, do we?' she said.

She reached for her glass, drank from it and set it down again. Looked across at him.

Her blue-green eyes, so striking, so expressive, were now expressing something caustic.

'So there's no point us trying to get to know each other, is there?' she went on, her voice caustic too.

Vincenzo dragged his thoughts from her eyes and frowned slightly. 'I'm not used to getting to know people,' he heard himself say tightly.

He saw Siena's expression change. Become veiled.

'Especially women?' she said. 'After all, what's the point in getting to know them? You won't be sticking around, so why bother?'

The hostility was back in her voice, in her face.

His own face tightened. This was *not* what he wanted. His resolve not to make any reference back to their searing night together vanished. This was another part of her wall—like it or not—and he had to dismantle it if he could. In the same way as before.

'Do you want an apology for that, too?' he asked. 'For not staying to have breakfast with you?' He didn't wait for a response, but spoke bluntly. 'It wasn't possible. I had a business meeting at eight-thirty, and after that meetings back to back all day—it's what I do when I come to London: max out my time here. And as for that eight-thirty meeting—I had made the appointment,' there was a caustic note in his voice too now, 'long before I met you.' There was an infinitesimal pause. 'I had not envisaged that the previous night would be as it was.'

She broke eye contact. 'Make that both of us,' she said. Then, almost immediately, her eyes flashed back to his. Full-on. 'Despite your charming assumption that it's a way of life for me.'

Antagonism bit in every word.

Vincenzo stilled.

'I believe,' he said tightly, 'that my original apology to you covered that issue.'

'Did it?' Her challenge was open.

'Yes.' He spoke with precision. 'However, if you wish me to clarify, I herewith apologise for any inference I drew that you make a habit of spending the night with men you have only just met, so that identifying the one who might be responsible for any consequent pregnancy would require extensive paternity testing. It was a slur on your character as unmitigated as it was unwarranted.'

He paused again, then half lifted an eyebrow.

'Will that do?' he said.

She didn't say anything but he could see her face working, as if conflicting emotions were cutting across it. He saw her swallow painfully. On an impulse he didn't understand, he let his hand start to reach towards her, then he pulled it back.

He spoke again. But in a different tone of voice now.

'Look, shall we just accept and believe that each of us acted out of character that night? That, for whatever reason, our id got the better of us—if you want to analyse it in Freudian terms. That seems as good a way as any, but do choose any other that makes sense to you personally. We succumbed to something we very probably would never have done under other circumstances. And...' he drew a breath '…if we accept that, then maybe we can also accept that what happened just happened, for whatever reason, and put it behind us.'

Even as he spoke, making himself sound reasonable and rational, he was conscious of a level of hypocrisy deep within him. But he set it aside. The fact that whether she was dressed to kill, as she had been that night, or dressed deliberately plainly, as she was on the present occasion, her looks would always draw his attention was completely irrelevant to the current situation…

I have to ignore that. Because it is the very last thing that I can allow into the situation we are trying to deal with.

He could see the same conflicting reactions playing across her face.

'I did put it behind me,' she said.

Her voice was low. Troubled. She wasn't making eye contact with him, but looking down at the tablecloth.

'It was the only way I could deal with it. Deal with what had happened. What I had *let* happen.' Abruptly, her eyes flashed back up to him. 'I made myself angry,' she said. 'I made myself angry about the way you walked out the next morning. Angry with you so that…' She paused, her face working again. 'So that I didn't have to be angry with myself for what I'd done.' She drew a breath. 'Because what happened that night was something that has *never* happened to me before. And…and it shocked me. Shocked me that I'd done it.'

Her face contorted suddenly and she squeezed her eyes shut, as if she were shutting out the world. Shutting him out with it.

Vincenzo's hand moved again, and this time he did not draw it back. Instead, he very lightly—very briefly—touched her cheek. Then he took his hand away.

'There is no need to beat yourself up about it,' he said.

His voice sounded different—he could hear it—but didn't know why. Didn't know why he had made that impulsive gesture of...

Of what?

Comfort? Was that it? Or collusion. Maybe that was it.

'And if it's any consolation,' he went on, 'you've probably pretty much described my own reaction.'

His voice was dry, but it was not dry with the acerbic tone he'd used before. This was self-knowledge. Belated self-knowledge. He, too, had used his anger at her—anger whipped up when she'd come to his office to tell him she was pregnant—to disguise his own shock that he had fallen into bed with a woman within hours of meeting her.

She had unscrewed her eyes, unscrewed her face, and was looking across at him now. Something had changed in her face.

'Men always think that it's OK to slut-shame a woman,' she said. 'While they themselves stay squeaky-clean and fragrant...'

Her voice had an edge—and with cause, he acknowledged.

He gave half a smile...a twisted one. 'Then they are hypocrites,' he said. 'And that applies just as much now, in the twenty-first century, as in any earlier period when women's sexuality was used as a weapon against them.'

He took a breath—a heavy one, but a releasing one too. Looked across at her. There was an open expression on her face now, and her eyes were meeting his. For the first time there was neither hostility in them nor challenge, nor reserve or guardedness.

'Siena,' he said, and he used her given name for the first time that evening, 'let's just accept what happened, shall we? We acted out of character that night, both of us. For whatever reason, it happened. Let's make peace with it.' He moved on, because it seemed the natural thing to do now. 'Just as we should make peace with your being pregnant and all that entails. We neither of us wished for it, but it happened. Let's at least try to keep on with what we've been trying to do this evening.'

He held her eyes for a moment. Hers were not veiled, but what was in them he did not know. Maybe it was simply exhaustion at hearing him out.

Whatever it was, their waiter was now gliding up to their table again, bearing his cheese board and Siena's *tarte*. He set them down, murmuring something about their coffee, and disappeared again.

'That looks good,' Vincenzo said, indicating her dessert.

It seemed a sufficiently neutral comment to make. He followed it with another one.

'In Italy, it's the custom to serve cheese before dessert, rather than after, as in England.'

She picked up her fork. 'Yes, cheese usually rounds off a meal here—unless you count the petit fours or chocolate mints that come with coffee and liqueurs.'

She echoed his neutral, conversational tone, and Vincenzo was glad. He felt in need of it. In need of something simple…easy…

The waiter was approaching again, bearing down on them with their respective coffees. Vincenzo made a start on his cheese. The atmosphere between them had relaxed. Or if not relaxed exactly, it had eased, at least. And he was grateful for it.

For a while there was silence between them, yet it was not a strained one.

We've moved on.

To what, he didn't know. But one thing he did know.

Wherever they'd moved on to, it had to be better than where they'd come from...

That, too, was something to be grateful for.

Siena went on forking up her dessert. Her mood was strange. She tried to find a word for it, but the only one she could come up with was 'exhausted'. Maybe that did sum up the situation. But another one came, too.

Relieved.

She wondered at it for a moment.

Relieved? Did she really feel relieved? And if so, why?

Because we've got something out of the way—something else.

Something other than the apology that she knew must have stuck in his craw.

But he made it all the same.

She frowned inwardly. Yes, he had. She had to give him that. And she had to give him something else—even if it stuck in *her* craw to do so.

He's making an effort.

Because he was—that was obvious.

And I have to as well.

She looked up...looked across at him. His face was unreadable again. Not closed, just...unreadable.

Suddenly, she wanted to read it. 'Were you really shocked that you fell into bed with me like that?'

The words were out of her mouth before she could filter them.

He met her eyes. 'Yes,' he said. 'It's not something I've ever done before.'

She looked puzzled. He had spoken calmly, but she'd picked up something in the timbre of his voice. 'It's not supposed to be something men think is a big deal,' she said slowly. 'Instant sex with a stranger.'

He set down his cheese knife. 'That depends on the man, doesn't it?'

She pondered his answer. Pondered her reaction to it.

She knew that she was if not glad, precisely, at what he'd just said, then she was not the opposite. She also knew she wanted to ask another question—needed to ask it. But it was riskier…much riskier.

'What is it?' he asked. His eyes were still resting on her.

'What's what?' she returned.

'What is it you want to ask me?' he said.

She was taken aback. *How did he know…?*

'Your face is expressive,' he said, as if he'd heard her ask that very question out loud.

There was a touch of dryness in his voice, but it was not harsh, or acerbic. It had the same quality as when he'd said, *'There is no need to beat yourself up about it.'* Then he had touched her cheek…

She swallowed. Her throat had tightened, but she didn't know why.

'If it's a difficult question, I will try to make it easier for you,' he was saying now, and there was still that different timbre to his voice, the new way he was letting his eyes rest on her. She didn't know what it was, but it made her take a breath. Risk asking the question. Blurting it out.

'If…if you hadn't had that early-morning meeting, would you…? Would you have…?'

'Yes,' he said.

She felt her throat untighten—and again she didn't know why. Only knew that as he went on talking something was changing.

'I would have been tempted to stay...to have breakfast with you.'

She heard his words. Heard the note of admission in them. Heard him continue.

'I don't know what would have happened had I not left as precipitately as I did.'

'Well, we'll never know now, will we?' she said.

'You're right. We'll never know, either of us, what might have come of that night together had I not walked out on you that morning...had you not found yourself pregnant. Which is why we can only deal with the situation as it is—not as it might have been, or might not have been. So...' he drew a breath '...here we are. Trying to find a way forward that is more viable than perhaps either of us thought at first, with my accusations and your anger.'

'I suppose we are,' she said slowly.

She picked up her spoon, absently started to stir the coffee in her cup. Decaf wasn't very appetising, but she took a mouthful anyway. Thoughts were going through her, and what might be emotions or might not—she wasn't sure. She wasn't sure of anything...

He said he might have stayed—at least for breakfast. He'd acknowledged what had happened between them. Acknowledged the night before and the morning after.

That was something. Maybe...

She realised he was talking again, and made herself focus.

'I was thinking...' he was saying, and she could hear the note of reserve in his voice, see the watchfulness in his eyes. 'Perhaps our next step should be to spend some time away. A few days together.'

She stared.

'Somewhere out of London,' he went on. He paused. 'Would you consider that?'

'I don't know,' she said slowly.

Could she cope with spending that kind of time with him?

'There is no rush to decide. I have to return to Italy to-morrow, and then I am in Geneva, and then Turin. But after that... Well, that might be a good time, if it's something you decide to do. Why not give some thought to where might be a good location?'

He left it at that, went back to eating his cheese and bis-cuits, and she went back to finishing her dessert. They didn't speak, but for the first time the silence didn't seem palpable.

She pushed her empty plate away, drained her unappe-tising coffee.

'Would you like a refill?' Vincenzo asked.

She shook her head. 'I'll have a fruit tea at the apartment. That way I won't miss the caffeine,' she said.

There was a rueful note in her voice, but it was only lightly rueful.

'Then shall I call for the bill?' he checked.

She nodded, and he summoned their waiter. The waiter came immediately, even though the restaurant had filled up and he was in demand. But then, she thought, Vincenzo Giansante was the kind of man who got waiters' attention whenever he wanted it. Or his wealth got it...

But he hadn't always been wealthy, had he? He'd said he'd made his money from scratch. So maybe there was a time when he couldn't just click his fingers and have wait-ers come running.

And there was also a thought in her head, disquieting and disturbing, that maybe there had been a time when he didn't have to be suspicious that any female interest in him was influenced by his wealth...

Like wanting to get pregnant by him.

He was putting away his fancy-looking credit card, getting to his feet. She did likewise. They fell into step as they headed back towards the apartment. The night air was cool, and she gave a slight shiver. A moment later he was draping his jacket around her shoulders.

'Oh!' she exclaimed, taken aback. Then: 'Thank you,' she said awkwardly.

It would be ungracious to divest herself of it—and besides, the warmth was welcome.

His body warmth...

It was a disturbing consciousness. Evoking memories...

They didn't speak as they walked—but, again, it was not a tension-filled silence.

At the entrance to the apartment block he stopped. '*Mi dispiace*, but I must relieve you of my jacket. My key is in the pocket.'

'Oh...oh, yes...'

Siena slipped the jacket from her, felt the beautiful soft silk lining sliding over her shoulders. Vincenzo took it from her, fetched out his key, and opened the door into the lobby.

'I'll see you to your door, then bid you goodnight,' he said.

And he did just that, ushering her into the lift, and then out again, and on to the apartment. By then she'd got her own key out of her handbag, and she used it to open the front door. Then she turned.

In the low light of the landing he seemed very tall, his face half shadowed, his profile thrown into relief. She felt something go through her, but she didn't know what it was.

Didn't want to know.

Because it's not relevant. Not any more. Nor is it appropriate.

'Thank you for dinner,' she said, self-conscious suddenly.

He'd shrugged himself back into his jacket as she'd

opened her apartment door. His eyes were resting on her. In the dim light she could not make out his expression. But perhaps that was just as well.

'I think the evening did some good,' he said. 'I will leave you now. You have my contact details, should you need anything, otherwise I will be in touch at the end of next week.' He paused. 'I would ask you to consider what I suggested. See whether you think that our going away together might also do some good?'

She gave a half-nod, not wanting to commit.

'I hope it goes well in Geneva and Turin,' she said instead. It seemed a polite thing to say.

He nodded in the same grave fashion. 'Thank you. And now, *buona notte.*'

'Goodnight,' she echoed, awkward again, and then stepped inside the apartment, closing the door. Shutting him out.

There was a studied expression on her face as she walked into the kitchen. It seemed a long time since she had set off from here earlier in the evening. As if she'd travelled a great distance.

But where she had reached she did not know...

CHAPTER EIGHT

THE SEA WAS a mix of grey and blue. Blue when the intermittent sun came out from behind a scudding cloud, grey when it went behind.

'Would you care to sit down? Are you feeling tired? We've walked some way.' Vincenzo's enquiry was polite.

'Thank you, yes.' Siena's reply was equally polite.

She lowered herself onto the empty bench they had paused beside on the paved promenade. Beyond the railing the tide was in, leaving only a strip of shingle below. Gulls swooped haphazardly, and though the sea breeze was light, white caps dotted the changing surface of the water. Further off shore Vincenzo could see a sailing boat, skimming west to east along the English Channel.

Memory pierced. He'd been watching the yachts off the Sardinian coast, having a leisurely lunch, when that call had come through and had ripped through his life like a cannonball through tissue paper.

And now...

Now he was here, at this genteel seaside resort in east Devon on the coast, sitting beside the woman who had changed his life completely. Changed it irreversibly and for ever.

'Are you warm enough?' he asked her now.

'Thank you, yes,' she said, in the same polite tone.

Politeness was their watchword, and each of them was applying it scrupulously. He was glad of it. Appreciative. They were making progress. But where they were going was still uncertain.

All he could do was keep on in the same direction, glad that she seemed to be acquiescing to his suggestion that they take a break from their lives, have some time away. She had chosen this place—he'd never heard of it—and it seemed acceptable in the circumstances.

'It's supposed to be the prettiest seaside town in Britain,' Siena had told him when she'd let him know that, yes, she would consider his suggestion of getting out of London for a few days.

Overall, Vincenzo felt the description justified. The resort dated, so Siena had told him, to the end of the eighteenth century, when sea bathing was becoming fashionable and resorts were springing up all along the south coast from Brighton to Devon.

Selcombe was small, and all the more charming for it, he thought. He had booked them into the town's main hotel at the far end of the promenade—a handsome white stucco-fronted house, with gardens giving direct access to the shingle beach beyond. Though hardly a luxury hotel, it was comfortable in an old-fashioned way, and he was not displeased with it.

'How are you feeling?' He turned to Siena, sitting beside him—she had left a good space between them, but not pointedly so. 'Can you make it back to the hotel, or shall we take a taxi?'

'Oh, I'm fine,' she answered. 'It's such a lovely day. Let's keep walking—it's only about half a mile, and flat going.' She turned her head to look at him. 'It's really important I keep myself fit, you know.'

'But you must not overdo it,' Vincenzo said.

'A leisurely stroll along a mile of promenade is hardly overdoing it!' There was no sting in her words. 'But it's nice to sit and watch the sea in the sunshine.'

He heard her pause for a moment, as if wondering whether to say what she said next.

'Do you like the seaside? I mean, in Italy? Is it your thing? Some people love the sea…some don't.'

'It's very pleasant,' Vincenzo said.

'Did you go to the seaside when you were young? We lived less than an hour from the coast, and my parents used to take my brother and me to the seaside for the day quite regularly. What about you?'

She was making conversation, he could tell. In principle, he welcomed it, because he was doing likewise. Had been doing so ever since he'd collected her the day previously, in the hire car he'd rented for the week, and headed out of London towards the west country. They had been civil to each other the whole time…polite, pleasant.

And guarded, too, he knew. Both himself and her.

That aspect rose to the fore now.

'No,' he said. He didn't mean to sound curt. 'Milan is not near the coast,' he went on.

'I suppose not,' she said, her gaze going back out over the sea beyond the railings at the edge of the promenade. 'But isn't it close to the Italian lakes?'

'Lake Como is the closest.'

He never went near Como—too many bad associations…

'Did you go as a child? I don't know whether one can swim in the Italian lakes… Not like at the seaside.'

'No,' he said again. This time he managed to make his voice sound less curt. 'And, yes, one can swim, but it is not that safe. The lakes are very deep. They are more appropriate for water sports—there is a lot of sailing, windsurfing, motor boats…that sort of thing.'

'Do you indulge?' she asked.

'No.' He paused, his eyes resting on a sailing boat skimming along the horizon. 'I never seem to have time.'

'That's a shame,' he heard her say. 'I've never done anything like that either.'

From nowhere, Vincenzo heard himself say, 'Perhaps we can do it here—go out on the sea. I've seen signs advertising boat tours along the coast. We could take one. Would that appeal?'

He looked at her again, and saw she had turned her head as well.

'It sounds nice,' she said. There was more than politeness in her voice now.

'Good,' he said. 'Perhaps tomorrow…if the weather is kind.'

'Yes, let's,' Siena agreed peaceably.

Almost subliminally, Vincenzo felt his mood improve, felt himself relax. He stretched out his legs, enjoying the sunshine on his face. It was not hot—that would be impossible compared with Italy—but it was warm, and the light breeze was ruffling his hair.

He let his glance go sideways to Siena. She had leant back on the bench, face lifted to the sunshine that had emerged from behind a scudding cloud, and the sunlight played on her face. She was wearing no make-up, but her hair was not confined to its usual ponytail. It was held back by a band, wisping a little in the breeze. Her eyes were closed.

Vincenzo watched her. With part of his mind he was taking in the delicacy of her profile, the sculpture of her cheekbones, the length of her eyelashes, the curve of her lips, the fall of her hair over her shoulders. He felt something stir within him, and knew what it was—knew he must set it aside promptly, immediately.

But her eyes were still closed, her face still lifted to the sunshine. Her features were in repose—exposed to him. He went on looking at her.

Knowing why.

Knowing he should not.

Deliberately, he dragged his gaze downwards. Her pregnancy was still barely visible—only the slightest roundness beneath the cotton sweater she was wearing over slimly cut trousers. But, barely visible though it was, her pregnancy was real. Increasing...

So the kind of thoughts he was having were simply...

Impossible.

Necessarily so.

After all, he reminded himself acidly, it was those thoughts—heated to a white-hot temperature—that had led to him sitting here, on a bench on a seaside promenade in Devon, rearranging his entire life on account of having indulged in them.

He frowned. She was looking so entirely different from the way she'd looked that fateful night at the Falcone. Not vamped up in the slightest. So why was he reacting in the same way?

He made himself look back out to sea again. That was better—safer.

Isn't this situation complicated enough, without adding any more into the mix?

The question was entirely rhetorical. The answer was obvious. And besides...

We are finally getting beyond all that ugly hostility, shock and anger. We are finally capable of being civil to each other, dealing with the situation we face in a calm, rational manner. So the very last thing it needs is disturbance.

Whatever his thoughts were when he let his eyes rest on her, he must keep them entirely private. She'd made it crystal-clear she regarded that night as a mistake.

And so do I—of course I do!

Yet even as he said the words inside his head he could hear refutation taking shape. Did he regret that night? Or only the consequences of it?

His thoughts went back to the restaurant on Holland Park Avenue, where she'd asked him whether, had he not had that prearranged business meeting, he'd have stayed with her... at least for breakfast.

What would we have said to each other had I not left her as I did?

Thoughts moved within him, raising more questions than they answered. Distilling down to one.

Would I have still ended up walking away from her? Putting her into a taxi and out of my mind? Going back to the life I lead. Writing off that night simply as a one-off aberration?

His gaze withdrew from the sea, went back to her face. His head turned.

Her eyes were still closed.

Her face was still lifted to the sun.

Still effortlessly beautiful...

Siena opened her eyes. She wasn't sure why. It had been so peaceful just sitting there, relaxed, her face lifted to the warmth of the sun, hearing the gulls cry and the waves break on the beach below, with the rhythmic sound of the shingle sliding and tumbling.

But for whatever reason she opened her eyes, turned her head slightly.

And then stilled completely.

Vincenzo was looking at her. Right at her.

No veiling, no guarding, no unreadability.

She felt his eyes on hers, holding hers. As if he could see right into her. Shock rippled through her. The last time he'd looked at her like that it had sent her into meltdown, pooling like honey at his feet... Liquid with answering desire...

For a second—just a second—she felt colour start to flare, her pulse surge, her heart thud. Then, with an effort of will, she dragged her gaze away, back to look out over the sea. Then she got to her feet.

'Shall we keep going?' she said brightly. Too brightly, but she didn't care.

She didn't wait for his answer, only started along the promenade in the direction of their hotel at the far end. The equanimity that she had so assiduously striven for ever since Vincenzo had turned up yesterday after lunch and they'd set off for Devon had evaporated like drops of water on a hot stove.

And she knew exactly what fuel that stove had been heated with...

No! Don't go there! Just don't! It's too dangerous, impossible, and totally inappropriate... Irrelevant...out of order. Embarrassing.

And embarrassment was the predominant reaction to that moment back there on the bench. Of course it was! What else could it be?

She'd been caught unawares.

So had he.

The words were stinging in her head, making her acknowledge them. Without realising it, she quickened her pace. Then, realising that might be revealing, she slowed again. Vincenzo fell into step beside her. For the first time she was horribly conscious of his physical presence at her side.

Conscious in that way...

No! She crushed the thought out of her head. That burning night had done quite enough damage to her life—the very last thing she must allow was that it should start smouldering again. She had done her best since Vincenzo had reappeared in her life—dear heaven, she had! Had managed to totally blank him in every way except one.

We just need to be civil with each other, that's all. We can afford no disturbances, no disruption, nothing else to cope with...

'Did you want to have lunch somewhere along the way, or back at the hotel?' she asked now, quite deliberately.

Lunch was a neutral topic, a safe one. Vincenzo seemed to agree.

'Shall we see if we spot anywhere likely as we go?' he said. 'And if we don't, we can always eat at the hotel. Dinner last night was perfectly acceptable, but maybe we don't want to eat there all the time. There may be other good restaurants around...cafés, even. That kind of thing for lunch?'

'OK,' Siena agreed.

She cast her eye across the road that ran between the promenade and the row of buildings on the other side. They were, she could see, Regency-style upmarket villas, a long terrace of them, interrupted every now and then by smaller roads leading away from the seafront. Although the upper floors of the former villas might now be apartments—holiday lets, probably, she thought—the ground floors were mostly either eateries or shops.

'What about over there?' Vincenzo said beside her, pointing to a restaurant with seating on the wide pavement, an awning overhead, and hanging baskets of colourful flowers.

'It looks quite Mediterranean,' Siena said.

'So it does—shall we give it a try? See what's on offer?'

There was a crossing nearby, and he ushered her across. The little restaurant did look nice. Quite a few of the tables were occupied, but Vincenzo guided them to one that was empty, and set back a little.

'Will this do?' he asked her politely.

She nodded with a half-smile and sat down. A waitress bustled up, proffering menus and asking cheerfully what they might like to drink. Siena gave her usual order, and Vincenzo ordered a beer. Siena noticed the waitress paying a lot of attention to Vincenzo. But then, a man with Vincenzo's looks would always draw female eyes...

Mine included...

She put the thought away. Been there, done that—and got the *Baby Bump* tee shirt for her pains...

She studied the menu, trying to replace such thoughts, and opted for a chicken and avocado salad. Vincenzo chose the house speciality—crab salad.

The waitress smiled. 'Fresh-caught this morning,' she said encouragingly, before disappearing with clear reluctance.

Vincenzo sat back in his seat, looking out across the road and the promenade beyond.

'I assume this must have been a fishing village originally,' he observed. 'Before it became a seaside resort.'

'Yes, I think so,' Siena said.

It was a good safe topic to discuss, and would help to keep her mind off the things it must be kept off.

All the same, a thought went through her head...

Had it really been wise to do this? Agree to Vincenzo's

suggestion that they spend some time together away from London like this? Well, it was too late now. Too late for a whole lot of things in her life…

Including my art degree…again.

But as she responded to Vincenzo's question about the fashion for sea bathing that had emerged in the mid-eighteenth century, leading to Regency resorts like this and any number of others along the Channel coast, she found herself thinking about something else. Found herself wishing she had her sketchpad with her. She would happily sit on a bench on the promenade…do some pencil sketching of the seascape.

The idea was appealing. Maybe she could find some kind of art shop here and buy some basic kit?

'Did they really have those strange caravans drawn into the sea by horses, so the bathers could walk down the steps right into the sea?' Vincenzo was asking, his voice amused.

'Yes,' said Siena. 'Bathing machines, they were called. I've seen prints and early photos. Women wore massive swimsuits—for want of a better word—that covered them voluminously from head to toe. Rather like a modern burkini, but even more encompassing! But it let them get into the sea, so it was probably worth it.'

'The *cold* sea,' observed Vincenzo.

'Well, a lot colder than the Med, that's for sure!' she said lightly. She gave a wry laugh. 'In England we say "bracing"—which translates as totally freezing!'

He gave a low laugh. It did things to her.

She went on hurriedly, because she must not let that happen. 'I'm wondering whether to be brave enough to go in myself,' she mused. 'The Channel can't be any colder than the North Sea—but then, of course, back then I was a child, and didn't care about cold water! Besides, after a while you warm up.'

He cast a sceptical glance at her.

She gave another wry smile. 'You could always just paddle. You know—take your socks and shoes off, roll up your trouser legs and wade in.' Now her smile turned to a laugh. 'You could also do the time-honoured old-fashioned English thing that men did a couple of generations ago, and that is to take a linen handkerchief, knot it at each corner, and put it on your head.'

He looked at her. 'To what purpose?' he enquired, nonplussed.

'To keep the sun off,' she explained.

'If the sun ever gets that hot, I shall purchase a hat,' he told her decisively.

She laughed again. 'Definitely more stylish. The knotted handkerchief was never a good look!'

'Thank you for the warning,' he said dryly. His mouth quirked. 'And as for paddling... I think I may give that a miss too. The hotel pool will suffice—it is heated.'

'Yes,' she conceded, 'I have to agree it sounds more tempting. But when the tide is out we can walk along the beach, at least. Feel the shingle crunching. It's a shame it's not a sandy beach,' she mused. 'Where we went as a child had a wonderful sandy beach, with dunes behind. My brother and I were delirious, making sandcastles, playing beach cricket, as well as actual sea bathing. My parents would sit on deckchairs, glad just to watch us, and my mother would knit, and my father would read a paperback, and then they'd call us back to them for a picnic lunch. We were always starving by then, and when it was finally time to go home we were treated to ice creams to eat before setting off.'

She realised Vincenzo was looking at her with a strange expression on his face.

'You sound as if you had a happy childhood,' he said slowly.

'I did,' she said. 'Very happy...'

'How old were you,' he asked quietly, 'when your parents were killed?'

'I was eighteen. My brother twenty-three. He'd just qualified as a vet and was newly married, and—'

She broke off. This was painful territory. The attentive waitress bustled back to their table with their drinks, and Siena was glad. She sipped hers thirstily, and Vincenzo took a leisurely mouthful of his beer. She looked away, over the other holidaymakers having their lunch, carefree and happy. Or were they? How could you tell just by looking? After all, who, looking at her and Vincenzo, would know why it was they were there, apparently together, apparently a couple...

When all we have between us is a baby that neither of us planned, envisaged, expected or wanted.

She felt her throat tighten suddenly, and slid her hand over her abdomen. It was rounding more day by day, making its presence felt. Inexorably, unstoppably...

She became aware that Vincenzo was saying something, setting his beer glass back on the table.

'It is hard to lose a parent at any age,' he was saying, and there was a quality to his voice that made Siena look across at him. 'I, too, lost my father at eighteen—a heart attack. My mother died when...'

He paused, and she had the impression he had stopped himself. She looked at him questioningly, sympathy in her eyes.

'She died when I was four,' he said.

'That is very hard,' Siena said slowly.

It seemed strange to think of Vincenzo as a child—as having a family at all. Hadn't he said he had 'none worth mentioning'? But if both his parents were dead…

We have that in common.

It was a painful thing to share…

Vincenzo was frowning. 'I don't have many memories of her. Just one or two. And they may be from my father telling me about her. It's hard to say.'

'Do…do you have any siblings?' Siena heard herself asking. 'For me, it was such a comfort to have my brother, and he to have me.'

Vincenzo gave a shake of his head. His expression had tightened. 'No,' he said. 'Which was one of the reasons why my father—'

He broke off, and Siena looked at him questioningly again.

'Why he wanted to remarry.'

'Did…did he remarry?'

'Eventually.' Vincenzo's voice was even tighter. 'I was thirteen.'

She was feeling her way forward. To hear Vincenzo open up like this was strange…

He wouldn't do it if we weren't in this situation. And nor would I.

But maybe it was important that they were doing so? Knowing more about each other. Coming to terms with each other.

'Did…did you get on with your stepmother?'

Something hardened in his face, making him look the way he had that nightmare day in his office, when she'd blurted out that she was pregnant.

'No.'

A single word. He reached for his beer, took another mouthful. Set down the glass with a click.

'Nor did I ever consider her my stepmother—nor do I still.'

'Still?'

He gave a shrug—a dismissive one. 'She took herself off when my father died…set herself up in a villa on Lake Como.'

Siena spoke slowly, carefully. 'That sounds…expensive.'

Vincenzo's eyes flashed. 'She took my father for everything he had left,' he bit out harshly.

In the silence, things reshaped themselves in Siena's head. Things were making sense…

Dark and difficult sense—but sense.

So that is why he made all those vile assumptions about me—thinking the worst of me…

Quietly, she spoke again, wanting him to hear—wanting him to believe. 'I'm not like that,' she said. Her voice was low, intense.

For a long moment—dark and difficult—his eyes held hers. She could feel her heart beating in her breast as she went on holding his eyes still.

Suddenly, his lashes swept down over his eyes, shutting her out, cutting off the moment. Then they opened again. His expression had changed, and Siena felt her stretched nerves ease. A half-smile, twisted, pulled at Vincenzo's mouth, as if in acknowledgement of what she had said.

'I should not need you to say it,' he said.

'No,' she agreed, still meeting his eyes, 'but perhaps it helps all the same…'

He gave a nod. 'Perhaps it does,' he echoed.

He glanced away for a moment, out over the promenade

across the road, then looked back at Siena. The wry expression in his face was there again.

'We have moved on again,' he said.

He was making his voice light, she could hear it, and she answered him in the same fashion. Wanting to for her own sake—and for his.

'Yes,' she said.

She reached for her own drink and took a draught, her mouth dry.

The arrival of their salads was timely, giving respite from what had been said…revealed. They were huge—Vincenzo's laden with flaked crab meat.

'Enjoy,' said their waitress, casting a look at Vincenzo.

He gave her a polite nod of thanks, but nothing more, and with her sigh almost audible the waitress headed away.

The waitress's were not the only female eyes to be lingering on Vincenzo, Siena could see. At least two other women sitting nearby were throwing him covert glances.

It was totally obvious why. The combination of his lethal looks, fatally augmented by his Mediterranean aura, made it impossible for anyone in possession of a double X chromosome to be unaware of him.

She let her eyes rest on him for a moment as he got stuck into his crab salad. He was casually dressed, but the style and expense of his clothes was unmistakable. The open-necked polo shirt bore a designer mark on the breast pocket that she vaguely recognised as that of a top Milan fashion house. It was worn with superbly cut but casually styled chinos, and rounded off with an even more beautifully cut and styled dressed-down jacket.

He looked cool, Italian—and devastating.

She gave a silent gulp, bending her attentions to her own salad.

Casting about for a safe subject, wanting an easier topic of conversation—less intense, less dark and difficult—she said, 'I wonder if Lyme Regis is very far. It would be worth seeing. The harbour has a high, protective breakwater called the Cob, made famous by Jane Austen,' she said.

Vincenzo raised a querying eyebrow.

Siena elaborated. 'She set a key scene there in *Persuasion*, her last novel. The heroine's sister-in-law, whom the heroine fears is going to marry the man she herself loves, but who no longer loves her, impulsively jumps down from the steps on the upper Cob to the lower and is nearly fatally injured.'

'Only nearly? No tragic ending, then?' he said sardonically.

'No, it's all right. The rival to the heroine does make a full recovery, but she falls for one of the hero's friends and marries him instead, so the hero is free to realise he loves the heroine after all, and they get their happy-ever-after.'

'That is reassuring,' observed Vincenzo. 'At least in novels there can be good resolution of life's problems.' Siena heard his voice change. 'Perhaps we must strive to do likewise in our lives too,' he said. 'Even when those problems seem…intractable.'

His eyes rested on her. His expression was grave.

'I appreciate, Siena, all that you are doing. Truly I do. You are meeting me halfway, and I hope I am doing the same.' He paused for a moment. 'Do you think this is helping? Time together like this?'

She met his gaze, and there was honesty in hers. 'Yes. It's strange—it can't be anything *but* strange. But, yes, I think it is helping.'

But helping us to do what? Helping us be civil to each other, yes—and to understand each other more, to see where we are coming from, each of us. But it can't change anything else. I still wish I had not got pregnant. And, given that I am, I still want to move somewhere on my own to have my baby, not be dependent on Vincenzo.

Her thoughts were turbid. If he could finally believe she wasn't interested in his money, now that she understood where that fear had come from—*that I might be like his father's second wife*—couldn't he accept her making a home for herself and the baby? If he wanted, he could visit from time to time—set up a trust fund or whatever, if he felt that was his responsibility. Wouldn't that be more feasible, now that they were not at war any longer?

She broke her gaze, letting it go back out over the bustling promenade. She was very conscious of Vincenzo's presence so close across the table. Conscious, too, that there was another reason other than her being independent for not giving him any grounds to think she was after his money, for why she wanted him at a distance once the baby arrived.

Because anything else is dangerous...

She felt her gaze wanting to return to his face, and that was proof itself of the danger she felt flickering around her.

He was dangerous to me that night at the Falcone—disastrously so. And for all that the hostility and accusations between us are gone, that danger is still there.

Lethal. That was what Megan had called his darkly handsome looks—and it was an apt word. Didn't just sitting here having lunch with him demonstrate that, with every female around turning their heads just because he was there?

I have to keep myself safe from him, safe from the danger he is to me...to my heart. It's not as though he would ever truly see a future with someone like me—if he sees a future with anyone at all. So it's safest, surely, just to focus on what we are doing now—getting used to each other, let-

ting there be some kind of peace between us. Asking nothing more than that. Wanting nothing more than that... Not letting myself want more.

Because that would only spell danger.

She gave a silent sigh. Life was already far too complicated to allow anything more into it. All she must focus on was the baby—nothing else.

Nothing else at all...

Least of all the man she had been unable to resist that fateful night, who had brought her to the now she had to deal with.

CHAPTER NINE

LYME REGIS WAS just as Siena had said. They walked along the Cobb, with Siena pointing out the steps that featured so dramatically in the Jane Austen novel. Out at the far end the sea breeze was stronger, buffeting them both. Vincenzo put his arm around Siena's shoulder to steady her. He'd made the gesture without thinking about it, but the moment he did he almost drew back. She'd stiffened, tensed.

'I don't want you blown into the sea,' he said.

'It is definitely windier here,' she allowed.

He felt the tension in her shoulders subside fractionally. All the same, as soon as the gust passed he lowered his arm.

They stood awhile, braced against the buffeting wind, watching it whipping up the water. The sun was bright, turning the sea to scintillating diamonds.

'We could take another boat trip if you like,' Vincenzo said.

They'd done so a few days ago, cruising sedately along the shoreline and back again. It had been pleasant, sitting against the gunwale, watching the other passengers taking photographs of the shore passing them by.

'It looks a bit too bumpy today,' Siena said. 'That's quite a strong swell. I think.'

'Then we shall pass,' Vincenzo said. 'Perhaps we could

try our hand at fossil-hunting after lunch?' he asked. Fossils, he had learnt, were something Lyme Regis was famous for.

'That might be fun,' Siena said.

She was still being careful with him, Vincenzo could tell. But then he was being careful with her. Scrupulously polite, courteously conversational.

They stepped off the Cobb and headed towards the town, choosing a pub that served fresh-caught fish for lunch, eating indoors this time, as the wind was so brisk. The low-pitched, smoke-darkened beams were atmospheric, and although the place was designed to cater for tourists, the fresh fish was indeed very tasty.

Afterwards they ventured along the start of the Undercliff, having purchased a guide to Lyme's fossils from a handy souvenir shop. The raised beach was strewn with boulders, and difficult walking terrain, so Vincenzo kept his eyes fixed on Siena, who took her steps carefully. They spotted a large rounded rock, suitable for perching, and did so. Vincenzo opened the fossil guide and they discussed the fossils the place was famous for, and what might yet be found.

'As it's called the Ammonite Pavement,' Siena commented, 'I guess that's what we'll see most of.'

It was—and quite spectacularly so.

'It makes one realise,' Vincenzo said slowly, 'how brief a span of time we occupy on this earth…how short a lifetime is…'

She was silent a moment. Then: 'Some are very short indeed…'

He could hear a strange note in her voice—something that made him look at her.

'What is it?' he asked quietly.

But she only shook her head and changed the subject.

They went on, strolling carefully, but not going too far, before turning and retracing their steps. There were plenty of other fossil-hunters along the way, or just walkers—a good few with dogs in tow. One dog—a large one, rushing around off its leash—came bounding up to them, jumping at Siena.

Vincenzo thrust it away ungently, speaking sharply to him in Italian. The dog gave a bark and bounded away again.

'Are you all right?' Vincenzo asked Siena.

She looked a little shaken, for the dog had been large, and had taken her by surprise.

'Yes, fine… I think he was more friendly than anything.'

'Uncontrolled,' said Vincenzo sternly.

The dog was careering towards them again, clearly over-excited. As it approached, Vincenzo held out an arm, simul-taneously warding it off Siena and giving it another order in Italian. The dog stopped, then sniffed at his outstretched hand. It gave another bark. Then licked Vincenzo's hand and bounded off, hearing its owner calling belatedly to it.

The woman came up to them. 'He's just being friendly,' she said.

'But not everyone loves dogs,' Vincenzo pointed out severely. 'And you—' he addressed the dog directly now, which was licking his still outstretched hand again '—are a fearsome beast!' His voice was severe but the dog knew perfectly well that he was being praised, and barked hap-pily again.

Siena, beside him, held out her own hand for him to sniff. 'But no jumping!' she admonished.

The fearsome beast's owner smiled apologetically. 'I'm sorry…he does get over-enthusiastic. But he mustn't jump up, I know—especially when you are in your condition.' She smiled again. 'When's it due?'

Siena looked taken aback.

'I'm a midwife,' the woman said with another smile. 'I'd say…' she cast a professional eye at Siena '…you're around sixteen weeks.'

'Seventeen,' confirmed Siena.

The woman's smile broadened—her dog had gone bounding away over the beach now, clearly done with them.

'Your first? How wonderful for you both! You must be so happy and excited! I know it will seem like ages and ages yet, but believe me…' her voice warmed '…when it finally happens you'll both be over the moon. I promise!' Her smile included them both. 'I wish you all the very best—this is such a special time of your lives, so enjoy every moment!'

'Thank you,' said Vincenzo with difficulty.

Siena said nothing.

The woman moved to go, pausing only to say, 'I'll keep my dog well away from you, but do take care on this stony beach. You really don't want to trip and fall at this stage.' She smiled again one last time. 'And congratulations!' she said warmly.

She walked away, calling to her dog. For a moment there was only silence between him and Siena. His eyes went to her. There was an expression on her face he had not seen before.

'I guess to others it does look like that,' she said, and he could hear the strain in her voice. 'As if we're just a normal couple starting a family. When we're not even a couple. And a family is the last thing we'll ever be.'

She started to walk, picking her steps carefully. Her shoulders seemed to be hunched, Vincenzo thought.

There was a tightness in his chest as he walked after her and his eyes followed her—the woman who had in one fateful moment, on one fateful night, set him aflame with something he had never felt before. Something for which he had no explanation, no excuse, no exoneration, but which had consumed him with its intensity.

It should never have happened—it had been insane self-indulgence—but he'd gone for it all the same, taking his fill, yielding to the flame she'd lit in him. Burning in it.

He'd kept that woman ruthlessly away from the one now walking away from him. Locked her away in the past, to that single night.

He quickened his pace. That woman's voice—the midwife's—in his head now, warning that Siena should not stumble or trip.

Siena who had ignited that flame in him and Siena who was pregnant with their child.

He did not allow them to be the same person. How could they be?

Once so physically intimate—yet a stranger.

But now?

No physical intimacy—nothing of that burning flame could exist—yet no longer a stranger.

So who is she to me?

The question hung in his head. He should answer it, but he had no answer to give.

Siena was sitting at a little ironwork table, sketchbook propped up, watercolour pencils to hand, newly purchased that morning. Her gaze was going from the view of the hotel's gardens and the sea beyond to what she was capturing of both on paper.

Vincenzo was in his room, touching base with his office, catching up with his affairs. They'd been here nearly a week now. The days were slipping by, undemanding and unhurried, as they toured around, sightseeing and exploring the lush Devon and Dorset countryside and the scenic coastline.

Day by day it was becoming easier between them, Siena acknowledged. So their time here was achieving its purpose. Defusing the toxic hostility that had been so destructive.

She was still conscious of the tension within her, though. Of her continual awareness of Vincenzo…of what he could arouse in her—which she must not allow. She suppressed it as much as she could, but it was there all the same, all the time…

She dipped the nib of her pencil in the water jar, refocussing on her sketching, pulling her thoughts back to safer ground. It was good to be working again. OK, it wasn't the kind of testing artwork she'd have been striving for at art school, but it was enjoyable enough.

The familiar stab of regret, that being pregnant had destroyed her hopes of finally getting to art school a second time around, came now. She pushed it away—because what was the point of dwelling on what could not be? Reached instead for a deep crimson, ideal for a splash of flowers in the foreground.

'That's very good.'

Vincenzo's deep, accented voice behind her made her start.

She turned her head.

And gulped silently.

The sunshine was bright—bright enough for Vincenzo to be sporting shades. She gulped again. Oh, good grief! What *was* it about men and sunglasses? They could turn the most unprepossessing male into someone to look twice at. But when sunglasses adorned a man like Vincenzo…

She crushed her reaction down. She could allow it no place.

Belatedly, she realised he'd spoken to her. 'Oh, thank you,' she said, hoping her voice was normal.

He was standing behind her, looking down at her sketch. 'It *is* good,' he said again. 'There's a talent there you should not ignore.'

Siena gave a flickering smile. It was an awkward subject. 'I enjoy it,' she said. 'But that's all.'

He gave a quick shake of his head. 'Talent should always be developed,' he said. His gaze rested on her speculatively.

'You've never really told me about yourself—what you've done with your life so far. Can it be that it's this?' There was a quizzical note in his voice now, and he gestured towards her sketchbook.

She took a breath. Why make a secret of it? Once she'd have said it was none of his business—that she didn't want him knowing anything about her because she didn't want anything to do with him ever again, after the way he'd treated her. But now—well, there was no reason not to tell him.

'I was going to study art,' she said. 'In fact, the reason I was in London, staying with Megan, was because...' She took another breath. 'I was going to start an art degree this autumn. Obviously because of the baby that's all gone now...' An edge slid into her voice that she could not stop, and she gave a shrug. 'But I'll survive. I gave up on it once before—'

She stopped abruptly.

'Why was that?' Vincenzo was asking frowningly.

But that was a place she did not want to go...

Too painful.

She got to her feet, packing away her pencils, emptying the water jar on the grass, picking up her sketchpad. 'I'll finish this off later,' she said. 'Isn't it time for lunch?'

She was glad he followed her lead—grateful. He got to his feet again, fell into step beside her as they headed indoors.

'Did you have a productive morning?' she asked, conscious that her voice was too bright.

He took her cue, and she was glad of that too.

'Thank you, yes. I can be clear now for a while. Tell me... what might you like to do this afternoon?'

They settled on an excursion further west along the coastline, meandering along country lanes, stopping for a cream tea at a pretty thatched olde-worlde teashop nestled in a sheltered valley, with glorious views over the sparkling English Channel. It was leisurely, undemanding, like all their days.

Serving the purpose for which they were here, Siena acknowledged. To come to terms—civil, unhostile terms—with the situation in which they both unwillingly found themselves.

No other reason.

Her eyes went to him now, as they headed back in the late afternoon. His focus was on the winding road as he drove, strong hands curved around the driving wheel, his face in profile.

But what if there were another reason they were here like this?

What if we were here together because we wanted to be with each other? Just Vincenzo and me, without a baby to complicate everything between us. What if we hadn't met at that party, with me dressed to kill and all that instant heat between us? What if we'd got to know each other slowly— taken things at a slower pace—romanced each other gradually? Spent time with each other the way we're doing now? Got to know each other first, without falling into bed so fast, the way we did...?

But it hadn't happened like that, had it?

She felt something tug at her inside, wanting admission.

She pulled her gaze away, moved it back over the passing countryside.

She felt a heaviness within her.

A sense of loss for what had never been. Never could be now.

I am here with him only because I am pregnant with his baby.

Anything else had been.

And gone.

Vincenzo eased back on the accelerator—these winding West Country roads were not designed for speed, with their thick hedgerows and blind corners. But the landscape was highly appealing, lushly green and rolling, with sheep and cattle placid and contented, the villages quaint and picturesque.

Touring around, sightseeing like this all week, had been very pleasant.

And it had achieved its purpose.

He flicked his glance to Siena, sitting beside him. She was gazing out of the window, an abstracted quality about her. She looked effortlessly lovely…

For a second he let his gaze linger, before returning it to the winding road. But his thoughts stayed with her. What was it about her that made him want to look at her the way he did? He had known beautiful women before, but with Siena there was something…

Something that wasn't just the way she'd looked that night at the Falcone.

Something that drew his eyes to her even as she was now, her hair held back by a simple band, wearing a short-sleeved cotton shirt and loose cropped cotton trousers, not a scrap of make-up, doing nothing to adorn herself. But there was a beauty to her, a glow about her, that made him want to turn his head again.

Perhaps it's pregnancy that makes her bloom?

If it was, then he welcomed it.

He drew his thoughts up short. Decided to speak instead. On a safer subject.

'Shall we dine at the hotel tonight?' he asked conversationally. 'I understand there's a special tasting menu, provided by assorted local producers to showcase their offerings. It's something of an occasion. What do you think?'

He glanced at her again. That abstracted quality had vanished, and she had turned towards him.

'I think it sounds good,' she replied. 'Does it require dressing up?'

'Nothing formal—just smart casual, I would think. I won't wear a tie.'

'Well, I think I've got something that will do, then,' she answered. 'There was a little charity shop next to where I bought my art materials this morning, and there was a summery dress in the window for only a fiver. It's got a loosely elasticated waist, so it will give as I get bigger.'

'That sounds just right,' he approved.

He had spoken politely, but he was conscious that he would like to see Siena in something more beguiling than her habitual tops and trousers. And he was conscious of why...

He pulled his thoughts and his glance away.

Refocussed on his driving and on his reason for being here with Siena. The only reason he should admit to.

As the mother of my child. Only that...

Yet even as he said the words to himself he knew that with every passing day it was not the only truth.

It is for herself...

'Thank you—but only a little.' Vincenzo held his hand up decisively.

The rep from the cider farm smiled encouragingly and poured some of the amber coloured apple brandy she was tempting diners with after their meal.

'Do try,' she said hopefully, clearly wanting him to take a taste while she was hovering.

He did so, and the spirit bit at the back of his throat. He dared not think what proof it was, but it was strong.

'It's very good,' he said to the rep, and she beamed.

'It's ten years old and matured in cognac barrels,' she said. 'Bottles are available in the lobby if you are interested.'

'I will consider it,' he said gravely.

The rep smiled, then turned her attention to Siena. 'What about you?' she said hopefully.

'Alas, no alcohol at all for me,' said Siena ruefully.

'What a shame,' the rep said, and regretfully abandoned them for another table.

Siena looked across at him. 'What's it like? I don't think I've ever heard of apple brandy before.'

'Strong,' said Vincenzo. 'And, yes, very good. But...' he made a slight face '...so many of the producers here seem to feature alcohol!'

'Devon is famous for cider,' Siena told him. 'But wine production is newer. I would have happily tried that white wine you had earlier. Though my blackberry crémant was very good. And I'm definitely tempted by the blackberry vinegar that was in the *jus* accompanying my lamb, which was also very good. In fact, I don't know about you, but I thought all the dishes were really good! Of course, I don't have your gourmet palette, but I do hope you didn't think the menu beneath you.'

'On the contrary,' Vincenzo assured her.

He meant it too. The tasting menu had been varied, and inventive, and a good showcase for local producers. The dining room was full, and dinner was not yet over. Another rep came by, this time with a tray of handmade chocolate truffles.

'Ah, those I can indulge in!' Siena said happily, and took two, promising the rep that she would certainly be buying a box for herself.

Vincenzo sat back with his glass of apple brandy, his gaze resting on her as she bit into the luscious-looking truffle, her eyes half closing in appreciation. He let his gaze linger. He had, he knew, imbibed more alcohol than he would normally have drunk over dinner, but it had seemed churlish to refuse the plentiful offerings—from a gin cocktail infused with countryside botanicals, through to a really very palatable English vineyard dry white wine with the meal, followed by a very good, sweet dessert wine, and now by the simultaneously fiery but mellowing—and indeed very strong—apple brandy.

The effect was lowering his guard.

And that was dangerous.

He felt his eyes drift over Siena's face. Memory came, infusing the present with the past.

The dangerous past.

The *very* dangerous past.

The past that had brought him to this very moment, sitting opposite her in this Devonshire hotel, late in the evening, after a leisurely dinner, comfortable and replete, his appetites sated.

Except for one appetite.

An appetite he could feel rising within him. Welling up in him, reaching out into his limbs, his whole body.

He let his gaze rest on her. The dress she was wearing, which she'd told him she'd bought in a charity shop, might not be a designer number like the one she'd worn that night at the Falcone, but it was every bit as effective. With a scooped neckline and cap sleeves, worn with a lacy wrap around her shoulders, it had a blue floral print that brought out the haunting colour of her deep-set eyes, the long lashes dipping on her silky skin. She'd left her hair loose, fastened at each side with a small clip, exposing the tender lobes of her ears.

He took another slow mouthful of apple brandy, letting it warm his blood. His eyelids drooped, his gaze resting on her as he leant back in his chair, fingers curved around his glass.

Looking at her…

Desiring her…

He should not let himself…should not indulge himself. Should straighten, look away, make some anodyne remark to break the moment.

But he did not.

He tried to think of all the reasons why he should keep his guard high—all the reasons that had pressed upon him every time he'd caught himself looking at her, remembering that searing night he'd spent with her. They were good reasons—he knew they were. His brain knew them at any rate.

Because the situation between us is complicated—uncertain—unprecedented. Because so much is at stake and I have to tread carefully, watching each step.

But right now he didn't want to think of all that. He wanted only to go on doing what he was doing, letting his gaze rest on her, absorb her, linger on her…

His gaze dipped to her neckline. It was hardly a dramatic decolletage, but for all that it shaped the swell of her breasts…breasts that were now more generous. His eyes narrowed infinitesimally as he took another slow, leisurely mouthful of the potent apple brandy. Her whole body was more generous too, rounding and ripening. Making her even more beautiful than ever…

He felt desire rise within him, quicken in his heated blood.

She swallowed her truffle, opened her eyes.

Looked straight into his…

CHAPTER TEN

WEAKNESS WASHED THROUGH HER. It was as if every bone in her body were dissolving…as if the room around them were vanishing…the whole world vanishing…evaporating…and all that existed was Vincenzo's gaze on her…consuming her.

Memory flared, hot and instant, sending colour coursing into her cheeks, then draining it from them just as swiftly.

He had looked at her like that before, with those long-lashed, hooded eyes of his, so dark, so impenetrable, yet with an open message in them that had made her very bones, then as now, dissolve… He'd looked at her as they had finally finished dinner that night at the Falcone, *knowing* there was only one way the evening was going to end… and that end was coming. Coming as he had got to his feet, his eyes never leaving her, their sensual glance weakening her, so that when he'd held out his hand to her she had put hers into his, and he'd drawn her to her feet, and she had gone with him…

And now it was happening again…

She felt the fatal weakness wash through her, more dissolving still…

She must fight it. Surely she must give it no room, no space. She must deny it…resist it. Because how could she not? How could she let happen again what had happened before? She must reject it…find the strength to do so.

But she had no strength—none…

His lidded gaze was on her still, holding hers, and heat flushed through her still. She was helpless to pull her eyes away. Quite helpless…

A voice beside her spoke. 'May I offer you some coffee?'

It was one of the waitresses, coffee jug in hand, smiling politely at her.

Siena turned her head, clutched at the lifeline.

'Oh…er…um, have you got tea instead?' she asked. 'A mint tea?'

Did she sound breathless? She must, surely. She fought for composure, to beat down the flaring of heat inside her.

'Of course.' The waitress smiled. Then turned her attention to Vincenzo. 'Coffee for you, sir?' she enquired.

'Thank you,' he answered.

His voice was mechanical, Siena could tell. But his gaze—his disastrous, dissolving gaze—had been switched off. She realised her heart was beating in an agitated manner, and sought to subdue it, to subdue the colour flushing in and out of her cheeks.

The waitress poured coffee into Vincenzo's cup, offered milk, which was refused, then promised Siena she would return with her mint tea. She moved off to the next table.

Urgently, Siena cast about for a safe thing to say, to take them away from the moment that had been so dangerous…

No, don't think it—don't allow it in—don't even think about thinking it. Just go… Before it's too late…

She felt herself get to her feet. 'I think I'll pass on the mint tea after all,' she said. 'It's been a long day. I'll head up to bed. Enjoy the rest of your apple brandy. Thank you for dinner.'

Her voice was staccato, and she knew it, but it was the best she could do.

With a smile that took more effort than she'd thought she was capable of she turned away, heading towards the dining room doors, walking rapidly, wanting only to get away…

Because she must.

Because anything else was too dangerous…

Far, far too dangerous.

But even as she fled, footsteps came after her.

Vincenzo had knocked back the last of his apple brandy and got to his feet, and now he strode after her. She'd paused by the lift, and his eyes went to her. She was running from him—and he did not want her to.

Silhouetted against the metallic doors of the lift, she was more beautiful than ever, with her long hair curving over her shoulders, the lacy fall of her wrap, the soft drape of her summer dress, her slender calves, bared arms…

So beautiful…

He felt the breath tighten in his lungs as he came up to her. She started at his approach, her head turning swiftly to him, eyes flaring.

'Let me see you to your room,' he said.

He could hear a husk in his voice…knew why. She looked up at him. Her eyes were wide, and in them was apprehension—and something else entirely.

'No…no, it's fine…really…'

He ignored her. The lift doors were opening and she stepped inside. He followed her. He could feel his heart thudding in his chest. He stabbed the button for their floor. His room was at the far end of the corridor, but hers was closer to where the lift disgorged them, and as she walked to her door, her gait quickening, fumbling for the key in her handbag, he closed in on her.

He did not speak. Then, as she turned the old-fashioned key in the lock, he said her name, his voice more husky yet.

She turned, lifting her face to him. Her eyes were wide. Pupils dilated.

'Vincenzo...' Her voice was faint, so faint. 'No—we can't...we mustn't...'

He took no notice. And as her hand pushed open the door, he reached out his hand to her...

She had no breath in her body—none. His hand was curving around the nape of her neck. He said her name. Low and husked. She saw his eyelids dip down over his eyes, watched him lowering his mouth to hers.

It was velvet on her lips...soft, infinitely seductive...and as his mouth moved on hers he pulled her to him, drawing her inside her room. A thousand sensations blinded her as he shut the door behind them. A low, helpless moan came from her, and she felt her limbs dissolving as the velvet of his mouth weakened everything about her. Her hands went around him, to hold and support her, for she had no strength at all. The hard wall of his chest pressed against her breasts, and she felt, with a dim sense of helpless fatality, how they engorged and flowered...

Another moan came from her and her mouth opened to his as his kiss deepened, her hands winding around him, holding him against her. He said something to her, low and husky in his native language. A kind of madness was coming over her, and as he scooped her up into his arms she let him do so. The room had disappeared, the world had disappeared, the whole universe had disappeared. There was only this...only now...only Vincenzo. He was carrying her to her bed, lowering her down upon it, coming down beside her, his mouth never leaving hers.

She was in meltdown—she knew she was. It was as if she had been taken to another existence, one in which only the sweet bliss of *now* was real. For bliss it was, and sweet it was, and all that she craved…

Somewhere, dimly, in what was left of her consciousness, she knew that this time with Vincenzo was far different from the way it had been before. Then it had been an urgent, burning flame, fierce, white-hot, incandescent, sensual, ecstatic, with each of them feeding upon the other, hungry for each other, unleashed upon each other. There had been no time for anything else. Desire—raw, visceral, physical desire—had burned, had blazed between them, wreathing them in its flames, stripping the clothes from their bodies, making them uninhibited, greedy for the sensations that naked intimacy aroused between them, their bodies winding around each other, flexing and writhing, feasting wantonly and wildly.

Now there was no wildness, no hungry urgency. Now there was a slow, sensuous coming together, with each touch of his lips, his fingers, his tongue, his palms, celebrating the beauty of her body—a body that ripened under his as his hands splayed out over her abdomen, smoothing its soft roundness. His mouth lowered to trace its gentle contours, softly and sensuously. Then his hands were lifting to her breasts, filling his curving palms.

She felt her limbs loosen, his body moving over hers. And in the darkened room, their clothes long shed, she gave herself to him, taking him in return, his long, lean body covering hers, hers yielding to his. They did not speak, and yet she heard soft murmurous Italian from him as his mouth kissed her breasts, her throat, her lips. His kisses were deep, impassioned, yet without frenzied urgency, only with slow, sweet bliss. A bliss he drew from her as he moved his body within hers, setting not a raging fire but a low, warm flame, melting and dissolving her, fusing her to him and him to her.

And when her moment came, it was a warmth, a sweet, liquid pleasure, that spread from her very core to every cell in her body, even to the tips of her fingers, with a honeyed glow that made her cry out softly...so softly...her body lifting to his, her hands pressing the sculpted contours of his back to hold him close, so close...

She felt him surge within her, felt her own body flex and pulse, drawing him in yet deeper, fusing with him, becoming one with him, as still her own moment went on and endlessly on.

And when it finally ebbed, tears were wet upon her cheeks.

Tears for so, so much...

Vincenzo stirred, sleep gradually leaving him, consciousness gradually returning. Daylight was filling the room—the curtains were undrawn since the night before. His arm reached out across the double bed.

The empty double bed.

Instantly, he was fully awake, his eyes searching the room. The empty room. The door to the en suite bathroom stood open.

The empty en suite bathroom.

He swung himself out of bed.

'Siena?' His voice was sharp, urgent.

No answer came.

No answer was going to come.

Siena had gone.

He slumped back against the pillows, staring out into the room. Heart thudding.

He heard his phone—still in the pocket of his discarded jacket, dropped somewhere on the floor near the bed. Instantly he went to it, snatched it up. A text—from Siena.

He read it, and frowned, then dropped the phone on the tangled bedclothes. But the words in the text were crystal-clear in his head.

I can't do this. I can't do any of it. I'm sorry—I just can't. I'm sorry.

Siena sat in the railway carriage, heading back to London. Words were going over and over in her head, in rhythm with the wheels of the train over the track.

I'm sorry... I'm sorry... I'm sorry.

It was all that was in her head. All that she would allow. All that she dared allow.

She urged the train onwards. She had to get to London before Vincenzo could. Had to get to the apartment he'd taken for her. Had to get there, pack her necessities, and get out. The holiday clothes she'd taken to the seaside would have to be packed by one of the hotel maids, unless Vincenzo did it. And either he would bring her small suitcase with him, her newly purchased sketchbook and pencils, or have it sent on to her.

Wherever she was.

But where would that be?

Into her head a new question formed, repeating over the relentless sound of the train wheels.

Where can I go? Where can I go? Where can I go?

She did not know. Not yet. But she must think of somewhere. She must.

She *must...*

* * *

Vincenzo was in Milan. He might as well be. There was no point being in England. Not any more. Siena had made that clear. Crystal-clear. He knew where she was, and for now that must do. He was not out of touch with her—not completely. She sent him brief monthly updates, reports from the midwife appointments she went to. Her pregnancy was progressing healthily—that was all he knew.

He knew he must allow her this. Allow her time and space and distance.

Because she does not want anything more from me.

He felt emotion stab at him, but he crushed it back down. There was no point allowing it…permitting it.

I have to accept that she wants nothing more than what she has made clear—completely clear.

And he must respect that—he had no choice but to do so. All he could do was what he was doing now. Leave her be.

The way she wanted.

Until…

When her time comes I shall be there. Be there for her.

On that he would insist.

CHAPTER ELEVEN

SIENA WAS WASHING UP, looking out of the kitchen window into the garden at the back of the little terraced house. In the summer it was a holiday let, but she had rented it for the winter. In the garden, a robin and a blackbird were hopping about. She must put out some more food for them.

She moved slowly towards the back door that opened on to the garden. Her gait was ponderous now…gravid. Her feet had disappeared from view, and sitting down and getting up was a slow business.

As she scooped up some more birdseed and scattered it on the paved area beyond the back door she felt the baby move and turn within her. She stilled a moment, letting the movement subside.

Her time was coming…her due date approaching. No longer weeks—only days.

She walked slowly, ponderously, to the sink, filled up the kettle, set it to boil. A cup of tea to while away the time. She could do some sketching—but what for? She'd done a little, from time to time, but had no heart for it. The one of the garden and seascape that she'd made at the hotel in Selcombe had never been finished. She did not want to think about it. Didn't want to think about the time she'd spent there that had ended so disastrously…

She felt a twisting inside her—like ropes pulling tight, into knots.

Isn't this enough of a mess without...?

She tried to pull her thoughts away, as she had been training herself to do ever since she had fled, so urgently, so desperately, to find refuge here in this anonymous little house. Somewhere she could hole up...hide...

But how could she hide? This place, this time, was a respite only. Nothing more than that. Soon—and it was coming ever closer—in a handful of days, she must see Vincenzo again. She might wish with all her being that she need not do so, but how could she deny him?

Impossible to do so.

Her words, hurled at him so long ago now, speared in her head.

'I am handcuffed to you—shackled to you!'

Emotion twisted inside her again. The irony of it was hard to bear.

I didn't want anything to do with him because I loathed him. Now...

She stared blindly out of the kitchen window as the kettle started to boil. Outside the birds pecked hungrily at the seed she'd scattered for them, unseen by her. Emotion came again—a physical pain, stabbing at her. Unbearable to bear—and yet she must. For what else could she do but bear it? What else but endure the ultimate folly she had committed?

Not her pregnancy—not that at all.

A smothered cry of anguish broke from her and she turned away, hand pressed against her mouth, tears starting in her eyes.

How can I bear it?

But it was beyond answering.

* * *

Vincenzo pulled the car against the kerb, turned off the engine. He looked at the small terraced house he'd parked outside in this market town in a popular tourist area of East Anglia. He knew what to expect—he had checked it out online, on the holiday letting agency's website, when Siena had given him her new address. He'd offered to pay for it, but she'd refused. She was refusing all financial support and he had accepted her refusal. As he had accepted everything else...

He felt himself tense. This would not be easy, but it had to be done. Her due date was imminent and he would be here, at her side. Literally so—for he'd rented the house next to hers, also a holiday let, and would stay for the duration. Stay while he could be of use to her.

And then...

No, he would not go there. Not yet.

Impossible to look beyond what was about to happen.

Starting right now.

With a determined movement he got out of the car, walked up to her front door, rapped on it with the knocker. She knew he was coming. He had texted her when he'd set off from London, having flown in the day before. He'd told her his ETA here, then texted again, pulling over on the outskirts of the town, to say he was making his way to her house.

She'd simply texted back:

OK

His mouth pressed. 'OK' was not what it was...

But there was nothing he could do about it. Nothing except what she wanted him to do.

Accept her decision.

The one she'd made all those months ago, when she was fleeing from him...

Siena heard the door knocker, tensing immediately. For a moment she did not move. Then, heavily, she levered herself up and out of the armchair she'd sunk into to watch something mindless on TV. It took her a while to get up—it increasingly did now. Ponderously she made her way out of the living room, down to the front door, steeling herself to open it.

He was standing there, tall against the wintry dusk. She felt her stomach clench, her senses reel from his physical presence after so long a time, but she stood back so he could come inside.

For a moment, though, he was motionless. Siena assumed he was taking in just how very different she looked from when he had last seen her.

'I told you I would look like an elephant by this time,' she said.

She kept her voice neutral, and so was his reply.

'Hardly,' he replied, temporising. 'But you are very near your time now.'

He walked in. The narrow hallway only just let him pass her. The brush of his sleeve made her stiffen, and as he walked past she caught the distinctive trace of his aftershave. For a second she felt faint with familiarity...with memory.

Memory she must not allow.

Too dangerous.

Too pointless...

Because he is not here for me! He is here only because

I am about to give birth to the baby I have conceived. No other reason.

No other reason at all.

And I must have no other reason either! Must allow myself none.

She must match him in the way she was with him now.

'It still could be up to another fortnight,' she said, following him as he stepped into the little sitting room. 'I hope it isn't, though—I just want it over and done with.'

He turned to look at her, his face unreadable.

'How was the drive?' she asked, to take her mind off what it did not help her to think about. 'It's not the easiest part of the world to get to.'

'It was fine,' he said. 'Sat nav did it all.' His eyes were on her still, and still unreadable. 'How have you been keeping, Siena?' he asked.

'OK,' she answered. 'My ankles have swollen a little, but—'

'That's not good!' he cut across her sharply, frowning.

She shook her head, negating his reaction. 'I'm within normal range. No sign of pre-eclampsia. All my readings are fine. I saw the midwife this morning, and she's happy with everything. She said that if I'm not in labour by midweek she'll come again to check on me.'

She didn't want him fussing.

'Can I make you a coffee?' she offered, to stop any more questions. 'This place comes with a coffee machine—though it's probably a bit basic for you. Come into the kitchen and see.'

She led the way, knowing she was waddling, but there was nothing she could do about it. Absently, her hand touched her distended abdomen, as if she were patting a puppy that did not know how much disruption it was causing, but whose feelings she did not want to hurt all the same.

Because it's not your fault, little one. None of this. You couldn't help being conceived the way you were!

'There's a choice of coffee pods,' she said, opening an ornamental tin box beside the coffee machine on the worktop. 'I've used all the decaf ones. And anyway, these days I prefer something that's more easily digestible. I'll make a mint tea for myself.'

She went to fill the kettle, memory filling her head as well. She'd asked for a mint tea at the end of that tasting menu dinner at the seaside hotel and had never drunk it.

She had run instead.

Knowing she had to.

It had been too dangerous…much too dangerous…to do anything but run…

But I ran in vain.

She snapped the memory off. There was no point to it… no purpose.

He was stepping forward to make his selection of coffee pods and Siena moved away. For the first time she was glad of being the size she was. She could not have looked more different than she had that night at the hotel in Devon. Then, pregnancy had given her a bloom, enhancing her looks.

Dangerously so.

Disastrously so.

She pulled her thoughts away again. She must not indulge them. However hard—unbearable—it was to have Vincenzo here now, at this time, she had to endure it. He had a right to be here.

It was not his fault any more than it was her baby's fault that her life was now the mess it was. The mess that was infinitely worse than she had ever thought it would be the day she'd found herself pregnant.

Anguish bit again.

She took a breath as she flicked on the kettle, steadying herself as she often must now.

Vincenzo switched on the coffee machine, turned to look at her. 'I was wondering,' he said, his voice careful, 'if you would like to have dinner with me tonight?'

She shook her head. 'I get very tired now, and I go to bed very early. Do try the pub in the market square for yourself, though. It's supposed to be pretty good—at least by local standards.'

'Thank you—I'll try it out.' His eyes were resting on her, still unreadable. 'And how are *you*, Siena?' he asked. 'Not just physically, but—'

'I'm fine,' she said, cutting across him. There had been concern in his voice, and she did not want that. She could cope with him being here only by keeping well clear of anything personal. 'Like I said,' she went on, 'I'm just keen to get a move on now.'

He nodded in acknowledgement. 'That I can understand,' he said. He paused a moment. Then, 'Do you want to tell me what your birth plan is? I… I would like to be there… or close by…if you will allow me.'

She looked at him uncertainly. 'I… I don't know. If you want to be at the hospital while it's all going on, I guess I don't mind. As for a birth plan… Well, nothing out of the ordinary. I assume I'll want pain relief at some point. Other than that…just as it happens, I suppose. My grab bag's all ready—by my bedroom door. That's it, really.'

The coffee machine finished just as the kettle boiled. She turned off both, making her mint tea while Vincenzo reached forward to take his coffee. An ache filled her. To be here with him, like this, in such circumstances...

Isn't it enough of a mess already? Without me messing it up even more?

Anguish clutched at her again. Why, oh, why had she allowed what was already an impossible situation...one she'd never wanted...to become so much worse?

'Siena?'

Vincenzo's voice made her start. Hastily, she grabbed her mint tea. 'Come into the sitting room,' she said, heading heavily for the kitchen doorway.

'Are you all right? You look...upset.'

Concern was in Vincenzo's voice. It hurt to hear it.

'Just tired,' she said, making her way to the armchair and lowering herself ponderously into it.

'I'll leave you in peace as soon as I've drunk my coffee,' Vincenzo was saying.

She was grateful. This was an ordeal, and it was hard—so very hard.

But I have to get used to seeing him again—to him being around. I have to!

He was sitting himself down on the sofa opposite the armchair, crossing one long leg over the other. She wanted to gaze at him. Gaze at him and drink him in...

But I can't. He isn't mine to gaze at. He's just the man who fathered my baby, and he is concerned only for that reason.

That was all she had to remember.

She took a sip of her mint tea, aware that he was speaking again.

'Is there anything that you might like to do over the weekend?' he asked.

'Not really.'

She didn't mean to sound indifferent, but the weekend

was just another two days to get through—two days closer to her due date.

'Well, then, I wondered...' His voice was cautious, speculative, his eyes resting on her with the same careful expression. 'I wondered whether you would feel up to an outing by car? Nothing strenuous. And only if you would like it.' He paused. 'You told me you grew up in this part of the country. Is that why you chose to base yourself here?'

'It seemed as good a reason as any,' she answered. 'I know the district hospital has a good reputation, and I had to settle somewhere—at least for the duration of my being pregnant. What I'll do afterwards I don't yet know...'

Her voice trailed off. She could feel Vincenzo's eyes resting on her, and wished they would not.

'I would still like to help you—' he began.

'No.' Her voice steeled. 'Vincenzo, please—we've had this discussion. I... I need to make my own way after...after the baby is born. Deal with it in my own way.'

Deal with so much more than simply having a baby...

She gave a sigh. It was all such a mess. A mess from beginning to end. Vincenzo had said that it need not be—but it was.

Longing filled her, intense and hopeless. This whole situation was wretched—her unwanted pregnancy, her poor, benighted little baby being born into such a mess, with neither of its parents welcoming its arrival but seeing it only as a problem, a difficulty...

And now, on top of all of that—

She thrust it from her. What was the point of brooding over it? She had to cope with it—and she had to get used to coping with having Vincenzo showing up. What else could she do?

After all he would be doing it for years ahead. Years she could not bear to think about.

'Maybe,' she heard herself saying now. 'Going for a drive tomorrow might be OK.'

His expression altered. Lightened fractionally. But it was still careful.

'If the weather is sufficiently clement, we shall do so,' he said. 'Would setting off at, say, eleven suit you? We could drive out somewhere, maybe have lunch, then circle back? Have a think about where you might like to go. This part of England is all new to me, so I am happy to be guided by you.'

He drained the last of his coffee, set the cup aside, stood up.

'I will leave you in peace now,' he said. 'Settle myself in next door. No, don't get up. I can see myself out.'

'Thank you,' she said, glad she did not have to lumber to her feet.

At the door to the narrow hallway he paused, looking back at her. 'You must phone me,' he said, 'at any time, if you have any need—'

'I'll be fine,' she said.

For a moment longer he let his unreadable gaze rest on her. Then, with a final nod, after bidding her a murmured goodnight, he took his leave.

Leaving her alone.

Alone, alone, alone…

Tears welled in her eyes. Such useless tears…

Vincenzo rapped on Siena's front door. It was a bright, sunny day, promising spring. A good day for a drive in the countryside. He was glad she'd agreed to it. She had not looked very well yesterday, he thought. Not ill, thankfully, but not…not *blooming*.

In her earlier stages, and at the seaside, there had been a radiance to her—a glow playing over her natural, effortless beauty which had been noticeably absent yesterday. Yes, of course her figure had ballooned, this close to full term, but it was more than that. There was an air about her of…not weariness, precisely, but lassitude, perhaps.

He frowned. Depression? He could understand that she was impatient for her due date to arrive, but there had been no eagerness for it.

His face shadowed. Nor could there be for him.

How could there be?

Bleakness filled him. The situation was damnable…

The door opened and Siena was there.

'Ready to set off?' he asked. He forced his voice to sound light.

She nodded. She was wearing a padded but lightweight knee-length coat that emphasised her bulk, but which was presumably warm enough for winter walking. Stout and solid-looking lace-up shoes were on her feet, and she was wearing fleecy trousers. Her hair was bunched back on her head, and her skin looked blotchy.

For a second Vincenzo wanted to ask if she was OK—because it looked as if she had been crying. He started to frown, but he got no chance to say anything, because Siena was talking, constraint in her voice.

'I need to sit on a towel over a polythene bin bag,' she said, and he saw she was holding both items.

'Bin bag…?' Vincenzo stared.

'And a towel, yes. I'm only a handful of days away from my due date.'

Comprehension dawned. 'I'll put them on the seat,' he said, and took them from her.

Settling her in to the passenger seat took some time, but it was done in the end. He helped her draw the seat belt around what once had been her waist. Then, finally arranged, she stretched out her legs and turned towards him.

'Have you had any ideas where you might like to go?'

He could still hear that constraint in her voice, and could see it in the way she sat. Would this outing work at all? He could only try...

'I'm easy,' he said. 'Do you have any preferences?'

'Probably best not to try for the coast but stick to inland.'

She gave directions and Vincenzo followed them. The flat, arable landscape was very different from that of hilly, pastoral South Devon, but he made no reference to it. Their time there—the way it had ended—lay between them, unspoken of and impossible to mention. Instead, he asked general questions about the area, and Siena politely gave answers, her air of constraint still palpable.

As for him...

Their encounter yesterday had not been easy, but he had not expected it to be. What had been achieved between them—their comfortable companionship during their time in Devon—had gone.

I destroyed it.

And now—now all he could do was what he was doing. Being here to support her in whatever way he could, whatever way she would allow. Ready to take on the responsibility of a parental role he had never looked for but now had to shoulder.

However impossible that might be.

As he drove his eyes slid to her, sitting beside him, her

face in profile, her gravid body expectant. Soon—within days—his life would change irrevocably and for ever.

It already has.

But not just because of the baby...

'Shall we find somewhere to stop for lunch soon?'

Siena gave a little start at Vincenzo's voice.

'Yes, good idea,' she said politely.

His question had interrupted her thoughts, which had been drifting, formless and shapeless, as they'd motored on. Though it had brought painful reminders of their time in Devon, it had been soothing, in a way, to drive around like this. She hadn't been anywhere except to the local clinic and for hospital appointments.

Absently, as it so often did, her hand went to the swell of her body, as if with compunction.

Poor little mite. Coming into the world like this...

'What about that place coming up?'

Again, Vincenzo's voice interrupted her thoughts.

She looked to where he was indicating. It looked a decent enough place, typical Suffolk pink, prosperous-looking, with a blackboard sign outside saying *Good Food!* It would do as well as anywhere.

He pulled across to it, driving the car into a small but busy car park—another encouraging indicator. Getting out took a while, and she flexed her legs, feeling elephantine and regretting, for a moment, having come out at all. But they were here now, and she was feeling hungry. Besides, she could do with using the facilities...

Vincenzo guided her inside. Memory pierced of how they'd toured the Devon countryside, explored the Jurassic Coast, how they'd walked along Jane Austen's Cobb, in

Lyme, and then tried out the Ammonite Pavement to look for fossils. How that midwife with the jumpy dog had told her to enjoy being pregnant, said how excited she must be feeling, and Vincenzo too, how happy they must be...

How hollow that had sounded, even then.

And now—

It was a thousand times more hollow...

'Will this table suit?'

Vincenzo's polite enquiry interrupted memories that only brought pain.

'Yes, it's fine. I'll join you in a moment.'

She disappeared off in the direction of the washrooms. She felt self-conscious, walking across to them, but there was nothing she could do about that. On her way back to the table a few minutes later she caught a woman seated at another table giving Vincenzo the once-over. He was oblivious to it. As she approached the table the woman saw her, saw how pregnant she was, and looked away, consigning Vincenzo to the category of 'taken'.

But he isn't, is he? And one day—one day when he is simply doing a duty visit to the baby he never asked for, never wanted, would never welcome but only feel responsible for—he will meet a woman who will captivate him, who won't mind that he has a spare son or daughter somewhere in England, by a woman he only ever spent two nights with...

She dragged her thoughts away. Why torment herself with them? To what purpose?

None.

She sat down heavily in the chair Vincenzo had stood to draw back for her, murmuring an awkward thank-you.

If the baby arrives on its due date, then in a couple of weeks' time Vincenzo will be gone. He'll be back in Italy. Back in his own life. And I—

But she didn't want to think about that.

Could not bear to.

Vincenzo finished his beer. His mood was bleak. He and Siena had made stilted conversation over lunch, and now she had disappeared off to the Ladies' again. The rest of the day stretched ahead. And all the days until her time finally came.

Had it been a mistake to turn up like this? Should he rather have left Siena alone at this time, not insist he be there?

Heaviness weighed him down. The situation was impossible.

And he had made it so.

That night in Devon—

He stamped down his thoughts. They were to no purpose. The situation was as it was.

Damnable.

Memory speared in him—the words Siena had hurled at him all that time ago.

'I am handcuffed to you—shackled to you!'

His eyes lifted from the menu.

Dread filled him at the future looming for him.

But it had to be faced. No escape from it.

His eyes went across the room. Siena was emerging from the Ladies' room, making her way towards him. He got to his feet, holding her chair for her to sit down. There was an odd expression on her face. Puzzled...

'I'm sorry if this is TMI—too much information—but I seem to be bleeding.' She frowned. 'It's not much, but it's definitely blood. I'm not sure what to do. Probably best to ignore it. I'll phone the midwife when we get back. I'm sure she'll just say it happens sometimes and tell me not to worry about it.'

She moved to sit down, but Vincenzo forestalled her. 'I think we ought to go,' he said.

She looked at him. 'Don't you want a pudding?'

He shook his head. 'I'll pay the bill,' he said, picking up the chit.

He crossed to the bar.

'I'd like to pay,' he said.

The barman, who was pulling a pint for another customer, nodded. 'Be right with you.'

'Now,' said Vincenzo.

Whatever he'd put into his voice—and he'd done so quite deliberately—it got results. Moments later Vincenzo was walking back to Siena. She was resting her hand on the back of her chair, as if leaning her weight on it.

He held his arm out to her, and though she hesitated for a moment, she took it. She was soon leaning on him, and frowning slightly.

They left the pub, Vincenzo ushering her into the car deliberately unhurriedly. He helped to settle her, ensuring, as she stipulated, that the towel was thickly folded over the bin bag. Then he got into his side of the car, but did not start the engine immediately. Instead, he keyed a destination into the sat nav.

'What are you doing?' Siena asked beside him.

He turned towards her.

'I'm taking you to hospital,' he said.

CHAPTER TWELVE

'*HOSPITAL?*' SIENA'S VOICE was a protest. 'In heaven's name, why? I'm perfectly all right! I haven't got a twinge or anything! Absolutely nothing that might be even the start of a contraction! Not a real one, anyway. I've had the Braxton-Hicks false ones from time to time, but that's perfectly normal.'

He was gunning the engine, heading back on to the road.

'Vincenzo, please! This is quite unnecessary. The hospital will only send me away again! They haven't got room to keep a load of pre-labour women hanging about till their due dates!'

His response was to speed up and throw a glance at her.

'Phone your midwife,' he said.

It was not a suggestion.

Her brow furrowed, but she fished her phone out of her handbag, flicked into her contacts file and hit speed dial. As she waited to connect, she pressed her free hand over her abdomen. A thought struck her, and her frown deepened. When had she last felt any movement?

A moment later her midwife was answering.

And when she hung up, a couple of minutes later, Siena felt fear like ice in her veins…

Vincenzo's grip on the steering wheel was whitening his knuckles. In his head, one word was stabbing:

Damnable.

That was what he'd called the situation. And now, with that single announcement by Siena, the word had been wiped out of existence. Totally overridden.

He dropped his eyes to the sat nav screen. Twenty miles still. Twenty miles to drive as fast and as smoothly as he could. Whether he broke the speed limit or not he neither knew nor cared. If the police stopped them—well, maybe he'd get a blue light escort to the hospital...

He'd glanced at Siena as she hung up from the midwife. Her face had been pale. He'd asked her to put the call on speaker phone, and the midwife had been very good. Not alarmist, but insistent.

'We need to check you out at the hospital,' she'd said. 'Phone again when you are closer.'

What she had not said was what she was going to be checking. But Vincenzo knew perfectly well. What had immediately stabbed in his head—what could be happening...

Placental abruption—the separation of the placenta from the uterine wall...and how dangerous that is...

A knife twisted inside him and his grip on the steering wheel tightened again. More than anyone, he knew that childbirth could be dangerous...

He depressed the accelerator further. 'How are you feeling?' he asked.

He heard her swallow, but she said, 'Fine. I feel fine. It's just that—' Her voice changed. And he could hear the thread of fear in it now. 'Vincenzo, I can't feel the baby moving—and the towel I'm sitting on feels damp.'

'I'll get you there.' His voice was grim.

The miles passed with punishing resistance, and without the sat nav he'd have been lost. It took them right to the hospital turning. Without wasting time parking, he steered straight to the entrance for the maternity unit, pulled up short. Siena had phoned the midwife again, and was on the phone to her now.

'She says she'll be in the lobby—you should grab a wheelchair. They'll take me straight up.'

Her voice was shaky.

He launched himself out of the driver's seat, hazard lights flashing, saw a row of wheelchairs under a shelter and grabbed one, coming round to Siena's side of the car. She was already opening the door and he helped her out, helped her into the wheelchair, hurried her through the automatically opening doors.

A woman in scrubs was hurrying towards them.

'You made good time—well done.' She nodded at Vincenzo. 'We'll take over now—get your car parked and come on up. You can be there for the examination—we don't know what's happening yet.'

Then she turned her attention to Siena and pushed her across the lobby, clearly hurrying.

Vincenzo went back out to the car, slamming the passenger door shut, throwing himself in on his side His glance went to where she'd been sitting. The towel on the seat was pale grey—except for the large bloodstain in the centre...

He felt sick suddenly. But not because of the blood...

Less than five minutes later he'd disposed of the car and was back inside the maternity unit lobby, pushing through the doors where Siena had disappeared.

A medic of some sort walked past him, and he grabbed his arm. 'Possible placental abruption—where would she be taken?' His voice was urgent.

The medic turned. 'Follow me.'

* * *

Siena heard the words, but scarcely comprehended them. Yet they were clear enough.

Emergency Caesarean.

She stared, white-faced, heart thudding, the ice in her veins colder still, at the consultant obstetrician, summoned by the midwife, who'd said those words to her.

'It has to be now. Right now,' he said.

His voice was calm, but insistent.

The door to the examination room swung open and Vincenzo was there, striding in.

'Vincenzo!' she cried.

He came to her at once, lying there on the examination couch. She was aware she was hardly in any state for him to see her, but she didn't care. All she cared about was what the obstetrician had just announced.

Vincenzo took her outstretched hand, squeezed it. Turned to the obstetrician.

'It has to be a C-section delivery straight away,' the consultant told him gravely. 'The placenta is coming away and the baby is becoming increasingly at risk. Hypoxia is—'

'Yes, I know.' Siena heard Vincenzo's voice cut across him, sounding not curt, but short. 'Potentially—'

He didn't complete the sentence, and Siena gave a terrified moan. Her free hand flew to her abdomen. As if her bare, splayed hand could keep her baby safe. Alive...

The baby she had never welcomed...

Her eyes flew to the obstetrician.

'Do it!' she cried. 'Just do it now! Do whatever it takes!'

The consultant nodded, and she saw his glance go to Vincenzo.

'I want him with me!' she cried, and clung to his hand in desperation.

'Of course,' said the consultant. He turned to the hovering midwife. 'Theatre One,' he said. 'Let's go.'

After that it was a blur. A blur that was a nightmare. She
felt herself being slid sideways onto a trolley and wheeled
off. Her hand still clung to Vincenzo's, as he kept pace with
the trolley, and it was all that kept her going…all that she
could hold on to in an ocean of terror.

So much more than terror.

Emotions poured through her like a tsunami sweeping
her up, convulsing her, buckling her into a tiny piece of
flotsam torn apart by the power of what was ripping her to
pieces. Words flew through her head—fragments, shreds,
rags and tatters—each one suffocating her with its terrifying intensity.

*I never wanted this baby. I was resentful and resis-
tant—appalled and self-pitying—angry at its conception.
A self-indulgent, irresponsible conception, by self-indulgent, irresponsible parents. All I cared about was that my
life was being changed for ever, that I was sacrificing my
dream of art college again. I never wanted this baby…my
poor baby…*

And now…

Terror constricted her again and she could barely breathe.

The medics seemed to be crowding round her, talking
over her, talking to her only to tell her what was essential.
Not one of them was telling her the only thing she was desperate to know.

Is it too late?

But she couldn't ask—and knew they wouldn't tell her
anyway. Her grip on Vincenzo's hand tightened. He was
saying nothing—not to her, not to the doctors. She knew
she had to let the doctors get on with it.

Silently, terrified, she urged them on.

Hurry—hurry—hurry!

She was being put into some kind of hospital gown, then turned on her side. Vincenzo was still holding her hand, and some kind of injection was being made into her spine. Then some kind of screen was being placed below her ribs and she couldn't see anything—anything at all—or feel anything except the tsunami of terror, of guilt, churning her into pieces…

Her other hand, which could no longer go to where it longed to be, started to flail helplessly, hopelessly, and Vincenzo caught it, pressed it with his own.

'Stay calm…they are doing what they must.'

His voice was strained, his expression strained too, and her eyes clung to his. There was desperation in her clinging. Despair in her terrified, whispering voice.

'We're losing our baby—oh, Vincenzo, we're losing our baby!'

Nothing else mattered. Nothing at all…

Only the fear, the terror, knifing her over and over again…

He pressed her hands, saying nothing—because what, she thought fearfully, could he say?

What was going on beyond the screen she did not know—dared not know. Knew only that it was taking an unbearably, agonisingly long time.

Until…

There was movement. Something was happening. Though she could still feel nothing…nothing at all. To the side of the screen she could see the midwife carrying something… something that made no noise.

She gave a broken cry, and Vincenzo twisted to see what he could, never letting go of her hands, which he was crushing with his own.

'What is it? What's happening?' Her voice was anguished.

But she knew. She knew what was happening...what had happened. Knew it because she deserved it... Knew it because suddenly the obstetrician was there, looking down at her. He was about to tell her, *I'm so sorry. We did all we could, but it was too late...*

Grief convulsed her, possessed her.

And then...

A cry...a thin, frail cry. A baby's cry...a cry of life...

'You have a little boy,' the consultant said. 'Congratulations.'

Another cry broke the air. Not a baby's cry—her own. Her face convulsed again, tears suddenly pouring from her eyes, blurring her vision completely.

And then she heard another voice. Vincenzo's.

Low, and deep, and wrung with emotion.

'Dio sia ringraziato,' he said.

God be thanked.

Vincenzo shut his eyes.

God be thanked.

It rang in his head, again and again. Relief such as he had never known knifed through him. Then he realised the consultant was speaking again, and made himself open his eyes, listen to what was being said.

The obstetrician was addressing Siena, but he threw an encouraging smile at Vincenzo as well. 'Now, I'm just going to finish off...tidy up. Then I'll zip you back up, make sure everything's tucked away neatly,' he went on, 'and then we'll get you into Recovery. But first...'

He turned away, beckoned to the midwife who was just scooping something up. She came towards them. A little mewing sound came from the white-wrapped bundle in her arms. The obstetrician disappeared behind his screen again.

'Here he is,' said the midwife.

And she placed into Siena's outstretching arms the most perfect human being who had ever existed...

Siena gazed and gazed as love—instant, overwhelming, overpowering love—poured through her.

'Oh, my darling...my darling one...my darling...'

The tiny, perfect face of her tiny, perfect baby looked up at her. And her love for him encompassed her, became her whole being for ever and for ever.

Then another voice was speaking, low and impassioned. *'Lui è perfetto. Perfetto! Il nostro piu prezioso—'*

Siena's hand pressed his arm. 'Our son,' she said. 'Oh, Vincenzo...'

He crouched down beside her, his eyes only for the tiny, so precious bundle in her arms. Tears stood in his eyes.

'I never realised—' he said.

She looked at him. 'Nor I...'

Then the midwife was speaking, smiling down at them both. 'He's doing very well, considering. I'm sorry it was all so dramatic, but these things can happen. We're going to pop him into Neonatal ICU, just to—'

Siena's eyes flew up, a cry breaking from her. *'ICU?'* Stark terror was in her voice suddenly.

'For observation only...just for a little while,' the midwife was instantly reassuring.

'There's something wrong!'

The terror was still in Siena's voice. Her eyes distended. Fear hollowing her out.

Something wrong! I knew there would be...that I couldn't... that I didn't deserve...

The midwife was speaking again, calmly and clearly. 'No, there is nothing wrong. I promise you. All the signs are good. We just want to ensure he gets a really good start after his rushed arrival.'

She felt Vincenzo's hand tighten on her shoulder. 'So there is nothing to fear?' he asked.

Siena could hear the same note of terror in his voice as had been in hers. Her hand clutched his sleeve.

'Nothing at all,' the midwife said firmly.

'Exactly so!' The voice of the obstetrician, busy behind his screen, corroborated the midwife's assurance.

Siena felt the terror draining away, felt Vincenzo's hand lighten on her shoulder.

She heard the midwife continue, brightly, 'So, enjoy this time with him, both of you, and then we can get all of you out of Theatre.'

She smiled benignly, then disappeared behind the screen again, where whatever was being done to her Siena could not feel, and right now did not want to know. Because all that existed in the entire world was what was here—for which she was so grateful…so abjectly, desperately, heart-wrenchingly grateful.

The precious, perfect baby in her arms.

Vincenzo stood by his parked hire car, still dazed. When he'd parked the car in daylight, all those hours ago, all that had been in him was the urgency that had possessed him since they'd begun heading to the hospital, the knifing fear he'd been trying to hide from Siena, because it would only add to hers. Now, the entire universe was transformed.

Slowly, he opened the car door, got into the driving seat. He felt overwhelmed, wrung out. And at the same time…

He closed his eyes a moment, feeling the emotion that

had possessed him ever since that first frail cry had told him that his desperate prayers had been answered possess him again, more strongly yet. Gratitude, thankfulness pierced him. And more.

Remorse.

I didn't realise—I didn't know.

But now he did. And it was a gift past counting.

The same words that had broken from him as he'd heard that thin cry, heard the obstetrician speak, were searing in his head again.

God be thanked.

His eyes opened, he turned the key in the ignition, reversed the car out of its parking space. He would return to the house next to Siena's. In the morning he would come to the hospital again, bringing her bag with him. She would need to be in hospital for a few days, but he'd asked for her to be moved to a private room when it was medically safe. As for his son...

My son!

The words rang in his head. Such incredible, wonderful words—so infinitely precious.

He'd been able to see him, cocooned in his neonatal protection, fast asleep, ignorant of all the monitoring of his vital functions. He'd reported back to Siena, repeating all the medical reassurances given him, and what they had already been told—that his stay there should not be long, and that on the morrow she could have him with her.

'Now, you get some sleep. Rest and recover.' He'd smiled down at her, then left.

She'd looked exhausted...

Emotion twisted inside him. He set it aside.

Drove away from the hospital.

CHAPTER THIRTEEN

THE PRIVATE ROOM was very comfortable, and Siena sat, propped up with pillows behind her back, gazing down at her baby son in his hospital crib beside her. Fast, fast asleep—and so, so tiny.

And safely out of ICU—blessedly.

He was completely safe. That was what the consultant had assured her when he'd called by this morning.

'His arrival was dramatic, but he has taken no harm from it...none at all. All his vital signs are totally normal,' he had told her.

'Are you sure? Are you absolutely sure?' Siena's voice had been fearful.

'Absolutely. He is completely healthy. No cause for any concern at all.'

She clung to the words now, as she gazed into the crib. Emotions flowed through her—a tangled, overpowering mix. So much emotion...for so many reasons...

A nurse tapped on the door, put her head around it. 'You have a visitor,' she said brightly.

Vincenzo walked in.

Siena felt something leap inside her—hold for a moment. Then it subsided. She made it subside.

He looked at her, but only briefly, as if in greeting, and then his eyes dropped to the crib, his expression changing. As if reluctant to look away, he looked quickly back at Siena. This time he smiled. But it was a careful smile, she could see.

'How are you?' he asked.

The concern in his voice was real, though, and she appreciated it. Appreciated it so much. Emotion turned over inside her.

'Fine,' she said. 'I'm on painkillers, and will be for a while. But they've made me walk about a bit already—they say it's good for me.' She glanced across at the crib. 'And, as you can see, he's out of ICU.'

Her voice had softened, relief open in it. She looked back at Vincenzo. So much was inside her, and to some of it she must give voice.

'Oh, dear God, Vincenzo…' Her voice was low, heartfelt. 'Thank God you realised what danger I was in—' She broke off, lifted a hand, then let it fall on the bedclothes again. 'I'd been trying not to look up every single thing that might make me alarmed unnecessarily! I thought it would just work me up into a bag of nerves! The midwife had said everything was fine, so I was determined not to let myself worry.'

'What happened could not have been predicted,' Vincenzo said. Concern was in his voice.

'But if you hadn't been there—' Fear was in her again.

Vincenzo held up a hand. 'You would have phoned, and your midwife would have called you in—just as happened. You would have taken a taxi to the hospital—you said you had the number on standby. So please do not think about it any more. Everything was safe in the end.' His gaze went from her back to the crib. 'How is he? He looks so peaceful. So—'

He broke off. Siena could hear the emotion in his voice, see it in his face.

'Perfect,' she said, her own voice softening, filling with love. 'Just perfect.'

For a moment they just gazed at him, so tiny, so perfect…

'Have…have you thought about names?' she heard Vincenzo ask. His voice was tentative.

So was hers as she answered. 'How about something for your father?' she ventured uncertainly.

'My father's name was Roberto,' he said slowly, as if trying it out.

She thought about it, tried it out too. 'Robert in English. Rob or Bob—or Bobby.'

It sounded good.

'And for your father? A second name?' Vincenzo was asking.

The shake of her head was instinctive.

Vincenzo frowned. Looked at her. His gaze searching. Perceptive. 'What is it?'

She didn't answer immediately—could not. Memory was knifing through her—and all the terrible emotions that went with that memory.

She heard Vincenzo draw a chair close, sit down beside her.

'What is it?' he asked again, his voice low. Troubled.

She plucked at her bedclothes, not wanting to look at him. Keeping her gaze lowered. Feeling the overpowering presence of the baby in his crib beside her bed. Her safe, healthy baby…

So utterly unlike—

'Can you tell me?' Vincenzo's voice was still low.

Her face worked. She didn't want to tell him, but knew she must.

There was so much she could not say to him—could never say—but this she could. And maybe she needed to say it for herself, too. To help her make sense of the way she had been since learning she was pregnant.

She took a breath, making herself look at Vincenzo. That itself was hard to do. Emotion twisted inside her—so much emotion—for so many reasons, so tangled and knotted.

But this was one she could unknot...make sense of.

'You asked me when we were in Selcombe why I hadn't gone to art school when I was a teenager.' She began, her voice low. 'I... I never really answered you.'

She paused again, looking away for a moment. Then made herself continue. It was so sorry a tale—so desperately sad...

'I didn't go,' she said, 'because my brother and his wife had just had a baby. And the baby—' She broke off again, then made herself look at Vincenzo, her expression bleak— for what else could it be? 'He was severely disabled,' she said heavily. 'There was a cruel, incurable congenital condition, inherited from my sister-in-law, that meant he was life-limited. He needed round-the-clock support, even when they could finally take him home. They were in pieces... distraught. And I...well, I stayed at home to help them. Practical care, emotional support... It was just...just dreadful.'

She paused again, then made herself continue.

'He was named after my father—and he...he died last year.' She swallowed painfully. 'His death, expected though it was, broke my brother and his wife. They...they emigrated to Australia, to put it all behind them.'

She broke off, unable to speak any more. Yet there was more that she must say.

'When they moved to Australia,' she said, 'I reapplied to art college, and was accepted again as a mature student.

I thought my life—on hold for so long—was finally start-ing. Until—'

She stopped again. Looked at Vincenzo, sitting beside her, his face sombre.

'I realise now,' she said slowly, 'that what happened to my nephew—which I never wanted to tell you about, or even think about, because it seemed like a dark, frightening shadow over my own pregnancy—affected my reaction to finding myself pregnant. Part of me felt guilty, I suppose, that I was having a baby and my poor brother and sister-in-law had just lost their child. And part of what I felt...' her voice caught '...was...was fear. Yes, I know that my neph-ew's condition was genetic, that he so tragically inherited it from his mother's side, not my brother's. But still I felt, I suppose, a kind of dread—even though I wouldn't admit it, even though I was having a healthy pregnancy—lest some-thing went wrong for me, too.'

She took a breath, like a knife into her lungs.

'And it so nearly, nearly did!'

She reached for Vincenzo's hand, clutching at it.

'I know... I know you say that even if you hadn't realised how dangerous that bleed was, my midwife would still have called me in, and the outcome would have been blessedly the same, but it was *you* who saw the danger—' She broke off again. Then, '*You* saw it! *You* knew it!'

And now it was Vincenzo's turn to speak. Heavily, som-brely. 'There was a reason for that. As your time approached, I ensured I had learnt as much as I could about late preg-nancy and labour. What risks might present themselves... What might go wrong.' He stopped. Then: 'You see, I knew things could. Knew things could go wrong. Because...' He took an incising breath. 'Because it did go wrong for my mother. She died.'

Siena could hear the hollowing in his voice.

'She died from complications in labour, giving birth to my still-born sister.'

She saw his eyes go away from her, out across the room, out into the past, to the mother he had lost, the sister he had never known, the father bereft of his wife and daughter. Then they came back to her.

'It was the last thing I wanted to tell you,' he said. 'And maybe...' he took a narrowed breath, '...knowing how my mother's death devastated my father, taking my sister as well, I felt anger somewhere inside...that...that we were having a baby so...so...'

'So carelessly.'

Siena's voice was flat. She held Vincenzo's gaze. Would not flinch from it.

'Both you and I,' she said, 'have tragedy in our families. Loss that should never have been. Not just our parents. Two children...loved and wanted and yet lost. While we—'

She broke off again. Her face buckled, her voice choking now. Emotion overwhelming her. So much emotion. Carried for so long. For nine long months. Suppressed, denied...feared. And now it was pouring through her in an unstoppable tide.

'To think I never wanted to be pregnant! Could only feel how wrong it was! So completely wrong! And then yesterday—oh, dear God, we nearly lost him! We nearly *lost* him!'

She felt the remembered terror of that breakneck drive to the hospital, the horror of realising what was happening—realising, like a blow, just how desperately she wanted this baby, how terrified she was of losing it...

Suddenly she was starting to shake. Tears began to convulse her. She couldn't talk—not any more—as sobs ravaged her. And she was shaking...shaking so much—

And then arms were coming around her. Arms that were strong and sure, folding her against him, holding her, holding her safe while sobs choked in her throat. He was speaking to her, but it was in Italian, so she couldn't understand. And yet she heard the passion in it, the vehemence. Her tears poured and poured until there were no more, and still he held her, gently now, soothing her, his hands warm and safe and protective.

For a long time he went on holding her as her tears ebbed, and it was the only place in all the universe that she wanted to be.

The only place she should not be...

She drew back. 'I'm sorry,' she said chokingly, tearily. 'I know I shouldn't...shouldn't cry. It's just that—' She broke off, unable to say more.

Her hands were still in his, and she was clinging to them, warm and strong. But they were not hers to cling to...

He pressed her fingers. 'There is no more need for fear,' he said. 'He is well and safe, our Baby Roberto. We can give thanks for that.' He took a breath—a scything one. 'That is all we must think of now. That—and the future.'

Something had changed in his voice...something that made Siena look at him. Her heart was still beating hectically, in the aftermath of her outburst. She felt a chill go through her. Nervelessly, she slipped her fingers from his.

She took a breath. A hard one. A difficult one. Infinitely hard. But one she must take all the same so she could say what she must.

For his sake.

'Vincenzo—it's all right. You...you don't have to say anything. I... I know what the future must be. I've always known.'

She could hear the hollow note in her voice...knew why

it was there, knew that it echoed the hollow forming inside her. She made herself go on, knowing she wanted to say it herself, not wait to hear him say it to her. Say what she knew she must.

The tragedy that had so nearly consumed them yesterday had ripped from her all that had meshed about her during her pregnancy: her fears and her guilt, her resentment and her resistance. Ripped them from her and transformed them into what had been so blessedly bestowed upon her—her precious baby son, alive and well and loved with all her heart.

But now she must face what remained to be faced.

For a moment pain lanced in her…and anguish. But she must go on. Because nothing had changed. All the drama and terror of yesterday—it altered nothing.

'I know that now we have to move on,' she said, making herself face him…face what had to be said. 'Move forward. You've been so good,' she went on, 'supporting me as you have. And yesterday…*thank you*…'

She felt her voice become unsteady, forced herself to make it sound more normal, less strained. She must not burden him with her pain, her anguish.

'And thank you now…for coming in, for the private room, for seeing me through to this point. Thank you for all your support! But now…' She swallowed. There seemed to be a stone in her throat, blocking it, making it hard to speak, but speak she must. To say what must be said, cost her what it would. 'Now I don't want…don't want to impose on you any longer—'

'Impose?' There was an edge in his voice suddenly. He pushed back the chair, getting to his feet. Looking down at her, his face shuttered.

She forced herself on. 'You have been so good to me— and yesterday…' She didn't finish—couldn't. Instead she went on: 'I am so, so appreciative. But now you will want to get your own life back.'

He cut across her. 'My own life——?' His voice was flat.

She spoke on, saying the difficult things that had to be said. Even now, after all the trauma, they had to be said. The abject relief of their baby's safe arrival could not last for ever. It had drawn them together in urgency, but now the reality of their situation must apply again. However guilty she felt now, for having come so terrifyingly close to losing her baby, guilty for how she had not welcomed becoming pregnant, had wished it had never happened, that did not blot out all that she must face.

She looked him square in the eyes—but her fingers were working on the folds of her sheet.

'I forced this on you, Vincenzo. Forced on you the knowledge of what had happened that night we spent together. And I know... I know you are grateful for our baby's safe birth, when it might have gone so dreadfully the other way, but I don't want... I don't want that to...to change anything. I mean, I don't want you feeling...obliged...in any way because of that.' She took a breath, made herself go on. 'I know you will always honour what you feel are your responsibilities, but...'

His expression had changed. She had seen it before, that expression—but not for a long, long time.

'Responsibilities? Obligation? Is that what you would reduce me to?'

There was a chill in his voice that reached into her veins. She stared at him, consternation in her face.

'Vincenzo...' Her voice was anguished, each word forced from her, halting and hesitant, but they had to be said— they *had* to. 'We know—we *both* know—that had yesterday been the tragedy it might have been, we...we would never have seen each other again. For there would have been no reason… And I know…' each word was a blade, cutting into her '…that…that our baby is all there is between us—nothing else.'

He was looking at her, and it was unbearable that he should do so. But she must bear it—she must. Even if it was a weight that was crushing her, stifling her…

He was silhouetted against the window, motionless and rigid.

'But that is not true.'

His words fell into the space between them.

His face was shuttered. His own words echoed in his head.

'But that is not true.'

Not true.

His eyes went to the crib on the other side of her bed. He felt his heart catch, turn over in his chest. His son…

And Siena's too.

But other words overwrote those.

Ours—our son.

Conceived on a night that was impossible to forget. That burned in him still. A night he had since seized a second time—taking her into his arms, into his passionate embrace…

The bitter irony of it tore him like a wolf at his throat.

That first night together it had been he who had left her in the morning, not wanting to face the truth about what had burned so fiercely between them. But that second night…

She left me. And, yes, I have had to respect her wishes, her decision. Had to let her be.

But now…

Now urgency filled him—impelling him to speak.

'That is not true,' he said again.

*That morning—that first morning—waking with her...
walking out on her. But if I hadn't? If I had stayed? And
that second morning—if she had not left...?*

But he knew the answer to that question. Knew it because he gave it now.

'Not true,' he said, 'because from the very first there
has been something between us.' He paused. 'And there
still is, Siena.'

Her eyes lifted to his, and in his she saw an intensity that
stilled her.

'From the very first,' he said again. 'It has been there.
And you cannot deny it, Siena—and no more can I. Neither
of us. You cannot deny that first night we spent together—'

'It should never have happened!' The cry broke from her.

'Why?' he challenged. 'Because you became pregnant?
That does not negate what brought us together that night!'
His voice changed. 'And nor does it negate that night in
Devon.'

He held up a hand, as if to silence her—but she could
not speak, not a word. Tumult was in her. This should not
be happening. He should be accepting what she'd said, that
there was nothing between them except the baby now sleeping, unconscious of the tormented circumstances of his conception and his birth.

Vincenzo was speaking still, his voice grave, guarded, as
if he were picking his words carefully, deliberately.

'When you left that morning in Devon I respected your
decision to do so,' he was saying. 'Respected that it sig-
nalled—could only signal—that you wanted nothing more
to do with me. That for you there was nothing between us
other than a pregnancy you had never wanted.'

'But there *was* nothing else! I've said that—known that—all along!' Siena's voice rang out.

'And I tell you that is not true,' Vincenzo said.

Something worked in his face as he stood there, his expression grave, looking down at her. His voice had changed—she didn't know how, or why. Didn't know why there seemed to be something in her throat. Something making it tight.

He was still looking at her. Speaking again. But all the while her throat was tightening yet more. As if to hold something back—something she dared not allow.

'What is it between us, Siena, that draws us together?' he asked.

There was an intensity in his voice now, beneath the gravity, and his eyes were still holding hers, not letting her go... She could see tension in his face, in the stance of his tall body. Felt her own face and body tense in return. Her throat was narrowing still more, making it hard to breathe, and in her chest she could feel her heart thudding.

She heard him answer the question he had just put to her—for she was incapable of answering it...incapable of saying anything...

'The child we created between us? Yes—but how did his conception come to be? It came, Siena, because when I first set eyes on you I wanted you, desired you. In an instant—a second! Overwhelmingly and absolutely. And it was the same for you. That night we spent together proves that beyond all question! And despite everything else that has happened since that night, that desire—that overpowering, overwhelming desire that burnt between us—has been there. And neither of us can deny it!'

He reached for her hands, holding them fast. His expression was no longer grave, but his eyes were still holding hers, not letting go...

'Desire, Siena—that is what draws us together. And has from the very first! In London and, yes, in Devon too—because why else should we have ended back together again as we did? Throwing all our caution to the winds! And there is more...oh, so much more that draws us together! Now we have the miracle of parenthood, so long resisted but now—oh, dear God—treasured and rejoiced in, as it should have been from the first, given to us as a gift beyond measure!'

His voice was shaken, intense—vehement. She could scarcely bear to hear it.

But he was not done yet.

He stood there, beside her hospital bed, so tall, his eyes never letting hers go, and she was helpless—just helpless to do anything but hear his words, feel the constriction of her throat, the thudding of her heart, the catch of her breath in her lungs.

How could she deny what he was telling her? Impossible.

And he was talking still, his eyes still holding hers... just as his hands, so warm, so strong, were holding hers...

'And there is one more thing that can draw us together, bind us, hold us.' His voice changed, softened. 'If we let it.'

She couldn't speak—could only sit there, eyes fastened on his. Her heart now thudding in her chest...ringing in her ears.

'And if you want it,' he said. 'That second night with you told me something—blazed it to me!—that I know now I can never deny. And even if you deny it, or do not feel it—which, if it is so, I must accept, cost me what it will—it changes nothing. Not for me.'

His eyes were pouring into hers, and she was reeling from what was in them. The drumming in her ears was making her feel faint…or something was. But she must speak. She *must*. No matter what it cost her to say it. To dare to say it…

'But for me,' she said, and her voice was so low it was almost a whisper, 'it did change everything. Oh, Vincenzo, what is this "one more thing" that might be between us?'

Anguish was in her eyes, in her face, as she asked him. Asked him the question she could now dare to ask him—risking all.

He gave a slow, grave smile. Lifting his strained features. Transforming them.

'You know its name, Siena, and so do I. So say it.'

But she could not. Could not speak at all. Could only let her hands cling to his, her heart thudding in her chest like a hammer.

'Then I will say it for you,' he said. 'It's the missing piece. We started with desire—instant, blazing and consuming—so strong, so powerful, that we both did something we had never done before to consummate it. And then we jumped straight to parenthood. But we missed out the bit in the middle—the bit that binds the one to the other. I thought… I thought we had had found it, that night in Devon, but—' He broke off, his voice twisting. 'When I woke to find you gone—'

Words burst from her.

'Vincenzo, it's why I fled from you! I couldn't bear it—couldn't bear the realisation! Couldn't bear that it might mean as little to you as our first night together!'

A rasp broke from him—remorse and self-castigation.

'That first night was just desire! Because I would not let it have a chance to be anything more! I feared it—I admit that now. It was only when we had to spend time with each other, because of what that first night had created, that it started to grow. So slowly at first… And then—'

He lifted her hands, clasped them in his, raising first one to his lips and then the other.

'But on our second night... *Then* I knew—oh, I *knew*—' He took a breath—a ragged one. 'I knew, Siena, that I had come to feel for you so much more than mere desire.'

He paused, her hands pressed in his, his eyes pouring into hers. And they were telling her what he now said in words, his voice softening, catching.

'Love, Siena—that is the missing piece. Love that leads from desire to what we have now. Binding the one to the other, bringing us together, now and for ever.' His gaze went to the crib at her side. 'With our son. Our precious, beloved son...'

Tears were sliding down her cheeks. Tears that spoke of so much. Of love given—with anguish in her heart—as she fled his bed after that night in Devon. When she had known that she had fallen in love with him...when she had known that to him she was only a woman of fleeting desire and unwilling parenthood.

Her tears were for hopeless love, and the anguish of her months away from him, alone and pregnant, knowing that for all her days, the rest of her life, she must share the child she had conceived with a man who would only ever desire her...and nothing more.

And now she felt her heart blossom and flower, and sweet, sweet air fill her lungs, dissolving the unbearable ache in her throat. And now her fears, her anguish, had vanished, were no more, and never again would be. For now the love she had thought only she felt was his too—for her. Love given and returned...

She said his name haltingly, through the tears sliding down her cheeks. He lowered himself beside her, leaning over her to kiss them away softly, gently, tenderly.

Lovingly.

'No more tears, Siena,' he said, kissing the last away.

'It's my hormones,' she said, and her voice held a shaky laugh through the tears.

'And love, Siena. Love—what else?'

Through the mist of her tears she saw his eyes were moist, as they had been when their precious son had been placed in her arms.

She gave a choke, words falling from her. 'I left you that morning in Devon because I could not bear that after such a night you would think it a mistake…regret it as you did our first night! I could bear it that first time, but not again—not when I awoke in your arms and knew that I was in love with you. And that is why…why I have kept away from you… kept you away! Because I could not bear to know that at best you would never want from me anything more than desire, and at worst…not even that. All these months without you have been agony—agony because I knew that I had fallen in love with you, and that for the rest of my life it would be a torment to have you being the father of my baby but never anything more!'

'And that is what I thought I faced too!' His voice was rough with emotion. 'These last hellish months, with you keeping me at bay, when all I wanted in the world was to come to you, be with you, stay with you—' He broke off, taking a ragged, razored breath. 'Damnable! That's what it's been! Damnable to know that I loved you and you could not bear me near you. Damnable to think that I would have to face all the years ahead, sharing with you our son—but nothing else! Damnable to think that one day you would find someone to love of your own, and I would have to stand aside and let it happen! Damnable!'

A sob broke from her. 'Oh, Vincenzo—what fools we've been! What *fools*!'

She gave another choking cry and held him closer to her yet, her lips pressed against his. Emotion was pouring through her, filling her to the brim, overflowing...

So much emotion. And with one name—only one.

Love.

He had said it, declared it, and she had too. So what use was it for her to try and deny it still—to deny what he had said?

None.

And never again would there be denial. *Never.*

She clung to him as he kissed her, possessively, cherishingly, and she kissed him back, just as possessively, as cherishingly. Tears sprang in her eyes...tears of diamonds, of rainbows...

He drew back a little, but only to lift his mouth from hers and smile at her, looking deep into her eyes. She said his name, low and loving, and for a long and timeless moment he simply held her, his gaze pouring into hers. Then his eyes slipped from her, going to the crib beyond the bed. Their son slept still, oblivious to all that was taking place around him. She saw Vincenzo's expression soften. Saw the lovelight in his eyes for her and for their precious son, loved and adored by them both.

'He brought us together by his conception—and now he brings us together by his birth,' he said.

'And now,' Siena said softly, her gaze aglow with all the love filling it, filling her whole being, lifting her into a joy she had never known or thought possible, 'we will stay together as he grows, and be there for him all our days.'

She leant back against her pillows, taking Vincenzo's hand, holding it fast. So infinitely much was filling her.

She gazed at him.

The man she loved.

The man she had desired, then hated, then, oh, so slowly come to feel love for—then fled from in fear of those very feelings. And now... Oh, now...

'Is it possible to feel happier?' she asked.

He shook his head. 'No,' he said. 'Unless...' His eyes held hers. 'Siena, I once, in my arrogance, said we should marry.' His voice was rueful, eyes glinting. 'Now,' he said, 'I simply ask you. Be my wife, Siena. Take me for your husband so that the only day we will be happier than we are right now will be on our wedding day.'

She gave a laugh of joy, of love, of a happiness that stretched into the infinity around them. And as she did so another sound came. A tiny mewing sound.

Their eyes flew to the crib.

Their son was waking.

Carefully coming around the bed, Vincenzo lifted him up to place him into her arms.

This token of their love for each other.

This living symbol of their love.

The cause of their love for each other.

For without him...

Thankfulness poured through her as she put her precious infant son—*their* precious infant son—to her breast.

Her joy was complete.

And gently...so gently... Vincenzo—the man she loved, with whom she had made the long, strange, difficult and tormented journey to where they now were and aways would be—brushed his mouth on her forehead as she nursed their newborn son. The reason and the proof and the future of their love.

EPILOGUE

SIENA STOOD IN the quiet churchyard, her hand resting on the arm of the man beside her. They both stood looking down at a tiny grave, its little white headstone nestling between two other graves.

Tears choked her voice as she spoke. 'Thank you...*thank you* for coming,' she said. 'It means so much to me.'

The man beside her pressed the hand on his sleeve with his own hand. 'And to me, too. I am glad to be here.' He paused a moment, his eyes going back to the little white headstone. 'He's safe here, isn't he? With his grandparents. And that is the way I shall think of him and remember him—here, at peace, out of pain and illness. Knowing that you and his new cousin will keep watch over him. And knowing that he will have a brother, soon, who will live to be strong and healthy and with a full term of life.'

Siena heard the emotion rich in her brother's voice and lifted her face to his.

'I am glad more than I can say that you'll be parents again, and that genetic counselling means a healthy baby this time.' She gave a smile. 'When they are both older, the cousins, we'll come and visit you in Australia, I promise. As soon as Bobby's big enough to cope with such a long flight!'

'Try him out on short-haul first—to Italy,' her brother said smilingly. 'I'm glad you're happy about living in Milan,' he added. 'And that you're definitely going to be picking up your art studies in Italy—it's the ideal place for it, after all.' He patted her hand again. 'You're going to Siena for your honeymoon, Vincenzo tells me. Lots of art there—and all with your name on it!'

She nodded. 'It seemed the perfect place to go.'

'Well, then, let's get you married, sis. Come on—time for me to walk you down the aisle.'

They moved away, towards the church familiar to them both from childhood. The three graves marked sadness— but today there was only gladness. It would be a small wedding—just her brother, to give her away, and Megan as maid of honour—and to hold Bobby during the service— enraptured that so happy an ending had come about after such a storm.

They reached the church door.

'Ready, sis?' her brother asked.

The strains of the ancient organ struck up.

'Ready,' affirmed Siena.

They stepped through and Siena's eyes went, like a homing arrow, to the man standing by the altar rail.

Vincenzo. The man she loved with all her heart and soul and being.

He turned his head to smile at her. And in that smile was all the love he held for her and always would.

The organ swelled and on her brother's arm Siena walked beside him. To marry the beloved father of their beloved son and be his wife—his beloved wife—for all eternity.

* * * * *

BOSS'S HEIR
DEMAND

JACKIE ASHENDEN

MILLS & BOON

This one is for the real work wives,
Maisey, Nicole and Megan.

Love you guys.

CHAPTER ONE

DOMINIC LANCASTER LEANED BACK, placing one elbow negligently onto silk cushions of the Roman-style couch he was lolling on, and debated pouring himself more wine from the jug that sat on the low table near the couch.

Not that he needed any more wine since he'd already had a few goblets and was feeling perfectly pleasant. Then again, it was a *very* good French red and this *was* a bacchanal and he was the host. What kind of bacchanal would it be if the host himself didn't bacchanate?

Not that bacchanating was a word...but still, the point applied.

He held a bacchanal every year during midsummer, in the forest of his stately home, and it involved the usual—togas, masks, white silk pavilions in the forest, couches, grapes, wine—and then devolved into lots of sex.

People in his circle, the social elite of Europe, loved it and around the time the invites went out, the gossip columns were full of speculation as to who would be invited and who wouldn't, and why. It was a very select group.

There was no rhyme or reason to the invitations. Dominic chose guests purely on a whim, because there was nothing better than messing with people's heads, and he enjoyed the speculation and jockeying for position when invite season came around.

Tonight, though, was different, because he'd decided this would be the last bacchanal. Twenty years was long enough to retain ownership of his childhood home, and now was the time to get rid of it. Sell Darkfell Manor and the forest that surrounded it to anyone who would give him a good price, and then, with any luck, whoever bought it would raze the whole thing to the ground, thus saving him the bother of doing it himself.

Dominic surveyed forest from his couch, the white silk pavilion around him moving slightly in the night air. He'd had the pavilion put up to the side of the clearing and in the centre flamed a torch that leapt and flickered, casting strange shadows against the trunks of the ancient oaks.

More torches marked the paths that led to other small clearings, and other pavilions, all with couches and pillows, and wine and food. He could hear some of his guests laughing and shrieking, most of them already drunk.

A pity, really, to get rid of the forest—he'd had a lot of fun here after all—and maybe he could put a caveat on it or something. Or maybe not. Maybe it should go, along with the manor and everything else his father had touched.

Thoughts of his father never helped Dominic's mood and he was determined to enjoy himself tonight, so he leaned forward and poured more wine into the thick pottery goblet he only ever used for his bacchanals. Then he leaned back on the couch again, sipping at the wine.

Beyond the darkness of the trees came a squeal, which could only be Marissa. She was a lovely French socialite and Cannes regular, who'd begged him for an invite in various inventive ways, and she'd made it clear already that if he wanted to make it a night to remember she would be happy to oblige him. From the sounds of it, she was already occupied. Then again, it wouldn't be a bacchanal if he couldn't join in.

He sighed, wondering if, in fact, he could be bothered. He liked a good orgy as much as the next man, but sometimes it could be such a faff. Not to mention boring. It was nothing he hadn't done before, many times, and there were occasions where he couldn't see the point. Sexual pleasure was nice while it lasted but it was always so fleeting, and it had been years and years since he'd lost himself entirely in sex. That had been a young man's game, and he wasn't that young any more.

Besides, sex was also beginning to bore him. Parties were beginning to bore him. Even Lancaster Investments, the investment business he'd started around fifteen years ago, after he'd sold the last of his father's assets, was beginning to bore him. He had more money than he knew what to do with and when he sold Darkfell Manor, the last piece of his father's poisoned legacy would be gone and, after that, what challenges were left?

Dominic lay back on the couch and stared at the white silk above his head. He could go into space, or maybe buy a submarine. Or perhaps build a bunker in Iceland and retire there in solitary splendour. He could get himself a camel and ride off into the desert like Lawrence of Arabia, or maybe go exploring in the Amazon…

Really, the possibilities were endless.

At that moment Marissa squealed again and then came bursting through the trees on the far side of the clearing opposite him, laughing breathlessly as she came to a stop in front of Dominic's pavilion.

She wore nothing but a short white tunic and an owl mask, her long glossy black hair wild down her back, every bit of her long, golden body visible through the tunic.

A lovely woman.

Yet he wasn't moved. He'd seen her body before, knew everything it could do in bed and the sounds she made and the things she preferred. There was nothing about her sexually that he didn't know and nothing about the rest of her that interested him.

No one interested him, not these days.

So as she moved slowly and gracefully over to his couch, despite the flaring torchlight making her tunic seem half transparent, he remained…bored. He'd been bored for a long time, he suspected.

His lack of interest in her should have bothered him, but it didn't. In many ways, it was even a relief.

'Dominic,' Marissa purred in her sexy accent. 'I've been looking for you everywhere.'

'No, you haven't,' he said, surveying her as she walked over to his couch, hips swaying. 'I'm still here, where you last saw me.'

She laughed, stopping before his couch, her blue eyes shining through the eyeholes of her mask. 'Have you been waiting for me?'

'Actually, I've been contemplating the mysteries of the universe.' He smiled, trying to muster up some enthusiasm, since this was last bacchanal and he'd told himself he should be having fun. 'Including the mysteries of the female gender.'

Marissa gave a little shiver—one of her trademark moves—then she reached for the small clasp on the shoulder of her tunic and undid it, letting the fabric flutter to the ground. 'Well, here I am,' she said softly, standing naked before him. 'You can contemplate me.'

Since she was right in front of him, he could hardly do anything else. She was beautiful, he couldn't argue with that. But he'd spent the last twenty-five years of his life contemplating the mysteries of the female gender and, as he'd already thought to himself, there was nothing about this particular example that intrigued him.

Perhaps that was why he felt bored.

There was no mystery in anything any more.

Dominic was an expert in the art of dissembling, yet Marissa must have picked up on his lack of interest, because she suddenly darted forward, leaning over him and brushing her mouth over his. Then she backed away, giving him a sultry smile. 'You can have me if you catch me.'

Then she turned and ran off naked into the forest.

Maude Braithwaite stood in the darkness, pressed against the trunk of one of Darkfell Forest's ancient oaks, and held her breath as the naked woman ran past her, barely a metre away.

The woman must not have seen Maude because she didn't pause, giggling as she disappeared into the darkness.

Maude let out the breath she'd been holding, shivering a little in her bare feet and nightgown. It wasn't exactly cold—it was midsummer—but it was still one in the morning and pitch black, so not quite warm either.

She'd been asleep in her little bedroom in the game-keeper's cottage right on the edge of the forest, and had been woken abruptly out of a dream by the sound of someone screaming.

Tonight was the night of the Midsummer Bacchanal, and while she'd been told that the guests had been warned to keep away from the cottage, she supposed some of them hadn't followed the rules.

This was deeply annoying because, while hauling herself out of bed in the middle of the night to investigate wasn't mandatory, management of the forest was one of her responsibilities and she did want to make sure that her employer's rich friends hadn't accidentally set fire to something they shouldn't.

Maude was one of four women who ran Your Girl Friday, a company that offered speciality services to those rich enough to afford them, and her area of expertise was landscape design and forest management, anything to do with the natural world basically.

She loved nature, so when a groundskeeper contract for Darkfell Forest had come in, she'd jumped at the chance. Groundskeeper work had sounded intriguing, with the bonus of being responsible for the management of the forest. Her personal goal was rewilding a piece of land that her grandparents were going to leave her, and for that she needed, not only a touch more expertise, but also money. Handily, the contract she'd signed, which was for a year, paid exceptionally well.

However, what she had not loved was preparing a section of said forest for the bacchanal, since it involved turning a beautiful, wild place into what was essentially a party venue, i.e. making nature palatable for a whole bunch of rich people who didn't care.

It was always this dichotomy that bothered her while working for Your Girl Friday. Despising the rich and privileged, while also taking their money. She'd early on decided that money would go back to her rewilding project, and in return the people who employed her could stand to have a few lessons in caring for nature. Most of the time they were grateful, so she couldn't complain.

She was definitely going to complain about the drunken idiots currently cavorting around in these woods in the middle of the night, though. The forest wasn't inherently dangerous, but the fools could hurt themselves and someone had to make sure they were okay. That someone being her.

Anyway, she hadn't found anyone injured in the vicinity of the cottage, so she'd ventured a bit further into the forest itself, just to be certain.

She'd moved as many of the animals away from the bacchanal area as she could, but animals didn't obey human rules and one of them could have strayed somewhere it shouldn't and frightened someone. Not that she cared about humans. They could look after themselves. It was the animals she was concerned for.

The bacchanal was supposed to be a very private affair, with a specially curated guest list, and she'd been told—all the staff at Darkfell Manor had been told—that they shouldn't go into the forest while the bacchanal was being held. Maude hadn't wanted to anyway—she didn't care about bacchanals—and she'd been on the pointing of turning back to the cottage when the naked woman had run by her and she'd been forced into immobility.

The sound of the woman's progress gradually faded and Maude glanced back in the direction she'd come from to make sure no other naked people were in her immediate vicinity. Then she glanced back to the clearing beyond, where the torch flamed, causing dramatic shadows to leap and flare. A Roman-style couch had been placed artfully near the torch, beneath a pavilion of white silk, the curtains of which had been pulled back and held with jewelled ties.

A low table containing goblets, a bowl full of grapes, a jug of wine, and a platter of various finger foods had been placed near the couch, along with another low chair.

A man lolled indolently on the couch, on his back. He wore nothing but a white toga draped around a body that could have belonged to a Greek god, all hard, sculpted muscle and smooth tanned skin. A crown of golden laurel leaves rested in his hair.

He held a goblet in one large, long-fingered hand, the light of the flaring torch outlining the perfect lines of his face. Like his body, he was beautiful, but not in the way, say, Apollo or Hermes was beautiful. This man wasn't a boy. He was Zeus or Poseidon, or even Hades. An older god, stern, ruthless. Utterly masculine and completely in control of the universe he ruled.

Straight nose, long ink-black lashes, high cheekbones. There were lines around his eyes and his mouth, and through his short ink-black hair—from the severe widow's peak of his forehead all the way to the back of his head—ran a white stripe.

Maude's breath caught.

That stripe was famous. She didn't keep track of celebrity gossip and barely even checked social media.

The world of humanity didn't interest her. Yet even so, that stripe marked him.

Dominic Lancaster, one of Europe's most notorious playboys, if not *the* most notorious. Owner of Darkfell Manor and the forest that surrounded it.

Also, her boss.

She'd never met him, only one of his assistants. She'd seen a few pictures of him—she didn't much care about the people she worked for, it was the landscape that mattered—but those pictures hadn't done him justice.

This was the first time she'd seen him in the flesh and…

Maude stared at him, transfixed.

If he'd picked up a thunderbolt and thrown it at her, she'd have let that bolt go straight through her.

It was baffling. She'd never felt that way about a man before.

She'd always been the odd one out, even with her closest friends, the other three of the Your Girl Friday team. Irinka, the team's secretary, who came from a Russian family and provided the rest of them with the connections they needed to the rich and powerful. Lynna, who was from Wales and had been raised in Greece, and who could make magic with food. And Augusta—known as Auggie—the sole American in the team, and who'd recently done a stint as a stewardess on a plane.

None of the others liked plants or forests the way she did. None of them liked communing with nature. And she knew they all considered her a little odd.

She was okay with that. She liked being odd.

She'd spent most of her early years in a Scottish commune with her mother, which had involved living very close to nature and not much in the way of schooling. Then her maternal grandparents, disturbed by the way she was being brought up, had forced her mother into giving Maude to them to raise. They'd tried to tame her with urban life, with concrete and rules and TV and homework instead of bonfires and storytelling and dancing.

Maude had found it tough, but eventually she'd managed to behave the way they'd wanted her to. Except for the fact that nature had got deep in her soul and now it was so much part of her, nothing could get it out.

It was nature that commanded her attention and, really, it was more normal for her to stop and stare like this at a tree, or a magnificent flowering shrub, than a man.

In the clearing, Dominic Lancaster put down his goblet and sat on the edge of the couch. Maude tensed. Perhaps he was going to run after the woman, in which case staying put was probably a good idea. She didn't particularly want him to find her creeping around in the forest, especially when she'd been told not to intrude.

He didn't move for a moment, the torchlight running over his skin and the carved lines of his torso revealed by the loose toga, bathing him in gold. Then he rose from the couch with a deliberate muscular grace that had Maude's heart racing, and walked slowly to where a white scrap of fabric lay in the leaf mould of the forest floor. Bending, he picked it up then continued over to where the woman had disappeared into the trees.

'You forgot something, sweetheart,' he called as he tossed the white fabric into the trees. 'You also forgot that I never run after a woman.'

A shiver ran unexpectedly over Maude's skin. His

voice was deep and velvety and rich, with a darkness threading through it that seemed to connect with something inside her.

He stood very close and he was much taller than she'd expected. Much taller than she was. The crown of laurel leaves on his head, gleaming in the torchlight, and the way he held himself, as if he were indeed king of the gods, made her pulse begin to beat in a hard, insistent rhythm.

Men hadn't featured in her life. She hadn't met one she'd been even remotely attracted to and wasn't interested in meeting one. Men as a whole didn't interest her.

So this man, this complete stranger, shouldn't have warranted a second glance.

Yet she couldn't take her eyes off him.

She couldn't even take a breath.

He'd gone very still, as if he was listening, and Maude wouldn't have been surprised if it was her heart he'd heard thumping like a drum within the confines of her ribcage.

Something whispered in her brain, something dark and seductive, that was drawn to the man standing so close. A deep part of her that couldn't stop looking at the broad width of his shoulders and his powerful chest. That wanted her to run her hands across his olive skin, feel the prickle of crisp hair and then move further down, to the corrugated lines of his stomach left bare by the drape of the white fabric, the only thing that clothed him.

The forest bowed to him, the darkness in her head whispered. He was the king here. He was primal and raw, and if he wanted to chase a woman, she had no chance. He would bring her down onto the rich earth and take her, connect her so deeply to this forest and to him, she'd never escape.

There was an ache between Maude's thighs, an insistent ache she couldn't recall feeling so intensely before. She couldn't have moved if she'd wanted to.

'But you,' he murmured without turning his head, the velvety texture of his voice deepening. 'You, I might just make an exception for.'

He couldn't be talking to her, could he? No, it wasn't possible. She was hidden in the shadows of the trees, in the darkness, he couldn't know she was there. In the forest, she was unseen. She was *always* unseen.

He's a god, remember? He could find you anywhere.

Her palms were damp, her heartbeat loud in her ears. She should melt into the trees and slip away, go back to bed. Pretend she hadn't seen him.

Yet…she didn't.

He turned his head slowly, looking in her direction. His face was shadowed, but somehow she could see the gleam of his eyes, black in the night. It wasn't possible for him to see in the dark, yet she was certain all at once that he knew she was there.

She had no idea how he knew, because she hadn't made a sound. Just as she knew that if she ran the way that other woman had, he would follow.

He would chase her through the forest until he caught her and then she would be his.

And he would be yours.

It came over her unexpectedly and very suddenly then, a wild thrilling rush of adrenaline, and before Maude was even conscious of doing so, she'd turned and had started to run.

CHAPTER TWO

IT HAD ONLY been once he'd got to the edge of the clearing that Dominic had felt he was being watched. And it wasn't Marissa; he'd have to have been deaf not to hear her crashing through the undergrowth as she'd run from him.

No, someone else was watching him.

He'd stood there a moment after he'd thrown Marissa's tunic after her, having decided he couldn't be bothered to chase her, staring into the darkness, feeling the weight of someone else's gaze on him.

Then he'd caught a scent, earthy and musky and delicate, and very female, and abruptly everything male in him had sprung to instant life.

It was a sensual, deeply sexual scent, banishing his boredom, flicking switches inside him, turning on a current of pure electricity that he'd thought was long since dead.

It had been nearly fifteen years since he'd wanted anything. A long time since his life had been more than simply following a whim. Years since he'd taken his father's vast property development company and sold it off, piece by piece, netting himself huge profits and a sense of deep satisfaction.

He'd thought he'd come to the end of wanting any-thing, since whenever he had a hankering for some-thing, he simply bought it or did it, letting nothing hold him back. He indulged himself at every opportunity, because why not?

Apparently, though, he hadn't come to the end of wanting after all, because someone had been watching him in the darkness, a woman, and every little piece of him had been intrigued.

He'd turned and stared into the shadows near an oak not far from where he stood, and though his night vision had been impaired by the light of the torch, he'd been able to make out a slender figure by the trunk of the tree.

A wood nymph.

There had been a second where he'd been sure he'd seen her eyes gleaming in the darkness, and an inexpli-cable need had risen up inside him. A primitive, basely masculine need, primeval almost.

So much so that when she'd turned and run, it had been instinct to run after her.

He'd told Marissa the truth. He never ran after a woman. He never ran after anyone. They all came to him and he liked it that way since it gave him all the power, and he liked power. Especially when he had it and other people didn't.

Which made his sudden mad dash after a woman he hadn't even laid eyes on completely inexplicable. Yet there was also an inevitability to it. As if she'd been in this forest for years, perhaps was even part of it, and had been waiting for him.

Waiting for him and him alone.

She made no sound as she ran, white fabric of her

tunic or whatever she was wearing billowing out behind her, a pale figure in the night. Her bare feet hit the soft earth soundlessly as she dodged trees and leapt fallen logs, agile as a deer.

He felt strangely outside himself, as if he'd left Dominic Lancaster, renowned investor and notorious playboy, back in that clearing, and he were someone else now. A man with no past and no future, who was concerned only with the here and now. With the sound of his breathing, fast and hard, and the beat of his pulse, steady and strong. With the scent of the forest around him, spicy and dark, and the woman running ahead of him...

Thoughts gathered in his head, mundane thoughts. What was she wearing? All the guests wore either a white tunic or a toga and this was neither, and yet it was white, so maybe she'd styled it differently. Who was she? Why hadn't he noticed her earlier when he'd greeted everyone like the good host he was? He surely would have noticed her...

He pushed the thoughts aside. Those questions didn't matter. Nothing mattered. Nothing except running after her, a primitive hunter's instinct waking up inside him, pouring adrenaline through him. A wild excitement building inside him and an anticipation he hadn't felt for a long time, if he ever had.

He wasn't sure why he was feeling these things now, but he didn't question them. This was new, this was different. This made him feel as if he were sixteen again, and Craddock, the gamekeeper, had taken him deer hunting for the first time. He'd loved it, the thrill of the chase. Of course, he hadn't been able to shoot the deer when he and Craddock had finally tracked it down, and his father had sneered at what he'd deemed Dominic's 'softness'.

He wasn't soft now, though.

The forest around them thickened, becoming denser, which meant they'd moved out of the area he'd specified for the bacchanal, but he didn't care. The only thought in his head was to catch her, bring her down, so when the white fabric of her tunic caught on a branch and she slowed to release it, he put on a burst of speed and before she could free herself, he was there, catching her in his arms and pulling her hard against him, her back pressing against his front.

Her breathing was wild and her hair was in his face, a skein of raw silk that smelled just as delicious as she did. Christ, he'd never felt a woman as hot or as soft as she was.

She twisted in his grip, panting, but made no real effort to get away, nor did she speak. He bent his head, nuzzling against the side of her neck, her musky, feminine scent making him harder than he'd ever been in his entire life.

He didn't understand why he'd run after her, or why she was making him so hard, but, again, that didn't matter right now. What mattered was that she was in his arms and he wanted her. He wanted her more than he'd wanted anything in a very long time, and that was something to be savoured. He'd thought he'd lost the ability to feel anything more than mild pleasure and boredom, but clearly not.

'You were watching me, nymph,' he said, his voice rough and uneven. 'You think I didn't see you standing there in the darkness?'

Her breathing had slowed, and he could feel little trembles running through her, and for one timeless second they remained like that, her panting while he held her tight, his own breathing fast, inhaling the dizzying, intoxicating scent of her.

Then abruptly she turned in his arms and lifted her hands, her fingers in his hair, and she pulled his mouth down on hers.

And just like that Dominic lost his grip on reality.

Everything slid away. His father. His company. His guests. His party. There was only the forest, dark and still around him, and the woman in his arms. Her mouth, hot and hungry, and the taste of her igniting something in him he'd thought long dead. Something desperate and raw.

He slid his fingers into the silken warmth of her hair and closed them into fists, gripping her, holding her still as he devoured her, pushing his tongue into her mouth and exploring her heat and her taste. So sweet and yet with a tart edge that excited him, that made him want to kiss her deeper, harder.

She made an animal sound, throaty and husky, and it wasn't in protest. Not when her hands were on his bare chest, running over his skin, her nails scratching him as she reached down over his stomach and further down. He wore nothing but his toga and a growl escaped him as her fingers found the achingly hard length of his shaft and closed around it.

The touch was too much. He wanted to get rid of this excess fabric between them, have her skin next to his. He wanted to taste her. Lick her. Bite her. And only then, once he'd had his fill, would he give her what she so clearly wanted.

She didn't make a sound as he took her down onto the forest floor, onto a pile of bracken that God himself couldn't have positioned any better, and then he was casting his toga to the side before tackling whatever it was that she was wearing, tearing it straight down the middle and off. She reached for him as he pulled it away from her, hungry in the night, but he took her hands and pinned them above her head with one hand, while with the other he began to map her body hidden in the darkness.

She was delicate and slender, yet the curve of her breast fitted his palm to perfection and her skin was warm silk. She moaned as he brushed his thumb over her hard nipple and then gasped as he slid his hand lower, to her hip, fingertips lightly brushing over it, touching the side of one thigh, then exploring between them. She shuddered, her sharp intake of breath loud in the night air, as his fingers found damp curls and slick, hot skin.

She smelled like sex and the forest itself, and he found himself raising his fingers to his mouth and licking her flavour from them. A flood of intense hunger swept through him, drowning the last remaining piece of Dominic Lancaster, and now there was only him. Only the trees. Only her. Female to his male. Raw and primeval as the forest itself.

He released her hands, but only to grip her thighs and spread them wide. Then, pinning her hips in place, he bent and began to devour her like the beast he'd become.

Maude lay on her back, conscious of nothing but the feel of his strong hands holding her pinned to the bed of soft bracken, his hot mouth between her thighs. Of his tongue exploring her delicately and yet with an insistence that made her tremble. And of the sharp, agonising pleasure, winding tighter and tighter.

It was a mystery how she'd ended up here. Why she'd run from him instead of calmly walking out from behind the tree and telling him who she was, before going off to her cottage alone. Why she'd kept running through the forest, filled with a totally alien and yet wild exhilaration, part of which was delicious fear and yet another part excitement.

Something sensual had awoken within her as she'd run headlong into the dark, an awareness that had seemed to saturate the forest around her. An awareness too of the man pursuing her.

He might have said he didn't run after a woman, yet he'd run after her, somehow staying close behind her even though a man of his size and power shouldn't have been able to run as fast or know the forest as well as she did.

When the branch had caught her nightgown a simple rip would have pulled it free. She hadn't needed to slow down, yet she had. Maybe she'd slowed deliberately. Maybe a deep part of her had wanted to be caught. Wanted *him* to catch her. Not just any man, but him.

Zeus, the king of the gods.

The god of the forest.

He *had* caught her then, his arms closing around her, pulling her back against him. All the breath had gone out of her, all her awareness captured by the male body behind hers and the power of his arms banded about her. The heat of him had been incredible and he'd felt so hard, like rock, and so tall. He'd towered over her, like one of the trees she'd been hiding next to.

There was no hiding from him, though.

He was a god.

Now, she stared up into the darkness of the tree canopy, seeing nothing but stars as he lay between her thighs and did something wicked with his tongue, causing everything to light up inside her, making her feel like one of those torches, flaming in the night.

She cried out, shaking as the pleasure crashed through her, and she was still trembling with the aftershocks when he rose from between her thighs and stretched himself out above her. His toga was long gone, but the laurel leaves in his hair were still there, gold gleaming against stark black and that snowy white stripe.

What are you doing? He's your boss. You don't even know him.

The thought was dim, the sound of it reminding her of her grandmother and all the rules she'd been given. Rules she'd had to follow if she wanted to stay with them and, since she'd had nowhere else to go, she'd stayed. And followed their rules. But she was tired of that. Tired of rules.

So what if he was her boss? So what if he was a stranger? He was part of the forest and she was too, and she didn't care what she should and shouldn't do. She'd never been in a man's arms before, never wanted to be, but this felt right. This felt primordial and so was she.

A current of intense sensual awareness ran through her, making her conscious of her own sexuality in a way she'd never been conscious of before. Of how right this was and how natural to come to full awareness of herself as a woman right here on the forest floor, beneath the trees she loved. With a man who seemed part of the forest himself.

He was above her now and he smelled so good, warm and earthy and spicy. Somehow familiar and yet intoxicating. Sexual. Carnal.

He lowered his head, his teeth at the side of her neck, and he bit her like an animal, making her shudder, waking pleasure inside her yet again. Then she felt the touch of his tongue against her skin, as if he was tasting her the way he had between her thighs, and another rush of heat flooded her, prickling over her entire body.

Obeying an instinct that came from deep inside her, Maude lifted her arms to him, pulling his big, powerful, muscular body down on hers, finding his mouth and kissing him with wild abandon. She tasted herself on his lips and that was as it should be. Right. Powerful. *She* felt powerful, the primal feminine to his masculine, a goddess in her own right and now demanding his surrender, as she'd given him hers.

She had no idea what she was doing, but she didn't care. Tonight there were only the rules she made herself and if this kiss involved sharp teeth and tongues, then it did. They were animals tonight, connecting in their purest form.

He made a low, guttural sound as she bit his bottom lip and then his hands were in fists in her hair, holding her still as he kissed her back with raw savagery, nipping, biting, licking, tasting.

She moaned, her hands pressed against the velvety skin of his chest, all heat and the prickle of hair as she touched him. He was naked but for the crown of laurel leaves and he was magnificent, and even though the darkness hid most of him, his crown deemed king in this forest.

Tonight, she would be his queen.

He shifted his hips and without hesitation pushed inside her, hard and deep, and it felt right to wrap her legs around his waist and arch beneath him, making him slide even deeper. Sensation rushed through her as she felt herself stretch around him and tighten, holding him inside her. Glorious pleasure with a slight edge of pain to make it sweeter.

She groaned, inner muscles tightening around him, and then his mouth was on hers again, the kiss savage, passionate, wild. He moved, inevitable as the turn of the earth, as the change of the seasons, the rise of the sun and the fall of night.

There had always been this darkness inside her, a hint of primitive savagery that she hadn't wanted to uncover. But now she did. Now she went deep into that darkness and found him there waiting for her.

He moved faster, harder, and she moved with him, the forest surrounding them, glittering with the wild magic they were generating between them.

And it was magic. It was glory. It was a connection she'd never dreamed she'd ever have, but it was happening right now and she was losing herself to it. Losing herself to the pleasure and the night.

When the orgasm came for them both, it blazed hot through each of them, leaving them flaming in the dark. Both, like torches.

Dominic opened his eyes to find himself lying on his back in the middle of the forest, completely naked. Dawn was filtering down through the forest canopy above his head, dew chilling his skin.

For a moment he had no idea where he was or why he was lying naked in a forest. He felt…relaxed. Which he shouldn't have considering the location, and yet, he did. Alcohol and other such…substances, didn't usually leave him feeling so boneless and sated, though they were usually the reason he woke up somewhere he didn't expect.

But he wasn't hungover or anything else. In fact, he felt oddly energised.

He sat up at the same time as a beam of sunlight shone through the trees, falling on his skin like a benediction, and that too felt good, so he stayed there for long seconds, enjoying the feeling of sun on his skin.

Then memory began to filter through, of the darkness and warm skin, of breathless cries and intense pleasure…

Abruptly, he looked around for the woman he'd spent all night having sex with like an animal in the dark, but there was no sign of her.

He was alone.

Damn.

He'd never had a woman like her in all his life and he'd had more women than he could count. All beautiful. All skilled lovers. All ready to do whatever he wanted.

But *that* woman… She'd been all passion. All heat. Fire between his hands. She'd taken what she'd wanted from him, no holding back, matching him passion for passion. He'd taken too and she'd let him just as he'd let her. She hadn't asked him what he wanted or watched him to make sure he was enjoying himself or watched herself to make sure she only looked sexy. She hadn't cared. It had been dark, admittedly, so neither of them had been able to see, but she hadn't teased him or taunted him, or tried in any way to engage him. No, she'd used him, he suspected. Taken what she wanted as if she owned him.

And he'd found himself giving as good as he got, his reward her cries of pleasure, her nails digging into his back, her teeth against his shoulder.

They hadn't spoken. They'd let their bodies speak instead and it had been...

He let out a breath, closed his eyes, and tilted his head back, feeling the warmth of the rising sun on his face.

He felt...bloody amazing. His body sated. His mind at peace.

That hadn't happened in years.

The pursuit of pleasure had always been one of his interests, and he hadn't cared where it came from. The urge to fill the gaping void inside him with sensation. It was always there that void, or maybe it wasn't a void. Maybe he was just dead inside and sex and pleasure were the defibrillator he used to jump-start what was left of his soul.

In which case, the sex he'd had last night had been one hell of a charge. He could feel it still, passion burning in the depths of him, embers of a fire that had ignited the night before and were smouldering away still.

Who was she?

It didn't matter. What mattered was something coming alive inside him as he'd run through the forest in the dark, an exhilaration, an excitement. The instinct of a hunter, chasing sensual prey.

He'd never felt it before, not at any of the bacchanals

he'd held in years gone by, and some of them had been good. But this…this was something else. This was what a bacchanal was *really* about, wild, savage, carnal.

He'd taken her down to the forest floor and when he'd pushed inside her, he'd felt as if he'd come home almost.

Christ.

He could go over the guest list again and find out who she was, but there had been something magical, mystical even, about not knowing. As if finding out who she was would break a spell.

Fanciful even for him, but perhaps it was best if what happened at the bacchanal stayed at the bacchanal. After all, he knew how passion played out. Eventually it died, no mysteries left, and cue the boredom.

He didn't want that to happen.

Dominic sighed again, took a deep breath of the dawn air, then pushed himself to his feet. His ridiculous laurel crown had come off at some point in the night and he found it under a fern. He picked it up, settled it on his head, found his toga and threw it over his shoulder. Then, not far from the bed of bracken he and the nymph had slept on the night before, he found the remains of more white fabric. It was not one of the togas or tunics that had been issued to the guests.

It was a white nightgown. And was ripped right down the front.

Which meant only one thing.

The woman he'd spent the night with in the forest had not been one of his guests at all.

CHAPTER THREE

MAUDE PAUSED A moment along the forest path that ran up the side of the hill and took a breath. It wasn't steep, but she'd experienced a distinct lack of energy for the past couple of weeks and it was annoying. She'd be turning over earth, or raking leaves, or doing any one of the thousand tasks involved in managing the grounds of Darkfell Manor, and she'd suddenly find herself needing a lie-down.

Normally, she was fit and had boundless energy, so it was puzzling.

Or rather, it wasn't puzzling, not if she really thought about it, but she didn't want to think about it, and so puzzling it remained.

Nothing at all to do with the wild night in the forest five months earlier, where she'd lain in the bracken with the god of the forest.

Thankfully she'd woken up before he had, long before dawn, and had hurried back to the groundskeeper's cottage. She hadn't wanted to shower the scent of him from her skin, but her feet had been dirty and she'd been cold, so she'd stepped under the warm water and let it do its work.

Afterwards she'd stood in front of the mirror in the

tiny bathroom, gently touching the marks he'd left on her body, her only proof that it had actually happened. She'd let her boss, a stranger, run after her in the woods and she'd let him catch her. Let him take her to the ground and have her.

A reminder that, for one night, she'd been wild.

Her grandparents would be appalled if they knew, but she'd thought then that with any luck they'd never find out.

Unfortunately for her, though, luck wasn't her side.

It had been six weeks after her last period that she'd eventually taken herself off to see the doctor in the little village twenty miles from Darkfell. The doctor had given her the news she'd dreaded, along with various pamphlets and instructions on what to do next, and Maude had decided that the question about what *exactly* she was going to do wasn't one she could answer just yet.

Sonya, her mother, was still in the Earthsong commune, in Scotland, and that was off grid, so she was uncontactable. Not that she wanted to contact her mother, since her mother hadn't bothered staying in contact with her after her grandparents had taken her away. Even apart from that, there was also the fact that Sonya didn't know what to do with a baby, especially when she hadn't wanted the one she'd had.

Maude couldn't talk to her grandparents about it either. They'd ask too many question about the baby's father, and the truth wasn't something she could tell them, not if she wanted the piece of land they were going to leave to her. They'd always been very clear that they didn't want her going down the same path as her mother had.

There were the other Your Girl Friday girls, but although they were her closest friends—they'd all been to university together—Maude felt weird about telling them. They wouldn't be judgmental, but they'd be worried and she couldn't bear the pressure of their concern.

Really, if she told nobody, then maybe she wouldn't actually be pregnant?

Don't be stupid. The doctor told you that you are.

Maude sucked in a breath of the rich, forest-scented air and continued her trudge up to the small picturesque waterfall that emptied into a perfect small pool. The waterfall was surrounded by trees and it was peaceful. Grasses and wildflowers grew around it and Maude would often bring her lunch up there for an impromptu picnic whenever she wanted to sit and think.

It was hot for early autumn, and even with the slight bite in the air, Maude was sweating by the time she got to the top of the hill.

Soon she'd be twelve weeks. Soon she'd have to admit to the reality of this baby and, since she hadn't made a decision earlier, soon she'd have to decide what she was going to do about it.

And him? What about him?

Despite the heat, she shivered.

She couldn't tell him. After that night, he hadn't returned to Darkfell, and she hadn't asked about him. There was limited Internet at the manor and none at all in the groundskeeper's cottage, so she was able to dismiss him from her thoughts entirely. Out of sight, out of mind.

But she couldn't keep telling herself that for ever.

Maude sat down at the side of the lake and dipped a

finger in the water. It was cold, deliciously so, but not too icy for a swim.

She hadn't brought her bathing things—she'd intended to come here for some peace to decide what to do about the baby—but the waterfall and pool were very isolated, and no one except Mr and Mrs Harris, who managed the manor, were in residence, so the chances of someone seeing her were just about zero.

Still, she gave a cursory look around at the surrounding woods to make sure she was completely alone, then she kicked off her worn boots before stripping off her muddy jeans, T-shirt, and underwear. Then, standing naked by the pool, she glanced down at the small rounded bump of her stomach.

Her child, conceived on the floor of Darkfell Forest. She touched her stomach gently, and allowed herself to finally think about her baby.

He or she was a gift from the forest and they belonged here with it, she felt that suddenly and quite strongly.

Child of the man who owns the forest, too.

That was true, but what little she did know of Dominic Lancaster was that he wasn't a family kind of man. After that night, she'd indulged herself once he and all the guests had left, taking advantage of the manor's Internet and doing a few Internet searches on her laptop.

There were gossip sites and discussion threads dedicated to his sensual exploits, with numerous pictures and videos of parties and clubs he'd attended, and in every single one of those videos and pictures the charisma he gave off was so palpable it mesmerised her.

She'd touched those powerful shoulders. She'd kissed his beautiful, hard mouth. She'd had him inside her…

Now his child is inside you too.

A thick, hot feeling gathered in her throat. She'd really tried to be what her grandparents had wanted. Hardworking, honest. Reliable. Thinking through her actions before she made them and being alert to the consequences. She'd never been a rebellious teen, since her grandparents had made it very clear that they wouldn't put up with what they termed 'any nonsense'. They hadn't wanted her to turn out like her mother, who'd left home at sixteen after falling pregnant to a much older man and then running off to join the Earthsong commune.

Sonya had been wild, reckless, and could never be told what to do. She'd also been distracted and impatient, and had preferred socialising to parenting and Maude had often ended up being looked after by other people in the commune.

Maude's grandparents had put up with what they saw as their daughter's irresponsibility for ten years before finally coming to Earthsong and taking Maude away permanently.

She didn't like to think about that day, because she'd loved the commune. She'd loved not going to school, loved one of the older ladies who'd managed the commune's garden and who'd let Maude play there all day if she'd wanted to. She loved her wild, reckless mother too.

But Sonya hadn't loved Maude enough to keep her. She'd let her parents take Maude away with only a shrug. Then she'd cut off contact with them and Maude without explanation. Permanently.

After that, Maude had often felt untethered as a child. As if she'd lost an anchor and the current had been dragging her and she'd had nothing to hold onto. She'd had no real home to go to, no place where she'd felt she belonged. She'd tried to fit in all through the rest of her childhood and into adulthood, had tried to find her place in the world. But the only place that had felt like home was the forest, and Darkfell Forest in particular.

She didn't want to leave, didn't want to give up her job, but it was a fixed-term contract and maternity leave wasn't part of it.

Gran would have told her that it was her own stupid fault and she should have known better. That she had too much of her mother in her, and did she really want to waste her life the way Sonya had?

Now, the thick, hot feeling in her throat tightened and her eyes prickled, but she forced the feelings away. Hard.

Having a baby *wasn't* a waste of her life and she *wasn't* going to leave, either. This child was part of the forest and she couldn't think of a better place for it to be than with her, here in Darkfell. Maybe she could manage things with her job so she could stay with the baby.

No, there was no maybe about it. That was exactly what she was going to do, and she'd fight tooth and nail to make that happen.

Braced by that thought, she bent down and picked a wildflower, weaving the stem into her hair on a whim. Then she picked another and another, weaving more flowers into her hair as she went, covering herself with parts of the forest.

She was going to have to tell people, she knew that.

First her friends, then… Well, maybe just her friends for the moment. The one thing she certainly wasn't going to do was tell Dominic Lancaster.

Picking a couple of forget-me-nots, she wound them into her hair beside each ear, then picked her way around the lake to the rocks where the waterfall splashed down. It was only a little waterfall and not very powerful, delightful to stand beneath and let the water wash over her like an outdoor shower.

She tilted her head back and closed her eyes, letting the gentle pressure of the water ease away the tight knot of fear that had settled in her chest. Letting the calm of the forest enter her soul and soothe it.

After a couple of minutes she turned and dived cleanly into the pool. Arrowing down to the sandy bottom, she touched it lightly, a little ritual of greeting to the spirit of the pool and waterfall, then pushed herself back up to the surface. Then she turned onto her back and closed her eyes, floating for a time, letting her mind settle.

Then Maude slowly became aware that she wasn't alone. Someone was standing in the trees beside the lake, watching her.

A very tall, powerfully built man, with a white stripe running through his black hair.

Dominic wasn't sure how long he'd stood there watching the woman. He'd been in the forest, showing a developer currently interested in the property around, and had been intending to show him the waterfall and the pool, but as they'd approached, he'd caught a glimpse of bare skin and long golden hair and had quickly decided the developer should return to the manor without him.

Obviously, he hadn't gone too, since if there was a naked woman bathing in his pool, he wanted to know exactly who she was and why she was there.

Not that he needed to ask her, since the knowledge had been sitting in his subconscious for months now, and had since become part of him.

There was only one woman it could possibly be and that was the beautiful wood nymph he'd caught in the forest on his last bacchanal. And of course it was her. He hadn't seen her face, hadn't spoken to her, knew her only by her scent, the soft sound of her cries, and the silken heat of her skin, but it was her all the same.

He knew it like he knew his own name.

He'd watched her turn her face to the waterfall as it cascaded over a delicately curved body, with honey-gold skin, and then he'd watched her dive gracefully into the pool before rising onto the surface and rolling onto her back.

Wildflowers were tangled in hair the colour of ripe wheat and caramel, long tresses like golden kelp fanning around her head as she floated in the water. Her body was framed beautifully, high, rounded breasts with pretty pink nipples, the curve of hip and thigh proportioned with perfection. A slender woman, yet he remembered the way she'd felt, delicate but with a subtle strength in the arms that had wrapped around him and in the thighs that had closed around his hips.

He felt like a voyeur watching her now, but he didn't move. His scruples had always been few and scant enough that he couldn't bear to drag himself away. She was a beautiful wood nymph crowned in wildflowers, and she was bathing in his pool.

Abruptly, as if sensing she was being watched, she rolled onto her front, the water splashing as her head turned in his direction and her gaze met his. She had warm brown eyes, flecked with the same gold as her hair. They made his heart feel as if it had missed a beat.

Her mouth opened and her eyes went wide with surprise, and she submerged herself to her shoulders in the water, obviously trying to hide herself.

He should have looked away. He really should, but he'd never been a gentleman, not once, and why shouldn't he look anyway? The darkness had hidden her that night in the forest, but now the sun was shining and she was naked, and he couldn't tear his gaze away.

'Hello, nymph,' he said. 'What are you doing in my pool?'

Her features were as delicate as the rest of her, small and precise, with a full mouth and high cheekbones, and slightly winged dark gold brows. An ethereal beauty, almost otherworldly, and subtle enough that he might not have noticed it in another context. But right here, right now, it was all he could see. Those gold-flecked eyes of hers held a strength and a fire that caught his interest and held it.

'I'm swimming,' she said. 'What does it look like?'

Her voice held a husk to it that went straight to his groin, but her tone was decidedly un-nymphlike. Which also went to his groin. He'd always liked a woman with spirit.

'You appear to have forgotten your bathing suit,' he pointed out. 'Did you perhaps think you could hire one? Alas, neither this pool nor the manor are open to the public.'

'I'm not the public.' She eyed him with deep suspicion. 'I work here.'

That gave him pause. She worked here? It was possible, he supposed. He had many houses dotted all over the globe, most of them fully staffed, and he didn't know the names of all those staff. But he did know the names of the Darkfell staff. They'd been there since he was a child. John and Polly Harris. Those were the only two. Except...

John had been getting on in years and had told Dominic that he should hire a gardener and someone to do forest upkeep, so Dominic had instructed John to employ whomever he thought best. Dominic trusted his judgement. But this...sprite could *not* be the person John had hired, surely?

She couldn't be the woman in the woods that night either, right?

Dominic wasn't often surprised, but he could feel shock working its way through his body now.

He'd found that nightgown the next morning, but he hadn't bothered finding the owner. In fact, he'd put it out of his mind. Yet every now and then he'd find himself looking over the guest list of that last bacchanal, studying the names of the female guests and wondering.

It hadn't been any of them, he was sure, which meant he should keep looking. Because if that woman hadn't been a guest then perhaps he'd involved someone else, someone unsuspecting who hadn't known what was happening. Then again, she hadn't protested, hadn't pushed him away. When he'd caught her, she'd kissed him just as savagely as he'd kissed her. There had been nothing reluctant about her, nothing at all.

She was staring at him now, her gaze wary, her shoulders still underwater.

'Please tell me,' he said, 'that it wasn't you that night.'

She flushed. 'What night?'

'You know what I'm talking about.'

'I don't.' She glanced away, her chin jutting at a mutinous angle. 'It's cold. I need to get out. Which means you need to bugger off.'

He decided to ignore that. 'You're John's hire, aren't you? From that agency. You're the gardener.'

She glanced back again, her jaw tight. 'I prefer groundskeeper. Since I also look after the forest, not just the garden.'

Hell. It *had* to have been her, in that case. There was no other possibility. As the thought hit him, a shock of sexual desire pierced him, so intense it took his breath away, and for a moment he had to fight to get it under control. Which hadn't happened for twenty years. In fact, he couldn't remember the last time he'd been in the grip of such intense sexual hunger.

He'd spent the last fifteen years indulging his appetites shamelessly, letting himself have whatever he wanted, and why not? He deserved it after the long battle first to gain control of his father's company, then to break it up piece by piece. After the years of his childhood where everything had come with a price, with strings. Short strings, long strings, but *always* strings. Everything had been a negotiation, a deal. Everything a quid pro quo. His father had taught him to be ruthless and hard when it came to getting what he wanted, to negotiation, and, since it was the only power he'd ever had as a child, he'd learned.

He'd learned to control his emotions too, to not let need or desire get in the way of getting the best deal possible. Of course, now he'd achieved what he wanted, he'd lengthened the leash he kept on his appetites, seeing no point in not indulging them. But he never let them get too out of control, never let them control him. He remained in command of himself always.

Except apparently he hadn't with this woman. Who, despite having been under him for one whole night, made him want to have her again. And again, and again...

Dominic knew he should walk away. Should turn and go back to the manor, sign the papers that would sell this godforsaken property, and leave without a backward glance, never to return.

But he didn't.

Instead, he strolled over to the edge of the pool and looked down at the woman in it, her hair a golden veil around her face, the remains of wildflowers, blue and pink and purple, still caught in the wet strands.

She stared back, the gold flecks in her eyes glittering with temper.

'It was you,' he said, and he didn't make it a question this time. 'That night in the forest.'

She gave him an aggravated look. 'Can you please go away? It's cold and I want to get out.'

But he was in a position of power now, his favourite position, and he was finding it far too satisfying getting under her skin. She'd turned him inside out that night and apparently still had magic enough to do the same thing now, and what was sauce for the goose was good for the gander, et cetera.

So he merely folded his arms and remained where he stood. 'Then by all means get out. Don't let me stop you.'

The golden sparks in her eyes glittered brighter, and again he felt that delicious rush of excitement and anticipation. It would be glorious if she got out, only to run again, naked and dripping wet. He'd run too, and this time he'd make sure to catch her sooner, so that they could get to the pleasurable part quicker, her mouth on his, all raw heat and honey, with a sharp edge.

He hadn't had a woman since that night. He'd been busy with a new startup in LA and had told himself he hadn't had the time to find a new lover. Lies, of course. He'd had the time, he just hadn't had the inclination, and now two months of celibacy were starting to bite.

That had to be the reason he felt this way. The *only* reason. If she didn't get out, it didn't matter to him. He'd find someone else to lose himself in…wouldn't he?

You want her, though.

She was staring at him furiously from the water, and, yes, he had to be honest with himself. He wanted her. He wanted her badly.

'I can stand here all day,' he murmured. 'You, on the other hand…'

'Bastard,' she muttered, shooting daggers at him.

Oh, she had spirit. He liked that *very* much. 'I'm your boss. I could fire you for that.'

'Fine. Fire me. Now go the bloody hell away.'

'I've touched every inch of your body. What does it matter if I see it?'

'This is sexual harassment.'

'Take it up with HR.'

Her full mouth compressed. If looks could kill, his broken body would be floating in the water next to her.

What are you doing? You're usually much better with women than this.

It was true. Then again, he liked power games, and

the pettier the better, especially with women who were as fiery and stubborn as this one.

Still, making her sit in cold water to gratify his need to win was perhaps too petty, even for him. He really should turn around and let her get out, and then they could have a proper conversation.

The water of the pool was clear and as he prepared to turn around, he could see the pale shape of her body beneath the surface. She had her arms crossed protectively over her chest, and maybe it was a distortion of the water but it seemed as if her stomach was…

A shaft of ice pierced him and he took a step closer to the edge of the pool before he could stop himself. 'Get out,' he ordered.

People always did what he told them when he used that tone of voice, and this woman was no different. Her eyes widened and she'd already half risen out of the pool before she realised what she was doing, brown eyes flashing with anger as she sat again.

But it had been enough for Dominic.

Enough to see the water glistening on the bare skin of her belly, revealing the small, rounded bump of early pregnancy.

Dominic met her gaze, every inch of him suddenly burning with a fury he hadn't thought was possible for him to feel these days.

'Get out of the water,' he said coldly. 'Get out of the water *now*.'

CHAPTER FOUR

MAUDE EYED HIM WARILY, her heart beating far too fast and far too hard.

He stood by the edge of the pool, his arms crossed over his broad chest, every line of his tall, powerful figure drawn tight with anger. It burned in eyes dark as the night too, turned his beautiful mouth hard, and made a muscle leap in his strong jaw.

He was dressed casually, in faded jeans that sat low on his hips and did wonderful things to his thighs, and a simple black T-shirt that clung to his muscled chest. The clothes should have made him less intimidating, but somehow they only highlighted it.

Dominic Lancaster. Her boss. Her god of the forest.

The father of her baby.

A baby she'd thought he'd never know about…at least until now.

The moment she'd locked eyes with him as she'd floated in the pool, she'd known she wasn't going to get out of this with her secret intact. Not given how the tension that had been there that night in the forest had suddenly leapt between them again, electric and resonant.

She'd tried to stay beneath the water as he'd strolled to the edge of the pool, but his dark gaze had seen too much. She should have pretended she was a lost tourist and not given away the truth that she was his employee, but he'd surprised her. She'd been surprised too by her own reaction to him. It had been months since that night in the woods, yet the moment she'd made eye contact with him, she'd felt as if she couldn't breathe.

She knew she shouldn't have got angry with him. She knew she shouldn't have called him a bastard. Her grandmother had instilled in her the importance of being polite to people and calling him a bastard wasn't at all polite. But, God, the way he looked at her made her skin feel so tight she wanted to crawl right out of it.

And that wasn't even counting the secret she was trying to hide from him. The secret curled up in her belly that she desperately hoped he hadn't noticed.

Clearly she'd hoped in vain. He must have seen her stomach when she'd half stood in instinctive obedience to his command, and had made the right assumption. That was why he was so furious.

Yes, she really *should* have pretended to be a tourist.

It was too late for that now, though. Too late to pretend anything, even that she wasn't the woman he'd spent the night in the forest with, not with this electricity crackling between them.

She really didn't want to obey him, since it felt as if she'd spent her entire life doing what people told her, but she was freezing, and if she stayed any longer in the water, she'd probably die of exposure.

Also, she'd never been good at pretending.

Gritting her teeth, Maude rose slowly from the water and he watched her, fury snapping in his dark eyes. She didn't look away, deciding she wasn't going to let him intimidate her, no matter that she hadn't told him about the baby. She had a stubborn streak in her, a streak her grandparents had tried first to whittle away and then to grind down, sanding off its sharp edges. Yet the moment Dominic Lancaster's dark eyes met hers, all those sharp edges snapped back into life as if they'd always been there.

She didn't bother to hide the rounded shape of her belly as she stepped from the pool and walked over to where her clothes lay, discarded on the grass. And she didn't speak as she picked up her T-shirt, fighting to stay calm as she dried herself off with it.

He merely stood there, his eyes dark, that muscle in his jaw leaping and leaping. It should have been threatening, the way he stared at her. Should have cowed her, made her feel ashamed of keeping the secret of their child from him, but strangely it had the opposite effect.

It put steel in her spine. If he was going to watch her dress, then he could watch. She wasn't going to hide herself or be ashamed. Because he was right, his hands had been all over her body, touching her hungrily and desperately. He'd wanted her and, from the growing flames in his eyes now, despite his fury, he wanted her still.

If he'd been the god of the forest that night, she'd been the goddess, and goddesses did not hide.

So she took her time, pulling her knickers up slowly, then putting on her bra. Easing into her damp T-shirt then stepping into her jeans. He watched her the whole time, saying nothing, filling the air with a complicated mixture of hunger and fury.

She sensed somehow that he wasn't going to break the silence, that he wanted her to do it. Well, if so, too bad. If he could play silly games to keep her freezing in the water, then he could stand being the one to break the silence first.

Maude sat on the grass to put her shoes on—slowly—and only once she had did she get to her feet and stand facing him, meeting his hot black stare. She didn't speak. She only raised an eyebrow.

A thick, crackling silence filled the space between them.

'You're pregnant,' he said at last, and Maude experienced a brief thrill at making him break first.

'Gosh, really?' she said dryly. 'I had no idea.'

His jaw hardened still further. He took a couple of steps towards her then stopped. 'It's mine.'

Again, it wasn't a question, making his certainty needle at her. 'Is it?' She shrugged. 'Actually, it could be anyone's. There were a lot of men in the forest that night.'

Unexpectedly, he closed the distance between them and reached for her, gripping her upper arms, his fingers pressing hard against her skin, holding her fast. She tensed, staring challengingly up at him.

'It *is* mine,' he said in a low, hard voice. 'You did not sleep with anyone else. You were with me the whole night.'

A small thread of excitement wound through her, as if she liked his anger, liked the hard press of his fingers against her skin and the black flames that leapt in his eyes, the skein of darkness that wound through his voice.

That darkness that connected to something inside her the way it had that night.

It made her breathless, made her want to push him, make him savage as she had five months earlier. She had no idea why. Perhaps it was all about trying to rec-reate what she'd felt that night, as if she'd shaken off the rules society had imposed on her, free of everything but nature's own law.

'You don't know,' she said. 'I might have—'

'Don't lie to me,' he interrupted fiercely. 'Not about this.'

Get a grip. You can't lie about your own child.

Cold shock hit her as reality reasserted itself and she realised what she was doing. She'd enjoyed flexing her power over him, but she'd let it go to her head and that was a bad thing. That night with him, she'd let the fire inside her, the darkness, overcome her good sense and that was why she was in the situation she was in now. She needed to control herself.

Maude swallowed. 'Fine. Yes, I was the one in the forest that night and, yes, the baby is yours. I mean, probably.'

'What do you mean "probably"?'

He was very close, his hands burning her skin, the rich, spicy scent of him, the scent of the forest, all around her. He was tall, like one of the oaks towering over her, and very powerful, and she could feel the electricity of his presence, an elemental and raw thing that seemed to put its fingers around her throat and squeeze.

'Let me go,' she said, suddenly needing to put some space between them, because if she didn't get away from him, she wasn't sure what would happen. 'Let me go, *now.*'

Instantly, he released her, allowing her to take a cou-ple of steps back. But fury in his eyes and the set of his powerful figure didn't change.

'Okay, okay.' She was breathing faster than she would have liked. 'Yes, the baby is yours.'

'You just said probably. Do you really want me to insist on a paternity test?'

She hadn't thought of herself as a proud person, but, as it turned out, she had a fair streak of pride in her too. 'No,' she snapped. 'It was you. I was a virgin that night.'

His dark gaze flickered. 'A virgin. That seems…apt. All things considered.'

She flushed, which annoyed her, and opened her mouth to make some retort, but he went on before she could get a word out. 'What the hell were you doing in the forest that night?' he demanded. 'The staff were warned to stay away.'

'I heard someone scream outside the cottage,' she said defensively. 'So I went out to check they were okay.'

'Screaming in the context of that particular party is nothing to worry about. Again, you were told—'

'I was worried,' she interrupted, defensiveness giving way to anger yet again. 'The forest isn't exactly safe at night and I wanted to make sure no one had fallen and broken their leg.'

'I see. And after that, you decided a little experiment with voyeurism was necessary?'

Again, she felt herself flush. Technically, he was correct, she'd been warned to stay away and she hadn't. Also, she realised belatedly that she hadn't thought about his perspective at all. He'd clearly thought she was a guest and had acted accordingly. He hadn't known she wasn't one, or that she was his employee. She'd been too caught up in the moment, in the magic of the forest and the night, and so had he.

That was why they were here, having this conversation, after all.

It's your fault and you know it.

Maude's jaw ached. She felt like she had at thirteen, when she'd had her one and only rebellion, and had sneaked out to a party given by one of the older kids at school. Her grandparents had somehow found out and her grandfather had come to get her, taking her by the scruff of the neck and marching her to the car. Then there had been an interrogation in his study the next day, with her grandmother standing beside his desk, arms folded. They'd had identical looks of disapproval and disappointment on their faces as they'd explained to her that she couldn't do the things that other children could. That she had her mother's wild blood in her and she had to be careful. She had to watch herself, had to learn to take responsibility for herself, had to learn self-control. They'd always made it clear that they were doing this for her own good, because they loved her, and so she'd tried. God knew how she'd tried, and mostly she'd succeeded.

But that night, none of the lessons had stuck.

And look what happened. Perhaps you're just like your mother after all.

Maude ignored the snide thought. 'I didn't know you'd run after me,' she said, knowing she sounded as if she was making excuses and, well… She was.

'Yes, you did,' he snapped. 'You wanted me to. You wanted me to catch you, too.'

'I was a virgin. Was I supposed to be carrying condoms, or—?'

'I thought you were a guest. All guests had personal

responsibility for their own birth control. Condoms were also provided.'

'But not in the middle of the forest, clearly.'

He said nothing, dark eyes still burning with anger, the muscle in the side of his jaw flexing. The white stripe in his hair seemed brilliant in the sunlight, making the rest of the ink-black strands seem even darker, and she had the oddest thought that he looked like an angry badger.

'What are you smiling at?' he barked.

Maude hadn't realised she was, in fact, smiling, and stopped. 'Nothing.'

'I'm glad someone finds this situation so amusing.'

'It's not that. I just… Well, you looked… For a minute… Like…an angry badger.'

He blinked. 'A badger,' he repeated blankly.

'Yes. You know, with the stripe in your hair and—'

'I'm familiar with what badgers look like, thank you very much.' He tilted his head back slightly, looking down his aristocratic nose at her. The fury in his eyes had abated somewhat but the embers of it were burning still. 'And as much fun as this conversation is, I think we've come to the end of what we need to say to each other about that night.'

Relief washed through her. 'Oh, that's great. Okay, well, I'll just nip back to the—'

'You will come back to the manor with me, Miss…' He paused and frowned. 'What the hell is your name?'

She was very tempted not to give it to him, but that would be pointless considering he could find out very easily anyway. 'Maude,' she said. 'Maude Braithwaite.' She took a breath. 'And I'm sorry, but I'm not coming anywhere with you.'

* * *

Dominic couldn't remember ever being so furious. Furious enough that during the conversation with the nymph—*Maude*—he'd done a terrible job of keeping a grip on his temper.

That never happened to him. Normally he allowed himself to care just enough to be mildly peeved when things didn't go his way, but certainly not enough to provoke rage. Then again, 'normally' wasn't a word that could be attributed to his current situation, since there was nothing normal about it.

She was pregnant and the child was his, and *of course* the child was his. The fact that she'd even had a stab at pretending otherwise had incensed him, and he wasn't even sure why.

He wasn't sure how she managed to get under his skin so badly, but she did. There was something about the way she'd looked at him, all suspicion with an edge of wariness, and a slight hint of disdain that just…needled at him. Then that had faded to be replaced by anger, the gold in her eyes glittering bright, only for that then to vanish and be replaced by, of all things, amusement. Then anger again. So many emotional currents moving through her lovely eyes and flowing over her delicate features like a fast-moving stream.

If he hadn't been so furious himself he would have watched them move, captivated. But he was furious. Furious that she'd kept this pregnancy from him, and furious at himself that a) he hadn't used any kind of protection that night in the forest, and b) he'd suspected she wasn't a guest and he hadn't bothered to find out who exactly she was.

When problems occurred, Dominic dealt with them swiftly, since problems left unsolved usually compounded themselves, and so he was very aware that he had to deal with this particular problem just as swiftly.

He also didn't want to deal with it standing beside the waterfall, staring at Maude's T-shirt clinging damply to her body, making him remember how she'd looked standing naked in the water. She'd had a forget-me-not stuck to her skin just above one soft pink nipple and he couldn't get the sight of it out of his head.

With five months of celibacy weighing heavily on him and his grip on his temper not what it should be, being here alone with her was a bad move and one he needed to rectify.

'Do you really want me to chase you again?' he asked, ruthlessly tempering his tone. 'Because we both know what happened the last time I did that.'

Her golden brows drew down and there was a long moment of silence. Then she said, 'Okay, fine.'

Part of him was disappointed at how easily she capitulated, his body wanting yet another chase, but he ignored that part of him. He wasn't going to make *that* mistake again, not considering the consequences of their last meeting.

Without another word, he turned and headed into the forest again, following the path back to the house.

Darkfell Manor had been built of grey stone in the late sixteenth century, and, in addition to the forest behind it, was surrounded by beautifully kept gardens, including a walled garden, a courtyard terrace, a formal parterre, a small orchard and a few fields.

Dominic had spent the majority of his early life here,

and, after his father's death, he'd spent a not so small fortune ripping the interior out and getting a designer to redo the entire place.

Gone were the tiny, dark servants' quarters in the attic that his father had sometimes locked him into as a punishment. Gone were the hulking pieces of furniture that had crowded all the rooms, making him feel as if he were suffocating. Gone was the chill that had seemed to settle into his bones during winter because he'd failed in a negotiation with his father to keep the heating on.

Gone was the dark green wallpaper and the smell of old, damp stone, and the rooms that had felt as though they were echoing with the sound of his own loneliness.

Now, the manor's stately interior was all white, with polished floors and thick silken rugs, and light flooding through the tall, mullioned windows. It smelled of the beeswax that Mrs Harris used on the wood half-panelling and the lemon furniture polish she used on everything else. And it was warm, the interior redone with the best central heating system money could buy, that he could turn on whenever he wanted.

It was a jewel now, and, if Dominic was honest with himself, he almost regretted his decision to sell it. But only almost. This was the last remaining piece of his father's legacy and soon it would be gone, and good riddance to it.

After that, he'd finally be free.

He showed Maude into the formal sitting room with its view over the pretty parterre garden outside, sunlight flooding the windows and making the white walls glow. There was a deep window seat full of bright cushions, and a series of low white linen couches set in a box shape around the huge fireplace.

He gestured wordlessly to one of the couches and Maude sat on the edge of one of the cushions like a bird alighting on a windowsill, ready to take flight at any moment. There was a belligerent look in her eyes, which sent a strange thrill of anticipation through him, as if he was looking forward to whatever challenge she was going to throw in his way, and maybe he was.

The ennui he'd felt at the bacchanal had afterwards turned into an odd restlessness that he couldn't pinpoint or satisfy. It had been bothering him, and maybe, if not for the pregnancy, he might have turned all his attention on seducing this mysterious, oddly alluring woman, but...

Well. There was the pregnancy.

You're going to be a father.

The thought was cold and sharp, like a piece of thread edged with razor blades winding through his soul, cutting him in places he didn't expect. Places he'd thought were invulnerable.

He'd never wanted children. Never wanted to be a father, not after the hell his own father had made for him. He wouldn't have known how to be one even if he'd wanted to be anyway, yet it seemed now that he wasn't going to be given a choice.

Perhaps that was why he was so angry. He hadn't had a choice because she hadn't given him one.

It's not her fault. She wasn't expecting anything like that to happen that night, but you were.

The accuracy of the thought was so painful he ignored it.

'Why didn't you tell me about the baby?' he asked at last, after the silence had reached screaming point. 'No, scratch that. Were you *ever* going to tell me about the baby?'

A flush had crept into her cheeks, turning them deep pink, making her brown eyes seem lighter. 'No,' she said without hesitation. 'I wasn't.'

That turned up the heat on his already simmering temper, but he kept a tight grip on it. 'Bold of you to assume I wouldn't want to know.'

'I read a few articles about you on the Internet, Mr Lancaster.' She was sitting straight-backed, with her hands resting on her thighs, fingers gripping her knees. 'And from what I read, you don't strike me as the family type.'

She wasn't wrong. He wasn't at all the family type. Yet the way she'd decided all of this, as if he had no say in how things were going to be, slid under his skin like a shard of glass.

She didn't know him and when she'd found out she was pregnant, she must have realised he was the father, and had clearly made some kind of judgement call based entirely on what the media wrote about him.

She hadn't bothered to speak to him personally, not once.

Why does it matter? When you never wanted kids in the first place? Throw some money at her and let her go on her way.

That was exactly what he should do. Yet he couldn't bring himself to do it. Something about the rounded curve of her stomach, the vulnerability of it, the knowledge that there was a little life curled there, a life he'd helped create, had hit him hard. Had woken something possessive and territorial in him that he hadn't known was there. He was never either possessive or territorial, since he didn't care about anything enough, but for this baby... Apparently he cared about that.

Maybe it was a primitive response to that night in the woods, with her virginity and how it had felt to be with her, sacred almost. Or maybe it was only biology kicking him in the teeth. Either way, he didn't like the intensity of the feeling or how it messed with his control.

'So what type am I, then?' he asked, still struggling to control his temper.

'Rich.' She said the word with distaste.

'You don't like rich people?'

'Not really.' Her stare was flat. 'I didn't like what I read about you either.'

'You assume the media always tells the truth?'

She frowned. 'There were lots of pictures of you at parties and—'

'You don't know anything about me, nymph,' he interrupted gently. 'Which means you have no idea what "type" I am.'

The belligerent expression on her face didn't change. 'So when was I supposed to "know" you?' she demanded. 'When you caught me in the forest after chasing me? Or maybe when you pulled me down on the bracken? Were we going to have a conversation about whether we wanted children or not then?'

His anger felt like a live wire, spitting sparks whenever he tried to grab hold of it, and he couldn't stop himself from saying, 'Perhaps if you'd bothered to tell me you weren't one of my guests, we wouldn't be in this position now.'

'Well, I didn't,' she snapped right back, her own temper clearly not within her control either. 'I was a little too busy being chased.'

Dominic opened his mouth to say something ill-advised, then thought better of it and closed it with a snap. This was getting them nowhere and being angry wasn't going to help matters. Because while he might not have chosen it, the child was his. He'd had a part in creating it, regardless of whose fault it was. The baby's presence was a fact, he couldn't change it, and being angry with himself that he'd been so careless, that he'd let his own desires take control, was pointless. He couldn't punish the child or Maude for his mistake.

His Greek mother had been one of his father's many lovers, and he himself the result of one night of passion and a careless attitude to contraception. She'd had him then had left him with his father, vanishing into the ether, never to be seen again. Jacob Lancaster had been very open with him, telling Dominic that he'd been going to put him up for adoption, but had then changed his mind. He'd needed an heir and now he had one.

Except Jacob hadn't been any kind of father to Dominic. He'd set himself up as a kind of business rival instead. Everything Dominic had wanted had had to be earned, had to be worked for or negotiated. Food. Clothes. Books. Toys.

Jacob had done this to teach him about the value of things and how to survive in the 'real world', where money was everything and the art of the deal the force that generated it. He'd wanted to turn his soft-hearted, sensitive son into an heir worthy of the great Lancaster

Developments, with properties all over the world, that he had built up from nothing.

It had been a terrible childhood, but one thing Dominic would give Jacob: he'd become one hell of a businessman. But as to being himself a father, he had no idea how to do it, and he was too old now to learn, so claiming this baby as his was likely to be a mistake. He'd probably only end up repeating Jacob's mistakes. But…he couldn't walk away. Personal responsibility was something he believed in, and he was responsible for this.

'So, what were you going to do?' he asked at length. 'Bring the child up yourself?'

'Yes, actually.' She lifted her chin, stubborn as a mule. 'That's exactly what I was going to do.'

'I see. And you were going to bring up the child, in addition to your workload, here? Were you going to apply for leave to have the baby? You're only on a year's contract, remember, so you won't have much. What did you think would happen afterwards? And how were you going to manage childcare? Or did you think you could fob the baby off onto Polly while you worked?'

Instantly the golden sparks in her eyes ignited. 'I was not going to *fob* the baby off onto anyone! I'd only just started to think about—'

'Only just? What are you? Twelve weeks? Thirteen? More? You've known about it for a good—'

'There's a chance of miscarriage, you bloody idiot,' she retorted hotly. 'I didn't think there was much point—'

'Not much point?' he found himself interrupting yet again, his temper slowly slipping from his grip. 'A child isn't a damn puppy! You can't just give it back if you find you don't like it!'

'You think I don't know that?' She surged to her feet. 'If you've only brought me here to shout at me, then thank you but I think I've had enough.' She turned to the door and took a step towards it, but before she could take another, he reached out and grabbed her arm, holding it firmly, stopping her.

She rounded on him, her face pink, the gold flecks in her eyes molten with fury, turning the warm brown into bright guinea gold. 'How dare you?' she spat and tried to jerk away from him.

'Wait!' Dominic growled, holding on tighter. He didn't understand what was happening, how his usually expertly controlled temper had slipped so completely out of his grip. But no, of course he understood.

It was her and her temper. She was a flame and he dry tinder that kept igniting whenever she got too close.

She pulled her arm away but didn't keep walking. Instead, she faced him, her expression pure fury. 'Don't you manhandle me *ever* again,' she snapped furiously and then, much to his surprise, instead of leaving, she took a step closer. To him.

And Dominic found himself staring into her golden-brown eyes, watching the sparks of her fury turn into something else, feeling the air around them burst into flames with the same desire that had consumed them back in the forest that night. The same animal hunger.

He swore, then reached for her at the same time as she reached for him, and her mouth was on his before he'd even managed to close his arms around her. Hot and desperate, feverish, needy. As if she'd been as starved for him as he was for her.

He'd never experienced anything like it.

She bit his lip hard, pulling a growl from him, and then he was on one of the couches, and she was beneath him, and he was giving as good as he got, biting the softness of her full bottom lip, making her jerk beneath him as he devoured her.

She clawed at him, trying to pull aside his T-shirt as she squirmed and wriggled like an eel beneath him. He pushed his thigh between hers and leaned forward, pressing it against the sensitive place between her legs, making her gasp and writhe even more.

Then with quick, hard motions, he jerked her T-shirt up and over her head, then swiftly wrapped it around her wrists and pulled it tight, before pushing them up and over her head and down onto the cushions. Then he held them there.

She stared up at him, a golden-eyed fury, wildflowers still scattered through the heavy honey-gold skeins of her hair. The pulse at the base of her throat beat hard and fast and the heat between her thighs was insane, soaking through the denim of his jeans.

'You want this?' he demanded, his voice harsh gravel and rough sand.

She said nothing, but her eyes were full of anger and heat, her hips moving sensually against the hard press of his thigh.

Dominic was a businessman through and through. His father had raised him to be ruthless, and ruthless he was. He had the soul of a predator and, right now, that predator was hungry.

'You have to tell me, nymph,' he said. 'And then you'll have to make it worth my while.'

CHAPTER FIVE

MAUDE LAY ON the couch beneath Dominic Lancaster's hard, hot body, a dim part of her screaming a warning. She couldn't quite work out how she'd got here, only that one moment they'd been shouting at each other, and she'd decided to leave, then the next she'd turned and thrown herself into his arms instead.

His mouth had been on hers and she'd still been furious.

Furious that he'd made her feel bad for how she'd acted. Furious that he'd made her feel afraid. Furious that, apparently, he wasn't going to laugh off her being pregnant with his child and let her resume life as if nothing had happened. Furious that he'd made her feel stupid for not considering her future, when a very deep part of her was still in shock that she was pregnant at all.

Furious that she wanted him so badly it was almost painful.

It was easier to kiss him than to talk to him. Easier to bite him and scratch him than it was to swallow her fury. Easier to channel that fury into desire than to keep hold of her temper and try not to lose it, not to be at the mercy of her wilder emotions the way her grandparents had always warned her about.

The way he touched her, with firm mastery, felt so good. Made her feel as if she could rage out of control, give into her darker impulses, and it would be fine, because he was there. He was strong and powerful and he could take anything she threw at him.

The way he'd bound her wrists made her feel contained and safe, which was weird since being tied up usually indicated the opposite.

He wouldn't hurt her, though, she knew that deep in her soul. He was the god of the forest and she was under his protection.

His dark brown eyes, so much darker than her own, bordering on black, stared down fiercely at her. Flames in them.

'Well?' he demanded, his rich, deep voice as dark as his eyes. 'What's it going to be?'

She took a gasping breath. 'Make it worth your while? What do you mean?'

'If it's sex you want, I'll give it to you. But then you will give me a calm, rational discussion about this baby.'

She did want sex. She wanted him to give it to her. But to talk about the baby…*their* baby…

'You can just walk away, you know,' she said thickly.

'I know. But sadly for you I'm not a man who walks away from his responsibilities.'

'You can walk away from this. I won't hold it against you.'

'No, but you'd rather other parts were against me, wouldn't you?' He shifted his thigh between her legs, pressing delicately. 'Like this, hmm?'

Maude shuddered, the pressure causing the most exquisite pleasure. 'You don't want…children…'

'How do you know? I could want a whole horde of them.'

'But you…you don't.' A sound broke from her, torn from deep in her throat as he shifted again, the friction making her want to lift her hips against him.

He bent his head, his mouth close to her ear. 'Keep telling me what I don't want, nymph,' he purred. 'I'm sure you know better.'

This was insanity and she knew it. From the minute he'd shown up at the edge of the pool, watching her, she'd known it. Then being in this room, feeling as if the walls were closing in on her, because he was in it too, taking up all the space, all the air. Standing there like a king, with his arms folded, his black eyes accusing. As if she were one of his subjects and had to do what he said.

She didn't want to do what he said. She wanted to push him as much as he was pushing her, throw all her anger and frustration at him. She'd never felt so out of control and wild as when he was close, his electric presence making her feel as if she had a million ants under her skin.

It was ridiculous. As he'd so astutely pointed out, she didn't even know him.

Except…he made her feel *so* good. He made her feel alive and wild, the way the forest did, and she wasn't sure that was a good thing. But she couldn't think. He had his thigh right *there* and she was… God, it felt just right. It made her want to give him anything he wanted.

She struggled to take a breath. 'I…okay. A calm, r-rational discussion… That's…all?'

He shifted his thigh yet again and she writhed as sparks of pleasure shot along all her nerve endings.

If this was what sex was like for everyone, then she couldn't think why anyone ever did anything else.

'You should have told me,' he said in that dark voice again, purring and soft. 'What kind of man do you think I am?'

His eyes were so dark, so deep she could fall right into them. Like Alice down the rabbit hole, she was falling and falling.

'I...don't know.' She was hardly aware of what she was saying, all her awareness concentrated on that delicious pressure between her thighs and the lines of his beautiful face. 'I looked on the Internet... Like I said... there were pictures...of you...'

'Not father material, hmm?' He moved and she gasped as a jolt of pure physical pleasure electrified her. 'Is that what you thought?'

She couldn't remember what she had thought. It was all becoming very hazy. 'I...just wanted to do it myself,' she said, her voice uneven. 'I...don't need you...t-telling me what to do.'

'Is that right?' For a moment he remained still, looking down at her, his dark eyes utterly impenetrable. Then abruptly he pushed himself away from her and off the couch, standing once again at his full height. 'In that case let's proceed straight to the discussion about the baby and you can give yourself an orgasm later.'

Maude blinked up at him, her arms still bound over her head, her legs lying open, the ache between them insistent. No. What was he doing? He couldn't just leave her like...this... Could he?

And apparently he could, because he didn't move, his

arms folded across his broad chest, regarding her coolly, his expression giving nothing away.

A small pulse of fury hit her, that he could look so unbothered while she was lying here, desperate and hungry for him to finish what he'd started.

She swallowed and glanced down his body, looking for and finding evidence of his own arousal, pushing against the denim of his jeans.

He glanced down too, following the direction of her gaze, then shrugged, his mouth curving slightly. 'That's easily remedied. In the shower later.'

Bastard. He looked so unaffected while she felt… undone.

Did he want her to beg? Was that what he was doing? Or had he been offended when she'd said she didn't need him? Was he trying to prove a point?

In which case, he could go to hell. She *didn't* need him and maybe *she* was the one who needed to prove it.

Trying to get herself under control, Maude gave him her own version of his cool stare. 'Untie me, then. I'm not having a discussion with you like this.'

'Pity,' he murmured. 'You do make a pretty picture.' But he reached forward and untied the T-shirt around her wrists. As the fabric fell away, Maude sat up, slightly startled to find him crouching in front of her, and before she could move, he took her wrists in his strong hands, chafing them gently.

His touch was warm and not at all sexual, and it took her by surprise. So much so that she just sat there as he glanced down at her wrists, presumably checking the blood flow.

Her grandparents weren't physically demonstrative.

There were never hugs or affectionate touches, or kisses for her. There hadn't been comfort or reassurance. It was as if they didn't know how to express it. The most she'd ever had out of them had been the few times when she was sick or had a cold, and her grandmother would bring her a glass of water and some watery soup in bed.

So it was a little shocking to have Dominic Lancaster crouching before her, gently coaxing the feeling back into her fingers, his dark head bent, the stripe in his hair glaring white. There was a hint of grey at his temples too.

He was very close and he smelled so good, as he had the night they'd spent together. Of the spice of the forest and good, warm earth, and something else, something inherently masculine that made her mouth water.

'Why do you have a stripe in your hair?' she asked, the question popping into her head and then out of her mouth without any thought.

'I'm not sure,' he answered, as if he'd been asked the same thing many times. 'I've always had it. My mother had the same.'

She stared at the stripe, itching to put out her hand and touch it. As if touching him was natural. As if he'd already allowed it. She stopped herself, though, her hands clenching into fists. No point in encouraging him.

He noticed of course and glanced up at her, his dark eyes enigmatic. 'If you want to touch me, nymph, you have to earn the right.'

Maude glared at him as he rose to his full height once again. 'I don't want to touch you.'

'Is that why you clenched your fists? Because you don't want to touch me?'

'The baby,' she said, deciding they had to get this conversation started so it could end and as soon as possible. 'That's what we were supposed to talk about.'

'Oh, yes,' he murmured. 'That's right. There's a baby. Almost forgot about that.'

'You were the one who—'

'I will not be cut out of my child's life,' he interrupted, his tone hard as iron. 'Do you understand me? I will be involved. You might not need me, Maude Braithwaite, but my child will.'

At the sound of her name, spoken in that voice, all darkness and heat, she felt another electric pulse. As if part of her had liked what he said and wanted it, which couldn't be true. She *didn't* want him involved. Her mother had brought Maude up on her own, without any help from Maude's father. In fact, her mother had never even told Maude *who* her father was, not that Maude cared.

Her grandparents had thought Sonya hadn't done a good job with her, but, despite that, her memories of the commune were good ones. She certainly hadn't suffered through lack of a father, and she'd make sure her own child wouldn't suffer either.

Except the look on Dominic Lancaster's face and the iron in his tone made it clear that he would brook no argument.

Her heart gave an odd little thump and, while she didn't want to admit it, a part of her was almost admiring of his willingness to step up and take responsibility for his child.

However, he also was who he was. A man with too much money, who apparently liked clubs and parties, all things that Maude didn't care about, and who almost certainly didn't value the things she did or wouldn't even be interested in them.

She didn't want him to be part of her child's life.

The child was *her* responsibility. She'd made a mistake, it was true, and she should have never done what she had in the forest that night. But now there would be a baby, and she couldn't shake off the feeling that somehow this child was a gift from the forest. It had been conceived in a way that still felt magical and sacred, even now. Perhaps if the man standing in front of her had been as deeply connected with nature as she was, then she would have felt differently. But he wasn't.

He was from the city and inhabited a different world. The same kind of world that her grandparents inhabited, and she didn't want her child to have the same kind of upbringing she'd had. Where she'd been told what to do and how to be and how to behave. Been stuffed into the little box they'd prepared for her and never let out. Forced to grow into a shape that wasn't her own.

She wanted her child to be free to be their own person.

How do you know he doesn't feel the same way you do about it?

Well, here he was, already ordering her around and laying down rules, so of course he didn't feel the same way she did. That wasn't even a question.

'Why do you even want a child?' she asked belligerently.

'I didn't. But we can't always get what we want, can we?'

'Unfortunately,' Maude muttered. 'I can take the child away. You can't stop me.'

He lifted one dark brow. 'Do you really believe I can't stop you?'

Maude wished that she didn't, in fact, believe him, but there was a steely glint in his eyes that made her think that would be a mistake. He was a billionaire, with mountains of money and a whole bunch of lawyers on speed dial. Of course he could stop her.

He could take the child from you if he wanted to.

Something cold settled in the pit of her stomach. He had a hard edge, this man, a harder edge than she'd expected. He was rich and liked parties, but that didn't mean he was stupid. In fact, she had a feeling he was the opposite, and that while she had a stubborn streak a mile wide, he had a ruthless one as stark as the white stripe in his hair.

'Fine,' she bit out, trying to mask her trepidation. 'What kind of involvement are you talking about, then?'

'I want the child to live with me.' His eyes glittered. 'And that includes you as well.'

Maude's brown eyes widened and she blinked, her mouth opening slightly. Which satisfied Dominic far more than it should. About time he surprised her, because he was tired of her doing the same to him.

She wouldn't like what he suggested, he knew that already.

It was a tactic of his, to make outrageous demands and then see what the response was. Usually the response was a refusal, which was then his cue to start proper negotiations. From there, he would gradually give ground until it looked to the other party as if they'd got the best deal, when, in fact, they'd ended up giving him everything he wanted.

She would refuse, he knew, and sure enough, after a moment of shocked silence, she said, 'Are you kidding? I'm not living with you.'

There was no reason to feel a slight prick of irritation at that, yet he felt it all the same. 'It's not as if you'd be living on the street,' he said. 'I've got a substantial house in the middle of London and—'

'No,' she said before he could finish. 'I'm definitely *not* living in London.'

He wanted to argue, which was insane since the next step in his tactic was to concede minor ground until he got what he *actually* wanted. And surely what he actually wanted was *not* her living with him.

But then you'll have the child. And you'll have her in your bed. Why not?

He could think of several very good reasons why not. He'd only suggested it because it was the most outrageous demand, and one she'd never agree to. Yet now he'd demanded it, he couldn't stop thinking about it.

That moment on the sofa just before, with her writhing beneath him, obviously desperate for him, had been the most intense aphrodisiac he'd ever experienced, and it had taken almost everything he had to pull away.

But he'd never been intending to take it further. Again, she'd pricked his temper with her arguments and stubbornness, and he'd wanted to give her a taste of her own medicine, make her desperate, make her stop pushing him. Perhaps even make her beg for him.

Yet it had almost backfired on him. He'd become so distracted by the thought of her begging that his intention to stop had fallen by the wayside. At least until she'd insisted she didn't need him and…yes, again, he'd found that unreasonably annoying.

Everything about her was unreasonably annoying.

It had taken everything he had to pull away, but he'd managed it, and her look of surprise and irritation as he'd done so had made that worth it.

Except he was still hard and he ached, and he resented both of those things. That night in the forest he'd lost control and he'd found it freeing in the moment. But that moment was gone and he didn't want to want it again. He didn't want to want *her*. Every interaction with her felt fraught, as if he were walking a tightrope between his control and her undeniable physical pull, and even the slightest wrong move would cause him to lose his balance and fall.

He'd never experienced a feeling like it and he hated it.

He hated, too, that the thought of her living with him, or, more accurately, her being in his bed, was far too tempting to ignore. He'd been so restless lately, not wanting any woman in particular, and it wasn't until that moment on the couch that he'd realised that he did, in fact, want a particular woman: Maude.

'What's wrong with London?' he asked, trying to cover his irritation.

'I don't like the city,' she said. 'I never have. And I don't want to bring my baby—'

'*Our* baby.'

'*The* baby up in a city.' She was glaring at him again. 'He or she is connected to the forest and needs to grow up as part of the natural world.'

The muscles in Dominic's neck and shoulders were getting tense. He uncrossed his arms and thrust his hands into the pockets of his jeans instead. 'The baby can visit the natural world in London,' he said tersely. 'There's parks and woods, all sorts of natural phenomena.'

'It's in the city,' she said insistently. 'Those parks and woods are surrounded by houses and roads and train tracks and streets. We created the baby here and he or she needs to live here.'

Dominic stared at her, utterly bemused. Her hair was drying into a wild tangle of curls and waves, and the bedraggled remains of wildflowers were still caught in amongst the golden strands. The gold in her eyes was glittering, her delicate features flushed with temper, and she looked very much like a wild creature he'd somehow caught. There was something wild about her, too, something untamed, that made him want to catch her, tame her to his hand…

Maybe his demand that she live with him wasn't so outrageous after all. Maybe that was what he *did* want, so he could have that magical experience of that night in the forest again. And again and again…

'Well, he or she can't live here,' he said. 'Because I'm selling the manor and the forest along with it.'

'What?' She paled. 'But you can't do that.'

This time her obvious shock didn't give him any satisfaction, because if he wasn't much mistaken that was a glint of pain in her eyes. As if he'd taken something precious from her and ground it into the dust.

'Why not?' he asked, feeling vaguely as if he'd made

a mistake and resenting that too. 'It's my manor and my forest. I can do what I bloody well like with it.'

'But…' She stopped and her mouth compressed into a hard line, her chin jutting mutinously. 'Who are you selling it to?'

'I don't know yet.'

'I'll buy it.'

He nearly laughed. 'Oh? You have a few million pounds lying around, do you?'

She flushed. 'No, but I'll… I'll save up. My grand-parents were going to gift me some land further north that I was going to use to rewild. But I can sell that.' She shoved herself off the couch after a moment, standing in front of him, all righteous indignation. 'I'll go to the bank and borrow as much as I can. I'll do unpaid work. I'll sign a contract—'

'Why?' he asked, cutting off the flood of words, mystified by her sudden passion. 'Why on earth do you care so much about Darkfell?'

She was silent, biting her lip. Then she said simply, 'I love the forest here. It feels like…like…home. Like… I belong here. The baby was conceived in the forest and so the forest is connected to it. I know that sounds strange and I don't expect you to understand, but that connection to nature is important. I feel very strongly that this child needs to be born here and that he or she needs to grow up here.'

She was right, he didn't understand. That she, who had no connections to this place, should feel so passionately about it, while he, who'd actually grown up here…

For years he'd put Darkfell to the back of his mind, visiting it only in midsummer, for the bacchanal. He never thought about it when he wasn't here—it was very much a case of out of sight, out of mind. But it had always felt like a millstone around his neck, dragging him down.

It wasn't so much the place itself, though that was part of it.

It was what it represented.

His father, Jacob Lancaster. Who'd made him beg for everything he'd needed. Or rather, not so much beg—the distinction was important—but explain why he'd needed it. List the pros and cons, present a case for payment, 'sell the idea', as Jacob had put it. Dominic had had no money with which to pay for it, and so everything he'd made a case for had had to be put on his 'tab', a growing debt that he could never pay off.

When he was thirteen, his father had presented him with a full accounting of that debt, expenses incurred throughout his childhood, including food, clothing, schooling and the wages of a nanny when he was very young.

To Dominic back then the debt had seemed astronomical. He'd had no hope of paying it back, or so he'd told his father, weeping. But Jacob hadn't cared. It was a lesson in how to do business and was it unfair? Yes. But life was unfair. Life was also open to negotiation, so state your case, negotiate the costs, cut them down, change my mind and on and on. Stop crying. Harden up. Figure out the deal.

So Dominic had. He'd hardened up, had figured out the deal, and had cut the costs of his upbringing in half by the time he was fifteen.

At seventeen, when his father had died of a heart attack, Dominic hadn't expected to inherit Lancaster Developments. He'd been sure his father had put one last obstacle in his way and, indeed, Jacob had. The will had specified that, since Dominic still owed him for his upkeep and hadn't proven himself adequately, the company would instead go to Jacob's second in command.

But Dominic had been waiting for this moment, planning, and doing deals just as his father had taught him. He'd used those lessons to wrestle the company back under his control and then, once he'd had it, he'd broken it up into tiny little pieces and sold every last one.

Now, he owed his father *nothing*.

Darkfell was the last of it.

'How strongly?' he asked, his brain turning over.

'What do you mean?'

'I mean, what would you do to stop me from selling it?' He arched a brow. 'What would you give me?'

She looked puzzled. 'Are you asking about money? Because I don't have—'

'It's not money I'm talking about.'

'But… I don't have anything else.'

With another woman he might have suggested sex, since it was clear that she wanted him every bit as badly as he wanted her. But she wasn't another woman and he didn't play such games with innocents like her. She was far too sincere, too honest, and, apart from anything else, he'd lost control of himself so completely the last time they'd had sex, he had no desire to do it again. Especially given the severity of the consequences the last time it had happened.

That didn't mean she had nothing to give him though.

'Yes, you do.' He allowed his gaze to settle on her

stomach, where their child rested. 'You have plenty to give me, nymph.'

Instantly fire leapt in her eyes, and she put a hand protectively over her little bump. 'You'd really use our child as a bargaining chip?'

Both the gesture and the sharply worded question sent an unexpected arrow of discomfort through him, and he found himself brought up short by a sudden realisation.

This game they were playing together, he'd just fallen into it. The game of negotiation and bargaining, of making a deal, was as natural to him as breathing. He did it all the time, in his work and when he was with a woman, bartering and negotiating for money or pleasure, it was all the same to him.

But this, with a child in the mix and a woman who didn't play games…

You can't do that with her. It's wrong and, worse, it's no better than what your father did with you.

The arrow of discomfort turned cold and sharp.

How lowering. To be like his father in any way, shape or form. Especially when he'd always seen himself as the very opposite.

'Of course not,' he said coldly, drawing himself up. 'I would never use the child. The bargaining chip is Darkfell, the manor and the forest. If you don't want me to sell it, then I'll hold off until the child is born. You can also continue to live in the groundskeeper's cottage. But in return you will make no argument about any obstetric care I see fit to employ or any discussions about custody arrangements once the child is born.'

Her eyes narrowed, her hand still curled protectively over her bump, which angered him for reasons he couldn't articulate. Did she really think he was dangerous? That he would hurt her or their child? He would never do that. *Never.*

'I want paid maternity leave for when I have the baby,' she said flatly.

Normally he would have loved that she'd joined in his negotiation, giving him demands of her own, but there was something about the way she still had her hand over her stomach, protecting their child from him, that incensed him and, worse, made him feel ashamed of himself.

'Naturally.' He tightened his grip on his temper that kept on lunging like a rabid dog on a short leash. 'I'm not a monster. The child is mine, after all.'

She studied him for a moment, chewing her bottom lip, and he didn't like that at all. He had his armour, the facade of the jaded, bored playboy that he'd been wearing so long it had become part of him. But now she was looking at him as if that armour wasn't there at all, as if she could see through him, all the way to the small, angry, hurt boy he'd once been.

'Well?' he demanded, the word sharp as a pistol shot.

'So, what?' She was seemingly oblivious to his mood. 'You'll sell Darkfell after the birth?'

Dominic snarled inside his head and choked the life out of his temper. Give nothing away, that was key to this, the key to any good deal. Maintain a good poker face.

He shrugged. 'Perhaps. And perhaps not.'

It was only marginally satisfying to see how that needled her and it must have, because she scowled abruptly. 'What does that mean?'

'It means that, unfortunately for you, I'm the owner and I get to say whether I sell it or not.'

'Why do you want to sell it?'

'None of your business.' His temper was still there, snarling behind the bars of the cage he'd set around it, which meant that probably the best thing for him to do right now was to leave. 'Well?' he asked, with the merest hint of his usual insouciance. 'Do we have a deal?'

She wrinkled her nose. 'I suppose so,' she said at last.

Normally he would have reached out and shaken her hand, sealing the deal between them and leaving her with a sensual reminder of his touch. But her hand was still guarding her stomach and her gaze was wary, and for some reason that was food for an anger that had no reason for being and no outlet, and he was tired of it. Tired of her getting under his skin. Tired of being here in this house and her hand over her stomach as if he was a threat.

So he didn't shake her hand.

He only gave her a sharp nod, then turned on his heel and walked out.

CHAPTER SIX

A WEEK LATER Maude sat at the kitchen table in the manor, glowering at her laptop screen and all the emails she hadn't responded to. It was the Your Girl Friday team all wanting to know what was happening with her and why she hadn't been sending anything to the group chat.

It made her feel tired.

She really should let the others know that she was okay and that everything was fine, and she *should* tell them that she was pregnant, but she couldn't face it. Not when all she could think about was Dominic Lancaster storming out of the manor sitting room in a huff the week before.

And yes, he *had* been in a huff.

She wasn't sure what she'd done to annoy him so much, but it had been something. He'd been all barely repressed heat right up until the moment he'd started bargaining with her about the manor and then, quite abruptly, he'd gone cold. At least his voice had been cold. His dark eyes, on the other hand, had been full of banked embers, as if she'd offended him in some way.

Perhaps he wasn't used to people talking back to him. Then again, John and Polly had never had a bad word to say about him, and they were pretty free with their opinions if they didn't like something.

He'd certainly been angry when she'd told him not to use their child as a bargaining chip. In fact, that was when his voice had turned to ice, so in retrospect, yes, she *had* offended him.

Maude bit her lip, annoyed with herself. Why was she thinking about him? She had a million tasks to do today and not one of them included thinking about Dominic Lancaster. Yet she hadn't been able to get him out of her head. The bold white stripe of his hair. The touch of his fingers as he'd gently chafed her wrists. The heat in his eyes as he'd bargained with her, only for that to disappear in a flash of temper as she'd put her hand on her stomach protectively.

He really hadn't liked her accusation or her being protective of the baby, and she suspected he hadn't liked that because… Well, the only logical assumption was that she'd offended him by assuming their child needed protection from him.

Maude leaned on her elbow, hand tucked beneath her chin as she stared sightlessly out of the large kitchen windows and into the walled garden beyond.

He had *not* appreciated her assumption that he was a threat, and she supposed she could understand that. In her defence, though, she didn't know him and their little confrontation in the sitting room had been one shock after another. All she'd been able to think about was protecting her child—that had been instinct. She didn't believe he'd *actually* hurt her or anything else, yet…

The god of the forest will claim his due.

The thought whispered through her head, sending little prickles of heat flooding over her skin. His hard thigh between her legs, pressing insistently against her…

Her mouth dried and she swallowed.

No, she couldn't allow thoughts like that. And she especially couldn't allow him to see his effect on her, to think he got under her skin, because she had a feeling that if she allowed him any quarter, he'd take all of it. He'd take everything and she had little enough as it was.

All this week she'd been uneasy, waiting for him to text or to call or email or contact her in some fashion, to talk about these 'custody arrangements' he'd mentioned the week before, yet she'd heard nothing.

A doctor had turned up a couple of days after Dominic had left and had given her a thorough examination, which she'd allowed since that was what she'd promised. The doctor had also asked if she wanted to know the gender of her child and she'd automatically said yes without really thinking about it.

A boy, apparently. She was going to have a son.

Dominic should know, of course, but she'd decided to wait until he came back to Darkfell so she could tell him face to face, and instructed the doctor accordingly.

But the uneasy feeling wouldn't leave her, and she wasn't sure why. She couldn't settle to any task, not fully, and even walking in the forest, which usually soothed her, hadn't helped. She felt like Damocles waiting for the sword to fall.

Abruptly, she pushed the laptop shut and leaned back in the chair, folding her arms.

She needed to make a decision. She needed to figure out just what she wanted when it came to the baby and his demands to be part of the child's life, because when he did come back, he'd no doubt try to steamroll her into doing whatever he wanted, and that wasn't going to happen.

She'd had years of being told what to do, of having to bend herself into the shape other people expected of her, and she wasn't going to start doing it again for him.

So. The first thing she was going to insist on was that the child be brought up here, at Darkfell. The forest was where he had been conceived and that and the manor were part of their legacy, and Dominic Lancaster would sell it over her dead body.

She was responsible for, not only the child, but the forest as well and she'd protect them both, no matter what he wanted. Of course, if that was her position, then she was going to need to think of how she could get him to agree.

She needed some kind of leverage, something that he wanted that she could use to extract a promise from him that he wouldn't sell Darkfell. And why did he want to sell it anyway? The manor was lovely, and the gardens around it were amazing. How could anyone get rid of it?

She glanced around the kitchen, which had been renovated very recently and very sensitively, she thought. There was lots of light and big windows. White cabinetry and polished wooden floors. A lovely, airy space.

Him wanting to sell, not only the house, but the forest too, mystified her. She'd asked him why, but he hadn't been in any mood to tell her, that had been clear. Was it money? Had he made bad investments somewhere? Then again, the articles she'd read about him all pointed to him being exceptionally good with money, so maybe not that. But what other reason could it be?

Not that she was interested. That was a side issue.

All she needed was his agreement not to sell it, and in order to get that, she needed to find out what he wanted. Except the only thing she could think of was the baby, and she couldn't—wouldn't—use her child in that way.

Perhaps she could guilt him into it by pointing out that Darkfell was his child's legacy, and getting rid of it was wrong. Surely, he couldn't argue with that. But…what if he did? What other things could she use?

Maude continued to stare fiercely out of the window as her thoughts spun.

What could she use to nudge him in the right direction? What did she have that he wanted, apart from the child?

You know damn well what he wants.

Her breath caught. Lying under him on the couch, her wrists tied with her own T-shirt, his dark eyes full of hunger as he looked down at her…

Her. He wanted her.

Heat returned, prickling over her skin once more as her thoughts spun a little faster, and this time she didn't force herself to stop thinking about it.

Could she use their chemistry to get him to keep Darkfell? Use his physical response to her in some way? Perhaps seduce him into keeping Darkfell? It was certainly worth considering. He had all the power here, that was the problem. He was her boss and a well-known, infamous billionaire playboy, while she was just a contract worker. Still, she wasn't without weapons. She wouldn't use the baby, but she could certainly use her femininity.

She'd never thought of her sexuality in that way before, mainly because she hadn't cared about her sexuality before. It had felt like one of those traps her grandparents had warned her about that could lead her down the wrong path if she gave into it. At that stage, she'd still been trying to be what they wanted, so she'd been a good girl and had concentrated on her schoolwork instead of boys. Then, when she'd gone to university and met the other Your Girl Friday women, the vagaries of sex and dating had felt too complicated. Sex had just seemed to make people unhappy and, anyway, she'd much rather be out in the woods than in some bar trying to pick up some guy.

But things were different now. He'd made them different. He'd woken something in her, something dark and hungry, and the thought of using that hunger to make him do whatever she wanted held a certain…appeal.

Careful. It might backfire on you.

Yes, that was a risk. She wanted him, too, and the tricky part was that, while she was fairly confident she could seduce him, she had no experience of staying in control herself.

And she had to stay in control. That was the only way with a man like him. He'd bound her hands that moment in the sitting room, and she'd felt strangely safe rather than afraid, but she didn't want that to happen again. Didn't want her own hunger to take the reins. She couldn't cede him any control, because once she did that, well…

You'd be powerless again.

A memory returned, of her standing by her grandparents' car where she'd been told to wait while they talked to her mother. Of her not knowing what was going on and trying to ignore the growing suspicion in her gut that, whatever it was, it wasn't going to be good. No one had told her what was happening. All she'd been told was that her grandparents were taking her out for an ice cream, and she was to go with them and not cause a commotion.

She'd stood by the car and watched as her mother had glanced once at her, shrugged, then walked away.

That had been the last time she'd seen Sonya.

Her grandparents had bought her the promised ice cream but then they'd told her that she would be living with them from now on. Then she'd been thrust into a new living arrangement, in an unfamiliar environment, with people she'd barely known. She'd cried, of course, heartbroken at being taken away from the commune and her mother. Her grandparents had ignored her the way they always did when she 'made a fuss'. She'd never felt so powerless and she was not going to let that happen again.

Just then, Polly came bustling into the kitchen, breaking the train of Maude's thoughts.

'Well, Mr Lancaster is on his way,' Polly said as she began opening cupboards and putting things away. 'He'll be staying a couple of nights.'

Maude was conscious of a little shock arrowing down her spine. 'H-he is?'

'Yes, just got a text from him.' Polly straightened and gave her a concerned look. She was a motherly woman and Maude liked her quite a bit. 'You're looking a bit peaky, love. Are you quite all right?'

The Harrises didn't know about her pregnancy. No one knew except the doctor and Dominic Lancaster, and Maude didn't particularly want to tell Polly now. Not when there were so many things undecided.

'I'm a bit tired.' She pushed the chair back and stood, picking up her laptop. 'I might go and have a lie-down.' She paused a moment. 'He won't want to see me, will he?'

Polly shook her head. 'Oh, no, I shouldn't think so. Not sure why he's here. Probably something to do with the sale.'

Maude stilled. 'You know he's planning on selling?'

'Oh, yes. He's been talking with John and me about it for a couple of months. A good thing if the manor goes to someone who will actually live here.' Polly pulled open the dishwasher and began unloading it. 'The house needs a family and Mr Lancaster isn't about to start one any time soon.'

Maude found her hand was creeping to her stomach again. 'You don't think he will?'

'No, love,' Polly said, her attention on the dishwasher. 'He's not a family man.'

She should go, let Polly continue cleaning up, but she didn't move. 'Do you…know him well?'

If Polly found her curiosity startling, she didn't show it. 'Known him going on about ten years now,' she said, methodically unloading some teacups. 'When John and I took over management here. This was his childhood home, apparently, but he never visits. He only comes for his midsummer parties and that's it.'

Maude's curiosity deepened. She hadn't known he'd grown up here at Darkfell. Interesting. And perhaps another thing she could use to get him to keep the place.

'Do you know why he's selling it?' she asked.

Polly shut the dishwasher. 'No and it's not my business either. John and I are due for retirement, so I won't be sorry. It's a big place to look after with just us.'

As if on cue, the rhythmic thump of helicopter rotors came drifting through the air, and Maude was conscious of a sudden electric thrill pulsing through her.

'Oh, that's him,' Polly said. 'Better get on with airing out the bedroom.' And she vanished out of the kitchen door.

Maude took a breath as the sound of the helicopter came closer and closer.

He was coming and he would want to talk to her, in which case she'd need to prepare herself, as well as decide what demands she was going to make. Because there *would* be some demands.

She just hoped he'd be prepared for them.

As his helicopter settled on the grassy lawn at the front of Darkfell Manor, Dominic stared grimly out of the window and wondered for the millionth time just what the hell he was doing.

He didn't need to visit his childhood home physically. He could have rung Maude and talked to her or sent her an email or even a text. Except he hadn't. He'd organised his helicopter and here he was, and he still didn't understand why.

He'd spent the past week keeping busy with client meetings and investigating a couple of new investment opportunities—something he normally loved doing. He'd also thrown himself into attending multiple parties, including the opening of an exclusive new club in London. There had been the usual celebrities, socialites, a few royals and captains of industry all in attendance. Again, usually something he enjoyed.

Yet as he'd sat in the VIP area with more than a few

beautiful women all vying for his attention, he'd felt...
dissatisfied. And, worse, bored. The same boredom that
had been dogging him for months, along with the same
restlessness. It was infuriating.

He'd wanted to enjoy himself with a few casual liai-
sons, yet every time he even looked at a woman, all he
could see was the challenging glint in Maude Braithwaite's brown eyes and the way her hand had curved
over her stomach. All he could think about was the feel
of her in the forest that night, and how then she'd looked
up at him when she'd been beneath him on the couch,
her face flushed with heat and passion...

None of the other women he'd met had that same
glint in their eyes, and while they definitely looked at
him with heat and passion, it didn't move him. It didn't
make him hard.

His nymph had put a spell on him and now she was
all he thought about.

Ringing her to discuss the baby hadn't even occurred
to him. Neither had simply sending her an email or a
text. All he'd thought was that any discussion with her
had to be conducted face to face, so he'd let Polly know
he'd be visiting, and now he was here, he wondered if
he'd made the right choice.

Then he wondered why the hell he was doubting himself, when he never had before.

It was her that was the issue. It was all her and the
baby.

He'd thought about the baby, too, in the past week.
About how he was going to be a father and what that
would look like. Not like his own father, that was for
sure. He wouldn't keep his child secreted away like an

afterthought. He wouldn't go away and leave them for weeks and months, rattling around in this big ancient house. And he certainly wouldn't be presenting them with itemised bills for their own upkeep or making them negotiate for everything they wanted.

The child would live with him in London and he'd give he or she whatever they wanted, whenever they wanted it. And as for Maude, well, she could come and live with them too. He hadn't had a mother, since his own had up and vanished, and he'd never known why she'd just walked away—his father had never mentioned it and Dominic had never asked—but maybe his life would have been less lonely, less difficult, if she'd stayed. He certainly wanted his own child to have their mother around.

One thing for certain, though: neither of them would live here.

The helicopter settled and Dominic leapt out, heading for the path that led to the groundskeeper's cottage rather than the manor, since he might as well get this meeting with Maude over and done with, and as soon as possible.

The cottage was a ridiculously picturesque brick building on the edge of the forest, not far from the manor house. It was small, with a slate roof and ivy climbing up the sides and pots of lavender just outside the front door.

He hadn't been here for years, he realised suddenly as he approached the cottage. Not since he was a boy. Craddock, who'd been his father's gamekeeper, had lived in it, and Dominic had loved visiting him, though Jacob had disapproved. He hadn't liked his son mixing with the staff.

Jacob would have a fit now, Dominic reflected as he knocked on the door, if he'd known that his son was now having a baby with said staff.

There was a pause, and he was about to knock again, when the door opened and Maude stood on the threshold, her warm brown eyes meeting his.

And he felt it again, that gut punch of desire, leaving him breathless, his heart racing in a way it hadn't raced for any of the women he'd surrounded himself with back in London.

His fingers itched to shove the door open, grab her and pull her close, press his mouth to hers and taste her again. But he crushed the urge. This was not about sex. This was about the child.

'May I come in?' he asked, when she didn't say anything.

'You didn't tell me you were coming,' she said, eyeing him.

'No,' he agreed. 'I didn't. Do you really want to have this discussion on the doorstep?'

She stared at him a moment longer, then turned without a word, and went down the little hallway. He stepped inside, closing the door behind him, then followed her through another doorway and into the tiny living area.

It was a cosy little room, with a sofa facing the fireplace and an armchair to the side. There were throws of various brightly coloured fabric draped everywhere and lots of mugs on the small coffee table in front of the sofa. Books were stacked in piles on every available surface, as well as magazines open at the crossword section. A comfortable room, full of cheerful clutter, that made him feel at ease, though he wasn't sure why.

Maude stood in front of the fireplace, her arms folded, regarding him warily. Her hair was loose and she was wearing a flowing, wraparound dress of deep scarlet that shouldn't have been so sexy, since it was very plain. Yet somehow it drew his attention to every one of her feminine curves, including the generous swell of her breasts and her little bump, making him feel once again that primal sense of possession.

Yours. She is yours.

He gritted his teeth, ignoring the thought. The baby was his. *She* wasn't.

'Why didn't you warn me that you were coming?' she said, as if *he* were the problem.

He sat on the arm of the sofa, ostensibly casual, trying to find his usual lazy, bored facade. 'Should I have?'

'I would have appreciated some preparation.'

'Preparation for what?'

She opened her mouth as if to speak, then, clearly thinking better of it, she shut it. But he didn't miss the way her gaze darted down over his chest and lower, before returning once again to his face. Colour bloomed in her cheeks and the little glints of gold in her eyes gleamed brighter, and the rush of possessiveness and desire tightened its grip on him.

She wanted him too, that was obvious.

'So,' she said after a long moment of silence. 'Are we going to have a discussion about the baby? Since I assume that's why you're here.'

Straight to business, was it? Probably a good thing, considering the attraction that he'd hoped would have eased in the week he'd been away apparently hadn't eased at all.

It irritated him, dug beneath his facade, made him want things he shouldn't and now he was starting to regret coming here. Why had he thought face to face was better? This could have been a phone call.

'There will be no discussion,' he said flatly. 'I have made my decision. The child will come to live with me in London.'

Hot temper leapt in her gaze. 'Absolutely not. You will not be taking my baby away from me.'

'I'm not going to be taking the baby away from you,' he said. 'You'll be coming too, naturally.'

Her arms dropped and she took a step towards him, every line of her radiating anger. 'No,' she snapped. 'I'm not going anywhere. The baby should be brought up here, in Darkfell, close to the forest, not in a city. Not in London.'

'As I said, this is not a discussion.' He tried to keep his tone mild and his expression bored. 'My son or daughter will be with me and since I will not be living here, neither will they.'

'Why do you think living in London is better than living here?'

'Why do you think living here is better than London?'

A moment of silence fell, tension seething in the room. She was breathing fast and he found his gaze drawn to the deep V of her neckline and the shadowed valley between her breasts. It wouldn't take much to get her naked. Just a tug on the tie holding her dress together and it would fall open…

Get your head out of the gutter.

Dominic gritted his teeth. 'You promised me you wouldn't argue. I distinctly remember that.'

Her chin jutted. 'That was when you said this would be a discussion and not just you telling me what to do.'

Taking a slow, even breath, Dominic gripped hard onto his temper. It was ludicrous that she should have such an effect on him and ludicrous that he should let her. He'd had decades of perfecting his control and he wasn't going to let one young woman get under his skin so easily no matter how lovely she was.

'Well, you can't stay here, nymph,' he said at length. 'I will be selling the manor once the baby's born, as I've already mentioned.'

Her eyes glittered with heat. 'Polly said this was your childhood home.'

'Yes,' he bit out, even more annoyed now. Polly should never have said anything. 'It is.'

'Then why do you want to sell it? Don't you want to pass it on to your child?'

'No.' The word was far more emphatic than he'd meant it to be. 'My child will have nothing to do with this place.'

'Why not? It's their legacy.'

Why was she asking so many questions? He didn't want to talk about Darkfell, especially not with the mouthful of angry, bitter words that had somehow gathered in response. In fact, it was surprising just how bitter and angry they were, considering all the time that had passed. His father shouldn't still have such a hold on him, not after so many years.

'It's not a legacy I would wish to pass on,' he said after a moment, choosing his words carefully.

She frowned, as if she found his response puzzling. 'Why not?'

He forced himself to smile. 'Let's just say my child-hood here wasn't a happy one and leave it at that.'

She studied him for a long moment, the temper dying slowly in her eyes. 'I…feel the same way about the city if you must know,' she said, a little hesitatingly. 'My mother used to live in a commune in Scotland, but my grandparents didn't approve of me being brought up there so they came and took me away to live with them.'

He could have sworn he wasn't curious about her, not in the slightest, and yet now he found himself studying her in much the same way as she'd studied him, as if she were something new and interesting he'd never seen be-fore. Strange when there was nothing new and interest-ing about people in his experience. They all wanted the same things, which pretty much boiled down to money, power, or sex. He didn't care to know about their motiva-tion for pursuing one or all of those things, not unless it applied to a deal he was doing, so it was quite astonish-ing to find himself almost intrigued by what she'd said.

Clearly being taken away to live with her grandpar-ents hadn't been a good experience. Was that why she was resisting him taking their child to live in London with him?

'I only want happiness for our child,' he said slowly. 'I don't want to take them away from you. A child needs a mother.'

Something shifted in her eyes, though he couldn't have said what. 'But I don't want to leave here,' she said. 'And I don't want to live in the city.'

Frustration coiled inside him, but he crushed it. 'Oh? Why not?'

'I love being part of nature. It's important. The trees

and the forests, all the wild places, are important. They're part of me. And I feel responsible for them. I want to protect them, and I want my child to learn how to protect them too.' As she spoke, her eyes glowed, the warm brown like a sun-dappled forest pool, glinting with gold and amber.

She meant every word, he could see that. There was a passion and a sincerity in the words and in her expression too, that tugged at something inside him, something he couldn't quite articulate.

There was no sincerity in his world, no honesty. It was all games and power-plays, all deals and money, smoke and mirrors. And as for passion, well, there was none of that either. Passion was a weakness, a vulnerability for someone to exploit for their own gain.

Looking at Maude now, all Dominic could think of was that she shouldn't tell him these things, shouldn't show him such a vulnerability, because—and he knew himself far too well—he'd use that passion and sincerity against her. Use them to get what he wanted, because what he wanted, he got. He didn't know why he cared, but he did.

'You shouldn't tell me these things, nymph,' he murmured softly. 'You shouldn't reveal your hand before you've sealed the deal.'

Her eyes narrowed. 'Why not?'

'Because now I know what cards you're holding, I can use that against you. For example, you want me to keep Darkfell? Very well, I will. On condition that you and the child come and live with me in London.'

CHAPTER SEVEN

THE LIVING ROOM of the cottage felt too small, too claustrophobic. Maude felt as if she couldn't get enough air. Dominic Lancaster was standing in the middle of the room, filling the entire space with the taut electricity of his presence, and it was hard for her to think.

She'd thought she'd been prepared for him, but of course she wasn't.

She'd hurried into the cottage as his helicopter had come in to land, racing into her bedroom to pull out one of the few dresses she owned that she could still wear, a red one Irinka had once told her had looked beautiful on her.

Certainly, when she'd pulled open the door to his knock and his gaze had dropped to the neckline of the dress, she'd felt a small burst of satisfaction. That was until she'd taken him in and realised that no amount of preparing herself for meeting him was going to be enough.

He was in a suit today, perfectly tailored to his tall, powerful figure. It was of dark grey, with a black business shirt, and with a silk tie of washed gold. Beautiful clothes for the most beautiful man.

And he was beautiful. Not a god of the forest today, but a god of industry, or business. Zeus presiding on

Olympus, using the power of his charisma and authority to dominate the other gods.

Her heart had begun to beat fast, and she'd forgotten everything she'd meant to do, all the demands she'd meant to make. She'd intended to take control of the conversation, but he'd taken it instead, laying out his demands and leaving her to protest in a pathetic knee-jerk reaction.

It made her feel childish to have to say no like that, but what else could she do? She'd told him why she wanted to stay here, had let some of her passion for the forest show in her voice and she'd thought that might sway him.

But it hadn't, she could see it in his eyes.

He'd been right to warn her. She'd let slip too much and he was far too astute a businessman not to use that against her. Her plans for seducing him into not selling the house and leaving their baby with her probably wouldn't work either, not when she didn't have the experience to play that game.

There is another option: refuse to play.

The thought whispered in her head, appealing to the broad streak of stubborn inside her. He was bending her to his will with all this talk of deals, trying to make her use his language, operate by his rules. And she'd fallen into it without thinking.

But she wasn't a dealmaker and she didn't negotiate. She was a free spirit and he couldn't force her to be what he wanted her to be. She had to be herself.

Maude took a breath. 'No,' she said.

'No?' One winged black brow rose. 'What do you mean no?'

'I mean, I'm not coming to live with you anywhere.'

His dark eyes glittered. 'Then I will sell Darkfell.'

'Fine. Sell it.' She lifted her chin, her heart beating suddenly far too fast. 'I'll continue to live in the cottage.'

'I have money, nymph. More money and power than you can imagine. You think I won't use them to—'

'Do it,' she interrupted, digging down into that stubborn streak of hers. 'Get your lawyers. Sell this house. Have the police come to the door and try to arrest the woman pregnant with your child.'

The lines of his face had hardened, the air in the sitting room full of his thick, crackling anger. He looked like Zeus ready to pick up his thunderbolt and hurl it straight at her.

It was exhilarating to affect him this way, to make his bored, jaded mask slip a little.

'I'm not playing your game,' she said into the seething, tense silence. 'I won't. I've done what other people wanted me to do all my life and I'm not doing it now. This is too important.'

'Important to whom?' There was a certain lethal softness in his voice. 'Is this little performance really for your child's benefit or for your own?'

That caught at her in a place she wasn't expecting, a vulnerable place, making a thread of doubt wind through her. This was supposed to be about her child and yet…

You were brought up in Earthsong by your mother, because she wanted to stay. It wasn't about what was best for you, was it?

Selfish, that was what her grandparents had always said about her mother. Selfish of Sonya to bring Maude up in a place where there was no formal schooling and no other children, either. Living in the commune had been lonely, and Sonya had left a large portion of Maude's care with other people, if any were around. Most of the time she'd been left on her own.

Was she the one being selfish now? With her own child? Forcing her or him into a way of life that they might not necessarily want or might not be the best for them?

Maude turned around abruptly, facing the fireplace, not wanting her doubt to show, and especially not since he'd already warned her once about that.

She didn't want to be a mother like her own, who'd cared more about herself and what she wanted than she had about what was right for Maude. So…maybe her child would be better off in London. Dominic could certainly give him or her a much better life than Maude could give them on her own. And living in London didn't mean they had to be apart from nature. There were plenty of woods and lakes and wild places that were within easy reach of London, as he'd already said.

Abruptly, the familiar, intoxicating scent of the forest surrounded her and she knew he was there. She could sense him standing behind her and close. Like one of those mighty oaks in the forest, tall and strong. And she had the oddest urge to lean back into him and take some of his strength for herself, because she was coming to the end of hers and pure stubbornness wasn't a good enough reason to keep fighting him.

'Maude,' he said quietly. 'Tell me why this is so important to you.'

Dominic had made an error somewhere along the line and he knew it. He'd known it the moment she'd turned away suddenly, his little barb about her passionate outburst obviously landing somewhere painful.

He hadn't known what hurting her would do to him, because if he'd known, he wouldn't have done it. He hadn't expected to feel as if he'd kicked something small and vulnerable, and purely for cruelty's sake.

He couldn't believe he'd done the same thing as he had last week, letting himself be drawn into a fruitless argument because she was so stubborn, and then nearly losing his temper because she wouldn't give in and because no one said no to him.

The problem was, she'd called his bluff. She'd absolutely refused to negotiate, leaving him no choice but to bring out the threat of lawyers, knowing, even as he'd said it, that he wasn't going to do that. He wasn't going to tear the child away from her or trespass her from Darkfell.

He wanted to sell this place, that was true, get rid of the last vestiges of his father, but it surely didn't matter when he sold it. It wasn't as if he needed the money. He was insisting purely because she aggravated him so much.

He was letting his emotions get the better of him.

He wasn't in the habit of caring about other people's feelings, so it was odd to care about hers. Or at least to have her hurt bother him as much as it did. Perhaps it was because of that passion, that sincerity. The honesty burning in her eyes as she'd told him that nature, the forest, was important to her.

It was foreign to him, that honesty, that sincerity. In the past, in the boardroom, they had been ammunition in the negotiating war, and he'd used both to win. But he wasn't in a boardroom now, and she wasn't a businessperson who knew the rules of engagement.

She was pregnant and it wasn't a deal they were negotiating, but what would happen when their child was born. She was right, this was important, and they needed to find an understanding between them, not relentless arguing.

So his request to know why she was so insistent about staying here had been a start of the bridge they had to build between them, a small olive branch to begin with. Also, he was curious.

She didn't move and he realised he was closer to her than he should be. Enough to be aware of the scent of lavender that seemed to come from her hair and another delicate, very feminine scent that was uniquely her own.

It made his mouth water, woke everything male in him into a state of almost painful alertness.

'I grew up close to nature,' she said, without turning around. 'I spent a lot of time in the commune's gardens and in the woods nearby. It was a…child's paradise. The commune didn't have a school or lessons of any kind, so I was free to follow my own interests. Then my grandparents took me away to live with them. And there were schools and lessons and timetables and…rules. I tried to live with them, tried to fit in, but it never felt the same as being in the commune. It never felt like…home. Not the way the forest does.'

Finally, she turned around and looked up at him, her brown eyes dark, the forest pool shadowed. 'I wanted that for our child. I wanted him or her to experience the same freedom I had at Earthsong, to not be bound by rules and timetables, even if it's only for a short time.' Slowly the gold in her eyes began brightening. 'It's important for our future society that we come to an understanding with nature, with this planet we live on. Because this is our home, and we need to take care of it.'

Dominic found himself momentarily transfixed, caught by the passion in her voice and the glitter of it in her eyes. And he realised, almost with shock, that although she'd revealed a significant vulnerability to him, he wasn't going to exploit it for his own gain, use it against her to get what he wanted.

And not only he wouldn't—he *couldn't.*

She believed what she said, believed in it totally, and her refusal to play the little game he'd started made him feel something akin to shame for his own part in it. She had more integrity than he did, it seemed, and part of him admired her for it.

'Then,' he said quietly, 'you should stay here.'

She blinked, as if she didn't quite understand what he'd said. 'You mean stay here? In the cottage?'

'Yes.'

'But what about selling Darkfell? I thought you were adamant the child has to live with you.'

'I'll hold off selling the house for now.' He was still standing far too close to her, and it was all he could do to keep his gaze on her face and not the neckline of her dress. 'All of this is a moot point until the child is born anyway. We can decide what the future will look like then.'

Shock rippled over her features and he couldn't deny that pleased him. 'I don't understand. What changed your mind?'

'You did,' he said simply.

'But I didn't offer you anything.'

'You did, though. You offered me your honesty and your sincerity, and I found that a…compelling argument.'

Her forehead creased. 'Why?'

'Because honesty is a scarce commodity in my world. So is sincerity. It's refreshing.'

She studied him for a long moment, the currents of her emotions shifting and changing in her eyes. 'It wasn't honesty that I was going to offer you,' she said at last.

A soft husk now threaded through her voice, making everything in him go very still. 'Oh?' he murmured. 'And what was it that you were going to offer me?'

Colour flushed her cheeks. 'You changed your mind without it, so I don't need to offer it now.'

A sharp electric jolt went through him, as if he were a hunter and had suddenly caught the scent of prey. Surely she could not be saying what he thought she was saying? 'Now who's playing games?' he said softly. 'Tell me.'

Her mouth curved in a smile that maddened him, as if she knew a secret that he didn't, which was impossible. Because if, as he suspected, she'd been intending to offer him her body, then there was nothing he didn't know. He'd been playing the game of sex and seduction for decades now and he knew everything there was to know about it. Certainly more than this little nymph did.

'If I tell you, that'll leave me with nothing to use against you later.' Her gaze dropped to his mouth and then back up again. 'I need to have something in reserve.'

Her skin was warm, her scent utterly intoxicating. There was something about it that seemed to grab him by the throat and not let go.

'If it is what I think it is, then you're not the only one with a weapon,' he murmured, lowering his head until his mouth was bare inches from hers. 'You have to be careful, nymph. If you play with fire, you might get yourself burned.'

Her eyes, so close to his, darkened and, as he watched, the lush softness of her mouth opened slightly. 'I don't mind,' she whispered. 'Especially if you burned with me.'

Again, there was that honesty, reaching inside him as much as her scent did. Though it didn't grip him by the throat so much as it wrapped long fingers around his heart. And he didn't know why.

Another woman would have kept playing with him and he would have enjoyed it. He would have won in the end, of course, because he always did, taking things to their logical conclusion, which would be in the bedroom.

But Maude wasn't playing now. She'd given up the game, even though she'd barely started, and now had handed the win to him. Yet he couldn't shake the feeling that he hadn't won at all, that she had.

Heat glittered in her eyes, and hunger. For him. She didn't look away and she didn't try to hide it. She wanted him and he felt a strange sort of protectiveness well up inside him in response.

'You shouldn't look at me like that,' he said. 'You shouldn't show any kind of vulnerability to a man like me.'

'Why not?'

'I already told you. I'm a businessman and I'll exploit any weakness I find if it serves my interests and gets me what I want.'

'Would you though? Would you really?'

It was a genuine question. He could see it in her eyes. 'You put your hand over your stomach last week,' he couldn't help but point out. 'And you told me not to use our child as a bargaining chip. So you tell me. Would I?'

She studied him for a long time, desire bright in her gaze and yet also, shining through that, a sharply acute intelligence that made something in his heart skip a beat.

You want her to say, No, you wouldn't.

He wasn't sure what that thought had to do with anything. Because he knew the truth, which was yes, of course he would. He'd exploit any weakness, because, like it or not, that was the lesson he'd learned from his father. That was how he'd survived.

And it still hadn't been good enough for him.

The thought was snide, stealing through his brain, but he shoved it aside. Then he let go of her and stepped back, because maybe, after all, he didn't want to know what kind of man she thought he was.

'Don't answer that,' he said smoothly. 'And I should leave. You're a pretty thing, but I've already had everything you have to offer. I don't need to revisit it.'

It was a cruel thing to say, but he had to put some distance between them. She also needed to know that he wouldn't allow anyone to have power over him that he didn't grant them. And the only thing he'd granted her was that she could stay here. He hadn't given anything up.

He thought she would back away, thought that she would be hurt, and he'd intended both. Except she didn't back away and it wasn't hurt that glittered in her eyes, but anger.

'Is that right?' She reached down to the tie of her dress and casually pulled it. 'I suppose you won't care about a reminder, then.'

The fabric fell slowly open, revealing the fact that she was wearing nothing underneath it. Not a stitch. Only warm golden skin, pink nipples and the sweetest thatch of golden curls between her thighs. Only the swell of her stomach where their baby lay.

Your baby.

She lifted her chin and stared straight at him, openly challenging. And Dominic found that he'd been right, she *had* won this little game they were playing, and that he didn't know quite as much about sex and seduction as he'd thought he did.

Because right now, he couldn't move. He couldn't breathe. Desire and hunger had tightened their grip around his throat and were slowly, relentlessly squeezing. The raw possessiveness of that night in the forest was welling up inside him, an animal feeling, turning him into nothing but instinct.

He knew he should turn around and walk away, prove to her once and for all that she had no power over him, and especially not sexual power. *He* was the master of that, not her, and yet...

She let the dress fall slowly off her shoulders and flutter to the ground, and then she closed the distance he'd put between them, not once taking her gaze from his. As bold as she had been that night in the woods, only this time it was bright daylight and he could see her. He could see every bloody inch.

Christ. He wanted her.

She halted in front of him, and laid one small hand on his chest. 'I think you're a liar, Dominic Lancaster,' she murmured. 'I think revisiting it is exactly what you want to do.'

CHAPTER EIGHT

MAUDE WASN'T QUITE sure what she was doing. Somehow the conversation had got away from her and somehow her control had got away from her, too. Somehow he'd taken it and he'd done it simply by existing. By being close. By telling her she could stay at Darkfell, that he wouldn't sell it after all, and without demanding anything in return.

Her honesty, that was what she'd given him apparently, and that was what he'd been happy with, or so he'd said.

Except she didn't believe him. He'd told her that he was a businessman and that he exploited every weakness, and yet he hadn't exploited hers. He could have used her love of the forest against her to get her to do anything he wanted, but he hadn't.

She knew what he wanted though, and a part of her wanted him to admit it. To test whether she actually had the power she thought she did, power over him. He'd tried to distance her with words, but he hadn't meant them, she knew that. Not when she could see the blatant heat in his eyes.

It was bold of her to strip naked before him, but it wasn't anything she hadn't done before. He'd seen her by the pool and, in the forest that night, he'd run his hands over every inch of her. So she felt no embarrassment or shame, even though perhaps she should have felt both.

She only wanted to see if she was as powerful as she felt in this moment. Prove to herself, and maybe to him too, that the power she remembered from that night in the forest was still hers. The power of a primal goddess.

She needed it. Needed to know once and for all that she could unsettle him as badly as he unsettled her.

Desire flared in his dark gaze now, like embers of a banked fire igniting into life, and it made her heart race. The heat of his body burned through the cotton of his shirt and into her fingertips where they rested on his chest. He smelled so good, like all the wild places deep in the forest, where she could lose herself if she wanted...

'You shouldn't do this,' he said softly.

'Why not?' She lifted her other hand and placed that on his chest too, testing the hard muscle she could feel beneath his clothes. 'It's nothing we haven't done before.'

'Sex will...complicate matters.'

'Really? I thought you were an infamous playboy.' She stepped even closer, the tips of her breasts grazing the cotton of his shirt. 'You're not supposed to care about sex complicating things.'

The fire in his eyes leapt higher and yet still he didn't move. 'Consider the last time we did this.'

'I am considering it.' She ran her fingertips down the front of his shirt, to the waistband of his trousers. 'What's the problem? It's not as if I'm going to get pregnant again.'

The breath hissed in his throat as her fingertips dipped

lower, over the hard length of him she could feel through the wool of his trousers.

'I have never been a possessive man.' His dark voice had roughened. 'But I should warn you that I'm feeling very possessive now. I'm not sure you would appreciate me wanting to own you.'

He was doing it again, trying to put distance between them. Trying to frighten her, she thought. Sadly for him, she wasn't easily frightened.

She looked up into his eyes as she let her fingers trace the outline of his hard shaft, watching the flames in his eyes leap even higher. 'I think you're afraid,' she murmured. 'Is it me you're afraid of?'

He bared his teeth. 'I didn't say you could touch me, nymph.'

It wasn't exactly an admission, but he'd betrayed himself all the same. He *was* afraid, though what of she didn't know. Because as she'd already told him, he was an infamous playboy and sex was the one thing he shouldn't be afraid of.

Maude dropped her hands and stepped back. 'That's fine. I don't have to touch you.' She turned. 'I'll get my—'

But she didn't have a chance to finish. His fingers closed hard around her upper arms and he pulled her around to face him. 'I didn't say leave,' he growled, then his mouth was on hers in a kiss so hot and hungry, she almost lost her mind.

Then again, perhaps she'd lost it already, because the moment his lips met hers, she was up on her toes, sliding her arms around his neck, pressing her body against his as she opened her mouth to him, letting him take anything and everything he wanted.

Heat exploded between them, a conflagration burning high.

His hands came down on her hips, gripping her, turning her so that the couch was nearby and then he took her down onto it, crushing her beneath him. He was a solid, hot wall of muscle and there were too many clothes between them. She clawed at his shirt, ripping it open, and he cursed, grabbing her hands and holding them away from him.

'No,' he said roughly, black eyes molten. 'If you want this, then I'm in charge.'

She sucked in a breath, her heartbeat wild, her body trembling with need. It hadn't been like this between them in the woods that night. No one had been in charge then, they'd both taken what they'd wanted and it had been so good. But then that night they hadn't known each other, hadn't known what would happen and nothing had existed then but the moment.

They couldn't have that moment again. It was gone. And her god of the forest was now hidden behind the mask of Dominic Lancaster. A mask he seemed very set on keeping.

She wanted to ignore him, keep tearing at his clothes until she'd uncovered the man he was behind the mask, all raw heat and primal power, nothing but glorious essence, but there was iron in his black eyes. He wasn't going to yield. If she wanted this, she was going to have to surrender to him.

It wasn't a choice. She wanted him and if this was the only way he could give himself to her, then she'd take it.

So she nodded, the resistance bleeding out of her.

He shifted, rising up to his knees. With calm, deliberate movements, his black gaze not leaving hers, he undid his tie, pulled it off then leaned forward, looping it around her wrists and pulling it tight. Then he lifted her hands and took them up and over her head, pressing them back down onto the couch cushions.

She took a gasping breath as she lay there, looking up into black eyes full of flames. He stretched himself over her, his big, long body all muscled power and heat, and, really, she should have been frightened by how helpless she was. He could hurt her, he could do anything he wanted with her, and she could do nothing to stop him.

Except she wasn't afraid and she didn't feel helpless. He wanted her, his desire bright in his eyes, and that was where her power lay. In surrendering to him, in giving him her trust.

A strange thing to think about a man she didn't really know. Then again, it wasn't Dominic Lancaster she was surrendering to, but the man he was beneath that. The man she'd met in the forest that night.

That man hadn't hurt her, hadn't done anything she hadn't wanted. That man had given her everything she'd demanded and then had demanded the same of her. There had been nothing between them that night, nothing held back, nothing hidden. Trust given and pleasure received.

He still hadn't moved, searching her face. 'What are you thinking about? Are you afraid?'

'No,' she said truthfully.

'Why not? Some women would be.'

'They might, but… I trust you.'

His body tensed, something moving in his eyes, gone too fast for her to read. 'And why would you do that?'

'That night in the forest. We were strangers and yet there was trust between us. And you gave me no reason to regret it.'

His black gaze was pinned to hers. 'But we're not in the forest now.'

'I know, but I think you're still the same man.' She shifted beneath him, watching the flames in his eyes leap again. 'You don't need to hide him. Not from me.'

He stared at her silently, his gaze boring into hers and he didn't move. Not even when she lifted her bound hands and looped them around his neck. Not even when she pulled him down and kissed his beautiful mouth, giving him everything the way she had that night, holding nothing back.

Perhaps it was then that the mask of Dominic Lancaster slipped, because he made a sound deep in his throat, and abruptly his tongue was in her mouth, exploring, tasting, devouring, his hand between her thighs, stroking, exploring.

She gasped as his fingers slid over her slick flesh, teasing her as his mouth ravaged hers. There was no finesse to it, no art, but she didn't care. They hadn't had any the last time in the forest and they didn't have it now. But she didn't need it. She needed only him.

He paused long enough to open his trousers and then he was down on her again, holding her hips down on the couch cushions as he pushed into her in one deep, hard surge.

She groaned, wrapping her legs around his waist, her hands gripping hard to his shoulders, nails digging into the fabric of the jacket he still wore. He slid a hand beneath her rear, tilting her, sliding deeper and she made another sound, pleasure spreading through her like a wild, dark fire.

He didn't speak and neither did she. It was as if they couldn't talk again until this chemistry or need or whatever it was had burned itself out. She could only gasp as he rocked deeper and harder, her legs tight around him as the pleasure climbed higher and higher.

He kissed her neck and she felt the sharp edge of his teeth against her skin. It made her shudder. Made her remember that night again, and how they'd connected. At a base level, at essence, the both of them animals in the dark, their civilised skins left far behind.

She wanted that again so she turned her head to find his mouth, kissing back hungrily and hard, and then he was moving faster, and the pleasure was tightening, the net it had caught her in constricting around her. She didn't want it to end so soon, and yet she wasn't going to be able to last, she knew it.

His hand was down between them again, giving her that last bit of friction, and then the ecstasy caught her, dark and hot, and relentless as the tide.

Maude cried out as it hit, shaking and shaking, feeling his movements get wilder and almost out of rhythm until he lowered his head and buried his face in her neck, a groan of release escaping him, too.

Dominic lay there, knowing he was likely crushing her, yet utterly unable to move. It had been a long time since an orgasm had stunned him like that, if one ever had. But no, that night in the forest he'd been stunned, he remembered. Apparently being stunned was a theme with Maude.

Aftershocks of pleasure pulsed through him, the sweet, musky scent of sex and her filling his senses.

He hadn't meant to break like that so completely and maybe he should have been worried about how easily he had, but with the most blissful post-orgasmic sense of satiation filling him, he honestly couldn't bring himself to care.

He'd thought binding her hands would give him some control over the chemistry that had burned white-hot between them, at least until she'd told him that she trusted him. And then proved it.

It had been a gift, that trust. It had reminded him of that night with her, where they hadn't needed anything but each other. No rules, no barriers, and no reason not to give each other everything.

There had been such simplicity in that, and he'd realised as he'd looked down into her eyes that he wanted that simplicity again.

And she'd given it to him with no deals, no quid pro quo. She'd offered him pleasure, given him all her passion, holding nothing back, and, yes, it had been simple.

But he could feel the hard swell of her stomach between them, where his child lay, and that made this whole situation anything but simple.

He shifted off her, gathering her in close so that they were lying on the couch with her half on him, and then glanced down at the rounded curve of her belly. She said nothing, her eyes still half closed.

Feeling oddly hesitant, he reached down to trace that curve, touch where his child lay. It was a strange feel-

ing to know that between them they'd created this little
life, who now lay still, waiting to be born. Then, as he
was wondering that, another feeling swept over him, the
knowledge, sure and deep, that he would do anything
to protect that little life. Anything at all, even give up
his own.

He'd always been a selfish man. His father had taught
him that selfishness was the only way to get ahead, and
that was a quality Dominic had had to cultivate if he'd
wanted to be the heir Jacob had wanted him to be.

It had never been something he'd questioned… Until
now.

His child was more important, he understood. More
important than anything else in the entire world, and
certainly more important than he was.

Did your father ever feel this way about you?

The thought crept through his head before he could
stop it. And of course, he already knew the answer. No,
Jacob hadn't felt that way about Dominic. Because if he
had, he'd never have made Dominic's life such a misery.

Maude shifted and put her hand over his, moving it
slightly, and to his utter amazement he felt something
flutter against his palm. He looked at her in shock. 'Is
that…?'

Her lovely mouth curved in the most beautiful smile
he'd ever seen. 'Yes. I felt him kick for the first time a
couple of days ago.'

Instantly Dominic sat up, cold all over. 'I was lying
on you. I could have hurt—'

'No,' Maude interrupted. 'You didn't hurt him.'

'Him,' Dominic heard himself repeat stupidly.

She nodded. 'I had a scan last week. I wanted to know

the gender. I…was going to ask you if you wanted to know, but…'

He. Dominic was going to have a son.

Yet another feeling washed over him, colder this time and full of doubt. This baby was getting more real by the moment and he hadn't once thought about what kind of father he'd be. The baby had been only a thought, an abstract, but now…

It hit him then, like a thunderbolt straight from heaven, the certainty that he would *never* be the kind of father his own had been. His son would not be left alone, his son would not be handed an itemised account of the cost of his upbringing. Like Jacob, Dominic had never wanted children, but unlike Jacob, he would embrace being a father. He would give his child everything he'd never had growing up, attention, protection, tenderness and care.

This would be the purpose of his life now, because this was the thing he'd been looking for, the next challenge to throw himself into, and he would not fail. He couldn't.

'I'm sorry,' Maude said.

Dominic looked at her, for a second not processing what she'd said, his head too full of the epiphany he'd just had. 'For what?'

'For not telling you that we were having a boy.'

He blinked, her face suddenly leaping into focus. Delicate features, tawny gold brows, warm honey-golden skin, dark gold hair in soft waves around her face. His nymph.

Your child. Your woman.

The power of the thunderbolt was resonating inside

him, spreading out from the baby, spreading wider, becoming possessive and intense. Part of him wanted to deny it, because he never felt that strongly about anything and never wanted to, except it was there in his heart, as relentless and inevitable as the tide.

This woman and the child she carried were his now, and it was time for him to claim both of them.

Maude was looking at him with some concern. 'Are you okay?' she asked, sitting up slowly, her hair falling around her shoulders.

She was astonishingly lovely, naked like this, with the beautiful swell of her stomach beneath her full breasts, and his breath caught.

She was why he'd been so restless and tense. *She* was why he didn't want any other woman. Which made *her* the answer to the problem.

If he wanted any peace at all, he needed to be sleeping with her. No longer resisting her, but indulging himself fully and to the utmost, and with no one else but her.

It felt foreign to think that, to limit himself that way, yet, instead of feeling constrained, he suddenly felt as if he'd been given a freedom of sorts. As if it had been the resistance that had constrained him rather than the other way around.

'I'm fine.' His voice sounded rough even to his own ears. 'But I have decided something.'

Her gaze flickered and he could see the apprehension in it. She thought he was going to demand again her presence in London, that was obvious. Well, she was wrong. He'd already made that demand and she'd protested, digging in when he'd threatened, and he didn't want to make that mistake again.

Demanding things from her didn't feel right, not after what she'd given him just now on the couch, the gift of her trust. And it was a gift. She'd given him the same that night in the woods back then, but he hadn't realised its value until now. And now he knew...well. He wasn't going to throw that away.

'I understand why you don't want to come to London,' he said. 'In which case, I'll come here.'

Her eyes widened. 'What?'

'I'm tired of London. I'd rather be here where I can keep an eye on the baby, and where I can have you.'

A flush crept through her cheeks. 'Have me?'

He held her gaze steadily. 'I've been thinking about you for months, nymph. Thinking about that night. I tried to put it out of my head when I woke up and found you gone, because I thought I wouldn't see you again. Then there you were, swimming in the forest pool, and I knew it was you instantly.' He paused, letting her see that he was telling the truth. 'I haven't had a woman since you and I find I don't want one. The only woman I want at the moment is you.'

A shocked expression rippled over her face. 'But... why?'

'I don't know,' he admitted. 'You're unlike any woman I've ever met, and perhaps it's only physical chemistry, but... What I do know is that it's been impossible for me to think of anyone else.'

Her lashes lowered abruptly, veiling her gaze, but she didn't move. 'So...what are you thinking?'

'No, don't do that,' he ordered softly. 'Look at me.'

Her lashes lifted and she met his gaze, apprehension in it.

'You don't want me here?' he asked bluntly. 'Because if so, that might be too bad since I own this house and the grounds.'

'It's not that.' Her chin firmed in that stubborn way he was beginning to recognise. 'I'm not your girlfriend or your wife, and I don't want to be either of those things. And I won't be your...' she made a gesture with her hand '...brood mare that services you whenever you're in the mood, either.'

Strangely, now he'd made a decision, the restless tension that had been gripping him receded. Perhaps it was merely the aftermath of his rather stupendous orgasm, but he felt lazy and sated, and the sight of her pretty golden eyes sparking with temper amused him rather than annoyed him.

'A brood mare,' he said slowly as if tasting the words. 'Yes, you'd look very pretty with a halter on, in a stall. Though I think you'd bite so maybe you should have a muzzle.'

She scowled. 'I wasn't joking.'

He let his amusement go. 'I know. So how about this? I will live in the manor and you live in the cottage. We will have our own lives. But at night... I could sleep with you or you could sleep with me, I don't mind which.'

She sniffed. 'You're assuming I'm going to want to sleep with you.'

Dominic moved his hand slowly, giving her plenty of time to pull away, sliding his palm beneath one round breast and cupping it gently. 'You don't want to sleep with me?' he asked casually, stroking his thumb back and forth over her nipple in a lazy movement. 'Because of course, if you don't want to, I won't make you.'

She swallowed, her eyelashes falling again, a soft breath escaping her. 'I… I…might not want you.'

'You might not?' Very gently he pinched the tip of her nipple, making her gasp and shudder. 'You'd better be clear about this. I wouldn't want to make any mistakes.'

She'd begun to press herself into his palm, arching her back slightly. 'I mean…there might be times when… I don't want you at all…'

'Of course,' he murmured. 'In which case I'll respect your wishes. But you're a passionate creature and I think those times will be few and far between.' He bent and gently circled her nipple with his tongue, before drawing back and blowing gently on it, making her shiver all over. 'Don't you?'

She gave him a frustrated look from underneath her lashes. 'You're manipulating me.'

'Yes,' he said, unrepentant because he was getting hard again and all he could think about was being inside her. 'But all you need to do is say no and I'll stop.' He took his hand away. 'Shall I stop?'

Her chin jutted as she glowered at him. 'Did I say stop?'

She looked adorable just then, pink with arousal, golden eyes glittering with desire and frustration, and he couldn't help but take her hand and guide it down to the front of his trousers. 'Just remember that manipulation can go both ways,' he murmured. 'And what works on you, also works on me.'

Her expression changed, becoming thoughtful, and he couldn't stop the heated rush of anticipation that flooded through him in response.

You want her to have that power over you?

Not exactly. But he wasn't averse to it either. She had no guile, this woman. She wasn't going to use it against him, not the way he would. And it was odd to think that even as she'd given him her trust, he was giving her his.

'Try it,' he invited. 'Try it on me and see what happens.'

She didn't need to be asked twice and soon proved his point, much to their mutual satisfaction.

CHAPTER NINE

MAUDE CHECKED HER WATCH. It was nearly twelve-thirty, the time Dominic had told her to meet him by the waterfall. Apparently, he had a 'surprise' for her and she'd been thinking about it all day, conscious of a building anticipation that felt a lot like excitement.

She'd been experiencing that more and more often in the past week, since Dominic had relocated himself to Darkfell Manor.

When he'd first suggested living at Darkfell, she'd been instantly wary. She hadn't been sure why he'd wanted to be here for a start, and then she'd wondered if it was so he could be a control freak about the baby. Certainly, after the day they'd ended up having sex on the couch in the cottage, and he'd felt the baby kick, he'd suddenly started deciding things and expecting her to go along with them.

He was a man who liked to take charge of a situation, and yes, she'd been wary about what would happen when he arrived here. Not that she'd had a choice in the matter. He did own the place after all.

She'd thought the instant he'd moved back, he'd be at her door, demanding sex, since that seemed to be the implication after he'd seduced her again on the couch. Yet…he hadn't.

In fact, the day he'd moved in, he'd stayed in the manor all day and she hadn't seen him at all. She hadn't seen him the next day, either. The third day had come around with still no sign of him, and she'd felt…disappointed. And she'd hated that she'd felt disappointed, because what did it matter if he clearly wasn't as desperate for her as he'd led her to believe? It *didn't* matter. Not to her. She'd gone without sex long enough that another couple of days weren't going to make a difference.

It wasn't until the third night that he'd appeared on her doorstep. She'd opened the door to find him lounging against the doorframe, and all he'd done was raise an enquiring brow. That had been enough to find herself in his arms, her mouth on his, hungrily devouring him as he'd devoured her.

They'd spent the night together every night since then, and usually they didn't talk. They gave in to their own mutual hunger and let that guide them instead, and in the morning she always woke up to find herself alone.

That was good. That was what she preferred. Living her life bound by nobody's rules but her own.

Except she found herself looking forward to the evenings when he'd visit more and more. And sometimes, when they were in each other's arms, she'd catch herself wondering what he was thinking. Wondering why he wanted to sell Darkfell. Why his childhood hadn't been a happy one and why he didn't want to talk about it.

Maybe it was a good thing to be curious about him, though. She was having his child after all, and she should know more about him than that he was a billionaire with a hugely successful investment firm, who was also very good in bed.

She didn't know what this promised 'surprise' was, since this was the first time he'd wanted to see her during the day, but she could feel the familiar breathless excitement that she felt every night the moment she heard his knock on the cottage door.

Did he want to repeat their night in the forest, but during the day? Was that what the surprise was? If so, she wasn't averse to it, not at all.

She walked along the little path that led to the grassy clearing with its waterfall and pool, the trees eventually giving way and opening out ahead of her.

Dominic was already there, sitting on a blanket that had been laid out on the grass. Also on the blanket was a wicker basket with the top open, and he was getting out various containers of food.

A picnic.

Maude usually had picnics by herself—if you could call eating an apple beside the waterfall a picnic—and preferred it that way, since it allowed her to bask in the forest silence and peace in way she couldn't if anyone else was around.

So it was strange to feel a little shock of pleasure to find him sitting on a blanket, arranging containers of food, and she wasn't sure why. She was hungry admittedly, so the food was welcome, but it was clear that sex wasn't on the menu—or maybe not straight away—and that was unexpected.

He looked up as she approached and his mouth curved, and the smile he gave her was so warm and so unbelievably attractive, it felt as if her heart had turned a somersault.

'Afternoon, nymph,' he said and then gestured to the food. 'Polly made far too much lunch so, of course, I thought you might like to share a picnic with me.'

Not many people in Maude's life had ever done anything for her. Not her mother and not her grandparents. Her mother had remembered the odd birthday, and her grandparents had at least made sort of an effort for Christmas, but generally she had been expected to follow the rules and look after herself.

That Dominic had decided to put on a picnic for her, and at her favourite place in the woods, made her chest go tight for a second.

'Oh,' she said, trying hard to ignore how that tightness had crept into her throat. 'This is…lovely.'

He patted the blanket next to him. 'Sit and I'll get you something to eat. It's all pregnancy friendly, I made sure.'

She settled down on the blanket where he'd indicated, sudden anxiety clutching at her. 'Did you tell Polly about—?'

'No, I didn't.' His dark eyes searched her face. 'Not yet anyway. Are you worried about people knowing?'

She didn't want to be worried, and yet she still hadn't told anyone and she supposed there was a reason for that. A reason she hadn't wanted to talk about it with anyone else yet.

'I suppose I am,' she said after a moment. 'My grandparents at least. They're very old-fashioned and very strict. Mum was a single mother and they didn't like that, so I'm very sure they won't like me being one either.'

He took a delicious-looking sandwich out of a container, put in on a plate, then handed the plate to her. 'Why do you care?' he asked. 'It's your life and being a single mother isn't an issue these days.'

Good point. She didn't know why she cared. It wasn't as if they'd been very understanding of her growing up. They'd tried to do their best for her, she knew that, but still. They'd taken her from her mother on the pretext of wanting to give her a better life, yet she hadn't been happy. Apparently happiness wasn't included in a better life.

'They promised me a piece of land as a rewilding project,' she said, picking up the sandwich. 'And I'm pretty sure if they find out I'm pregnant, they'll change their minds about giving it to me.'

He gave her an enigmatic look. 'You can find a piece of land anywhere to rewild. You don't need that one, do you?'

She took a bite out of the sandwich and chewed slowly. It was indeed as delicious as it looked. 'It's a gift,' she said after she'd swallowed her food. 'I don't have money enough to buy my own.'

Dominic's gaze remained enigmatic.

He was casual today, in black jeans and a loose sweatshirt the same deep green as the forest behind him. The colour suited his olive skin and the deep, dark brown of his eyes. He looked on the surface like a civilised man having a picnic in the grass and yet there was another man who looked out from behind his eyes. Passionate, raw. Possessive and feral almost.

The man he was in her bed every night.

She could see that man now, glittering in the blackness of his eyes. In the subtle curve of his mouth. In the long-fingered hand he had propped on his knee. In the crackling electricity of his presence.

It made her want to know more about him, the reasons Dominic kept him so locked down.

'Ah, yes,' he said. 'Money is an issue. But there are solutions to that.'

Maude stared at him in surprise. 'Solutions? What solutions?'

Again he smiled, as if he knew a delicious secret that she didn't. 'I've been thinking.' He reached for a bottle of fresh orange juice and poured her some in a plastic glass, then handed it to her.

'Oh, dear,' she muttered, taking the glass. 'You thinking is never good.'

He laughed, the sound rich and full of genuine amusement. 'There aren't many people in the world who get to say that kind of thing to me.'

'Well, maybe there should be more,' she said, unable to resist smiling back, feeling oddly pleased with herself that she'd made him laugh. 'You could do with being taken down a peg or two.'

He laughed again and shook his head. 'You're not afraid of me at all, are you?'

She gave him a look over the top of her glass as she sipped her juice. 'Should I be?'

'Many people are. I'm very rich and quite powerful, you see.' He poured some orange juice for himself. 'I'm surprised you weren't that night in the woods. I was a stranger to you, after all.'

'You were, but... I wasn't afraid. It was the forest. It has a...power. At least, to me it does.' She bit her lip, wondering why she was telling him this. Her feelings about the forest always sounded stupid when she told people aloud, and they always looked at her strangely.

But Dominic was looking at her now with interest, not hiding his curiosity. 'A power?' he asked. 'What kind of power?'

'It sounds weird and you'll probably laugh.'

'I won't laugh.' His gaze didn't flicker and he wasn't smiling now. He meant it.

She let out a breath. 'At the commune, Mum wasn't around a lot, so I was left on my own. I used to hang out in the commune garden because I loved the flowers and the plants, and the woman who managed the garden would tell me what each plant was and what it was used for. But when she wasn't there, I'd run into the forest on the border of the commune. I felt as if the trees were...watching over me. As if they were protecting me.' She'd looked away as she'd said it, not wanting to meet his gaze, yet she couldn't help glancing at him now. 'It's weird, yes.'

But he wasn't laughing. He was looking at her in a very intent way, making all the breath go out of her. 'It's not weird,' he said. 'There were no other children there?'

'A couple of babies, but no, no one my age.'

'So, you were lonely.'

It wasn't a question and a small jolt of shock hit her. Was she that easy to read? 'What makes you say that?' she asked, cagily. 'I never said I was lonely.'

'You didn't have to.' His tone was matter-of-fact. 'An only child with no parent watching over them?' He let the question hang for a moment then went on, 'And I know this because my father used to do the same with me. He would leave me at the manor for weeks at a time, with no one here to watch over me.'

Maude was momentarily diverted. 'You were? And you had no one?'

'There was Craddock, the gamekeeper, who lived in the cottage you're living in now. He used to take me hunting.' There was an odd note in Dominic's voice that she couldn't quite interpret. 'I'll tell you a secret. I was always terrified of the forest.'

Maude blinked. 'You? Terrified?'

'Oh, yes.' The corner of his mouth had curved, but it didn't look like amusement. 'My father used to—' He broke off, and Maude was conscious of a sudden tension around him that hadn't been there before.

This was painful for him. She could tell that right away.

'Don't feel you have to tell me if you don't want to,' she said quietly. 'Just because I told you something about me.'

Dominic looked down at his plate and the sandwich sitting on it, remaining silent for a time. Then he said, 'My father turned me out at night a couple of times. Made me sleep in the forest. I had to "face my fear".' He glanced at her suddenly, his eyes full of an intense expression she couldn't quite read. 'He said that if you didn't control your fear, it would end up controlling you, and I suppose he was right.' He smiled, but it didn't reach his eyes. 'After the first couple of nights, I wasn't afraid of the forest any more.'

But Maude could hear the lie in his voice. Was it really the forest he'd been afraid of? Or was it his father perhaps? He'd mentioned that his childhood hadn't been a happy one...

'You must have hated your grandparents then,' Dominic went on before she could speak. 'Taking you away from your mother and the commune.'

It was a clear change of subject, and Maude decided not to press him about it. Certainly not if it was painful for him.

'They weren't easy people,' she admitted. 'But I didn't hate them. They only wanted what was best for me.'

'Sounded like being left in the commune was what was best for you,' he said evenly. 'Did they even ask you if you wanted to go? And what did your mother have to say about any of it?'

She met his dark gaze, feeling oddly defensive of her grandparents, even though that was what she'd always thought herself. 'They didn't ask, no. And my mother had nothing to say about it. If I'd stayed there, I wouldn't have had an education.'

'Ah.' He raised his glass and took a sip. 'So you preferred being with your grandparents, then?'

'That's what was best for me in the end.'

'That's not what I asked.' His dark gaze was disturbingly intense. 'I asked if you preferred being with them over the commune.'

She didn't like the question and how unsure and defensive it made her feel. As if she'd had a choice about whether to go with her grandparents or stay at Earthsong with her mother, which she hadn't.

'Does it matter?' she said, trying to sound casual. 'It was a long time ago.'

But that unnerving black gaze of his seemed to see

right inside her. 'I didn't ask to make you uncomfortable. I only asked because it's clear you love the forest here at Darkfell. And I wondered if you'd like to stay beyond the term of your contract.'

Maude stared back at him in shock. 'Stay?'

'Yes. Make the position permanent, so to speak.'

'But you said you were going to sell the place after the baby is born.'

'I did. And then I changed my mind.'

Carefully, Maude put down her plastic cup and clasped her hands together, trying to keep the sudden fearful hope inside her. 'You're serious?' She searched his face. 'You really want me to stay on here?'

'Yes, I'm serious. However…' He paused and she saw it again, the flash of iron in his gaze, making her heart tighten. 'There are strings attached.'

Her heart tightened still further. Of course there were. There were always strings with him.

'What strings?' she asked, unable to hide the wariness in her voice.

Dominic's dark eyes glittered. 'I want you to marry me, Maude.'

Dominic watched the shock blossom over Maude's lovely face, which he'd expected. He hadn't exactly been open with her about his idea.

He'd also been wanting to give her some space. It was why he hadn't gone to her cottage the moment he'd arrived. She was a wild creature, he'd decided, and with wild creatures you had to go slow. So he'd let her get used to him being around and only on the third night had he gone to her door.

He'd been meaning only to talk or to suggest, but then she'd thrown herself into his arms and that had been the end of that.

He'd spent every night in her bed since then, leaving in the early morning before she woke up, still wanting to give her that space. But he'd been thinking, over the course of the week, of the future and what would happen after their son was born.

It was real to him now, a future he'd never thought he'd want unrolling before him. But he did want it. He did. And he wanted her, too.

Marriage didn't mean much to him, since it hadn't meant anything to his parents. His mother had been his father's lover and she'd left him not long after Dominic had turned two. He had no memories of her. Yet he'd decided that his son should have what he hadn't, a mother and a father, and what better way to tie it all together than to be married?

The idea hadn't bothered him as much as he'd thought it would. In fact, he liked it. Liked the thought of Maude being his wife. It would mean he'd be stuck with only one woman for the rest of his life, but he found he rather liked that thought too. It had been nearly a week and he still wanted her with as much hunger as he had that first time. Their nights together were incendiary. Of course, over time, their passion would wane because it always did, and then they might have to have a discussion about finding other partners, discreetly of course.

Until then though, he didn't see any reason why not to make her his wife. There were certain legal protections she would enjoy and she'd certainly like to stay here in the forest. They could keep their own lives as they were doing right now… Surely she wouldn't find it a problem?

Her warm brown eyes were wide with shock. 'Marry you?' she repeated huskily. 'But…why?'

'It would give you some legal protection,' he said easily. 'But more importantly, it would give our son a family.'

'He already has a family.'

'A family who are together,' Dominic clarified.

She was still staring at him, shock echoing in her gaze. 'But…you don't love me. And I don't love you.'

He almost laughed. 'Of course not. But that's not the kind of marriage I was thinking of.'

She didn't look at all reassured. 'So what kind of marriage were you thinking of?'

'Our lives would go on as they are now. I'll live in the manor and you'll live in the cottage. We will continue to sleep together and, I have to admit, that's another string, because I'm not staying celibate. You will have our son and he will continue to live here with both his parents.'

Maude frowned. 'I…'

'Nothing will change.' He made his voice as reassuring as he could, because now that he'd put the idea to her, he realised he very much wanted her to say yes. 'You will have your life and I will have mine. The only difference from now is that you can stay on here as the groundskeeper.'

'I still don't understand,' she said. 'If nothing will change, then why do we have to get married?'

Irritation wound through him, but he quelled it. Getting annoyed wouldn't help his case here.

'Why shouldn't we?' he said. 'It would be better for

you financially, and, as I already said, would give you some legal protection if anything happens to me.'

'I mean...' Her gaze narrowed in that wary, suspicious way he was coming to dislike intensely. 'What are you getting out of it?'

He reached out and idly pushed a strand of golden hair back behind her ear, relishing the feel of the silky strands against his fingertips. 'I am getting you. In my bed every night with any luck.'

'But you have that already.'

'Except you will be my wife.'

'How is that different?'

Questions. She was all about questions. He couldn't resent that, though. She wanted to know and he liked that she had no qualms about asking.

'I've decided that I want a family,' he said, the truth coming out of his mouth before he'd even thought about it. 'I did think I'd never marry or have children, and I'd never wanted to. But now I'm going to be a father, I want to give my child the best start in life, and that's with a family.'

'Is it?' There was a crease between her brows. 'My grandparents were married and I didn't have a particularly good life with them.'

'So you had a better life with your mother?' he couldn't help saying. 'Who wasn't around, which made you lonely enough to go into the forest to find companionship?'

She flushed. 'That's not... It wasn't...'

'Nymph.' He reached for her hands and took them in his, because fighting like this wasn't going to help either of them. 'What are you so afraid of?'

She'd asked him that once, as he'd tried to resist her physically, still wanting to control his hunger for her, and he'd hated the question. But he had no qualms about turning it on her, since it was clear that the idea of marriage disturbed her and he didn't want it to.

She didn't pull her hands away, letting them rest in his, and he brushed his thumbs across her skin, wanting to soothe her, ease away her fears, whatever they were.

'I don't want…to be tied down,' she said haltingly, as if the words were difficult. 'I don't want to feel like I'm with my grandparents again, where I wasn't allowed to do anything or go anywhere. I had to be quiet, sit still, and not cause a fuss.'

He could understand that. It reminded him of his own childhood, bound by his father's rules, his behaviour forced into something that had never been natural to him. And, God, he'd told her about those nights in the forest, alone. He hadn't meant to, not when it exposed such a weakness in him. Yet still, he'd told her.

'I understand,' he said. 'But it won't be like that, I promise you. It'll be a legal marriage and that's all. You won't have to do anything or be anyone but yourself. Call it a whim of mine.' Her fingertips felt cold in his so he rubbed them gently. 'You can stay here. You won't have to leave. And when we tell people about the child, you can call me your husband. There'll be some surprise, because of my reputation, of course, but marrying me will make the announcement easier.'

She was nodding, but there was still a tightness around her eyes and her mouth, so he tugged her gently into his lap. She didn't protest as he put his arms around her, holding her, and it came to him, slowly, that though he'd held her before, he'd never held her like this. As a comfort rather than anything more.

He'd never felt the need to comfort anyone before or even made any kind of comforting gesture. Why should he? When no one had comforted him? And he was surprised how good it made him feel when she turned her head into his neck, accepting the warmth of his body and the strength of his arms.

'You're a wild thing, nymph,' he murmured softly into her hair. 'And I know that I need to be careful with wild things. I won't cage you, understand? But also know one thing. I will be your forest. When you're lonely and need someone to look after you, don't go into the woods. Come to me instead.'

She looked up at him, her brown eyes dark, and he couldn't have said what she was thinking. Then she lifted a hand to his hair, her touch light. 'Badger,' she said softly.

His heart tightened in his chest at the tender sound in her voice. The press called him all kinds of things, and he'd never paid any attention to them, but this... This was a name she'd given him and he rather thought she was owed.

'Logically I should be "satyr", since you're my nymph,' he pointed out.

She wrinkled her nose. 'No, I like badger better. Also, you're not being particularly satyr-like now.'

'I can be if you'd rather.'

Her fingers sifted gently through his hair, her mouth curving as she looked up into his eyes. 'That night you were the god of the forest. And I let you catch me.'

Strange, mysterious woman. Wild and passionate one

minute, stubborn and angry the next, then warm and almost tender the minute after that.

She intrigued him.

She'll be your wife if she agrees.

The thought gripped him tight as a wave of possessiveness swamped him. Yes, she would be *his* wife. No one else's, just his.

'You did.' He tried not to let the possessiveness bleed into his voice. 'And you know what that means.'

Slowly, like the dawn breaking, she smiled. 'No. What?'

'It means you're mine.' This time he couldn't stop that possessiveness from colouring his voice. 'And the god of the forest always keeps what's his.'

He thought she might protest at his blatant declaration of ownership, but she didn't. Instead her eyes darkened further, the gold eclipsed. Did she like it? Did she want to be claimed?

He stared down at her, and it came to him then that it was a fine line she walked. Because yes, she did want that. Her mother hadn't wanted her, and her grandparents hadn't either. They'd taken her away, but it hadn't been about her, he thought. It had been for themselves, because they hadn't liked the way her mother had brought her up.

But that night, she'd let him catch her, because deep in her heart she wanted to be captured. She wanted to be held. Even though she fought against it and wanted her freedom, she also wanted that tether.

He wasn't sure why what she wanted mattered to him, perhaps it was merely that she was carrying their child.

Regardless, he wanted to give that to her. Both the tether and the freedom.

And why not? When it suits what you want very well.

There was an element of snideness in the thought, but he dismissed it. Yes, it worked well for what he wanted too, but who cared? In the end, they both got an arrangement that suited both their needs.

Maude clearly liked the thought of him keeping her, because her fingers tightened in his hair, bringing his head slowly lower until their lips met.

Her mouth was warm and she tasted both tart and sweet from the orange juice she'd been drinking, and he could feel the autumn sun on the back of his neck, as soft and warm as her mouth and body.

'Here,' he murmured, easing her down onto the blanket. 'Let me have you here. I've caught you, nymph, so you have to give me whatever I want.'

She was still smiling, but there was a delicate flush to her cheeks now, a sure sign of arousal. 'Do I?' There was a playful note in her voice. 'And what is it you want, O great god?'

He was already pulling at her clothing, and usually he was more adept, but he felt oddly desperate and inexplicably clumsy, and so she had to help him. She laughed as she got tangled in her jeans and underwear, until he covered her mouth with his, taking her laughter for himself.

Finally they were naked and he was stretched out above her, where he preferred to be, looking down at her, this beautiful, wild, uncanny woman he'd found in the forest that night, and he felt himself teetering on the edge of a cliff he hadn't known was there. But the feeling made no sense, so he kissed her again, relishing the way she arched beneath him, letting him know she wanted more, and then her legs wrapped around his waist and that was the sweetest feeling yet.

He guided himself into her, loving how she gasped as he pushed in slow, deep, and then he stopped, buried inside her. He lifted her hands and threaded her fingers through his, before pressing them down on the blanket, on either side of her head.

She smiled. 'I like you like this,' she said softly, her voice husky with pleasure. 'Naked and in the sun. You look like you're meant to be here. Like me.'

He shifted his hips, unable to look away, trapped by the pleasure darkening her eyes as he moved. 'Do I?' he asked, rough and raw. 'Like a god, if I remember right.'

She gave a soft laugh that ended on a gasp as he drew out of her, then slid deep inside again. 'Oh…yes…' She sighed. 'You are, badger.'

He found himself smiling back at her, staring into her eyes, gone molten and soft with liquid gold. 'Don't kill the moment, nymph.'

She laughed again, a soft sexy little laugh that had him kissing her, wanting to taste the joyous sound of it and keep it inside him. He couldn't remember the last time he'd smiled at someone during sex. The last time it had been playful, and teasing, and tender.

He rolled suddenly onto his back, just for a change, so she was above him, the sun turning her hair into a golden glory. Her face was alight, her hands braced on his chest, and when he gripped her hips, moving her, she sighed, her inner muscles squeezing him.

Beautiful nymph. Beautiful Maude.

A groan escaped him as she tilted her hips slightly.

'You're killing me,' he murmured, the pleasure sharper, hotter. 'I like it. Do it again.'

So she did, and he growled, making her laugh yet again, her body shaking on top of his. 'Animal,' she breathed. 'You're my favourite kind.'

He was rapidly losing the ability to think, but he paused again, deep inside, tightening his fingers on her hips. 'I'm your favourite kind of animal?'

'I like a badger.' She rocked against him. 'Move.'

'What?' He pretended to look surprised. 'Me? Move? Move where?'

Another laugh and she bent forward, her hair a golden curtain around them. 'Make me come, O great god,' she whispered against his mouth, 'and I'll be your slave for ever.'

'Oh, well, in that case…' He gripped her harder, moving beneath her, watching the teasing light in her eyes slowly fade, replaced by the burning pleasure that they always experienced with each other.

And even though she was above him, he had the oddest impression that he was the one falling. Falling into her brilliant golden eyes.

'You haven't said yes, Maude,' he whispered.

Her gaze was shadowed russet edged with gold. Darkness and light. Midnight and midsummer. The wild part of her and the joy. She kissed him, giving him a nip. 'Yes,' she whispered.

Then everything fell away and there was nothing in the world but the pleasure and the fire that ended it.

CHAPTER TEN

THREE DAYS LATER Maude stood in front of the little mirror in the cottage and stared at herself in the simple, gold silk shift dress. It was cut on the bias, hugging her breasts, hips and little bump, before flowing out into a gold swirl around her ankles. A beautiful dress. Her wedding dress.

She still found it hard to believe that she'd agreed to marry Dominic, especially considering her first thought when he'd asked her was an immediate no. And not because she had strong feelings about marriage itself—her grandparents admittedly hadn't seemed all that happy in theirs, yet Polly and John clearly were—but because she didn't want to feel bound to anyone. To be constrained by their rules and their expectations. She'd moved on from that when she'd moved out of her grandparents' house, but it hadn't been until she'd come to Darkfell that she'd felt truly free. She didn't want to give that up, not for anyone.

But Dominic had been adamant that nothing would change between them and she believed him. He hadn't given her a reason to doubt him since he'd decided to live here so why shouldn't she?

It had still been a deal for him—he'd made no secret

of that—and while she felt an odd pinch of hurt for absolutely no reason, mostly she found that reassuring. No feelings were involved, it was still a business decision, and that she was comfortable with.

Taking his name for the sake of legal protection for her and the baby had even sounded logical, and if it meant they could both carry on as they had, with him in her bed when she wanted it, why shouldn't she?

It also took some of the pressure off when it came to explaining about the pregnancy. There would be questions, naturally, about how she came to marry such an infamous playboy, but at least she didn't need to say that her baby was the result of a night spent with a stranger in the forest.

Speaking of which, the others need to know.

Yes, the Your Girl Friday team really did. She'd been cagey on their usual Zoom calls, and while she'd had a few assessing looks, no one had asked her outright what was going on. They respected her need for space, which she appreciated.

She'd tell them later, after the wedding maybe. They'd be unhappy she hadn't let them know about either the baby or Dominic earlier, but too bad. It was her secret to keep for the time being.

Dominic, however, had insisted that Polly and John be told, and that the announcement should be made with her presence. She'd been reluctant, worrying a little about what the Harrises would think of her pregnancy and then her forthcoming marriage. But they hadn't been judgemental. In fact, they'd been thrilled, Polly even going so far as to give both her and Dominic a hug.

She hadn't expected that and it was relieving. It made

her wonder why she'd been worried about it at all. Probably leftover anxiety from her grandparents' judgemental upbringing.

Carefully, she picked up the length of sheer golden silk that was her veil, and put it on her head. She'd chosen the gown and veil from a website the day after she'd agreed to be Dominic's wife and he'd had them shipped to Darkfell. He'd also asked her what she preferred in terms of a ceremony and, since she had no strong feelings about it, having never thought she'd ever marry, she'd only shrugged. He'd nodded and then asked her if she minded him organising it, which she didn't. He'd surprise her, he'd said, which could have been a little worrying, but she felt oddly calm about letting him do it. He'd never do anything she wouldn't want. She felt that in her bones.

Stepping out of the cottage, Maude was surprised to see a lit torch standing in the ground outside the front door, flaring in the sunshine. An arrow on the ground, formed of sticks, pointed in the direction of the forest, and a crown of woven leaves and flowers sat in the grass beside it.

A strange little feeling gripped her tight, though she couldn't have said what it was, a wave of the strangest warmth. She found herself smiling as she went over to the arrow and picked up the crown. It was competently woven, the leaves fresh and green, the wildflowers bright. It was obviously for her.

Her throat felt tight for some reason and the warmth in her chest expanded. Dominic had done this and he'd put thought into it. He'd considered her, considered what was important to her, what she liked, and he'd made an effort. This marriage might be only a business deal, but he'd made it special.

Is marrying him really such a good idea?

Maude ignored both the thought and the tight feeling in her throat. She'd said she'd marry him and she would, and it wouldn't change their arrangement. It was for the baby anyway, and the baby was far more important than her own feelings.

She put the crown of leaves and flowers on her head, over the veil, then turned in the direction of the arrow and walked into the forest. There were more torches and arrows, pointing the way, and she soon realised where she was being directed. It made the warmth inside her glow brighter.

She moved deeper into the trees, mindful of her dress, until she came to the little path that led to the forest waterfall and pool, because of course that was where he'd directed her.

Her special place. And since the day she'd agree to marry him, where she'd sat astride him, naked and free, and brought them both to the ultimate pleasure, it had become *their* special place.

She stepped out of the trees and into the clearing, her heart thumping, that strange, warm feeling moving through her, to find Dominic standing beside the pool, waiting for her. Another man stood there smiling, obviously a priest, and Polly and John were also there. Witnesses.

Not that she saw anyone but Dominic.

The autumn sun had blessed them today, shining down onto the clearing and onto him. Tall and powerful. He was dressed in black trousers and a simple black shirt, but on his head was also a crown of leaves. His black hair gleamed like spilled ink in the sunlight, the white stripe almost glowing amidst the green of the leaves. His eyes were as dark as his hair, and he didn't smile.

But when he looked at her, she felt something inside her bloom.

This man, who hadn't laughed at her when she'd told him about how connected she felt to the trees and to nature. Who'd accepted both her stubbornness and her passion, her fire and her wild spirit, and hadn't punished her for any of it. Who hadn't forced her to be anyone but herself. And who'd created this beautiful ceremony just for her, taking all the things that she found important, and turning them into the most perfect moment.

Everything about this was for her and so was he.

He was the god of the forest and she was his chosen queen.

She walked slowly over to him, her heart feeling somehow larger and fuller in her chest, the warm feeling flowing through her and almost bringing tears to her eyes, making her throat ache.

He reached out to her and clasped her hand, his fingers threading through hers. 'Surprise,' he murmured. 'I hope this is adequate.'

She gripped his hand tightly, swallowing past the lump in her throat. 'Adequate? It's…perfect. Just perfect.'

His dark gaze roved over her hungrily. 'And so are you.'

She flushed with pleasure then reached up to touch his crown. 'Who made these?'

'I did.' He smiled then and it lit his face like the sun shining down on them. 'It wasn't as easy as I'd hoped.'

'I love them.' The warm feeling in her heart grew, putting down roots and sprouting new leaves.

'Good.' He gripped her hand tight. 'Are you ready?'

Are you? You're afraid.

No, she wasn't. Not of him, not of this. And this powerful feeling growing inside her was nothing. Simple pleasure at how he'd made this day so special. It was nothing more than that.

It's not and you know it.

But Maude ignored the thought, nodding at Dominic and then turning to face the priest.

It wasn't a long ceremony, but, try as she might, she couldn't ignore that feeling inside her as it grew and bloomed, wrapping strong roots around her heart and binding it tight.

When it was her turn to speak, the words were hoarse, and when it was time to exchange rings, she looked down to see her own ring was shaped as a circlet of oak leaves, in white gold.

Her vision wavered, tears filling her eyes unexpectedly. He'd thought of every detail. He'd made this special, this ceremony that was supposed to be only a business deal. This ceremony that was only about legal protection, nothing more.

Her heart thumped even harder and it was difficult to catch a breath.

The priest was saying words and then Dominic gave her another ring, his ring, and that too was a circlet of oak leaves. She pushed it onto his finger almost automatically, the roots around her heart tightening still further, choking her.

Then she found herself looking up at Dominic as the priest continued to speak. The sun was behind his head, throwing his face into shadow, but his eyes gleamed, and in them she could see the man she'd given herself to that night in the forest. The fierce, passionate man, behind his urbane and polished front.

The man you've fallen in love with.

The thought wound through her head, the roots in her heart piercing it right through. Roots wrapping around her bones, growing down into her soul. An unbreakable connection, a tether she'd never be free of.

Dominic bent his head and kissed her, the priest naming them husband and wife.

No, she wasn't in love with him. She *wasn't*. She loved her friends and the forest, and her unborn child, but she didn't want to be in love with a man. And most especially not a man like him. He gave, she couldn't deny that, but he also demanded things in return. Her honesty, her passion, her time, her attention.

It wouldn't matter if she hadn't wanted to give him those things, but she had wanted to, so she did. Giving him small pieces of herself, not realising what was happening, not understanding what she was doing until it was too late.

Love had rooted itself so deep inside her she was never going to be able to cut it out.

Her fingers were cold, and Dominic must have felt them, because as he lifted his head, he frowned. 'Are you okay?' he asked, concern in his eyes.

'Oh, yes.' She quickly pulled her hand from his and pasted on a smile. 'I'm fine.'

She tried to ignore the feeling as she and Dominic received congratulations from Polly and John, before Dominic took her hand and led her back through the forest to the manor.

She didn't speak the whole way, her throat tight, her chest hurting. She was acutely conscious of her hand in his, of the ring of oak leaves circling her finger, and, try as she might, she couldn't ignore the feeling in her heart, strong and aching, binding itself with her soul.

Love had never been spoken of in her grandparents' house. No one had ever said to her 'I love you'. It was only ever 'for your own good' or 'we only want what's best for you'. Even Sonya hadn't said those words to her, not even when her grandparents had taken her away from Earthsong. Her mother hadn't even protested, leaving Maude to watch her walk away without a backwards look.

Once Maude had realised that they weren't going back to Earthsong, that the ice cream had been only a pretext to get her into the car, she'd wept all the way to her grandparents' house, an empty feeling in her heart. As if the most beautiful grove of trees had been growing there, but now they'd been cut down and the grove razed, the earth salted.

At her grandparents' house, there had been no wild forests for her to find comfort in. No garden of flowers. No herbs. No trees or even plants. There had been only a concreted space for her grandfather to park his car and that was it. Living there had killed something in Maude's soul.

She'd tried to make the best of it, since she'd had nowhere else to go, tried to be a good girl for her grandparents. School, with its playgrounds of concrete and metal, with timetables and bells, and rigid rules around behaviour, had been its own special hell. She'd tried there too, because her grandparents had given up their retirement to make sure she'd have a better start in life than what her mother could give her. They were doing it for her, they'd said.

Yet it had never felt as though they were doing it for her. It had felt as if she was a millstone around their necks that they'd had no choice but to deal with. And her mother, for all the freedom Sonya had given her, had made her feel that way too.

Maude had never been a child either her mother or her grandparents had wanted. She hadn't been a child at all. What she'd been was a rope around their necks, dragging them down.

You'll drag him down too.

Yes, she would. Eventually. He hadn't chosen her because he'd wanted her. He'd chosen her out of necessity. For their baby's sake. And knowing that really shouldn't hurt, since the baby was more important than either her or Dominic's feelings, and yet…

Maude fought to ignore the abruptly painful feeling in her heart as they came out of the forest and walked over the lawn to the manor. Dominic turned then, not making for the front door as she'd expected, but heading along the little brick path that led to the walled garden. And when she stepped through the stone doorway into it, the feeling inside her became even more painful, because a white silk pavilion had been erected near the pond in the middle, a table and chairs set out beneath it. On the table was food, drink, and the most perfect little wedding cake.

Maude stopped, her eyes suddenly full of tears.

He's done all this for you and you don't deserve it— not any of it.

Of course she didn't. She'd saddled him with a life he'd never wanted and now couldn't get out of.

She was the one tying *him* down. Not vice versa.

Dominic, slightly ahead of her and still holding her hand, turned. Then, obviously noticing the look on her face, frowned. 'Maude? What is it?'

She let go of his hand. 'I… I'm not feeling well.' The lie rolled off her tongue so smoothly it was as if she'd been lying all her life.

His expression became concerned and he stepped closer. 'You're not? How so?'

'Just a headache.' She clasped her hands together so he wouldn't seem them trembling. 'It's nothing.'

'It isn't nothing.' He reached for her clasped hands and pulled them gently apart, the warmth of his skin against her numb fingertips. 'Your fingers are cold.' His frown deepened. 'What's wrong?'

'It's nothing,' she repeated and tried to pull her hands away.

Except he held onto them. 'It's something,' he said quietly. 'It's not a headache, is it?'

Maude tried to get a breath, tried to think of another lie, but the way he was looking at her now, she knew he'd never believe her. It was as if he could see right inside her head, read her mind, know all her thoughts.

'I just…' She jerked her hands out of his and stepped

back from him, putting some distance between them. 'What is this for?'

He made no effort to reach for her again, frowning. 'This? What do you mean this?'

'The ceremony. The crowns. The rings.'

His frown deepened. 'I thought you would like it.'

'But there's no reason for it.' Her heart ached and ached. She was ruining this, ruining this day he'd made perfect just for her, and she couldn't stop herself. 'It was only supposed to be a legal requirement. It didn't need to be...special.'

'It was for you,' he said, searching her face as if for clues. 'I thought you would appreciate it if we made it an occasion, and I thought it would be nice to have it in the forest with some things that were meaningful to you.'

You are ruining this by making a scene. Stop it.

Except she couldn't stop it. She couldn't seem to stem the words that were pouring out of her mouth. 'I didn't ask you to do it for me. I didn't ask you to make it special. And what about you? Why wasn't there anything meaningful to you in there too? Why did it have to be all about me?'

Dominic stared at the woman in front of him, so startlingly beautiful in her golden gown and crowned with leaves.

His wood nymph. His wife.

He didn't know what had gone wrong, but something had. Somehow, in the moment between when they'd said their vows and walked back to the manor, something had changed. Something had spooked this wild creature of his and he had no idea what it was.

He'd taken great pleasure in organising the ceremony, he had to admit. He'd put the kind of thought into it that he'd never put into anything but his business, and he wasn't sure why, but he had. It had felt important to create something that Maude would like, since he was the one who'd suggested the idea of marriage in the first place, and for it to be special for her, because he didn't want her to regret it.

When she'd stepped out of the forest, resplendent in gold, wearing the leaf crown he'd made, he'd felt the most acute pleasure that this beautiful, mysterious woman was now his. A pleasure that had only deepened when he'd put his ring on her finger, the possessive part of him roaring its satisfaction.

She was his wife now and she was pregnant with their child, and he would keep them, protect them, make sure nothing would hurt them.

He'd been looking forward to cutting the cake and eating the food Polly had prepared, and talking about their future and planning it together. Then, later, taking her to his bed in the manor for a change, and making her his wife in every way possible.

She'd looked a touch pale as they'd walked away from the pool and her fingers had been cold in his, it was true. But he hadn't thought she'd suddenly and angrily demand to know why he'd made the ceremony so special, or why it was all about her.

There was something else going on here, he was sure.

He studied her face for a moment. 'This isn't about the wedding, is it? Something's upset you.'

She was pale in the sun, all the warmth leached from her brown eyes. If he didn't know any better, he would have said she was afraid, though he couldn't think what she'd be afraid of. He'd promised not to sell Darkfell, and he'd also told her that things wouldn't change between them, so what else was it?

'You don't love me, do you?' she asked suddenly.

Frowning at the abrupt question, he reached out and grabbed her, his hands on her silken hips, pulling her close, as if that would make understanding what this was about easier. 'No. Love was never going to be a part of this, I already told you that.'

Despite the wild look in her eyes, her body was already softening against his, moulding itself to him. Recognising him the way his body recognised hers. 'Good,' she said, her hands coming to his chest the way they always did, as if she couldn't stop herself from touching him. 'I love our child, but…not you.'

The words felt like small slivers of glass pushed slowly beneath his skin and he wasn't sure why. Because he didn't want her to love him. He didn't want anyone to love him. Love demanded things, required things. Love was a list of expenses that he had to pay back. Love was a deal impossible to negotiate with. Love was an empty house and loneliness.

He didn't want that again, not for himself. He never had.

'Just as well,' he said evenly. 'Because I don't love you either.'

'But our child? You'll love him, won't you?'

Tension crept through him, making his muscles tight and his jaw ache. It was true, his heart had died the death of a thousand cuts. His father's cold words and his efforts to 'harden him up'. Little by little the store of love he'd had inside him had leaked away until there was nothing left.

Until he'd hardened himself entirely just as his father had wanted him to. As hard as his father had been. No, harder.

His father had turned him into the perfect businessman, the perfect CEO, and yet he'd retained enough of his 'soft' nature, as his father had termed it, to make it clear he wasn't a carbon copy.

It wasn't soft to enjoy pleasure, and so he'd cultivated it as carefully as he'd cultivated his business acumen, until finally he was both the businessman and the sybarite, because why not? Why couldn't you have your cake and eat it too?

Why couldn't you have all that, *and* love your child? None of it was mutually exclusive. He didn't need a heart in order to love. All he needed was to not be his father, and he'd already achieved that.

'Of course, I'll love him.' And to make the point, he smoothed his hand over her bump where their baby lay. 'He's my son.'

Abruptly, as if his touch had burned her, she pulled herself out of his arms, and took a couple of steps away.

He stared at her in surprise. 'Maude? What the hell is going on?'

'Your childhood,' she said, ignoring him. 'Why was it unhappy?'

'What's that got to do with anything?'

'If you want to be a good father to your child, then I want to know why you were so unhappy as a kid. So we can avoid making the same mistakes.'

Impatience twisted inside him. He had no idea where

she was going with this, or what had provoked it, and he really didn't want to continue the conversation. What he wanted to do was cut their cake and then take her to bed.

'Later,' he said, trying to temper his tone. 'Let's have some cake first at least.'

'No,' she said, oddly insistent. 'Now. I need to know who I married.'

He took a calming breath, trying to hold onto his temper, because she was clearly upset so maybe going along with this—whatever it was—would finally get him to the truth.

'Fine.' He thrust his hands into the pockets of his trousers so he wouldn't keep reaching for her, since clearly she didn't want him to. 'What do you want to know?'

She'd folded her arms across her chest as if cold. 'Everything.'

'Okay. Well, my mother was my father's lover. They weren't married. She walked out when I was two. My father was going to put me up for adoption because he'd never wanted children, but then he changed his mind. He decided he needed an heir after all and, lo, there I was.' The words had a bitter tinge to them, but he decided he didn't care. He *was* bitter and he had reason to be. 'Dad wanted a strong businessman for a son, so from an early age that's how he treated me. Everything I wanted, I had to negotiate for. Clothes, food, heating, toys, his attention, his time. Nothing came for free. I had to pay for it all.

'When I was thirteen, I was handed a list of expenses I'd incurred merely by existing and he expected me to pay him back.' He kept his tone casual, because, after all, while he might be bitter, all of this had happened many years ago and it had no bearing on what was happening now. 'My father wanted me to learn how to be a board-room warrior, how to be hard, to never let anything get in the way of a good deal, and that was his way of doing things. He told me that if I paid back the money he spent on my upbringing, I'd be named his heir.'

Maude was silent, her golden-brown eyes fixed on his.

'He died of a heart attack when I was seventeen,' he went on. 'But I hadn't paid him back yet—nearly, I was very close—so I missed out on being named as his heir. I suspect the game had always been rigged and he'd never intended to leave it to me anyway. I just didn't know it until then.'

Her gaze flickered, though what she was thinking he didn't know. 'What did you do?' she asked.

'I took the company back.' He smiled, though it was rather more savage than he'd meant it to be. 'I put into practice every lesson he'd ever taught me, and I fought the board of Lancaster Developments into submission. Then I took the company apart, piece by little piece, and sold all of it. Then with that money I started my own company, and built it so that it was larger than his ever was.' He'd always found some satisfaction in that, yet saying it out loud to Maude now, it almost sounded… petty. 'You could say that my father would have been proud of me,' he went on, ignoring the feeling, 'because I turned myself into him. Everything I learned I put to good use as a businessman and he wasn't wrong about a lot of things.'

There was a taut expression on her face. 'Will you teach the baby those same lessons?'

It was a fair question, though he hated she'd felt the

need to even ask it. 'No,' he said fiercely. 'I will never do to him what my father did to me. Never.'

The tension in her face had eased slightly, yet something was still wrong, he knew it.

'Is that what was worrying you?' he asked. 'You'd think I'd hurt our—'

'No,' she interrupted quickly. 'No, I don't think that, not at all. It's just… Well, I suppose we both have our issues, and I'm not going to be the usual kind of wife. So if you're expecting me to be a certain thing…' She trailed off, but he didn't need her to explain.

He'd been right, she *had* been afraid, and he could understand why. Her life with her grandparents had left its mark on her and she was worried he might do the same thing to her. He wouldn't, of course. All he expected of her was that she be the delightful creature she already was.

'I'm not expecting you to be anything but yourself, nymph,' he said gently, and when he took his hand out of his pocket and extended it to her, it was in invitation rather than as a demand. 'Come and sit down with me. Let's eat this wedding breakfast and talk about anything you want. Or not talk if that's your preference.'

For a long moment she stared at him, as if she were a wild creature unsure of whether to trust him or not. Then slowly she came to him and took his hand, and together they sat under the white silk pavilion and ate their wedding breakfast.

He told her about the forest and Craddock, and the stag he'd cried over. 'My father sneered at me,' he said, sipping on his glass of champagne. '"It's just a dumb animal", he told me. "If you can't handle shooting a deer, then how are you going to survive in the business world?"'

'Your father was the dumb animal, not you.' Maude's dark eyes were full of fire. 'What a terrible thing to say.'

'It was,' he agreed. 'Dad only had terrible things to say.' It didn't feel bad to talk to her about these moments of vulnerability. In fact, it felt as if he could tell her anything, anything at all. 'You should know,' he continued, after a moment's pause, 'that I haven't led a good life, nymph. Nothing was more important than my own pleasure, and even that was getting dull. At least until the night of the bacchanal.'

She leaned her elbows on the table, velvety eyes dark. 'So, what changed?'

He looked at her. 'You know what changed. You, being in the woods that night too. You, running from me. You, giving me all your passion even though I was a stranger to you.' He paused, because this was a confession that felt dangerous somehow, and yet he had to say it. 'You changed my life that night, Maude.'

Something flickered in her gaze, an expression gone too fast for him to read. But then she leaned forward and reached for his hand where it rested on the tabletop, her long, slender fingers twining with his. He hadn't asked for any of her confidences, so when she spoke, everything in him went still.

'When my gran came to get me from the commune, Mum walked away,' Maude said slowly. 'And she never looked back. Not even for one last glimpse of me. She just walked away as if I meant nothing to her.'

There was pain in her eyes as she spoke and he could see how deeply this had hurt her.

He stroked his thumb over the back of her hand. 'I'm sorry,' he said, which was pitifully inadequate, but it was all he could think of to say. 'That's a terrible thing for a mother to do.'

'We should have swapped places.' A faint smile turned her mouth. 'I would have loved to sleep in the forest. Instead, all I got was my grandparents' concrete garden, with no trees, or flowers or grass.'

'Poor nymph,' he murmured, and he meant it. 'That must have been hell on earth for you.'

'It was,' she said simply. 'Leaving that place was the best thing I ever did.'

There was a silence then, of mutual acknowledgement of the hurts they'd both suffered.

Then he said, to break the moment, 'So where did you go after that?'

The conversation turned to less painful subjects, though no less interesting to him, as she told him about her life after she'd left her grandparents' house.

Then they talked about casual subjects, mundane things such as their favourite foods and their favourite books. The music they liked and the movies they'd enjoyed. He told her how he'd hiked to Everest base camp once when he'd been younger, and she told him that she'd always wanted to see the Amazon rainforest.

Then he asked her what it was that she actually did in his forest, and that was enough to make her grab his hand and lead him into the trees, talking all the while. She named trees and plants as she went, and what their niche in the forest ecology was, and how everything worked in concert with each other. And he saw it all with new eyes. Saw her anew too. Glowing with passion, bright with interest and curiosity. Nature was fiercely important to her, he could see, and she knew so much about it. Everything was connected, she told him, everything on this planet was connected.

Perhaps it was. When she talked like that, perhaps he even believed her. He certainly felt connected to her in a way he'd never experienced with another person.

They were in a little clearing with bracken on the ground when he stopped and reached for her. She'd been talking about ferns, but he was impatient now, because she was golden and glowing, and she was his wife. He wanted her and he was tired of waiting.

She didn't protest as he laid her down on the bracken, taking off her gown and veil, but leaving on her crown. As he left on his. Because they were both rulers of this little piece of land, king and queen of the forest, and this would be their marriage bed.

This time, though, he lay on his back, with her astride him, her hair a golden mane down her back, her hands braced on his chest. And he thought he'd died and gone to heaven. Because surely heaven was this, making love to a wood nymph who was his wife, on a bed of bracken, in a forest clearing.

And he realised, as she rose and fell above him, the pleasure twining around both of them, that this had gone beyond mere sex. Sex he knew very well, because he'd had a lot of it in his life. But this, what they were doing right now, right here, wasn't sex. It was more, it was deeper. It was reverent and sacred. It was worship.

It wasn't just about bodies. It was about souls.

He had no idea why he was thinking this, because he

wasn't a man much given to poetry. But there was poetry in this. In her.

In her stubbornness and wild temper. In the joy she
took in the things that were important to her. In the way
her hand would rest on her bump every so often as if
soothing the tiny baby inside her. In her touching his
hair, warmth in her eyes, and calling him badger.

And in this, her gasps of pleasure, her eyes gone molten as he worshipped her, in the perfection of them moving together, slowly. Building this little castle of pleasure
and wonder between them.

He'd never felt anything like it and he knew in that
moment that he never would again. That for him it would
always be this woman. That any other partner wouldn't
be able to give him what she could. And he was at peace
with that.

She was his wife and she would never leave him.

He'd make sure of it.

CHAPTER ELEVEN

MAUDE SAT IN the sitting room of the manor, sipping the hot chocolate Dominic had made for her. The fire crackled softly in the grate, warming the room.

It had been a week since the wedding and though she'd hoped the new ache in her heart would fade, it hadn't.

She should have left him in the walled garden the day she'd married him. She should have turned and walked out, but she hadn't. She'd tried to provoke an argument instead, wanting to use it to poison those roots growing around her heart, but he hadn't given her one.

He'd told her about his awful childhood and his terrible father and what his father had done to him and listening to his history had somehow made those roots stronger, not weaker.

No child should have had to live through that, and yet he had. He'd survived, even thrived, and in his own stubborn endurance, she'd seen herself.

They were the same. And while their childhoods had left their scars, they'd both come through the fire strong, and if not completely whole, then at least near enough to make no difference.

Then he'd made her show him the forest, listening

as she'd talked about it, asking questions and being curious, inviting her passion about the forest to bloom. And it had.

Making love to him on the forest floor, the trees standing sentinel around them, had been one of the most pleasurable and spiritual experiences of her life.

She hadn't been able to leave him after that.

Learning more about him hadn't made her any less in love with him, and she didn't know what to do.

For the first couple of days, she'd looked for excuses to demand a divorce, or just to move away, but he hadn't given her any. As he'd promised, nothing changed. He came to the cottage at night and then left before she woke up the next day.

He'd mentioned something about a honeymoon, perhaps she might want to go to the Amazon? But she had a feeling that would only make her love him even more and so she'd put him off. He hadn't pushed.

She'd begun coming into the manor at night, usually to join him for dinner, and they'd spend a good couple of hours there, talking as they ate. He was interesting, had travelled to a lot of interesting places and done some interesting things, and she even found herself fascinated when he talked about some of the new startups he'd been an angel investor in. Plenty of them had been in eco technology, and she'd been surprised when he'd confessed that he wanted to put money into research for new tech that could help the planet and the poorer communities that lived on it.

He wasn't just some self-absorbed rich man at all. He had a good heart and he cared, and she loved him for it.

It was a problem, that love. She didn't know what to do about it.

He'd told her love wasn't a part of their marriage and she hadn't wanted it to be either, yet that made no difference to the feeling in her heart. She loved him all the same, and a part of her selfishly wanted him to love her in return.

Dominic came into the sitting room and sat down next to her, pulling her into his arms as he did so. He was very physically affectionate; she loved that about him too.

'You look pensive, nymph. Anything the matter?'

'No.'

A lie, of course. There was definitely something the matter, but she wasn't going to tell him what it was. He didn't need to know and while that selfish part of her wanted more, she had to ignore it. He didn't want love and she had no right to demand it from him.

You're being selfish, though. Lying to him because you can't bear to have that conversation. Because if you do, you'll lose him. Because you like keeping him tied to you without having to make any compromises yourself.

The thought whispered in her head, doubt eating away at her. It was true, wasn't it? She *was* being selfish. She was enjoying this marriage they'd entered into, where she could come and go as she pleased and have no demands placed on her, where she had him as well as all the freedom she wanted.

It was a business deal for him, and that made it okay, because then she wasn't a millstone around his neck, dragging him down.

Yet there was a small, painful, honest part of her that

wasn't happy. That wanted more. That wanted that last little piece from him, to be loved as she loved him.

Except she could never ask for that, not without revealing how dishonest she'd been since the day she'd married him.

He'll never love you anyway, not when no one else did.

She shifted again, that knowledge like a barb sticking under her skin.

'There is something the matter,' Dominic said, looking down at her. 'What is it?'

Maude took a breath. She didn't want to upset the delicate balance they'd found together with the truth.

'I'm just thinking about the future,' she lied. 'And what it's going to look like.'

He frowned slightly. 'Our future, you mean?'

'Yes. You and I, and the baby. Will I still be in the cottage? Or will we be here? Or…what?'

Dominic shrugged. 'It's up to you. I promised you things wouldn't change and they haven't.'

'I know, but…the child is going to find it odd if we're still in separate places when he gets older.'

'It's hardly separate,' Dominic pointed out. 'It's still the same property.'

'Yes, but you've got a foot half in the city.'

'So? You wanted your own life, Maude.'

This was not the conversation she'd wanted to have, yet now her own lie had taken on a life of its own and she couldn't let it go. 'I know and I still want that. But… our child will have the life we give him, and I want to know what kind of life he'll have.'

Dominic's dark eyes narrowed. 'Are you imagining me leaving for months on end like my father did?'

'No, of course not. But…you'll still leave.'

'And then I'll come back. What's the problem?'

The problem is that I'll be here without you.

Except she couldn't say that. This was about their son and that was all. 'I… He'll be lonely here with just me.'

'But that's what you wanted initially. Are you saying you want me to take him with me?'

'No, no.' She took a little breath, trying not to tangle the little web of untruths she'd woven. 'It's just…is this the way it's going to be for ever? Are we going to live separately for ever? And what about if you meet someone else? What about if you fall in love with—?'

'I won't fall in love with anyone,' he said tightly. 'I told you that love wasn't a part of this.'

'Not with me, sure. But what if you—?'

'I won't.' His voice was terse and there was something glittering in his dark gaze that made her chest constrict.

She didn't want him to be in love with anyone else. The very thought made her want to cry, and yet now she'd broached the topic, she couldn't seem to shut herself up. 'You might want someone else,' she said. 'Yet you're married to me. I told you I didn't want to be bound by anyone's rules, but you're also being bound, aren't you?'

'That's true.' His gaze abruptly became very focused on her. 'But when I said I won't fall in love with anyone else, I meant it. I won't want anyone else either. There's only you, Maude.'

She swallowed, a lump in her throat. 'But…why?'

'You're beautiful, fascinating, mysterious. You're passionate about the things that are important to you and you're honest. You're brave.'

The words felt like stones being thrown at her and suddenly she couldn't bear it. He thought she was all these wonderful things and she wasn't any of them. She was just a silly little girl left standing by a car while people who didn't want her argued about who got lumped with her.

Also, she was a liar.

Maude pushed herself out of his arms, unable to bear being so close to him when he didn't know the truth about her, sliding off the couch and going to stand in front of the fireplace.

'Maude?' Dominic asked, his voice full of concern. 'What is it?'

She wrapped her arms around herself as she stared into the flames. 'I'm not honest,' she said bluntly. 'I've been lying to you this whole time.'

There was a silence behind her.

'About what?' he asked eventually.

Maude took a breath. If she was really as brave as he thought she was, then she needed to face him. This was too important to tell the fire. He was too important.

Slowly, she turned around.

He hadn't moved from the couch, his expression un-readable, his dark eyes glittering.

Maude took her courage in both hands and held on. 'When I said I didn't love you, I lied.'

He said nothing, still staring at her.

'I've fallen in love with you, badger,' she said, the words falling into the silence like pebbles in a still pond, creating ripples. 'I know we said love wasn't a part of this, but… It's become part of it for me and I…' She swallowed, her throat aching. 'I don't want to be a millstone around your neck or drag you down. I know you didn't choose to have this baby or to have me as your wife. In fact, you didn't want a family at all. And I'm sorry that I put you into this position. I…just want you to know that, if you don't want any of this, if you want to walk away, I won't stop you. And I wouldn't blame you either.'

Dominic stared at Maude, standing with her back to the flames, her arms still wrapped around herself as if she were cold. She was in leggings and one of his sweatshirts, the dark green one, and it was giant on her, the hem extending down to her mid-thigh. Her hair was loose the way he liked it to be, in a wild golden storm down her back, and her face was flushed. She looked so beautiful, but what he didn't like was the anguish in her brown eyes.

Nor did he like the flood of words that had just come out of her mouth.

In fact, they'd shocked him.

Firstly, love. What the hell did she mean that she'd fallen in love with him? How? Why? He'd told her *specifically* that love wasn't a part of their marriage and yet that was exactly what she'd done.

Secondly, why the bloody hell would she assume that he'd happily walk away from their child and her if given the option? And now? After he'd married her?

He stared at her silently, his temper pulling at the leash.

The past week being married to her had been the

happiest he'd ever known, and he'd indulged himself shamelessly. Going to her cottage every night and holding her in his arms. Then for the first time, a couple of days after their wedding, she'd turned up at the manor, apparently looking for him.

He'd allowed the fierce burst of satisfaction that had brought him, inviting her in for dinner, and then the same the next night, and the one after that. He was hoping to entice her eventually into sleeping with him, in his room, and he'd thought tonight she might actually allow it, and now... This.

She'd ruined it. She'd turned this magical little affair they were having into something it shouldn't be and all because of that hateful four-letter word. Love.

Love demanded and demanded. Love was a rigged game that couldn't be won no matter how hard you tried. Love locked you outside and left you terrified in the dark. Love called you weak and laughed at your pain.

Love was a canker that had to be cut out, a weakness, a vulnerability.

He didn't want it. He didn't need it. Not any more.

And as for the assumption that he'd walk away from his child...

'If you think,' he said finally, acidly, 'that I would walk away from my son now, after moving to Darkfell and insisting on marriage to you, then you have another think coming.'

She'd gone very pale. 'It's a business deal. That's what you said.'

'Yes, it was. So why are you now talking about love?' He was suddenly furious with her. 'You wanted your freedom, Maude, so I gave it to you. And I never in-

sisted you be anyone other than who you were. You had
the life you wanted, so why the hell would you want to
change it?'

There were tears in her eyes, he could see them glittering in the light from the fire. 'I know,' she said thickly.
'I know I wanted all those things, and, yes, you gave
them to me. But…that's why I fell in love with you.
You're caring and you listen, and you've always accepted
me. You've never wanted me to be someone I'm not. And
when you make me promises you never break them.'

A tear ran down her cheek, sparkling in the light,
and for some reason the sight of it felt like a knife in
his heart. 'You're not really the man you seem to be on
the outside. You're someone else deep down, someone
who's as passionate as I am and cares as much as I do,
and who feels like my soul mate. That's why I love you,
Dominic. You gave me everything I wanted. Except then
I realised that what I really wanted was you.'

Dominic closed his eyes, not wanting to see her face
or her tears.

He'd gone about this all wrong. He'd made a grievous
mistake. He'd thought he could have his cake and eat
it too, the way he always did. The way he'd done suc-
cessfully for years. Business and pleasure, yes, he could
have both and did, frequently.

But marriage without love, a family without ties, was
apparently *not* something he could have. Which meant
he'd have to give something up, and that something
would have to be her. There was no other option.

She loved him and he couldn't allow that. Wouldn't
allow that. It would hurt her, and the thought of hurting

her made him ache, but he'd been a fool to think that none of this would come without consequences.

He'd hoped that making this marriage a purely business proposition would keep love and all its ensuing pain out of it, yet apparently not.

What else could he do, though? Keeping her, as that deep, essential part of him kept growling, was not an option, not when he couldn't give her what she truly wanted: his heart.

It was frozen, that heart of his, and it wouldn't ever thaw. He didn't want it to. It was far better to keep it on ice, keep it out of other people's hands, because, after the way his father had treated him, he would never give anyone that kind of power over him again.

He had to let her go. It was the only way. Wasn't that old saying 'if you love something set it free'? Trite and ridiculous, but that was the only way out of this.

So you'll actually do what she asked and walk away? From her? From your child?

The primitive part of him snarled in protest at the thought, but he crushed it. He couldn't walk away from his son, no, but he could walk away from Maude. He'd have to. Because that same primitive, possessive part of him was urging him to lie to her, to tell her that he loved her, then take her away to the city and keep her near him, and for always.

But he couldn't do that, either. He wouldn't be like her grandparents, taking her away from everything she loved, everything that was important to her, and surrounding her with concrete and metal. He would never take his wood nymph away from her trees.

As for his son…well, the child would be better living

with Maude than with him. In fact, he couldn't think of anything better for his little boy than to grow up close to the natural world with Maude as his mother. She would love him, care for him. He'd never be lonely with her.

Dominic's chest ached at that thought, the pain of it lancing deep inside him, but he forced it away.

'Dominic? Say something, please.' She was still standing in front of the fire, tear tracks shining on her cheeks, her brown eyes full of anguish.

An anguish he was going to make worse, and he hated himself for it. But it was the only way.

He met her gaze. 'Say something?' he repeated. 'Say what?'

'I don't know. Anything.'

'Fine.' Slowly he rose from the couch. 'Then how about this? I won't take you away from your trees. But you're right, I didn't choose this life and I didn't choose you. So maybe it is time for me to walk away.'

Her eyes darkened with pain. 'I… Yes, okay. And… our son?'

It was the first time she'd said 'our son' and that hurt too, but, again, he ignored it. 'He can stay here with you.' He had to force out the words, even as the snarling beast inside him ripped at the bars of the cage he'd trapped it in. 'I would never take him away from you and I'd… like him to be taught to care for the forest.'

'You can stay,' she said abruptly. 'It's not fair that you should have to leave, because of me. It's your house. I can go, I don't have to—'

'No,' he interrupted immediately, his tone fierce. 'I'm not forcing you to leave your forest. It's yours.'

Her brown eyes were full of tears, the gold drowned beneath them. 'It's not mine. It's your home.'

It was and yet he'd never felt at home here. Not until she'd come.

And while she's here, you can never stay.

Of course, he couldn't. This house and its grounds would be off-limits for him for ever. The temptation she presented would be too great, and he'd manipulate her, use her for his own ends, and end up hurting her worse than he was doing now. And he just couldn't allow that.

'It was yours more than it ever was mine,' he said and when she opened her mouth to protest, he added, 'I'm not arguing, Maude. It will be my legacy to my son. Keep it. For him.'

She nodded, standing rigidly in front of the fire as another tear slid down her cheek. And he wanted to close the distance, wipe that tear away then pull her into his arms and make her forget all about love and how it could hurt, but he didn't.

Instead he said, 'I'll leave tonight. No point in drawing this out any longer than it needs to be.'

She looked so fragile standing there in his sweatshirt, holding herself so stiffly it was as if she was afraid one touch would shatter her.

His lovely nymph.

'I would keep you if I could,' he said finally, unable to stay silent in this last terrible moment. 'I don't want to let you go. But if anyone deserves to be loved, Maude, it's you, and if I can't, you need to find someone else who will.'

Another tear slid slowly down her cheek. 'I won't,' she said, and he could hear all the force of her strong, stubborn will behind the words. 'There won't be anyone else but you, badger.'

He'd had no idea this would hurt so much or even why it did, but there was no other option. Walking away was all he could do.

His heart felt as if it were burning away, leaving nothing but ash as, without another word, he turned and strode from the room.

Yet he didn't hesitate.

And she didn't call him back.

CHAPTER TWELVE

DOMINIC HAD BEEN gone a week and Maude was worse than miserable, she was broken-hearted. She dragged herself around the forest, but not even the trees could comfort her, not this time.

She knew she'd done the right thing. She knew. But that little selfish piece of her kept crying and crying because he'd gone. Because he'd done exactly what she'd told him to do and walked away from her, and now there'd be emptiness in her heart for ever.

A just punishment, really, for how she'd lied to him and for how she'd given him nothing, while he'd given her the world and everything in it.

It was only fair that he walked away and only fair that he couldn't love her back. He'd been clear right from the start about the kind of arrangement they'd had, and if she was the one wanting more, then she should have stopped it right in the beginning.

Except she hadn't known she'd even want more, not until it was too late.

Eventually, she called her Your Girl Friday friends in a video call, and told them what had happened, baring her heart in a flood of words that left everyone silent for at least five minutes afterwards.

'So,' Lyanna said at last. 'Let me get this straight. You slept with a strange man in the forest at a midsummer bacchanal, found yourself pregnant with his baby, and then the strange man turned out to be your boss and one of the worst playboys in Europe. Then he asked you to be his wife and so you married him, and now he's gone, yes?'

'Yes,' Maude said, grabbing a tissue from the nearby box and dabbing at her eyes with it. 'That's pretty much it.'

'Well,' said Auggie, clearly miffed. 'You kept that very quiet.'

'Dominic Lancaster's midsummer bacchanal, hmm?' Irinka was all curiosity. 'And with Dominic Lancaster himself. Is he as good as everyone says he is?'

'He's better.' Maude blew her nose into her tissue. Then she took a deep breath. 'And I'm in love with him.'

There was a silence.

Irinka frowned—she had her background blurred so Maude couldn't tell where she was. 'You married the man, so how is being in love an issue?'

'Because our marriage was a business agreement,' Maude explained. 'It was for the baby. He told me love wouldn't be a part of it and I agreed. And then…' her chest ached '… I actually fell in love.'

'That was poor timing,' Lyanna muttered.

'Extremely poor,' Irinka added.

But Auggie, newly married to her own wonderful explayboy husband, only gave her a clear-eyed stare. 'So what are you doing about it, Maude?'

Maude stared back. 'What do you think I'm doing?

I'm not crying for fun, and, before you say anything, it's not pregnancy hormones.'

'What I mean,' Auggie said patiently, 'is did you just let him go?'

'Of course, I let him go.' Maude pulled out another tissue. 'He had a terrible childhood and his father was basically the devil, and he was very clear he doesn't want love. In fact…' she swallowed as another bubble of anguish rose '…he walked away rather than stay with someone who loved him.'

Lyanna frowned. 'How could he not stay with you? You're pregnant with his child, for God's sake.'

'It's not his fault,' Maude said, instantly wanting to defend him. 'I'm the one who fell in love with him. And I…refused to compromise about certain things. He's… just such a wonderful man. Yes, he has his flaws, but he accepted me in a way no one else ever has.'

'Hey,' Auggie muttered, along with various protestations from Irinka and Lyanna. 'We accept you.'

'I know you do,' Maude said, thinking of Dominic standing in front of her, his dark eyes haunted as he told her he was giving her Darkfell, that it was hers more than it had ever been his. Giving up the last piece of himself to her. Telling her that he didn't want to let her go, but he had to, and then walking away.

Alone. He was so alone. At least she had her friends, but who did he have? Perhaps he had friends too, but she was sure there was no one who loved him the way she did, with every part of her.

'But I'm not sure he has anyone,' she said into the silence, her chest sore. 'I… I wish he could feel what it was like to be loved. Just once.'

'So?' Auggie said. 'Why don't you go show him?'

Maude took a breath. 'He told me that—'

'Oh, who cares what he told you?' Auggie interrupted impatiently, provoking startled looks from Irinka and Lyanna. 'Men say all kinds of stupid things that they don't really mean. You're a wonderful person, Maude, and you deserve happiness. If you love him, don't let him walk away. And don't accept whatever silly excuses he chooses to throw at you, either. You go after him and you tell him that you can't live without him.'

Everyone else fell silent.

Maude stared at her screen, feeling her friends' words echo in her soul.

He didn't love her and he wouldn't, he'd made that very plain. And yet, regardless of that small part of her that was desperate for his love and had been hurt terribly by him walking away, she couldn't bear the thought of being apart from him either.

But he's gone and he's not coming back.

Yes, he had, but that didn't mean she couldn't go after him. She didn't go to the city, she didn't like it, she never had, but she couldn't leave him there alone amongst all that metal and concrete and glass. His father had left him like that, had made him negotiate for everything he'd wanted, but she would never do the same. She'd go to him, tell him that she loved him still and then she'd find somewhere to stay. And if he didn't want her, then at least she'd be close by with their child.

She would be his little piece of home, a little piece of wild Darkfell, in the vast city.

'Sorry,' she said to her friends. 'I have to go. I need to find out how to organise myself a helicopter.'

* * *

Dominic sat in his London office wondering what the hell he was going to do now. He didn't want to do anything, that was the issue. A couple of months ago he would have thrown himself into a party and taken one, two, or three women to bed, but he'd lost his taste for partying.

He'd lost his taste for anything that wasn't Maude, and his future looked so bleak he almost couldn't stand it.

You threw it away. You loved her and you threw her away.

Maybe. Maybe this painful, aching feeling in his chest was love. He didn't know. His heart had been frozen for so long he'd forgotten what it felt like.

But no, he couldn't tell himself that. He knew. It was the same helpless pain he'd felt when the man who was supposed to be his father had laughed at his anguish over the stag. Had shrugged when he'd cried over the itemised list he'd been given, all the expenses laid out of his upbringing. His relationship with his father reduced to pounds and pence, to cold, hard money. Dominic had never been given anything freely. He'd always had to pay for it.

She gave you her love freely. She didn't want anything in return.

He sat back in his office chair, London at his back, and shut his eyes.

He didn't want to think about Maude and the tears on her cheeks, telling him that she'd fallen in love with him, anguish in her warm brown eyes. She hadn't asked to be loved in return. She hadn't asked for anything. It had been him that she had been concerned about, telling him that none of this had been his choice, not her, not their baby…

Pain sat in his heart, eating at him with sharp teeth. *You fool. You bloody fool.*

Oh, he knew it. And it was poetic, almost, to finally know what he wanted in life, to finally understand his purpose, only for it to be out of his reach.

He loved her. He loved their baby. He wanted the future he'd been able to see for them both, living at Darkfell as a family.

But he couldn't have it. He couldn't bargain for it. He couldn't buy it, not this precious future. Because in doing so, he'd cheapen it, and he couldn't bear to do that.

So you're happy to hurt her instead?

His beautiful wood nymph, crying because she was in love with him, giving him freely what he'd never been given before.

And he couldn't take it. Because ultimately he was just like his father. Everything was about the deal. Everything was about money. About cold, hard cash and a cold, hard heart. There was no room for warmth or passion. No room for the living, breathing things of the forest. And no room for the little family that might have been his.

He would never sentence Maude to the kind of life he lived, and he wouldn't sentence his son to it, either. It would kill her, and it would kill him too.

You can change, you know. It's not too late.

Ah, but that was the kicker, wasn't it? He couldn't change, not now. He was too old for that kind of thing, had lived too much of his life in the boardrooms. His heart was nothing but a frozen lump in his chest and nothing was going to shock it back to life.

Just then, his intercom buzzed. 'Mr Lancaster?' his secretary said. 'You have a—wait! You can't go in there!'

At the same moment the doors to his office were pushed wide and a woman strode through them.

She was dressed in maternity jeans that still had mud clinging to the knees and his green sweatshirt that just about swallowed her. Her hair was loose in wild golden skeins down her back, and there appeared to be a leaf caught in it.

His frozen heart was still and quiet in his chest.

He couldn't move.

He couldn't breathe.

It was his wood nymph, come to the city.

She was carrying a bag and as she dumped it on the floor next to his desk, her nose wrinkled. 'I'm disappointed, badger,' she said flatly. 'I was expecting to find you in bed with lots of women. But here you are sulking in your den.'

He had to say something, he had to. 'Maude,' he managed, his voice full of gravel. 'What the hell are you doing here?'

'What does it look like?' She surveyed his office and then the view out of the windows. 'I want you to show me the city.'

He stared at her, his brain moving so very slowly. 'What?'

Her gaze came to his, a deep forest pool dappled with sunshine. 'I showed you my world. Now I've come to see yours.'

'But…but…' He stopped. He'd never been lost for

words before, not since he was a child, and he just couldn't comprehend what she was doing here.

'I was an idiot,' Maude said. 'I let you walk away without a word and I've never regretted anything more. I was afraid, badger. I wasn't your choice, I told you that, and neither was our baby, and I didn't want to be a millstone around your neck the way I was with my mother and my grandparents, so I…gave you a way out.' Her chin lifted in that stubborn way. 'But I was wrong to let you walk away. I love you, Dominic Lancaster, and I've been miserable without you. You don't have to love me back. You don't have to do anything at all for me. But I can't bear not being near you, so I've decided to move here. I can have the baby here and we can—'

'No!' The word burst out of him without any conscious thought, and he was on his feet, his chair pushed back so violently it lay overturned on the floor. And he was coming around the side of the desk to her, full of some fierce, burning emotion he couldn't quite comprehend.

But maybe he didn't need to comprehend it. Maybe he didn't need to think about it or analyse it. Maybe he simply needed to obey it and so he did.

Her eyes were shining as he put his hands on her hips and jerked her into his arms. 'Nymph…' His voice was so rough it was barely intelligible. *'Nymph…'* And then her mouth was beneath his, so warm and sweet with that delicious tartness he'd come to hunger for more than his own breath. And his hands were in the raw silk of her hair, holding on for dear life, as if he was afraid she'd disappear again.

He *was* afraid she'd disappear again.

He was afraid of that fierce, burning feeling inside him. Afraid of what it meant. Afraid to trust it. Afraid to trust her and the heart she'd given him on a silver platter. But that heart of hers was valiant, and strong, and generous, an unbreakable tether holding him fast. Coaxing a thaw in his own, making a wild rose suddenly bloom.

'I'm sorry,' he whispered against her mouth. 'I'm so sorry I walked away. I was a coward and a fool, and I have been for weeks. I should have trusted what we had that night in the forest. I should have accepted it for what it was.' He lifted his head and gazed down into her eyes. 'I'd never met you. I'd never even seen your face. But that didn't matter. You were my choice that night, Maude, and you're my choice now. You've been my choice all along. My entire life I've been struggling to find a purpose and now I've found it.' He slowly tightened his fingers in her hair, his heart a bed of wild roses. 'It's you, nymph. It's you and our son.'

She smiled, warm as the midsummer sun, her eyes full of tenderness. 'My forest god,' she murmured.

He kissed her again, unable to stop. 'I love you, Maude Lancaster,' he said against her mouth. 'I love you so much.'

She deepened the kiss, giving him a wordless answer that flooded him with heat and the most peculiar sensation that he had the odd feeling was joy.

A few endless moments later, he lifted his head, because, while he was desperate for her, even he had standards and taking her on his desk was not one of them.

'Let's go home,' he said. 'To Darkfell.'

But Maude shook her head. 'No. I told you. I want to see the city.'

'Stubborn nymph.' He kissed her again, already reassessing his standards and thinking that maybe he could lower them just this once. 'I hope you're not meaning now.'

The gold in her eyes glittered, a sure sign that she was going to dig in on this. 'Of course now. Don't sulk, badger.'

He sighed. 'Come on, then,' he said, reluctantly releasing her, yet keeping hold of her hand. 'If you insist.'

Maude's gaze became hotter and suddenly very wicked. 'Well… I suppose I could wait a little longer.'

But Dominic was already striding to the doors and shutting them, and locking them for good measure. Then he strode back to where she stood, and kissed her hard, letting the flames take them both.

It was going to be interesting, this new life of his. Interesting in ways he couldn't even begin to contemplate. But one thing he was sure of.

He couldn't wait to get started.

EPILOGUE

IT WAS HOT, and she was sweating, and Maude couldn't wait any longer.

As soon as they reached the pool, she pulled off all her clothes, climbed onto the rocks under the waterfall and dived head first into the water.

It was cool and refreshing after the baking midsummer heat, and she gave a little internal sigh of pleasure as she touched the sandy bottom of the pool in greeting to the water spirits, before arrowing back to the surface.

Dominic had stopped by the edge of the pool and had taken off the backpack with Robin, their twelve-month-old, in it. He was sitting now on the grass, holding Robin while the little boy tried to grab the white stripe of his father's hair in a chubby fist.

Ever since he'd been born, he'd been fascinated with it. He'd been fascinated with his father too, and Dominic had been equally smitten. Watching him with their son was one of Maude's special joys.

There was joy, too, to be had in the projects that she and Dominic chose together to invest in. Eco projects and technology, mostly, because she'd decided that she didn't want to save just Darkfell forest, she wanted to save the world too.

Since she'd already saved one disreputable playboy and turned him into a respectable family man, she didn't think saving the world was entirely out of reach, and certainly not with him at her side.

After all, he'd tamed a wild forest nymph and turned her into a wife and mother, so fair was fair.

But that wasn't all they were.

Sometimes, on warm nights, when the moon was full and the forest spirits walked, they'd go out into the woods and become forest spirits themselves, the god and goddess, wild and free and passionate, on a bed of bracken.

As Maude surfaced, Dominic waved at her and so did Robin.

Really, there was no end to the joy of her life, and soon enough it was going to get even more joyous.

Maude put a light hand to her stomach and smiled.

It would be a little girl, she knew it.

Dominic was going to be so happy.

* * * * *

MILLS & BOON®

Coming next month

BILLION-DOLLAR RING RUSE
Jadesola James

'Am I that obvious?'

'Weren't you trying to be?'

'Don't be so eager to rush a beautiful thing, Miss Montgomery.'

'Val,' she corrected, her heart thumping like a rabbit's. If this was happening, she couldn't let it happen with him calling her *Miss Montgomery* or, worse yet, Valentina. Not with his liquid, rich voice simply dripping with all the dirty things she presumed he could do to her—it was bringing to the surface something she wasn't ready to explore. Not with him.

And yet, her thoughts were going in directions she couldn't control, while she sat in the booth, heart thudding, mentally grasping at them as they floated beyond her fingertips into places that sent back heated, urgent images that took her breath away with their sensuality. His mouth on her neck, his lips on hers, the softness of his breath on her ear. His hands on her breasts, hips, bottom, thighs. Stroking. Exploring.

Gripping.

Her face bloomed with heat, and it left her body in the softest of exhales before he *finally* kissed her.

Continue reading

BILLION-DOLLAR RING RUSE
Jadesola James

Available next month
millsandboon.co.uk

COMING SOON!

We really hope you enjoyed reading this book.
If you're looking for more romance
be sure to head to the shops when
new books are available on

Thursday 27th March

To see which titles are coming soon, please visit
millsandboon.co.uk/nextmonth

LET'S TALK

Romance

For exclusive extracts, competitions and special offers, find us online:

f MillsandBoon

X @MillsandBoon

◎ @MillsandBoonUK

♪ @MillsandBoonUK

Get in touch on 01413 063 232

afterglow BOOKS

Afterglow Books is a trend-led, trope-filled list of books with diverse, authentic and relatable characters, a wide array of voices and representations, plus real world trials and tribulations. Featuring all the tropes you could possibly want (think small-town settings, fake relationships, grumpy vs sunshine, enemies to lovers) and all with a generous dose of spice in every story.

♪ @millsandboonuk
◉ @millsandboonuk
afterglowbooks.co.uk
#AfterglowBooks

For all the latest book news, exclusive content and giveaways scan the QR code below to sign up to the Afterglow newsletter:

SCAN ME

afterglow BOOKS

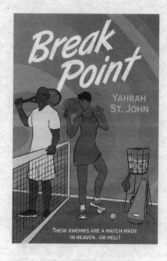
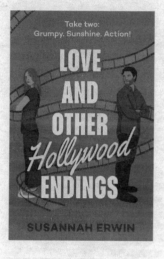

FOUR BRAND NEW BOOKS FROM
MILLS & BOON MODERN

The same great stories you love, a stylish new look!

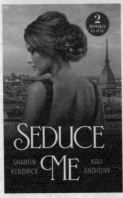

OUT NOW

Eight Modern stories published every month, find them all at:

millsandboon.co.uk

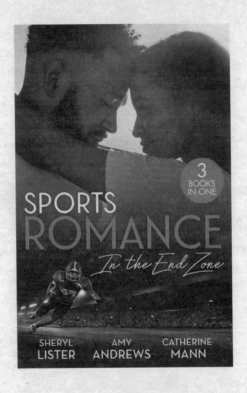